# THE
# FERTILE
# EARTH

# THE
# FERTILE
# EARTH

Ruthvika Rao

FLATIRON
BOOKS
NEW YORK

THE FERTILE EARTH. Copyright © 2024 by Ruthvika Rao. All rights reserved. Printed in the United States of America. For information, address Flatiron Books, 120 Broadway, New York, NY 10271.

www.flatironbooks.com

Designed by Steven Seighman

Library of Congress Cataloging-in-Publication Data

Names: Rao, Ruthvika, author.
Title: The fertile earth / Ruthvika Rao.
Description: First edition. | New York : Flatiron Books, 2024.
Identifiers: LCCN 2023046389 | ISBN 9781250899903 (hardcover) | ISBN 9781250899958 (ebook)
Subjects: LCGFT: Novels.
Classification: LCC PR9499.4.R367 F47 2024
LC record available at https://lccn.loc.gov/2023046389

Our books may be purchased in bulk for promotional, educational, or business use. Please contact your local bookseller or the Macmillan Corporate and Premium Sales Department at 1-800-221-7945, extension 5442, or by email at MacmillanSpecialMarkets@macmillan.com.

First Edition: 2024

10  9  8  7  6  5  4  3  2  1

*For Vikramaditya and Mithilesh*

For there is the law that the body, even if it is an Emperor's, must rest only on the floor, on Mother Earth.

—R. K. NARAYAN, *The English Teacher*

# 1970

———◆———

# Irumi, Telangana

# KANAKAM'S TALE

———◆———

T he village of Irumi sits on a small bluff rising out of a valley floor,
enclosed by the Eastern Ghats and the Krishna River, beyond
which the Nallamala jungle spreads, clinging to the mountain-
sides like moss. The farthest mountains in the range are blue, and as they
grow nearer and nearer to the valley, embracing Irumi, encircling it, they
plunge into hill ranges of darkest chlorophyllic green, hiding sandalwood,
crawling with tigers and tiger cubs.

Seasons distorted Irumi, as though the village were a living human
face, each season bringing out a different feature, a different expression.
In the winter, a fog descended from the Ghats and the villagers heard but
could not see hundreds of monkeys, swinging from hill tree to hill tree,
chattering like inseparable old women. In the summer, the earth cracked,
the dry riverbed showed. But when the monsoon arrived, the Krishna
rose and overflowed into Irumi's paddy fields, and the villagers stepped
into his rushing waters holding jasmine strands, camphor lamps, their
toes slipping on mossy river rocks.

On a cold winter morning in 1970, as dawn broke over the Ghats
and a feeble orange light flooded in, a row of severed human heads were
discovered hanging on pikes in a paddy field in Irumi. There were five of
them, fat, clay-like, swollen.

When the paddy farmer showed up for work, he dropped his iron plow
and shouted for the others. Soon, most of the village had descended on

his field. His crop was still young and the farmer asked the villagers to tread carefully, to not damage his seedlings. Wet land was precious, and he'd sown chitti mutyalu, a variety of sweet-smelling rice that needed gentle handling. But in their hurry to get closer to the severed heads, the villagers ignored him, they trampled his field, shoving, jostling, indiscriminately flattening and snapping the tender rice stalks.

The mounting curiosity amongst them was not about the identity of the victims; they all knew who the dead ones were, nor about the identity of the perpetrators; they all knew whose work it was. The only question that remained, therefore, was who had seen it happen. Usually, there was an audience for this kind of thing—they had heard tell—an audience and a hearing supposedly came before the execution. A "people's court," it was called. Judgments passed, wrongdoers punished. As they surveyed one another's faces, they paid no attention to a boy standing mutely just beyond the edge of the field, watching them.

The boy's name was Kanakam. He was eleven years old, and he was the only one who had seen it happen. He alone had seen the Deshmukhs die, seen their faces, the settings of their brows and eyes and lips and teeth in the fleeting seconds before life drained out of them.

Kanakam looked no different from other children his age, ribs protruding from beneath sun-beaten skin, a round belly, and those genes that gave him hair, eyes and gums, all the spectacular color of midnight. The villagers ignored him because even though he was from Irumi he did not truly belong there. He lived in a hut just beyond Irumi's boundary, in a small settlement abutting a shrine for Katta Maisamma; the village goddess tasked with protecting its borders. He'd lived in that settlement from the age of four—when his memory begins—to his now weatherbeaten age of eleven. Eleven was considered prime youth in his settlement. Death usually came around thirty.

In appearance, the huts in his settlement were no different from the two hundred or so huts in the rest of Irumi—low mud walls, thatched roofs made of dried coconut fronds and palm branches, earthen floors beaten smooth, an open area at the back for planting runner beans and sponge gourds in the winter. There was nothing in the outward appearance of this settlement that set it apart, and yet, the rest of Irumi shunned it. They shunned it because of the blackened earth beneath it. Polluted and ruined for perpetuity, the settlement sat beneath ghastly shadows of dead tamarinds and scavenging clouds of vultures. An intolerable stench rose from it—black tar pits, rows upon rows of curing animal skins folded with their flesh sides together, fat collecting in mud pots to be used for eating and for burning, chemical dye reacting in metal drums, decaying cow and pig carcasses, drying bone marrow, drained blood, sinew, and the rank hum of boiling animal flesh. It was a tanning settlement. Then too, the villagers had been taught from birth, to shun, to ostracize, and to not touch those born there.

Kanakam's father, like his father before him, was a tanner, and by that definition, a leather worker, a cow slaughterer, a dye master, a cobbler, and also, half-blind from adulterated country liquor. Death for him too, was coming at thirty, just as surely as it was to come for his father and had come for all the men before him. For reasons that the midwife from Irumi could not explain, Kanakam's mother died even sooner. The only thing he knew about her was what the midwife had told him: that she'd chosen his name months before he was born. That name—Kanakam—meant Gold; impossibly precious, a material of mythical significance, one that commanded desire. That had been her wish for his future, to be desired, touched, wanted. That he had caused the death of his mother, that she would be alive if not for him, was a thing imprinted on him, like a barbed tattoo against his wide cheeks and high forehead. But despite that, and despite his malnourished appearance and the ragged scars he bore on his back, Kanakam was special. He could, for example, perfectly skin a cow. Then, he could wash it, brine it, tan it, dry it, dye it and make a pair of perfect, full-grain leather shoes. He was capable of doing all of this with no help from his increasingly blind father. Even in that settlement of thatched huts, everyone remarked at his skill in his family's ancestral profession. Perhaps, they said, he was gifted.

The trick to skinning cows, he knew, was to breathe as little as possible, to sharpen his skinning knife beforehand, and to do it in the dead of the night, when everyone was asleep and the animals weren't frightened.

While the cows slept, he patiently raked his knife back and forth against the whetstone. Now and then, he'd pause to run his little finger against the edge of the blade. It was sharp enough only when it stung and drew blood. Then, he'd put away the whetstone, lay his knife on the ground, and look up, as he often did, almost as frequently as he blinked or inhaled or dreamt or prayed, at the structure towering over Irumi—the gadi.

A resplendent, fortress-like manor house on a flattened hillock by the river, he slept and awoke to the manifest sight of it, hovering above him, as though the gadi were the sun, and he, a lonely planet, never able to escape its gravity. Two hundred years old, it stood within a massive flagstone courtyard, beyond which lay several connected buildings: the granary, the cowshed, a stable where the horses and bullocks were kept, outhouses for farming implements and for the jeethas who minded the animals, and beyond all of it an orchard, spreading across the hillock, dipping down towards the riverbank. But from the tanning settlement, all Kanakam could see was the gadi itself. The terra-cotta tiles of its roof fitted together like puzzle pieces; the teak girders shone crimson in sunlight; the carved beams and corbeled pillars were etched with the images of gods and goddesses, lions and palmyras. A series of delicately latticed stone grilles descended over all the windows and balconies like a light summer veil.

From outside his hut, whenever his eyes fell on the gadi, Kanakam was flooded by a sense of immense, unbearable longing. He imagined that everything he didn't have, everything he could ever want was there, inside that splendid place that looked like a palace from a fable.

The Deshmukh family lived in the gadi. As the zamindars of Irumi, they were feudal landlords, rulers and administrators of law, taxation and cruelty. Former vassals to the former exalted highness, the last nizam, Mir Osman Ali Khan, Asaf Jah VII, ruler of the former princely state of Hyderabad, the Deshmukh family owned a hundred thousand acres of land spread across thirty-five villages all along the Krishna River, including the sum total of Irumi. For the villagers of Irumi—a combination of tenant-farmers, potters, weavers, barbers, smelters, tanners, washermen, manual scavengers, blacksmiths, toddy-tappers, cattle-keepers, cloth-traders, gypsy storytellers, well-diggers, stoneworkers, miners, tradesmen, small landholders, expelled tribesmen, indentured servants and bonded laborers—it was as though they could die merely from being looked upon by one of the Deshmukhs, as though their sight had the power to melt the skin off skulls.

The gadi's presence could not be escaped no matter where one stood in Irumi. It towered over Irumi and glared down at it. Its magnificent and intense beauty, its wrath and power, both drew and repelled the villag-ers. In that social order, in that fabric hewn from Irumi's centuries-old conscience, the villagers never raised their eyes to the zamindar. While entering his presence, they walked with their spines bent in a half bow, while speaking to him, they picked up their shabby, worn footwear and held them in their palms, and in his presence, they were not allowed to wear the color white. To him, they sent their harvested grain, thirty-five separate sharecropping rents and taxes, and when ordered, they sent their children, for vetti: lifelong, indentured servitude paid only in grains of rice. Their authority, their birthright, and their power over the lives of those who lived in Irumi was absolute. On the far edge of Irumi, on a low hill, stood a temple. The villagers might pray there, but the Deshmukhs were the real gods of Irumi.


The night that the Deshmukhs were executed, Kanakam had been work-ing. He'd been caught in one of those moments when he stared and stared at the gadi. At last, he forced himself to look away and return to work. Usually, when he went into the cattle shed to choose an animal, he chose one at random, awoke it and led it out. But that night, when he went inside and walked amongst the sleeping cows, his eyes were drawn towards one particular animal. It was sitting at the far end of the shed, under a spot where a section of thatch was missing. Under the black sky, its whiteness was ghostly. It struck him as strange that the cow was wide awake, it was even looking at him. He felt unsettled, briefly considered choosing another one, but out of sheer force of habit, he went towards it and ran his hands down its body. It was, as far as he could feel, near perfect: no blemishes, bug-bites, or parasite holes in its hide.

Outside, he coaxed the cow into kneeling on the ground, and with rapid movements, bound its legs and its mouth with jute rope. He had this way of laying his hand against the animal and covering its terrified eyes until it stopped being afraid, until it became as still as a temple sculpture. That, was his gift.

He produced a serrated dagger. Shorter and sturdier than his skinning knife, this one was heavier, with a hollowed wooden handle made for the purpose of directing the stream of animal blood, to allow the skinner to control the flow. He ran his fingers along the cow's neck, found that tender spot where the ligament met the top of its rib cage, a soft funnel-like muscle that took the life out of animals. He plunged his dagger into the spot, hooked the artery, and swung it upwards, letting the blood pool into the black mud under his feet. The cow began moaning and crying, struggling against its rope bindings. For a few minutes, he waited, watching it flail, the soles of his feet soaking in its warm blood. The cow shuddered one final time and did not move again. He was ready with his skinning knife. This part required supreme concentration, meditative in its spirit. All the smells and noises around him—the bubbling of the tanning pits, the melting blocks of dyes, the dripping of fat over fire, the rancid breeze whistling through drying animal hides, the cracking of tree boughs—disappeared, vanished until only he remained with his skinning knife. His hands were small, demure even, and their movements agile. He worked quickly, plunging a metal hook through the cow's jaw, under its pink tongue, then wound the chain of the pulley until the carcass was hoisted off the ground. He began at the top of the cow's head, and in swift motions, made a series of deep slits in its skin, around its front and hind legs, and a long, unbroken line underneath its belly from tail to jaw. He slid his blade beneath the deep cuts in the animal's skin, where he separated it from the slabs of fat and flesh underneath, severing the connective tissue. As he heaved and pulled, the skin began separating, sliding off; slowly, little by little, until only the dark, skinless flesh of the animal carcass remained on the hook.

A steady drip of blood was falling to the ground. He carried the hide to the brining tank and buried it in salt, where it was to soak until it could be dried. He was piling entrails fit for eating—hooves, eyes, ears, tongue, stomach—on a low wooden bench, when he glanced up, once more, at the gadi.

He blinked. The low bramble-strewn hillock on which the gadi stood was ablaze. Even at that distance, he could feel the heat against his face. The fire was spreading, brilliant tongues of it shooting up into the winter sky.

To run towards a burning building was a grave mistake, but inexplicably, as though in a dream, he found himself hurrying out of the tanning settlement.

When he came up the hillock, he stopped at the edge of the courtyard, near the stepwell where a banyan tree stood, within sight of the main doors. Only the eastern section of the gadi, the part farthest from him, was on fire. The rest of the gadi looked still and vacant. He smelled something odd in the air; it took him a few moments to realize that it was the smell of wheat. The granary was burning. He gazed at the gadi's massive doors, one of which was hanging off its hinges, the wood splintered apart as though with an ax. Set over the doorway's arches was an intricately carved wooden panel of a gigantic chariot. In the dim moonlight, he made out eight horses harnessed to the chariot.

He inched closer. Although he heard voices in the distance, no voice told him to stop. Nothing. Silence. He pressed on. Slowly, he reached the broken doorway, crept inside. As he entered, he touched the walls, felt the cold plaster under his fingertips, the dimpled stone under his bare feet. He was here, in the place he'd watched with longing every day of his natural life.

But when his eyes adjusted to the darkness, what he saw disappointed him. Broken pieces of wood, long pieces of rope, upturned furniture, shards of glass scattered across the floor. The contents of every dresser and drawer and closet appeared to have been overturned: books, vases, a gramophone, broken porcelain, even what looked like silver tumblers. He walked past it all and found himself at a connecting door. On the other side was an interior courtyard with a sunken pool. In the foot or so of water, his reflection rippled gently, staring back at him with excitement.

Then his eyes fell on a stairway, the varnished wooden banister leading to the floor above.

The stairs too were littered with broken glass, sparkling like chips of hail. He gripped the banister tightly as he crept from stair to stair. On the second floor, there was more light. He went down the corridor, passing room after room. Closets, daybeds, rattan easy chairs, bureaus, teapoys, most of it looking undisturbed. At the end of the corridor, he saw an open door. He reached it, slipped inside.

The first thing he noticed, stepping into the room, was the mounted head of a tiger on the wall. Its long, curved front teeth were bared as though it had been caught in the very moment of attack, the very moment it prepared to sink its teeth into the delicate neck of its prey. Its yellow, beady eyes were watching him. He could nearly hear the guttural snarl emerging from its throat. It looked alive. It was so arresting, so frightening that he felt as though it would pounce upon him any moment. But it was also beautiful, its fur looked soft, and around the base of its neck it was white. Like cotton. And its eyes were static, like large, round marbles. He could not tear his eyes away from it, nor could he stop himself from moving deeper into the room.

It was clear to him that he was in one of the back rooms of the gadi. He could hear the river. Through the window propped open on the far side of the room, he could make out the dark outline of the trees in the orchard. A cot was next to the window, its covers rumpled, trailing to the floor. He reached the cot and touched the sheet; it was cold, smelled like alcohol and something metallic he couldn't quite place. Half hidden amongst the rumpled sheets was an object. Still feeling the tiger's gaze on him, he picked it up.

It was as long as his forearm. Narrow, like a pipe, but heavy, its surface covered in silk. Not quite sure what it was, he shook it vigorously. It made a merry noise, like the rustling of a woman's anklets. He held it up to the moonlight; the silk was red, streaked with gold. He did not know what it was except that it was a glittering, beautiful thing: a treasure. The thought arose in him that he had to take it and leave right then, run home as fast as he could. The fire from the eastern section was catching, and its yellow light was pouring into the orchard below. Now and then, he could hear a sputtering, crunching noise; the timber rafters were burning and falling. The roof was beginning to cave. The air was getting thick with soot, he could taste ash. But before he could gather himself, he saw the Deshmukhs.

They were in the orchard. Hands bound behind their backs with rope, they were all kneeling in a neat row facing the river, first the men, then the women. At the end of the row was a girl. Her hands were not bound; she was so slight and so pale that she looked sickly. He could hear her sobbing.

There were at least a dozen people standing around, carrying rifles and stripper clips, dressed in green fatigues. One of them stepped forward and began speaking.

"It is a heinous crime to take this land away from the hands that till it, from the ones who toil in it and whose toil you reap. For this crime, and the crimes you have committed against the people of Irumi for all these long years, you, Surendra Deshmukh, the zamindar of Irumi, and your family, are hereby sentenced to death. This is the verdict of the people's court."

The man stopped talking. He walked towards the kneeling row of men and women and positioned himself directly before the first man. He raised his pistol, braced it against the man's head and fired. The muzzle flashed. Kanakam could smell the gunpowder.

One after the other, the Deshmukhs all fell the same way. The girl shuddered each time the pistol fired. Kanakam felt as though he had been dropped into a dream; this dream of stepping into the gadi, walking across its floors, touching what existed inside. But the dream had turned into a wild, disorienting nightmare, and the only thing that told him the nightmare was real was the object still clutched tightly in his hand.

At last, the girl let out a long drawn-out scream, a piercing cry filled with such agony that Kanakam felt the little hairs on the back of his neck stand on end. The man reached the end of the line, stood in front of the girl.

Kanakam stepped away from the window. He did not want to see any more. He stumbled from the room, knocking into the doorframe.

He sprinted down the corridor, down the stairs, across the broken shards of glass, the courtyard. Stumbling through the collapsed doorway, he ignored his bleeding heels. Outside, he ran, down the hillock, back to the tanning settlement, back to the safety of his hut, trying to prevent his mind from serving up the vivid memory of the girl whose scream still rang in his ears.

# PART ONE

——◆——

# 1955

# THE TIGER IN THE STUDY

---

In late summers, Irumi's heat is softened and tempered. The monsoon has passed, but the trees are still chirring with crickets. In the afternoons, the hills, though still green, are dappled in a golden, sugary light. There is a languor, a variegated stillness, as if Irumi was caught in a strand of time that was lush and decadent.

On one such afternoon, four whole years before Kanakam was born, fifteen whole years before the execution of the Deshmukhs, a boy was lying on the warm stone wall of the stepwell outside the gadi, looking up at the long tendrils of the banyan swaying over the stepwell's mouth as though ready to swallow it whole. At twelve, Krishna was a portrait of good looks in the miniature: a handsome face, toffee-colored skin, dark eyes that glittered like river pebbles.

At the distinct sound of a window clattering, Krishna jumped down from the wall, landing lightly on his feet. He dusted his knees and his uniform shorts and scanned the windows of the gadi. All the windows were firmly shut. Still, he had the feeling of being watched. A sensation arose in him; a sure knowledge that something was about to happen, as in that brief moment between the flash of lightning and the first drops of rain falling.

After letting a minute pass, he pulled himself back onto the wall. He peered into the well, at the water glinting merrily in the afternoon sun, and assumed the pose of a diver.

Soon, his mother would appear. Bearing the day's ironing in a large sack, her spine curving under its weight, she would ask him about the whereabouts of his brother. He would say he didn't know. Or he'd venture a guess. Ranga, older than him but only by a year, was never in the place he was supposed to be. Probably, he was off in the hills—trapping birds, collecting the shed skins of cobras and rattlesnakes, or catching black mountain lizards. Though now, with the man-eating tiger on the prowl, they were forbidden from going into the hills.

But the reason he was to come straight here after school, to wait for his mother, was not the tiger. It was because his mother believed that his destiny lay outside of Irumi—not hers, not Ranga's—his alone. Today had been his first day at the village school, and he was no longer allowed to make friends in the village, he was not to enter the village at all, but cut through the cotton fields and the paddy fields to reach the hillock on which the gadi stood. He lifted one foot and dangled it in the air before him. One wrong move, and he'd fall straight in. He took pleasure, in the delicious edge between falling and not falling.

Vijaya Deshmukh was sitting cross-legged on top of her rolltop desk, also still in her school uniform, kneecaps resting in the crooks of her arms. Her room was on the second floor of the gadi, and she'd dragged the desk close to the windows so that she could look out over the views of the courtyard, the stepwell, the flower gardens, and the lemon grove. The rock fountain with its carved ducks and swans, the curve of the hillock, Irumi below it, the hills beyond. She relished this sensation, of being high up on a peak, a vantage point from which she could see but not be seen, the world laid out before her.

She was watching Krishna, standing on the stepwell's wall, as though ready to dive. For weeks, she had waited for him to show up at school, ever since she'd overheard her uncle and her father arguing about him in the study. Sometimes, Krishna and his brother came inside the gadi, asked in by her mother in one of her peculiar moods, but she'd never been close enough to get a good look. Today she had, but it had all gone so badly.

At school, she'd been expressly forbidden from speaking to Krishna.

In fact, she was not to speak to anybody. And nobody was to speak to her. Even the schoolmaster's eyes passed over the space where she sat as if she wasn't there. Those were her uncle's rules, and her uncle's rules were law. But today, a boy in her class had come up to her and asked her to move to a different seat. He had wide-set eyes, a sly and friendly smile. She'd returned the smile and complied; glad she was spoken to at all. But he came up to her again. Asked her to move again. "Make room," he'd said. The others turned to watch, waiting for her to react. When she refused, he pushed her to the floor. She got up and shoved him back. That was the wrong thing to do. Before she realized what was happening, he used both hands and pulled her hair from the roots, dragged her across the classroom. She fought back, but he was stronger. While the others jeered, he slapped her, clawed at her neck with dirty fingernails. Then he sat on her.

The boy had smiled triumphantly across the room at Krishna. But Krishna hadn't returned the smile, hadn't jeered with the others. He came towards them and pulled the boy off her. He attempted to help her up, but she pushed him away. "I don't need help from a washerwoman's son," she'd said. Then she spat at his feet the way she'd seen her uncle do. There was a strange expression on his face. He looked offended at what she'd done, certainly, but more than that he looked puzzled, as though he did not know that he occupied a position in life that lacked in dignity. She'd grabbed her schoolbag and raced home.

If she told her uncle, the boy would never be seen at school again. If she told her father, he'd tell her that she could stop going to school altogether if she wanted. Both these things would make her mother happy, so she did neither. Only Katya, who'd been sweeping the courtyard, had seen her arrive home too early, her face streaked in tears, bloody scratches on the side of her neck. But she knew Katya wouldn't tell, wouldn't violate the cardinal rule between all children: never tell the adults anything.

Vijaya hesitated, then crept out of her room.

Downstairs, she passed the pool in the courtyard, and as was her habit, stopped to look at her reflection. Her braids were askew, her collar was soiled, there was an ink stain on her pinafore.

The living room was empty, the dining room was empty. In the front house, passing the accountant's desk, she ran into Katya again. Katya was holding a tray of kalakand.

"Wait," Vijaya said. The milk cakes were still warm, crumbly to touch. She picked out the largest slice with the most almonds and pistachios and strands of saffron. After a moment's thought, she slipped it into her pocket even though she knew the ghee would seep through the fabric.

Katya was often staring at her like this, as though trying to puzzle out something in her features. Though they were roughly the same age, Katya reserved this attitude only for her, and never for Sree, her four-year-old sister, whom Katya treated with adoration and with pride.

"What?" she said.

"Nothing, dorasani," Katya said and walked past.

Outside, she slipped past the stone fountain in the courtyard, and checking to make sure no one saw her, she darted into the lemon grove, threading her way through the trees, towards the stepwell. Panting a little, and certain that nobody had seen her, she reached Krishna.

He scrambled off the wall, straightened up, and observed her carefully. His uniform had retained its crispness even after a long day; it looked the way hers had in the morning, sharp, clean, spotless.

She hadn't been taught how to say that she was sorry. Nor did she know how to ask him to be her friend. But she knew what she had, and what he didn't. "Do you want this?" she said, carefully extracting the slice of kalakand from her pocket.

When he came towards her, she saw for the first time how much taller than her he was, his eyes so intensely black they seemed to glitter. She watched his eyes go over the scratches on the side of her neck. She was at the point of putting the milk cake back into her pocket, but he stepped closer and took the slice. Instead of eating it, he looked at it closely, extracted a strand of saffron from the top and put it in his mouth.

"What does it taste like?" she said. It had never occurred to her to taste saffron.

He tilted his head from side to side as though casting around for the right word. "Like blood," he said. Then he bit into the sweet, chewed thoughtfully, and gave the slice back to her as though it was a thing they'd decided to share.

At home, even Katya's eating utensils were kept separate from theirs—a beaten aluminum bowl and tumbler kept in the kitchen, next to the gunny sacks of onions and the floor brushes—this, even though she'd lived with them since she was a baby; the only one allowed to serve their food or handle silverware at their dining table. Instead of saying Vijaya mustn't, that it was engili—defiled food, as untranslatable as it was inviolate—she looked at the bite marks his teeth left in the kalakand, the ghee there shining slickly, and took a bite. It seemed the best apology she could muster.

He was watching her. She didn't think the sweet tasted any different from any other time she'd had it; first like caramel and cardamom, then like rosewater and sweetened, condensed milk. Nor did she think his spit tasted any different from hers. In fact, it tasted familiar, almost recognizable. She passed it back to him. He took another bite and returned it to her, his gaze never once leaving her face.

It was a visceral sensation, being looked at this way. She felt separated—momentarily, secretly—from the overwhelming sense of loneliness she continually endured; relief from which she only experienced when fantasizing about the tiger, sitting on her rolltop after school, on the lookout—*there—there it is!—orange fur! black stripes!—creeping between the boughs of trees, the grass crackling ever so slightly under the weight of its paws*. It was like that—*relief*—being looked at by Krishna. Yet there was also something else, like the wild exhilaration of going into her uncle's study when he wasn't there, to hold the hunting rifle that was always leaning against his bureau, its solidity weighing down her shoulder, the metal cold against her skin when she slipped her finger into the trigger hold. Whatever its name was, she wanted to bind herself to this feeling. And she sensed that it could only exist with Krishna, in the far away hills where the tiger prowled.

"Do you want to go into the hills with me?" Vijaya asked.

Krishna hesitated, as though waiting for her to look away or pretend it was a joke. "There is a man-eater out there," he said. "Don't you know?"

"We'll find it. Shoot it with my uncle's gun."

They heard the hinges on the gadi's doorway creak. Krishna threw a furtive look over his shoulder. "My mother is coming," he muttered. Still, she did not move. She waited for his answer. They could hear Pichamma's footsteps drawing close. He met her gaze. Slowly, he nodded.

"Will you tell anyone?" she said.

He shook his head.

"Promise?" she said, extending her open palm towards him. Krishna placed his palm over hers.

Then, Vijaya slipped back into the lemon grove and hid. She watched Pichamma pause at the stepwell, heard Krishna say, "How should I know where he is? Maybe he's in the orchard, he goes there sometimes."

"Sometimes?" Pichamma repeated, her voice high and alarmed. "He isn't allowed!"

Vijaya could not hear Krishna's reply. She picked her way through the lemon grove, crossed the flower beds. At the water fountain, she ran into her sister.

"Where did you go?" Sree said, her shrill voice rising over the tinkling of water spraying from the tips of numerous beaks and wings in the fountain. Sree's face was scrubbed clean and her hair was combed and braided. She had changed out of her school uniform into a green skirt that brushed her toes, and an even greener matching blouse, its neckline embroidered with pink roses.

"Be quiet!" Vijaya said, shushing.

But Sree only moved closer. Placing her hands on her hips, she peered up at her. "Tell me where you went, Vijaya, or I will tell Ma."

Ranga was winding his way around a copse of mango trees in the orchard. After the June rains, the mango trees had all borne fruit. The orchard behind the gadi had no perceivable shape, it merely spread as it pleased, across the hillock, down to the riverbank. It was a noisy place. Loud with the buzzing of beehives hanging off neem trees, with jumping bugs and tree frogs, with the ruffling feathers of nesting birds, the lulling of larks and the percussion of woodpeckers. Even the red earth under the orchard, covered by panes of dried leaves, made a deafening racket as though protesting against the feet that passed over it. Each tree, sapling and flower bush had been planted without order, and when the fragrance of the orchard faded each season, it was overcome, like a second, sweeter note in a symphony, by the fragrance of the next season. Summer crops were jumbled together with winter trees; black plums, jujubes, papayas, sweet limes, drumsticks and oranges sat irreverently amongst electric crossandras, marigolds, sunflowers, frangipanis, rosebushes; all encased in the brambly vines of a jasmine laden with snowy buds as thick as one's thumb.

Ranga was taller than Krishna. His long hair brushed his shoulders. Streaked and lightened by sun and river water, it fell in coppery locks around his face, almost matched his hazel eyes. His clothes were constantly wet, often streaked with mud, damp from scrabbling around the river spearing catfish, muddy from running into the lemon grove to fetch ripe lemons for Saroja-dorasani.

At this time of day, he knew that his mother was still working. He imagined her collecting clothes for ironing, waiting with her white cloth sack open on the floor. Later she would walk home, the treasured wrought-silver kada around her ankle glinting in the sunlight, Krishna trailing her.

Ranga had always known where he wasn't supposed to be on the low hillock above Irumi. For example, he was not supposed to be inside the gadi, but he was allowed to be in the vaakili—the flagstone courtyard— allowed to stand near the rock fountain, near the clusters of rosebushes and marigolds, near the flower beds, the lemon grove. He knew that he wasn't supposed to be in the orchard. However, because there were so many places to hide and it was impossible to tell who passed through it, he was nearly always in the orchard. He was, emphatically, not allowed to pick fruit from the orchard, nor flowers from the jasmine vine. The inheritance of all living things in Irumi belonged to the Deshmukhs alone.

But sometimes, there were aberrations. Ranga was summoned and taken inside by Saroja-dorasani. When she needed him to climb into the gadi's ancient attic space and pull out some object from amongst hundreds that lived and breathed there: a brass prayer pot that belonged to her great-great-mother-in-law, a carved wooden plank, window shutters long out of commission, old wedding clothes, a decorated wooden throne for a deity, foot stools. Once, Ranga had hauled from the attic a massive copper vessel so large he could have climbed inside.

Saroja-dorasani allowed him inside, but only when neither her husband nor her brother-in-law, the zamindar, were home. Often, she had both Ranga and Krishna come in. She talked to them as though they were adults, and she gave them treats, usually a handful of roasted peanuts each.

While Krishna ate his peanuts and answered all her questions, Ranga remained silent. As best as he could, he memorized and committed to his mind everything in sight: the courtyard's open-air roof; the sprawling holy basil swathed in turmeric in its center, its leaves so bright and blinding they appeared to be set on fire by the sun; the polished teakwood easy chairs and woven rattan daybeds surrounded by thick, embroidered drapes that hung over doorways; brass doorknobs. On a low table was a gramophone, its elaborately curved ear poised over the turntable. There was also a massive radio next to a large wooden box that held the accountant's supplies. Ranga amused himself imagining the things inside its belly; inkpots, fountain pens, a thick ledger, a counting frame. He drank with his eyes on these occasions, and often forgot the peanuts clenched in his palm.

He had another reason for wanting so desperately to be invited in by Saroja-dorasani. He was consumed by an intense curiosity about her daughters: Vijaya and Sree. He wasn't allowed to look at them directly.

In his short years, Ranga had discovered that if he stepped over the line quietly enough, often enough, and if his transgressions were of just the right dimensions; neither too small to give him any pleasure nor too large to demand a beating worthy of tapping into his endurance, he could get away with them. These transgressions were usually his presence in places he wasn't to be. Ranga reasoned that the Deshmukhs' reliance on him meant a respect for him, which in turn meant that he was allowed to transgress, if somewhat quietly and invisibly. Who else had his ability to crawl into spider-filled spaces in the attic and resist breathing in centuries-old dust? They had tried once to get a farmhand to locate a large brass plate in the attics. After nearly an hour, he'd come down empty handed and they had to ask Ranga once again. Because *he* was the expert on the gadi's attics. *He* had committed to his memory all the objects amassed in the hundreds of feet of attic space beneath the roof, their contours and locations, and could recall within seconds—given enough description of the requested object—its exact location for immediate retrieval.

In the orchard now, Ranga walked barefoot. The soil was dry on top and wet underneath. He purposefully walked on fallen leaves. In the copse of mango trees, in the still afternoon air, the fragrance of ripening mangoes was overpowering. Their unbearable perfume filled his mouth, laced itself around his teeth. Most of the fruit had been left indifferently on the trees. Overripe, droplets of sugar oozed from their stems, crystallized, and sat all along the curved, yellow sides of the fruit. When a sunbeam caught a mango, the sugar crystals splintered and re-fracted. A few, far too heavy and overripe, had fallen clean off, snapping branches, cracking stems that now leaked sap, dropping into yellow, syrupy heaps, attracting wasps and dragonflies, whose lazy wings sounded like low, steady drumming.

Ranga, hearing only the relentless buzzing of dragonfly wings, made the impulsive decision to climb a mango tree.

He knew full well that picking fruit from the Deshmukh orchard was for him, along with the rest of the vetti, expressly forbidden. But then, this transgression too, appeared to have the right dimensions. It was likely that he wouldn't be caught, but if he was and there was a beating, it would be earned, and it would be of an intensity that also had the right dimensions.

As he climbed, Ranga scraped his knee against the bark. It stung and bled. He ignored it. Balancing himself on a thick branch, he draped both legs around it and edged forward, reaching towards a large mango that hung low, so ripe and so full of syrup that he was sure it too would drop in no time.

He couldn't reach it. He slid forward and reached again. The branch creaked under his weight. Blood rushed to his head when he felt his fingers close around the fat mango. It came off the stem easily. He tucked himself back into the tree, and as though in a trance, ate without pause, biting into the taut, yellow skin, relishing the hiss with which each, painfully sweet bite fell under his teeth. He did not stop, even to breathe, until only the well-scraped, furry seed of the fruit remained in his hands. He breathed deeply and let his breath out in a whistle. He felt euphoric.

As he made to climb down, he caught sight of Krishna, watching him from below, terror on every feature of his face. "Want one?" Ranga asked theatrically from above, waving his arm across the fruit-laden branch. He laughed.

Krishna shook his head and motioned with his hands. "You aren't supposed to!" he mouthed. "Ranga. Please get down, before you are seen."

"I'll come when I want to," Ranga replied, his tone perfectly even, perfectly audible, rising over the loud buzzing of the wasps and the bees and the dragonflies.

Smoking a cigar at the window of his study, Zamindar Surendra Deshmukh watched the back of Ranga's head and torso, moving willfully between the boughs of the mango tree. It wasn't the first time he'd seen the washerwoman's older son walking in the orchard. But it was the first time he'd seen the boy climb a tree, steal. It didn't matter if the object was a matchstick or a bar of gold, stealing remained stealing. Sometimes, when he saw the utter lack of fear on the faces of the vetti, especially in the young, punishment was a duty. A bland task that gave him neither pain nor pleasure. Something that simply must be done. He sighed.

He was sitting in the easy chair that faced the orchard, where he liked to sit in the afternoons while smoking. For the last month, a man-eater had been attacking Irumi. A second villager—this one from the tanning settlement—who'd gone out at night hadn't returned. A severed human arm had been discovered near the forest. He had tracked the tiger for three hours that morning, out in the hills, the thicketed region around Irumi that wasn't the jungle yet. The hills were lower there, only gradually did they rise to join the Eastern Ghats, the rim that led into the deccan and into the heart of the Nallamala forests. But he had lost the trail. He bristled at his failure. In a week or so, the tiger would attack once more. A taste for human flesh, once acquired, never left a wild animal: the desire was exorcised only by death.

He and Mahendra usually set out together, at early dawn, taking a goat on a rope with them as bait, but today he'd gone alone. They'd almost had it once: they'd tracked it to a ravine. The path was narrow, and the horses were frightened. He wanted to press on but Mahendra said no, it was too dangerous. Mahendra was soft, that was what was wrong with him. Though it was called kindness, in the village—Mahendra-dora and his kindness. A kindness that existed only because *he* permitted it. Even encouraged sometimes. His brother had gone to college in Paris, and there he had lost whatever it was that gave one one's true identity. Mahendra and his library, he was alternately pitiable and despicable.

Usually, Vijaya came to his study after school. "Will you take me with you, Uncle?" she'd ask, looking up from that book of hers in which she wrote down everything he said about where he'd spotted the man-eater's prints, how deep into the forest he'd tracked it, how long on which day. In fact, he asked to see her book when he himself couldn't remember a detail. And he'd have taken her too, acquiesced if not for Saroja; his sister-in-law would never permit anything that Vijaya might enjoy. Once, he remembered, he'd taken Vijaya to the stables with him and gotten her on his favorite horse. He'd taught her how to hold the reins, told her that it was in the horse's nature to obey, but only as long as she showed no hesitation. But she was a natural. He and the jeethas stood around, watched in astonishment when Vijaya began first at a slow trot, circling them, and then faster, leaning forwards and steering the horse, her long braids in the wind, her head angled, her toes turned outwards and her heels pushed against the horse's sides, even though he hadn't told her that was how it was done. The look of happiness on her little face had taken his breath away. How bright that child was.

But Saroja had arrived, ordered her to get down, her tone so vicious that he found himself too stunned to say anything. It was as though Saroja nursed an inexplicable grudge against her own firstborn, lashing out at anyone who showed Vijaya affection; it seemed there were sides, and Saroja wanted everyone on hers. Such was the difference between how she treated Vijaya and how she treated Sree, that no one dared mention the striking resemblance between Saroja and Vijaya; they had the same classically rounded features, the same light brown eyes and the same dark skin. Just as no one mentioned the uncanny resemblance between Katya and Sree.

Though his own daughter was the same age, Vijaya evoked in him a tenderness that Tara could not. What was it about Vijaya? There was a steeliness in her eye, in her manner, by virtue of the blood that ran in her veins. To the manor born. Like Vani, his wife, dead so many years now. It was a resemblance that was not physical yet plainly obvious. She was like Vani in spirit; maybe not surprising given that Vani was Saroja's first cousin. It was only a fever, and Vani was convinced that she was merely under the weather right up until she died. But Mahendra was ruining Vijaya, sending her to that village school like a commoner.

There was a book on Surendra Deshmukh's desk that he'd brought from Madras specifically for Vijaya. An illustrated children's book of crafts. He'd even folded down the corner of the page he knew she'd like: how to make a kaleidoscope. He wanted to give it to her when she came to his study after school, but today she hadn't. He'd call Katya and send it along.

He continued watching Ranga, his progress through the fat, yellow mango, but he didn't make his way to the orchard. He waited to see if he would climb another tree, steal another.

And Pichamma, this thief's mother, had the gall to make a case for her other son's education, to send him to school instead of sending him to the gadi for vetti, and that too Mahendra had permitted. It was outrageous. This, after Mahendra built her that timber cottage outside Irumi, in that same palm grove where her husband had fallen to his death. A veritable palace, for someone of her standing. It would have been one thing, to give a young widow some money, but quite another to single out her son, grant such things, such station. As if it were a bargain, in her eyes, to be allowed to keep one son because she was giving up the other. The gall of the woman, the gall that Mahendra allowed, facilitated, enabled. It was just like the whole Katya business, all so utterly dangerous. Whenever he was with Mahendra, all his energy went into not showing his contempt.

He had been sure when he set out alone that morning that he would find the man-eater. Shoot it, mount its head in this very study, wear its claws set in gold around his neck. Now, as he smoked and watched Ranga, his frustration at his failure pressed up against his irritation at this boy eating a mango in a tree.

His gun leaned against the bureau, his boots were still on his feet, only splattered here and there with mud. Surendra Deshmukh waited until he felt calmer. On the way out of the room, he stopped to pick out another cigar from a silver case sitting inside the bureau.

He did not immediately approach Ranga, he took a more leisurely route.

"Are you done?" he said, when he reached Ranga.

The color drained from the boy's face. He scrambled down the tree, and as he did, he wiped his cheeks with the edge of his shirt, a gesture that was so child-like and sheepish that it gave him pause. But why was he wearing a shirt? Who did he think he was?

He dragged Ranga by his hair, threw him to the ground and began kicking him. First methodically, then indiscriminately.

As he always did when performing a routine task that did not require him to be present mentally, Surendra Deshmukh mulled over thoughts as he disciplined Ranga. Mercy, he often thought, without the presence of cruelty, had the valency of impotence. He had never been a man to be trifled with. No vetti peasant ever stood with his spine erect in front of him. No vetti peasant needed to be told twice not to do so. And no vetti peasant ever refused to run barefoot ahead of his horse when he left for the makta, as was required of them; their lot in life: running.

It was a lesson a master must know how to administer. In the eyes of the vetti, he knew that compassion and tenderness were peculiar things, just as the vetti mind was a peculiar thing, one that had to be conditioned with a constant stream of cruelty, so that his mind would expect it, as part of his daily life, just as naturally as he expected sleep to come for him at night, sweat to come to his brow when he worked the paddy fields or breath to move in and out of his lungs when he ran like a blinded horse in front of the veiled zamindari carts. The world was a complicated place, but what use is wealth that had no pride, and what use is wealth if it isn't worth guarding.

In moments like these, moments when he had to be the zamindar of Irumi, Surendra Deshmukh knew that he was not an adult and Ranga was not a child, that distinction between their respective conditions dissolved, and was replaced by their respective roles: master and servant. Punishment was expected of him. Just as surely as forgiveness without punishment made him unworthy of their respect, he knew that when the punishment was delivered, the boy would feel cleansed of his sins, and he, Surendra Deshmukh, would appear to his eyes to be a merciful and forgiving man, and indeed, he would appear, as he would to any peasant he had to discipline, like a honey-bathed god.

When he finished, his cigar was still burning.

A silent hum fell for a few terse seconds. "And what do you say now," Surendra Deshmukh asked Ranga, in a tone not framed as a question.

Ranga reached out and touched the mud-splattered boots with the tips of his fingers. "Dora, nee banchan, dora," he recited. *Master, I am your slave, master.*

Ranga waited until he could no longer hear Surendra Deshmukh's boots, the receding sounds of leaves crushing under them. Then, he sat up, wiped his bloody lip with the back of his hand. His hands were shaking. He could still feel the tip of the boot lodged in his ribs. His stomach throbbed, he felt light-headed, his vision blurred from the pain. The intensity of the beating had been severe, unexpectedly, unendurably so.

Krishna appeared from behind the neem tree. He looked petrified, as though afraid to even blink.

"It's nothing," Ranga said. "It's over. You shouldn't have looked, I told you to shut your eyes. Didn't you shut your eyes? Why didn't you shut your eyes?"

He stood up, biting the inside of his cheek in order not to wince. "This is a jujube tree, isn't it?" he said conversationally, walking past Krishna. He glanced around them, at the silent trees, then raised himself on tiptoes. He plucked a fat jujube from a tree branch. Brushing the small maroon fruit against his shirt, he offered it to Krishna.

"Here," he said. "Eat it. You will feel better."

When Krishna shook his head, he drew him close and shoved the plum past Krishna's lips. "How does it taste?"

"It is sour, Ranga," Krishna said, chewing reluctantly, "very sour. But a little sweet too, in the center."

"I will get you more tomorrow. The sweeter ones are higher up."

Ranga spat blood, then licked his lips. Underneath the blood, he could still taste the sweetness of the mango.

# THE KING AND THE
# KALEIDOSCOPE

———

B y the time they returned to the palm grove outside Irumi where they lived, Krishna knew what things he was going to keep quiet. Their mother was turning over the little coal pile she always kept burning. The air had a soothing aftertaste of ash. A bird was hooting as though falling asleep. He and Ranga stopped and shared a look. Then they turned to look at their mother again, at the timber cottage behind her, the forest beyond. Even from afar, their cottage smelled like earthen floors. Like camphor, like tea. In it was a character that wasn't grandeur. Afterwards, while their mother made dinner, and the scent of rice starch hung above the grove, he and Ranga sat on the porch, not talking, their knees touching.

He did not tell Ranga about Vijaya. There had been a grimace or a smile on Surendra Deshmukh's lips, he wasn't sure which, because they were clamped around a lit cigar. And when he went back to school the next day, he made sure his gaze never met Vijaya's, he felt so afraid. But while leaving, Vijaya slid a folded piece of paper across his desk. He waited until he was out of the school grounds before opening it.

It was a page, ripped carelessly from what he could guess was an expensive book, because the paper was thick, the illustrations in rich color and not simple black and white. Vijaya had underlined an item under "Things you will need to make a kaleidoscope" and made a note next to it, meant for him: *Krishna—bring this!—when you come to the stepwell today.*

His mother told him, nearly every day, that his going to school instead of being put to work in the gadi, like Ranga, was an uncommon gift. That he will never in life be given the things he deserves, but only the things he earned. It went without saying that he was never to squander or imperil this gift. He re-read Vijaya's note on the page; her absolute faith that he would do as she asked; the loop in the *K* she made when she wrote his name.

He folded the page, slipped it back into his pocket. The path that left the school grounds split into two, one into the village, through the bazaar and then to the bus depot, and the other towards the gadi, through the cotton fields. He stopped there and looked at the fields, it was that time of year when the bolls ripened and cracked, and every single field marker was covered in monkeypod vines. Krishna opened the page again. He found it strangely pleasurable to have her demand something of him, when she could demand anything of anyone.

He sensed someone coming up behind him. He turned around. It was the wide-faced boy who'd attacked Vijaya—his name was Linga, Krishna had found out. Though he was in their grade, he was older than Ranga.

Krishna held down the page, but Linga pulled it out of his hands so forcefully that the edge tore away. "Give it back," he said. Linga ignored him, holding the page out of his reach. Krishna saw his eyes go over the place where Vijaya had made her note.

Linga grinned at him. It was a sly, inviting grin, as though willing to make an insider out of Krishna. Then the grin became a grimace as spiteful as it was malicious. An image arose in Krishna's mind, of Linga finding Vijaya alone at the stepwell, standing over her the way Surendra Deshmukh had stood over Ranga.

Yesterday, the reason he hadn't stepped out from behind the tree wasn't because he was afraid, or had wanted to protect himself, but because Ranga wouldn't have permitted it.

"Do you want me to come with?" Linga said, crumpling up the page in one hand.

"What will happen to you, then, when dora finds out?" Krishna said.

Linga's expression changed. Krishna stood his ground; he thought Linga might grab hold of him, but he merely looked at Krishna with distaste, and pity. He threw the crumpled page at Krishna's feet. "You're like their dog, aren't you?" he muttered. "A faithful little hound that kneels when told to kneel."

Later, when Krishna arrived at the stepwell, he saw that Vijaya was already there, but not alone as he'd expected.

The little girl came up to Vijaya's waist. She was wearing a long silk skirt that brushed her toes, in a shade so violently purple that it seemed to punch a hole in the red earth beneath her feet. She looked to be no more than four or five years old.

Sree had until that point been kneeling on the ground, pressing her ear against the stepwell's wall. "He's roaring, Vijaya," he heard her say in an awestruck voice. "He's roaring! Come and listen!"

But as soon as she caught sight of him, she darted away and hid behind the stepwell's wall. Vijaya shook her head, from which Krishna gathered that he was not to acknowledge Sree's presence. "Did you bring them?" Vijaya said instead.

He nodded, extracting the shards of multihued glass he'd taken from the photo framers' in the bazaar.

"Good," Vijaya said. "Now I have everything."

Sree was leaning around the wall and gawking at him, but as soon as he looked her way, she hid behind the wall again. He knew there was a place there, alcove-like, where a pile of boulders sat stacked atop one another, so completely hidden that if someone looked down on the stepwell, even from a high window in the gadi, they would remain invisible. He walked around the stepwell's wall, knowing Vijaya would follow.

The banyan's branches were sparser here, as if the tree had tried to reach the spot but gave up. From this vantage point, they had sweeping views of the Ghats, nearly blue, running away from them in an almost straight line.

Sree was sitting cross-legged on the ground, looking up at him. She looked so different from Vijaya—an unusually pale face, a sharp and narrow chin, long jet-black hair braided and tied up above her ears with scarlet ribbons.

"Is it roaring?" he asked Sree.

"*He* is roaring," she corrected him. "And it's the same for walls. And for tumblers. And my father's desk. They all roar, you know, but only if you press your ear against them and close your eyes. Do you want me to show you?"

Before he could answer, Vijaya stepped in between them. "Do you still have the page?" she said.

He extracted the folded sheet from his pocket. He'd done his best to smoothen out the creases.

"What news of the tiger?" became a form of greeting between them. Krishna told Vijaya what he heard from Ranga, who was now being taken along as a tracker with Surendra Deshmukh. Or what he'd heard at school from the others. And Vijaya told him what her uncle said, and showed him the book in which she kept careful notes. As the months passed, flipping through the book, he stopped being able to distinguish his own writing from hers.

She always brought something with her when she came—usually sweets she snuck out of the kitchens. Warm laddus still dripping with syrup, halwa studded with almonds and strands of saffron, qubani in engraved silver bowls, sheer kurma so rich the taste of cream stayed in his mouth for hours afterward. They didn't eat the almonds, though. Vijaya made him bury them in the earth behind the stepwell. She said it was so fertile there, a tree would soon sprout. And she'd lay back on it, the fertile earth, close her eyes and spread her arms wide, as though she could hear the tree growing.

Often she said, "What is it like?" and he knew she meant, "What is it like in the hills, away from here?" He wished he could tell her.

If Sree managed to track Vijaya, "I *can* walk that far, you know?" would be her unasked response to everything. She said it was her special power, to be able to locate and track Vijaya at all times. Her other power being her ability to render Vijaya's name—*Vijaya, Vijaya, Vijaya!*—repetitively and percussively. Every time Sree came, she would press her ear against the stepwell and tell them he was roaring, demand that Vijaya sit alongside her and listen. She'd included herself in their plan without invitation, and it was no longer possible to exclude her; the words *I'll tell Ma* would rise to her lips.

The man-eater continued to remain elusive, sighted now and then near the tanning settlement, drawn there by the smell of the carcasses, the huts whose doors were closed merely with woven reed. In the middle of the night, Krishna caught his mother waking up to check the bolts on the door, to make sure that he and Ranga were fast asleep. If the night grew windy, and the door of their cottage thudded, he imagined it was the tiger, trying to nudge the latch open, its black and gold stripes shimmering threateningly from just beyond the borders of his imagination. The truth was that if Vijaya said she no longer wanted to go, he wouldn't press her. But she did, and he was careful not to express any signs of fear around her. He didn't feel as though it was in his power to stop himself from doing what she asked.

But now and then, they forgot. At the end of the summer, Krishna took his green marbles with him. He arranged the marbles in a pattern on the ground, then proceeded to lose all of them to Vijaya because her aim was so fierce. But she refused to take them. So, he took flat rocks he'd found near the river, stacked them on top of one another, and taught her palli patti; a game alien to her but familiar to him. He won every round, and he knew that made her happy.

And sometimes, they made up stories. His were mostly re-renderings of the burrakathas he went to hear with Ranga, narrated by the nomadic storytelling troupes that passed through Irumi. They weren't allowed to go to the performances, so Vijaya interrogated him: How exactly did the storyteller stand—how exactly did the secondary tellers stand: Did they mime? Did they play their instruments in the pauses, or for effect, or to quicken the rhythm? What did the little percussive drum look like? What about the long-necked string instrument that twanged and twanged?

Then Vijaya re-did them, the stories. She was the storyteller, but the stories were all her own, and they were marvelous.

He wondered how long it took her to concoct them. A minute? An hour? A day? When she came armed with one, she would say without preamble: *Do you want a story?* In a tone full of urgency, as though she was afraid the story would slip away from her and disappear if he didn't say yes. Her round cheeks and her round eyes, like a little, brown-eyed speaking doll.

It was late December by the time Vijaya finished making the kaleidoscope.

They were sitting, as they usually did, perched on the rocks behind the stepwell. Irumi, as it always did, spread underneath them. The kaleidoscope was sitting on her outstretched palm. It was wrapped in red silk. When he picked it up and turned it over in his hands, strands of sunlight splintered off the gold zari. "Press it against your eye," she said.

As he pressed it against his eye and turned it, she whispered into his ear, that she cut out the silk from her mother's wedding sari. Snuck it out of the closet, cut a strip from the inside, folded it back up, snuck it back in. That she'd taken an antique brass pipe from the library, slipped in the mirrors and the glass shards he'd given her. As he turned it, as the patterns gathered, swelled, shifted, the kaleidoscope made a pleasurable, tinkling noise. Vijaya whispered that she'd broken off pieces from her silver anklets and strung them around it with twine. Whispered all this because Sree had managed to come along and she didn't want her to overhear, because Sree could not be trusted with big secrets.

"Do you want to keep it?" she said, almost inaudibly.

"Can I see?" Sree interjected.

"Here," Krishna said, but Vijaya snatched it away before Sree could touch it. "It's not for you." She opened his schoolbag and placed the kaleidoscope inside. "Don't let anyone see," she told him. When he went home, he hid the kaleidoscope inside the batting of his bedspread, nestled it into a spot he remembered not to sleep on. It was the only place at home that he was sure would remain out of sight of both his mother and Ranga.

The very next day after she gave him the kaleidoscope, Vijaya came to the stepwell and asked without preamble if he wanted a story about a king who went hunting in the forest. It was as if she never wanted to meet him empty handed.

He was about to say yes when he noticed that her cheeks were flushed and red, her hands were shaking. Anyone else would have thought she looked angry. Krishna thought she looked distraught.

"Vijaya, what happened?" he said.

"Ma found out about the sari," Sree whispered.

"And who told her!" Vijaya snarled, glaring at Sree.

"Vijaya, I didn't!" Sree said, tears springing into her eyes. "I told you I didn't! I didn't tell Ma, I promise, Vijaya! Katya said Ma looks at it once in a while for no reason at all." But Vijaya glared at her until Sree lowered her eyes and looked at her feet. "I promise I didn't tell," she mouthed.

Vijaya turned to him, asked him again if he wanted a story. Her voice was brittle and shaky, but her face was resolute.

"Yes. Yes, of course," he said.

Vijaya stood up and told him to make the drumming noise. Sree, though she wasn't asked, made the twanging noise. Vijaya began to speak in a high, clear voice:

"Once upon a time, there was a kingdom whose king was just and kind."

*Are you listening, little children? Listen, listen. Pay close attention.*

"Once upon a time, there was a kingdom whose king was just and kind. It was a small kingdom. It had a river, a jungle, a palace, and fields and huts where the villagers lived. Each month, the king went into the nearby forest to hunt, for sport. The forest was full of overhung vines, tree bears, snakes, tigers, deer, birds, and beehives. Even so, the king always went alone, and even so, the royal palace guard was never worried about the king's safety. It wasn't just because the king was an extraordinary marksman; it was because the king took with him the swiftest horse in the entire kingdom, as well as the royal hunting dog. The presence of these two faithful animals eased the minds of the palace guard.

The hound was called Bhairav. Thin and long-limbed, Bhairav was bred for hunting. His name meant *dog*, and also a being who took the form of a dog, and when the king looked at Bhairav's short brown coat, his dripping, eager tongue, and thought of the name's meaning, it made him think how much he loved that dog.

On a hunt one particular morning, the king came across a doe. It was young, a pair of stubby antlers just beginning to emerge. He gently tugged on his horse's reins. Luckily, the doe didn't hear them. It was looking at its reflection in a pool of water, a glen, now and then dipping its neck low and drinking from the pool. Bhairav waited, his eyes fixed on the doe, his nose twitching.

Usually, the king shot rabbit or duck. Now, as he watched the doe, he thought of how much the princesses would love having it, feed it berries and sugar lumps perhaps. He decided that he would injure it as little as possible. All he wanted to do was to capture it. The king raised his bow. It was utterly quiet.

The doe was still staring at its reflection. The king heard his bowstring creak, the arrowhead pointed, with great accuracy, at the doe's hind leg.

It was a small or large wild animal. It made a frightening sound the very second the king's arrow left his bow.

Bhairav howled in fear, and the king's horse neighed and reared on his hind legs, causing the king to fall. He smashed his shoulder and crushed the bones on his right hand. In the ensuing confusion, the king's ankle snapped underneath his horse's hooves.

There was a river of blood, and all around the king fell his regalia: his ruby-encrusted sword, his filigree dagger, his bow, and his quiver of arrows. The king became unconscious.

When he came to, he heard a loud, heated argument between Bhairav and his horse. *What?* the king thought. Immediately, as though re-reading a sentence in a book, he tried to make sure what he heard was heard correctly.

'You made him fall!' Bhairav was shouting, pacing back and forth between the fallen king and the royal horse.

'But *you* howled!' the horse replied.

The king stayed where he was, terrified and unable to move; he did not let a single moan or murmur escape him. Like Karna before earning Parashuram's curse, the king bore the physical agony of his injuries in absolute silence. *Dogs do not pace*, he told himself. *And horses do not speak.*

'That was a tiger,' Bhairav was saying. 'The king has fallen, there is blood and soon it will be dark.'

'Should we leave him here?' the royal horse said, a look of terror on its long face.

'What if he survives?' Bhairav asked. 'He will have us executed for deserting him in a time of need.'

'Should we kill him, then?' the horse whispered in a low voice.

The king shut his eyes and waited for the illusion to dissolve. He waited and waited. Then, he felt Bhairav and his horse move towards him."

A cloud of parrots came flying towards the hill, and Vijaya stopped speaking. They were screeching and moving together as a flock, like a sheet of jade. After they passed, she turned to Krishna and Sree. "Did you see that?" Vijaya asked. "Did you see the parrots?"

"Forget the parrots!" he said. "What happened to the king?"

"In the story!" Sree said.

A gust of wind rolled over the hills and blew in their faces, carrying with it the smell of custard apples, which ripened only once a year, in late December, in the wild; a concentrated aroma of sugar and cream buried beneath wet leaves and bark. Vijaya inhaled deeply and met his eyes. She looked calm now. He knew what she was going to say.

"Why not tomorrow?" she said.

"What are you talking about?" Sree interjected.

"Krishna," Vijaya said, drawing so close that he could feel her breath on his face. "My uncle said that it has crossed over the ravine again. And he said the path was too narrow for an adult to follow, for a horse to follow. Do you know what that means?"

"Are you sure the tiger won't eat us?" Sree said.

Her eyes were bright and shiny. "*We can.* Krishna, *we'll* go hunting. *We'll* find it and shoot it. With my uncle's gun." She lifted up her arms and mimed holding the gun, as if she could feel the cold, burnished metal. The heft of it.

"What?" she said, observing his face.

He did not like how she was looking at him.

"You don't want to?" she said, frowning, dropping her hands into her lap.

Though he said nothing, Vijaya stood up and beckoned Sree with two fingers. Looking oddly pleased, Sree shrugged and followed. They walked around the stepwell and disappeared from his sight. He did not stop her. He waited several minutes to see if she would come back.

"Vijaya!" he shouted.

The thought passed through him that he mustn't be heard taking her name that loudly.

But again, he called her name, quite loudly and recklessly. "Vijaya!"

By the time he caught up with them, they were in the lemon grove. Vijaya was standing facing him, her hands folded across her chest as though she'd purposely chosen that spot to wait for him. Sree was stroking the sharp needles on the branch of a nearby tree.

"Okay," he said when he reached her, panting a little. "We'll go. I want to go."

"Tomorrow," she said. Her cheeks were still flushed, but there was a note of triumph in her voice. She extended her palm towards him, and he placed his own over hers. She shifted her hand slightly so their palms matched up. It went without saying that he was to tell no one.

# SPILLING THE PEARLS

A t dinner that night, while Katya laid down their plates, Sree
began to talk, excitedly, about their plan for tomorrow. What
an adventure it was going to be! To go into the hills! To hunt
down the tiger! Their parents were sitting on the other side of the dining
table, speaking in low voices. Her mother's hand was open on the table.
Her father tried to close his hand over hers, but she pulled away even
before he touched her. Vijaya knew that she was the subject of their conversation.

Sree peered around the table. She even tugged Katya's sleeve, waiting
for a reaction to what she'd said. But when excited, Sree spoke so rapidly
that her words tumbled and clattered like loose change in a tin can. It
was impossible for anyone to make out their meaning.

Sree started over. "What an adventure—!"

Vijaya reached over and pinched Sree's thigh under the table. Sree ignored her and continued speaking, but when Vijaya pinched harder, Sree
fell quiet. It seemed to thrill her, to share a secret with Vijaya, even if it
hurt a little. She put her finger to her lips and whispered, though quite
audibly, "Let's talk in *our* room, Vijaya."

Sharing a room was something their mother insisted they do, despite
Vijaya's daily, vehement protests, and despite there being so many unoc-
cupied rooms in the gadi. Usually, their mother did not deign to respond,
but once, she said, "Because Sree is your sister," as if that settled the matter

for eternity. "Maybe she isn't!" Vijaya had snapped, meaning only that they didn't look alike: Sree's face was heart-shaped, not round like hers; Sree's eyes were a deep black, not brownish like hers; and Sree's skin was pale and milky, not dusky like hers. And because anytime an opportunity presented itself, their mother remarked that everything about Sree—the delicate almond eyes, the slender nose, the fine fingers and feet—gave off the impression of being thoroughly refined, sieved for purity. Because such praise was never lavished on Vijaya. But her mother gripped her elbow tightly and said that Vijaya was never to utter such a thing again, letting go only when Vijaya cried out.

"And what will you talk about in your room?" their mother said now, looking over at them.

Sree fell quiet. Their father took a sip of water from his glass, pointedly not looking Vijaya's way.

When Vijaya's gaze met her mother's, she felt a curious prickling sensation—it ran up the sides of her neck and both her cheeks, her earlobes, rushing towards the top of her head where her roots still burned. It was as if she could still feel the impact of her mother's hands from the afternoon, striking her haphazardly, indiscriminately.

Vijaya looked down at her plate. Katya hadn't served the meat or vegetables yet, but she'd heaped the rice in a neat little mound. The rice was so hot that the steam rising from it blurred her vision, scalded the tip of her nose when she drew close. Knowing that her mother was watching her, Vijaya pushed her fingers into the center of the rice and held them there. She gritted her teeth, curled her toes and waited for her mother to exclaim—that Vijaya's fingers would sear—turn pink and blister—to shout for a bowl of ice-cold water—to say *Vijaya, stop.*

But her mother said nothing. Instead, she felt Katya by her side, their elbows grazing as though by accident. "Do you want some mutton, Vijaya-dorasani?" Katya said. She nodded, withdrew her fingers, waited for the pain to recede.

Her mother said, "Aren't I talking to you? Deaf, are you? Along with everything else that you are. What are you going to talk about in your room?"

Her father flattened the rice mound in his plate, blew on it. Sree looked at Vijaya as if she had no choice but to tell, she opened her mouth. Vijaya cut across, "Why do I have to share a room with *her*?" she said, knowing full well that it would enrage her mother, but also drown out curiosity.

"Because she is your sister!" her mother shouted, standing up. She looked livid. Her hair, usually combed and braided twice a day, was spilling around her face. She'd even taken out her nose ring. Vijaya did not remember ever seeing her mother's face without it. Her cheeks looked sallow, kindly even, without the light falling off the bloodred rubies coloring them. She stared at the bare piercing, the friendly-looking nub, slightly raised, slightly darker than the rest of her face. It made her mother seem both familiar and unfamiliar, like the time when she'd come home after a day in second form to find that her uncle had shaved off his mustache, how he'd been unable to understand why it made Vijaya burst into tears.

Her father motioned at Katya to add more meat to his plate, and Katya came between them, blocking her from her mother's view. Katya looked around at her and hissed, "What are you doing? Go upstairs! Quickly."

Vijaya pushed her plate away and went upstairs, throwing Sree a look of warning. *Say nothing. Or else.*


Upstairs, in her room, Vijaya sat on her bed and pulled up her feet. Her soles were grimy. Her cheeks were still tingling, her roots still burned, and now her fingertips throbbed alongside everything else. She felt miserable. Across the room, on her desk, was the book of crafts her uncle had given her, she'd tucked the page she'd ripped out to give to Krishna, the one on the kaleidoscope, into the middle.

When she returned home from school today, she'd found her uncle pacing in the front house, waiting for her. His eyes were gleaming when he told her that the tiger had crossed into the ravine again—cornered, surely—that he would get it this time, and Vijaya could come. She felt her conviction mirrored on his face. For one resplendent moment, Vijaya heard the horse's hooves hammering the earth, the wind whipping her hair, her hands clutching the reins. All she had to do was get her mother to permit it.

She went straight to her mother's room, entered without knocking, asked if she could go. Her mother was standing in front of the mirror. She had draped her wedding sari over the clothes she was already wearing, the long piece thrown over her shoulder so that Vijaya could see both fabrics held together, the pale lavender cotton clashing brilliantly against the red silk. Her mother was tracing the gold thread spilling out of the place where Vijaya had cut, her face wet with tears.

She could have apologized, but an apology also meant the rendering of an explanation; why she'd cut the sari; what she did with it; where it was. It *had* occurred to her when she'd made the kaleidoscope, bent over the piece of gold-and-red silk, that her mother might find out. That she needn't have cut up the sari at all. And she needn't have stolen the antique brass pipe from the library, nor broken pieces off her silver anklets with the stone pestle she'd taken from the kitchen, striking at link after link as loudly as she dared. And she needn't sneak out of the gadi every day after school to go to the stepwell. But she did it anyway. She could never say that she did all of it for Krishna, the one person who seemed to behold her in wonder, worthy of regard, even of endearment.

It didn't seem right to feign contrition, it felt dishonest. So she looked straight into her mother's face and did not answer. Her mother had arrived at the explanation that she'd done it simply to cause mischief. You have a cruel nature, her mother said. It felt like an indictment; an unmalleable definition of who she was. And all the while her mother was striking her, she made no noise. If nobody heard them, it was possible that it didn't happen.

She'd shut her eyes until she heard Katya, trying to intervene, pulling her out of her mother's room. When something like that happened, only Katya could intervene. Even her father did not—vaguely she had a memory of him saying that it was something between women, that he couldn't—shouldn't—interfere.

Afterwards, her uncle had found her in the hallway outside his study, sitting on the floor, crying quietly. She knew her mother wouldn't come here. It was the only safe place in the gadi. "Did you ask?" he said.

Then he drew her close and patted her hair. It felt so comforting to be held by him. His clothes always smelled like the outdoors; like starch and horses, his aftershave, and underneath it all like gun oil. She couldn't stop crying.

"Am I cruel?" she asked him.

He said she was spirited. As fierce and determined as he was. That she was like him, a born leader, his true heir, and that one day she'd learn to own lives. "And cruelty isn't a bad thing, Vijaya. It is a skill, one that cannot be taught. You must be born with it, and you'll learn to use it."

"Will you still take me with you?" she asked.

He shook his head. "You know," he added, holding her cheeks between his palms. "I have something for you, but only if you stop spilling all the pearls." It was something he said anytime he caught her crying. "Stop spilling the pearls, Vijaya. How ever will we gather them all up again?" It never failed to make her smile.

He went into his study and came back out with a small jewelry box. Inside were a pair of gold-wire earrings strung with oyster-colored pearls. "They look like jasmine buds," Vijaya said, holding one up to her ear.

"Don't tell your mother," he said. "At least not today."

Afterwards, walking down to the stepwell to meet Krishna, the story about the king and the hound and the horse had appeared in her mind fully formed, as they always did. Like a shadow falling away from her own body, it was simply there when she looked.


Katya and Sree came upstairs.

"Why did you have to say that, Vijaya-dorasani?" Katya said gently. "You knew it would make her angry. Now she has a headache, and she didn't eat either." She was holding a covered bowl. "It's for you," she added. "Eat, or you'll be hungry through the night."

"Did Ma send it?"

"Dorasani isn't mean. Only *you* make her so."

Vijaya asked again if her mother had sent the food.

Katya sighed. "Why do you have to make so much mischief, Vijaya-dorasani? Why can't you be sweet, like Sree-papa?"

Sree was at Vijaya's desk, about to open the jewelry box with the pearl earrings. "Don't you touch it," Vijaya snapped at her.

"You never do anything to make her happy," Katya said, pulling Sree away. "You could tell your father that you want to study with Tara's tutor instead of going to school. You know that would make her so happy—it would make even your uncle happy—but you won't do such a small thing either. Why is that, if not to vex her? It's as if vexing her is the only thing you truly want."

"She only wants me to stay home so Sree wouldn't have to go either."

"And why did you have to cut your mother's wedding sari? You could have cut another, any other."

"Katya, *she* could buy another. As many as she wanted."

"You don't understand," Katya said.

"She doesn't like me because I'm not beautiful," Vijaya said, her voice cracking. "Like Sree. Isn't it so?"

Katya let go of Sree, who darted back to Vijaya's desk. That familiar expression crossed Katya's face again, as though trying to puzzle something out in Vijaya's face. There was something in Katya too that Vijaya wanted to puzzle out, in that gentle way she had of speaking. Gentle and graceful, even while squatting in front of the woodstove. Once, Vijaya had asked her mother why Katya's name sounded odd. Her mother said that it was Russian, that Vijaya's father had picked it out of a book when Katya was a baby.

"I think you are beautiful," Katya said.

She motioned at Vijaya to show her hands. When she did, Katya drew close and held them open, asked her if it hurt. The pads of Katya's fingers were thick and calloused, she was wearing what Vijaya now recognized as clothes that used to belong to her—a brown skirt and a black blouse that did not go together. There was a burn mark on her sleeve in the exact shape of the handle on the rice pot. And she smelled of hay, like she'd been in the animal shed before coming here. "They look all right," Katya said. "They won't blister, but you mustn't have done that. You can't fix anything by hurting your own self."

Vijaya had the sudden, irrepressible urge to confess everything. About the kaleidoscope, about Krishna, about their plan for tomorrow. She even wondered what it would be like to ask Katya to come along—why couldn't she come along, anyway?—in fact, it would be better, to take Katya instead of Sree. She felt as if it would all spill out of her, she even had the terrific image in her head of oyster-colored pearls spilling out of her mouth when she spoke.

"But . . ." Katya hesitated. "You don't understand, Vijaya-dorasani. Your mother is supposed to wear her wedding sari on her pyre when she dies. It is irreplaceable. You took that away from her, and you should be sorry."

Vijaya pulled her hands away. "Who do you think you are, to tell me how I should feel?"

Katya's face hardened. Now there was no kindness on it. It was as if a ghost of someone else settled on it, making it unrecognizable; vindictive even. Katya wouldn't harm her, she knew this to be true. She couldn't, she wasn't allowed. But Vijaya still felt the little hairs on her forearms stand on end.

"What's a pyre?" Sree interjected. Neither of them answered her.

Katya left, taking the bowl with her. She and Sree changed into their night clothes and got into bed without talking. A full moon hung outside, its light filtering through the fret windows, beams splitting and falling across their feet.

"Vijaya, will you finish the story?" Sree asked, a somewhat ugly rag doll pressed to her ribs.

"Did you tell Katya anything?" Vijaya said. She'd caught them exchanging a meaningful look before Katya left. She supposed it could have been because Sree wanted Katya to kiss her cheeks before bed, something she knew Katya did in secret.

"No, I didn't. I promise. What happened to the king? Will you tell me?"

She didn't know how it ended. Not yet. But she didn't say so.

"Please?" Sree said.

A night owl swooped past the window, and Sree sat up. They could hear a lizard chittering on the windowsill. "Vijaya? Will you sleep in my bed with me?" she said.

"No."

# THE HILLS

———◆———

In the morning, instead of going to school, Vijaya and Sree snuck down to the stepwell. Sree had been remarkably quiet all morning, pressing her finger to her lips and looking into Vijaya's face to demonstrate how well-behaved she was being, except once, to ask Katya for the flower shape in her ribbons when she had her hair braided. As they waited for Krishna to appear, they took turns crouching low and casting glances around the stepwell.

It was early. The vaakili was bustling with people; with those who either came to wait their turn to speak to their uncle, or those who worked there in the morning, sweeping, raking fallen leaves and rinsing the flagstones with water and metal brushes until stone resembled liquid, and the gadi appeared as though floating on the surface of a gray lake. In the kitchens, woodstoves burned, copper boilers heated water, smoke and specks of ash dotted the air. It was cold underneath the banyan; Vijaya's palms were clammy, and the more she tensed, the tighter her grip became wrapped around Sree's hand. She had to make sure Sree didn't wander back into the vaakili where someone might see her.

"Will there be elephants in the forest?" Sree asked. "I want to see elephants, Vijaya."

"Hush," Vijaya said. "Don't speak!"

"How much longer? Can I speak when we go into the forest?"

Nearly an hour passed. As the sun rose higher, the winter mist that gathered over Irumi each morning disappeared, the sheet of water over the vaakili evaporated, the outlines of the hills and the Nallamala Range grew sharp.

Sree squirmed. "Let go of my hand," she whined. "It hurts."

"Don't you want to come with us?"

"I want to."

"Then don't move—"

"But my hand hurts!"

"If you move, we won't take you. Do you want us to leave you behind?"

When Krishna finally arrived, he wasn't alone. If Vijaya was upset that Krishna had brought Ranga, she didn't show it. She stared at the wild, copper-haired boy standing there, taller than any of them.

"Did anyone see you?" Vijaya said. What she meant was that Krishna wasn't supposed to have broken their promise.

"No," Krishna said, not meeting her eyes. "Where's the gun?" he added.

Vijaya motioned at her schoolbag, which partly concealed the barrel of the Ishapore Lee-Enfield Mk1, the polished metal glinting in the sunlight. Krishna moved her bag and crouched on the ground. "So heavy," he said, lifting it, holding it with both hands. He raised the gun and lowered the gun, his thin arms straining under its weight. He slipped his fingers into the trigger hold. He looked around at Ranga. Ranga gave an imperceptible nod. Krishna could read his mind; Ranga wanted to touch it, but not here, this close to the gadi.

They stood around the gun in silence, as though the gun was the fifth member of their hunting party.

Ranga ambled over to the rim of the stepwell. His shirt, although clean, was yellowed with age, and missing buttons here and there, the spots held together with rusted pins or with broken, mismatched buttons that Pichamma must have sewn. There was dust in his hair, dirt on his elbows, and a reckless attitude that recognized none of these things.

Sree drew close to Ranga. When he looked at her, she smiled into his face. Then she copied him, drawing herself up on the wall of the stepwell, beside him.

"So, do you think we will find the tiger?" she asked Ranga.

Krishna held Vijaya's arm and drew her aside. "Ranga knows the forest, Vijaya. He knows how to find the ravine."

Every time Vijaya had encountered Ranga around the gadi, she'd felt for him an intense jealousy she couldn't understand. Yesterday, her uncle had told her that she'd learn to own lives, but what that meant was still abstract and out of her reach, set aside for her adulthood like an inheritance. But she recognized that there was something not willing to be possessed in Ranga. Also, he made her feel afraid—of the forest, of the hills, of the tiger, of the solid fact that she had never been inside the jungle before.

"Without him, we'll get lost and never find our way home," Krishna said. "Vijaya, he won't tell anyone."

She'd obsessed for months over going, but now she was scared. Vaguely, she recollected that she'd even forgotten to bring the notebook in which she'd transcribed all the things her uncle told her: how to lay the bait and stay downwind of it, live bait being preferable; to stay away from water bodies where the tiger might come to drink; to be watchful of tracks in wet mud; to choose a vantage point that got sunshine or shade but not both; to aim for the heart. Her fists felt clammy and cold.

Vijaya picked up her schoolbag, slipped the straps over her shoulders.

Krishna looked upset. She noticed a crease form between his eyes. The light in his eyes, which always gave the impression of glittering, even in the shade, seemed to dim.

"Bait," Vijaya said, motioning at her bag. "Mutton. I took it from the kitchen without Katya noticing."

Krishna smiled, out of relief that she wasn't angry with him for violating their promise, and that by including Ranga, he hadn't really—not really—lied to his mother. Vijaya handed him the gun. When he took it from her, her fingertips brushed his, and their deathly coldness shocked him. Whenever their hands touched before, he noticed how warm they were, reminding him more than anything else of a bumblebee he'd caught once, feeling its soft body move inside his cupped palms, not knowing when it would sting. He wondered if it was possible that she was scared.

"Vijaya, are you afraid?" he asked.

In her eyes was such determination. "No. Are you?" she said.

Krishna slung the gun strap across his chest so the barrel rested against the back of his neck. He looked around at Ranga and nodded.

They started out after hiding Krishna and Sree's schoolbags behind the stepwell. Ranga walked ahead of the group. They crossed the lemon grove and descended the hillock. At the base of the hillock, they reached a dirt road. On the other side, the foothills of the Ghats began, rising and dipping, growing steadily in altitude while shrouded in jungle brush, and as far as their eyes could see, the world was only blue and green.

They crossed the dirt road and entered the Nallamala forest. The climb was uphill at first. While Krishna, Vijaya, and Sree slipped over rocks, Ranga climbed expertly; the worse the terrain became, the more sure-footed he seemed. He reached a spot at least five minutes ahead of them, crouched on the balls of his feet and waited for them to catch up, and as soon as they got close enough, he began his rapid ascent again.

Krishna, Vijaya, and Sree were soon out of breath. The three of them agreed without speaking that they were tired. Even the December sun was far too harsh. Their throats grew parched. On all sides, they were surrounded by rocky boulders, overhung vines and brush. The forest was still sparse, thin and rocky. "Ranga!" Krishna called, panting, bent double, his hands on his knees. "Slow down! We can't see you."

Ranga appeared as quickly as he'd disappeared, peering around a boulder.

"I'm here," he said, "and you mustn't shout in the forest when it is quiet like this."

Then they noticed how strangely quiet it had become. Even while he struggled to catch his breath, Krishna shivered. The gun was heavy, and the spot where the barrel rested against his neck was sore. Ranga wordlessly took it from him, slung it across his own shoulders.

As they walked on, the low hillock on which the gadi was built, then Irumi itself, shrank and fell away, smaller and less significant with each passing minute. After perhaps two hours, the village was still visible, but it was merely the width of their thumbs. Vijaya imagined her mother waiting for her to return from school. She imagined her panicking, climbing the high steps to reach the upper story of the gadi, calling Vijaya's name, searching her room, the library, the study, and the multitude of interconnected rooms in the upper floor. If she cupped her hands and called out, screamed even, her mother wouldn't hear her; no one in Irumi would hear her. Vijaya felt terror, then euphoria.

The forest surprised them, turning greener and flatter the deeper they went, but the earth was drier; like wet mud that had been sitting out in the sun for too long, the surface caked and stiff underneath their feet, covered in gravel and pebbles that tripped them as they walked.

Vijaya and Sree both wore shoes, but the heat and effort of climbing made them slip off. They took their shoes off and held them by their laces. Vijaya was careful not to slip on any rocks and tried to appear as though her breathing was normal, even though her lungs felt like they were filled with the very gravel she walked on. Sweat beaded on her forehead, around her lips, on her back, underneath her arms and shins. Occasionally, Ranga stopped to help Krishna climb up a particularly large boulder, standing atop it and hooking his elbow around Krishna's to pull him up. And Sree, who was so little that Ranga was able to lift her up by her arms; she smiled gleefully at Vijaya when this happened.

Crickets and grasshoppers were droning a chorus in the trees. Yellow-billed mynas whooped. There were holes in the ground, made by mole rats or rabbits or mongooses, they weren't sure. Sree's foot slipped into one of them, her narrow calf disappearing entirely. She waited, terrified, while Krishna and Vijaya pulled her up by her arms. In some parts, grass merely brushed their ankles, and in others, the brush was high, thorny, came up to the girls' waists, and they walked around whole sections to avoid snakes that no doubt nested there. All except Ranga tried to behave as though they did this every day, like this was not hard or unusual, not at all. But at one point, Sree screamed; she had mistaken a six-foot-long shed skin of a rattlesnake for a real snake.

They stopped and crowded around the snake skin, crouching low to examine it from every angle. Krishna brought a stick and poked it, turned it over. It was gray, streaked in black, with bumpy, close-set scales that ran its entire length, narrow at its tail end. Even though the hair on her arms stood on end, in fright and excitement, Sree reached out to lay a finger on the waxy, paper-like skin. Ranga jerked her hand out of the way, nearly slapping it. "Don't touch it," he said. "That's how its mate smells you and tracks you."

Then the sight of snake skins became common; their appearance growing more frequent and multihued the deeper into the forest they went. This one's a king cobra, they speculated bravely. That one's only a little grass snake, no poison in its fangs. But when they heard slithering in the dry leaves, no one wanted to stand still. They moved quickly, and everyone, except Ranga, was panting. Everyone, except Ranga, felt anxious, uneasy at not yet arriving at their destination. Perhaps it was all a mistake. Perhaps they should have gone to school, met later in the safety behind the stepwell. Perhaps they were headed in the wrong direction and be lost forever. The fact that three of them still wore their uniforms compounded their unease. When they caught sight of one another, they turned away; the jungle wasn't a logical place for a pale blue school uniform. Vijaya and Sree were both hungry. They felt embarrassed by their unfamiliarity with missed meals and did not voice the clawing feeling in their bellies. When they thought of their lunch boxes safely hidden behind the stepwell, their footsteps became slow and unenthusiastic.

Then, to their relief, the ground flattened out and all around them was the Nallamala jungle, wide tree trunks. At midday, when the sun blazed red, Ranga finally stopped and waited for the rest of them at the edge of the ravine.

They saw the ravine opening up behind Ranga. Shallow at first, deeper and deeper as it descended and rolled away from them, its bottom covered in so much undergrowth and brush that it was hard to say how deep it really was. Beyond the ravine, the mountain range continued like a fence, emerald colored and massive, rising ever higher. On one side of the ravine, to their right, was a steep hillside, and in between them was a narrow path. Crooked and winding, it disappeared around the curve of the hill.

"I'm thirsty, Ranga," Krishna said.

"There's a brook on the other side," Ranga said, standing up.

With the allure of water, they stepped onto the path and began crossing the ravine.

They walked sideways, their backs pressed to the hillside. Ranga, then Krishna, then Vijaya, and Sree at the very end. Their progress was slow. The rock was hot, and it burned the tips of their fingers, made everyone's faces pour sweat. A lone eagle cawed as it flew overhead. They stopped, looked up at its broad wings sailing over them, diving into the ravine like a falling kite.

When they reached the curve on the hillside, the path appeared disused, disappearing completely from view; they could not see where it went. The laces of Sree's shoes slipped out of her hand and tumbled into the ravine below. "You lost your shoes!" Vijaya cried. "What are we going to tell Ma!"

Even though she knew she mustn't, Vijaya looked over the edge. Beneath them, only the high tops of trees were visible. The depth of the ravine hurt her stomach and froze her feet. Even a gentle breeze threatened to hurl her over. "Don't look down," Ranga ordered, and she realized that on her either side, Krishna and Sree were looking over the edge too.

"Look at the mountains," Ranga said, "brace your palms against the hillside. Think of nothing but the texture of the rock under your hands. Follow my voice." As Ranga led them, they made it past the curve, and the path emerged once more, faithfully worn and brown.

When they reached the other side, Krishna fell to his knees and braced his palms against the ground, his heart was hammering so loudly in his throat that he could hear it. The forest floor was perfectly flat. It was lush and green. A shaded knoll. He exclaimed at the softness of the grass beneath his palms, delicate and tender as though never trampled by human feet. Vijaya was beside him, her hands braced against the ground like him. Her braids, as always, were falling loosely around her face. Her shins were bruised, the skin broken in spots where stray brambles had pierced it. She looked fatigued, but her eyes were gleaming. She grinned at Krishna, and he felt an overwhelming sensation of great well-being and success course through him. They would have a day together, an adventurous, wonderful day, clear and bright and happy.

Past the knoll, as promised, they could hear the brook gurgling. At once, Krishna, Vijaya, and Sree sprinted into the water without talking. They dipped their faces in and drank without stopping. The water was sweet and clear. Long strips of moss played at their feet. A game of splashing one another broke out. Ranga stayed on the bank, he took off the gun and placed it very carefully on the ground beside him. He drank from the edge and watched.

"This is the place," Ranga said, walking back into the knoll, speaking as though only his brother existed. Reluctantly, the three of them stepped out of the water and followed Ranga, Krishna and Vijaya still playfully jostling each other. Krishna brushed his hands through his wet hair and shook water out, Vijaya untucked her shirt and realized with a jolt that they couldn't return home until they were completely dry.

"I'm hungry," Krishna said.

In the quiet of the knoll, Ranga's voice, although the same pitch as Krishna's, sounded a few notes deeper. "Here," he said.

They had arrived at a clearing, a circle of grass surrounded by a group of dwarfish trees. The trees were thickly crowded together. The fragrance of custard apples reached them even before Ranga pointed to the trees. Although the bark on the trees was gray, the leaves were thick, deep green, and waxy. The custard apples grew in abundance amongst the leaves; purple, like laden teardrops composing themselves into perfect orbs. Some of the fruit was miniature, pale green, raw, and inedible. The ripest ones were streaked with black, their custard-like filling dripping out.

Although the fruit on the tree hung low enough, Ranga climbed the tree with the same sure-footedness with which he'd climbed the mango tree, one foot braced against the tree trunk, one hand dangling carelessly. He made Krishna stand underneath, plucking and dropping custard apples into his open palms one after the other.

They collected the fruit and made a small pyramid at the center of the clearing. Then, they sat in a circle, Vijaya in between Sree and Krishna, Ranga across from her.

Eating a custard apple was an acquired skill. Each section of the fruit had to be broken off, the soft bark-like shell scraped of cream, the seeds inside skillfully skinned with their teeth; it was a puzzle, to be solved with shut mouths, strained faces and self-conscious, ridiculous expressions. It took a while to eat and with Sree, even though they gave her the ripest ones, the sticky, grainy cream got everywhere, fingers, knuckles, elbows, cheeks, gumming up strands of loose hair.

"Now what?" Sree said.

"Now we wait for the tiger," Vijaya said. She shook the edge of her damp shirt, worrying the hem.

Vijaya opened her schoolbag and took out the mutton. It was wrapped in brown wax paper. She unwrapped the paper, and for a moment they quietly crowded around the slab of bloody meat. "The smell will draw it out," Vijaya said, laying the mutton on the ground. She stuck out her tongue for a second, then she picked up the gun. "You hide here, with Ranga," she said, pointing at the trees behind Sree. "Krishna and I will be on the opposite side."

Sree looked at the mutton and then at Vijaya and Krishna. "Why can't I be with you?" she said. Vijaya turned around and left as though she didn't hear. Krishna followed her.

By the time Sree's clothes dried, she and Ranga had been hidden across the clearing from Vijaya and Krishna for thirty minutes.

"Be quiet," Sree told Ranga. "The tiger mustn't hear us."

But Ranga was climbing the tree they were hidden behind. He plucked more custard apples and dropped them down at her. "Stop," she said, flapping her hands. "Quiet," she said again.

Across the clearing, she tried to catch a glimpse of what Vijaya and Krishna were doing. She could only see the edge of Vijaya's shoulder, the tip of the gun, Krishna's ear on the other side of the trunk, as if together they made up a single person.

Ranga did not heed her request to be quiet, did not speak to her. He wandered around the knoll, sometimes in Sree's line of sight, sometimes not, like a firefly going in and out of focus. Sree, bored, sat cross-legged and began pulling up clumps of grass. Then she wiped her hands against her skirt and lay back, cupping her hands around her eyes, turning them into small brown tunnels; binoculars with which one could watch birds flying in the sky. A few clouds drifted over. The sky was becoming overcast. When she blinked, all she saw were Ranga's eyes. Unnoticed, he had drawn close to her. He was squatting on the balls of his feet, looking at her intently. He came closer.

Sree uncurled her fingers A mixture of odors wafted downwind from Ranga—the leaves of the trees he had been climbing, the toughened bark that pierced the tips of his fingers, the skin lifted off his knees when they grazed tree trunks. He was close enough to see the pupils of her eyes widen. He could tell, from her expression, that she didn't know what he would do. But she surprised him. She raised a finger and touched his nose. It was warm.

"You smell like a tree," she said.

Ranga laughed. His laughter, as everything about him, had a wild quality, like the howling of wind through the tunnels of a solitary mountain. When he stopped laughing, Ranga raised his right hand. As though taunting a wild animal, as though to see what it would do, he drew his face close to hers, brought his fingers close to Sree's cheek. Sree didn't move, but her eyes were alert. Instead of touching her cheek, Ranga grasped the edge of her red ribbon and pulled.

"No!" Sree exclaimed. Frantically, she tried to re-tie the flower shape in her ribbon that Katya had made.

Ranga got up and walked away from Sree. Leaning against a tree trunk, he watched her as she tied and re-tied her ribbon, finally knotting it into a mess, the long, loose ends falling around her ear. She drew in her knees, pursed her lips, and glared at Ranga.

"Vijaya!" she called, shouting clear across the clearing, with the full intention of complaining. "Vijaya—Vijaya—*Vijaya*!"

Vijaya ran across the clearing toward them, Krishna following behind her.

"What is it? What is it?" Vijaya hissed when she reached Sree. "Why can't you ever be quiet!" she said with so much ferocity that Sree, still holding on to the long ends of her ribbon, looked at her feet, then looked up. Her eyes were filled with tears, the edges of her lips were drooping. "Vijaya, don't say anything—" Krishna warned, but it was already too late. Sree began sobbing.

"Stop crying!" Vijaya yelled. And Sree wailed, loudly now, at an earsplitting intensity, fat tears streaking down her cheeks. It was as if all this time, Sree had pretended that she wanted to come, only now realizing she'd rather have stayed home. "SHUT UP!" Vijaya screamed. "Shut up right now!"

Sree stopped crying, but only long enough to take deep gulps of air and ask why Vijaya didn't like her. Then she wailed again.

Krishna tried to calm Sree down. He touched her shoulder, patted her head, looked across the clearing at Ranga in puzzlement. But no amount of cajoling on Krishna's part could calm her down—as Vijaya knew it wouldn't. Sree continued to weep, sitting on the forest floor and drawing up her knees. After several minutes, "What do you want?" Krishna cried, exasperated. "Don't cry, Sree, please. Tell us. What do you want us to do so that you'll stop crying? Whatever it is, we'll do it, Sree."

Sree said that Vijaya must apologize.

Vijaya glared at her so intensely that Sree fell into another fit of weeping. "She doesn't like me. She's going to hit me," Sree said, "here, here, and here," she said, motioning at her cheeks one after the other, her mouth. "She'll pull my hair!" She pointed at the top of her head. "She'll say I have a cruel nature."

Vijaya froze.

It hadn't mattered then, how quiet she'd kept. Sree had seen it all.

"That's what Ma says about Vijaya," Sree said, looking first at Krishna, then at Ranga. "That's how Ma hits Vijaya."

Vijaya bit her lip, holding back the tears that were welling in her eyes. She looked at Krishna, caught him exchange a glance with Ranga. On both their faces, she saw embarrassment. How utterly humiliated she felt.

A gentle drizzle began to fall. Krishna grasped Vijaya's hand, closed his fingers around hers. She felt the lines of his palm against hers. "Vijaya," he said gently. She didn't move.

The rifle was at her feet.

Did she really think she would find the tiger? Maybe. Or maybe all she really wanted was to be out here, in the hills, with Krishna. To exist, however momentarily, secretly, in a world where she was not rejected by her mother. She wished she could live here forever and never return home. But a world like that could not exist. Sree had made it so.

"Krishna," Ranga said, "we better leave." He was looking up at the sky. Overhead, clouds were gathering, rolling into one another and curdling like milk. That unmistakable scent of rain falling in the distance: wet stones, torn leaves, mud. A gray sheet was visible over the ghats, but it was hard to say whether it would be wise to wait out the rain in the knoll, risk being stranded there, risk losing the time period within which Vijaya and Sree could plausibly be returning from school.

"Vijaya," Krishna said, "we have to go home."

Vijaya picked up the rifle and slung it over her shoulder and followed Krishna. The grass was moist and slippery; it squeaked beneath her feet. She wanted to put as much distance as she could between herself and Sree, but Sree stopped crying, sprang to her feet, and followed her so closely it was as if she wanted to adhere herself to Vijaya.

They hurried, reached the ravine. They began crossing, their backs to the cooling hillside. The path was already becoming muddy. Within minutes, the sheet of rain reached them, as though it too was racing, it too wanted to hurry, hurry, catch them out. Large, pebble-sized drops struck their faces and clouded their eyes, weighing down their hair, their clothes, and making their skin ache. When the wind shifted direction, the rain lashed their faces. Muddy water poured down the hillside in waves, crashing into the path, bringing small rocks with it. The path began to overflow, slipping away beneath their feet. It was difficult to say who was where. There was no place to stop and wait it out; they were approaching the curve in the hillside.

Ranga hooked his elbow around Krishna's, and they edged along together, their free hands pressed against the hillside. Vijaya and Sree trailed them. When they made it past the curve, Krishna looked over his shoulder. He could no longer see Vijaya and Sree.

Ignoring Ranga's vise-like grip around his elbow, Krishna stopped walking.

Vijaya came into view first. She slipped and fell to her knees. The rifle slid off her shoulder and tumbled into the ravine. He shouted for her to hold on. Vijaya pulled herself up, unable to tear her eyes away from the place where the rifle had disappeared. But Krishna shouted again. "Behind you," he said.

Vijaya turned.

Sree was holding out her hand. Vijaya ignored her.

"Please! Why won't you hold my hand?"

"Because you ruin everything!" Vijaya screamed.

A bolt of lightning flashed, thin and spindly like a tree branch, vanishing the instant she looked up. The accompanying thunder stayed longer, roaring with an intensity that shook the entire ravine. Vijaya knew what Sree would say next—that she'd tell Ma—this and everything else—that Vijaya would be in so much trouble. But when she looked, she only caught a glimpse of Sree's red ribbons, fluttering lightly in the wind before disappearing behind her. Then all she saw was mud, pouring down the hillside, thick as grease.

Sree was gone.

# RAG DOLL

———◆———

Vijaya was locked in her uncle's study, her body caked in mud. There was the window that looked in on the orchard, the easy chair in which he liked to sit in the afternoons to smoke his cigars. And there was the tiger. The head hadn't been mounted yet, and it lay on the desk across from her, its glass eyes, like yellow marbles, staring past her. Her uncle had caught the tiger, after all.

She was cold. Her legs were shaking underneath her, her elbows were twitching, mud was dripping off her, forming puddles around her bruised feet. The scent of wet grass was still with her, and it was mingling, horrifically, with the scents of the study: cigars off the walls, mineral oil off gun handles, animal pelt.

There arose in Vijaya's mind a memory of Sree as a newborn, brought home for the first time. She remembered how Sree smelled. Sree was sleeping, no bigger than a sack of flour, her small fists balled up in tight circles. She remembered begging to be allowed to hold Sree. She wasn't. Instead, their mother said she could stroke her feet, her baby toes. Without warning, she had swooped low and kissed Sree's cheek. Their mother had drawn Sree away. "Don't kiss her!" she'd exclaimed, gathering Sree in her blanket, hiding her from Vijaya's view. Vijaya remembered her mother's gesture. She also remembered stepping back, saying, "Sorry Ma. Sorry Ma." Afterwards, when she smelled her hands, they smelled like Sree, like newborn hair. Now, that memory felt like it belonged to another person. She didn't know when she'd stopped doting over Sree like that, had no memory of when she began owning a feeling that much closer to hatred.

The details of their return home were already becoming blurry, shapes and outlines of Krishna and Ranga becoming streaks, smudges of color; that childhood power of willfully fading unpleasant recollections was being exercised without her consent.

Somehow, on that disintegrating path, Ranga and Krishna had reached her. Ranga's hands around her shoulders, their grip cutting her. He'd shaken her; he'd shouted; trying to be heard over the sound of rolling thunder, the relentless rain and Vijaya's blind rendition of Sree's name. She was still seeing Sree's ribbons, the red streaks were as though burned into her eyes. "We have to find a way down!" Ranga had shouted. *A way down, A way down.* Even then, his arm was wrapped around Krishna's; through all this, he hadn't let go of his brother. "Vijaya. We have to go. We have to find her," Krishna had cried. Then Ranga had slapped her. His hands were rough.

And all the way down into the ravine, as she hurried behind Ranga, she'd continued to see the ribbons, and she could hear crying. Sree in the clearing, asking why Vijaya didn't like her.

The rain was still coming down on them. *Stop!* she cried. *Wait!* She did not know if she was screaming at the rain, or at Ranga, who was outpacing her. Everywhere she looked there were only fat tree trunks. Only vines. Branches. Dead leaves so wet they made no noise. She tripped, fell, got up. Kept running, only realizing that Krishna was calling her name and she was following his voice. They had found Sree. Past branches, past vines, trunks. She tripped, fell, got up. She kept running. Overhead, she saw the path on the hillside.

She came upon them. Ranga and Krishna. *Where is she?* she said. Then she spotted a rumpled mound at their feet, half-buried in soft mud—a figure, trapped like a large blue butterfly inside a pool of quicksand—*Is it her?* Krishna was saying. He looked at her and whispered. "Vijaya, it's her."

Gently, they turned her over.

One side of Sree's face was shattered. The bone was all so horribly softened it was difficult to say what was skin, what was flesh, what was mud. The eye on that side was swollen and shut. Her arms, gashed by tree branches and jutting rocks, were bloody and purple, a chunk of skin had peeled off her forearm. Then she saw the worst part. Sree's right leg, on which she had clearly fallen, was split in half. A piece of pale bone emerged from what could be her thigh. It was impossible to believe that this was her sister, the girl in the bright clean clothes and the shrill voice who followed her to the stepwell each day saying, *Listen to the stepwell, he's roaring.* She fell to her knees and cried her sister's name, but her voice didn't rise above a whisper. "Up," she whispered. "Sree, get up! Why aren't you getting up?" She was Katya, waking Sree in the morning. She was her mother, nudging her favorite daughter awake. "Sree, weren't you going to tell Ma what I did?" She was herself, never once failing to thwart Sree's affections. How she had failed to see it. It wasn't just Krishna, after all, to whom she appeared worthy of regard and endearment. "Here, Sree, look, I'm holding your hand. Please get up," she said. But Sree did not rise. She did not put her thin hands on her hips and peer into her face and say *Vijaya—Vijaya—Vijaya!*

Ranga wiped Sree's cheeks with the tips of his fingers. Then he put his ear to her face. She and Krishna helped lift Sree into his arms. After that they stopped only once, to wash the blood off Sree's face at a brook.

When they arrived back at the gadi, it had stopped raining. They'd been missing for hours already. The vaakili was so full of people that their arrival was not immediately noticed. Her uncle was standing in front of a group of jeethas armed with walking sticks and gas lanterns, clearly about to set out. Her mother was standing at his elbow. Her father was on his other side, he was the one who saw them first.

There was confusion—utter pandemonium—everyone talking over one another—shouting for water, for the doctor, for bandages, for quiet—surrounding the three of them: Ranga, in whose arms Sree did not move. Vijaya beside them.

She heard cries of shock. The phrase "Who is it?" mingled with

"Where is Sree?" echoed all around her. Then they saw Sree's school uni-form; her long, black hair falling almost to Ranga's knees. The soles of her feet, pale and white and unmoving, the silver anklets on them. That was when her mother screamed. A stillness fell. People made way.

Her uncle's fingers around her elbow had felt like a vise. She heard her father asking him to let her go. All the way to his study he'd dragged her, and all the way her father followed them. *Surendra, Surendra, don't. Stop.* Then her uncle shut the door, threw her against the floor of the study.

He said he'd ask her only one question: Did you go willingly?

She nodded without looking up.

But then he asked her another question, so quietly she barely made out the words: Did his brother come with you?

At the dirt path coming out of the forest, Ranga had ordered Krishna home. Going into the lemon grove, she glimpsed him still at the base of the hillock. He was sitting on the balls of his feet with his hands on his head. He was sobbing, shouting after them: *Ranga, please let me go instead of you.*

"I'm not going to repeat myself," her uncle said.

She looked up. His face was terrifying. All his volcanic anger was be-ing held at bay by the thinnest layers, and what still seeped through felt like it burned her eyes.

"No, he didn't come, Uncle."

"Liar. *You're a liar*," he spat.

He strode past her, but at the door, he paused and said without turn-ing around, "As long as you live in this house, I never want to cross paths with you again. Even when your name is uttered, I want it said out of my earshot."

It was almost with regret that he added, "I could have forgiven you if you told me the truth. Or lied on both counts."

Then he shut the door behind him. She heard the key turn in the lock. Her father standing outside, asking him to let her go, that she was a child who didn't know better. That they were all children who didn't know better. "She needs to witness this," her uncle replied. "She needs to witness what happens."

She felt paralyzed. It didn't occur to her to struggle, try the doorjamb, strike the door with her fist, scrape it with her nails and beg for it to be opened. To know what happened to Sree.

Not long after, Vijaya heard a scream that halted her beating heart. Without a doubt, she knew it belonged to Ranga.

On the northern edge of the orchard was a tamarind tree. The whipping tree. Thin, sharp vines fell from its highest branches. Those same vines were now around Ranga's ankles, his wrists. He was bound, facefirst, to the tamarind tree. Hung like a ritual doll. Around him, the laborers and vetti stood, a dozen of them at least. Around each of their arms was slung an upper cloth fashioned into a sack; a seru of grain, as payment for a day spent in the fields, a meal just sufficient to hold them over until they had to return to the fields once more. They watched, and Vijaya watched, as Surendra Deshmukh sliced Ranga's back with a whip, slowly, methodically.

Each time the whip struck, Ranga screamed. Blood was pouring down his back. Vijaya's eyes blurred. Each time she hoped that it was over, tried to convince herself it was over, Ranga screamed again. He was crying, chanting as though it were a funeral hymn: *Dora, please stop.*

Vijaya felt ill. She shut her eyes, but the terrible image refused to leave her. A weight, leaden and dead, began to grow over her heart. She felt as though she was being physically pulled, weighed down, by a hot, blistery feeling; a helpless anger, rage she could place with no one but herself. She turned away from the window and sank to the floor, pressed her knees against her ears. As Ranga's tortured screams assailed her, she knelt and put her face against the stone floor. Dried mud scraped her cheeks. She sobbed and tried not to be loud.

Nightfall. The orchard had grown quiet. The room was dark. Vijaya heard the sound of shuffling feet and imagined the villagers walking away, from the orchard, from the gadi, down the hillock and into their mud-walled huts. She imagined them untying the turbans, letting lengths of loose, grimy fabric fall gently around their shoulders as they sank to the floors, relief washing over them, words of pity falling from their lips. It was cruel, they would say, that Pichamma was made to watch.

Vijaya tried to focus; on this image in her mind, rather than the knowledge that Ranga was still there in the orchard, left to die.

This was her lesson—to witness. This was the reason her uncle had dragged her into this room and locked it.

Vijaya heard a voice outside—her mother's. And from the orchard—the sounds of heavy birds softly landing. Across her, the tiger continued to stare back, its eyes brighter in the darkness of the room.

Her mother opened the door and came inside.

"Be quiet," she whispered. "Your uncle doesn't know I'm here. Don't say anything. Walk right behind me."

They walked down the corridor, past the gallery. She kept her head down, looked only at her muddy feet. She was cold, she was shivering. At the landing of the stairway, outside the bedroom she shared with Sree, her mother stopped.

Katya was sitting on the floor. Her fists clenched, her knuckles white, she was glaring at Vijaya as though it was taking everything she had not to leap at Vijaya's throat.

"Look at me," her mother said.

Vijaya began to cry. She held her palms to her mouth and muffled her loud sobs.

"Look at my face when I'm talking."

She swallowed hard. She raised her head.

Her mother's face was scored by strain and worry.

"I know it was you. I know it wasn't that poor boy's fault. It is you. It is *always* you. I wish you were not my child. I wish you were never born. To be your mother is a long and painful imprisonment, Vijaya. One that I wait to be free of."

Vijaya bit her lip as hard as she could. She couldn't bear to look at her mother anymore, so she looked at the soles of Katya's feet, as pale and white as Sree's. She did not dare raise a hand to wipe away her tears.

Her mother said, "I need you to change who you are. Be only what I tell you to be. Even if it costs you your life."

Her vision was blurry. Her head throbbed from the effort it was taking to stop crying, to be quiet.

"Promise me, Vijaya."

She nodded.

"Say it. Out loud."

"I promise."

Vijaya felt her mother's sari brush her side as she walked away. It was so soft and warm. She wished her mother held her.

"Katya," Vijaya said, going towards her. "I didn't know—"

"Don't you speak to me."

Katya's tone wasn't like her mother's. Distraught or resigned. It wasn't even simple anger. It was like a vow. "You've no right to speak to me, ever again. She was beautiful, and you destroyed her. She will never be the same again. I know that you did it on purpose. Even if everyone else forgets, I won't."

She stood up. "*I* will make sure you pay."


The room smelled clean. The windows were open, it was cool and dark.

Vijaya didn't wake Sree, she didn't have to, because as soon as she entered, Sree spoke. "Vijaya. Did you come for me?"

Sree's entire face was covered in gauze bandages, except for a small, heart-shaped part, a single, dark almond eye searching Vijaya's face. Sree was covered in blankets, and from underneath the edges, a plaster cast showed. Of all the toys and dolls she possessed, it was Sree's rag doll that sat on top of her blanket. Katya must have put it there. Katya had made the doll herself, from scraps and loose bits of cotton she gathered. A gift for Sree alone.

"You took me into the forest with you, didn't you?" Sree mumbled.

"I'm sorry, Sree. I'm sorry. It was all my fault."

"It was such a good day."

Sree looked so utterly fragile that she was afraid to even breathe too close to her. She held her breath. "Does it hurt?" she said.

Sree closed her eyes.

Vijaya's heart felt heavy, full of a particular longing, a desire to reverse time. Unable to stop herself, she bent over her sister and kissed her very lightly on the cheek. Sree turned to look at her. "Will you finish the story?" she whispered.

She swallowed. "I will. But only after you get better."

Sree frowned, as though considering if it was fair. "But will you tell me if the king lived?"

"I will," Vijaya said.

# GUNPOWDER

---

Night was falling. Ranga was aware of going in and out of consciousness. It hurt to breathe. His mouth was full of blood, and also something sharp and acidic, like bile. There was a dull ringing in his ears. He wasn't sure how long it had been since the lashing stopped.

He'd bitten into the tree bark, scraped it with his teeth, and his mouth was full of splinters. His heels were slippery, caked in mud, and his own blood.

Wings rustling nearby. Heavy birds. Owls? No. Vultures.

The next thing he knew, he was looking into the face of Mahendra Deshmukh, Vijaya and Sree's father. He was free of the tamarind tree. Can you walk? he said. Ranga tried to nod. He couldn't remember if he did, couldn't remember what came next.

Then he was home, back in the palm grove. His mother was sniffling. He could hear her but not see her. The sting of something sharp in his arm. "He needs to sleep," said a man's voice. Sleep.

The doctor came again, in the morning.

"The danger now is infection," he said. "Send word right away if he gets a fever. Or yellow pus. Boiled water, only boiled water, to clean the wounds."

Their mother wasn't there. She was back at work, at the gadi.

He remembered very little of the night before. He'd lain very still on his side the whole night; to move was to risk excruciating pain. "And avoid bedsores," the doctor said, looking at Krishna. "Roll him over on his front now and then. This"—he handed him a pill bottle—"use sparingly. They are very strong sleeping pills. That's what we are using at the gadi. It is only for when the pain is unbearable."

He held his breath as Krishna rolled him over. He gritted his teeth and made sure no noise escaped him.

Thrice a day, Krishna fed him, crouching on his knees next to his cot, wiping his lips after. "Why does the food taste good?" he asked.

"Saroja-dorasani has been sending food," Krishna said.

"Why aren't you at school?" he asked.

Krishna did not reply.

All day long, Krishna stayed beside him, fanning his face with the reed mat, or opening the window, or closing it. Or asking him if he was cold or hot. If he was hungry. If he was in pain. Krishna boiled the water, like the doctor said. He boiled the rags too, and changed his dressings every other day. Every few hours, he put his thin hand against Ranga's forehead to check for a fever.

It felt as though Krishna was growing in front of his eyes, getting older by the minute. He did not smile, and even when Ranga attempted a joke, he did not laugh, that glint in his eye, one that appeared when he looked over his pebble collection, or crouched in the grove outside to watch ants move in single file—all of it was gone. Krishna looked haunted. His skin was sunken, his eyes were sunken.

Sometimes he fell asleep. Sometimes he threw up from the pain. Nights were worse. Red spots burst against his eyelids when he breathed too deeply. He bit into the pillow to keep from crying out, so that Krishna wouldn't wake. Krishna rarely slept for longer than a few hours. Kept checking Ranga for a fever, asking if he wanted his sleeping tablets.

She didn't look at him, their mother.

She left earlier than she normally did each morning. And stayed out of the house, sitting on the porch, entering only after he fell asleep. "Go back to school, I'll be all right," he kept saying, but Krishna only shook his head, so firmly it was as if he said no—Never. *Never.*

He healed. It was months before he was able to walk. He reached out and touched his back, the thick rope-like marks that would always remain a part of him from now on.

He went back to the gadi. He chose a time of day when he knew the laborers would be gone. It was dark when he reached the vaakili. Mahendra Deshmukh was standing outside. He did not look surprised to see him there.

Ranga knelt down and touched his feet. "Kal mokta dora, ne banchan dora," he whispered.

Mahendra Deshmukh said, "Come back in the morning. Talk to Nari about taking the cattle out to pasture. I will speak to my brother."

So, he went back in the morning, at the crack of dawn, before their mother was up. Krishna still refused to leave the cottage. Refused to go to school.

At the gadi, no one commented on him being there. The others who worked there—the jeethas, the others who came for vetti—avoided him. He went to the cattle shed and took the milch cattle out to pasture, stayed all day and took them back. It still hurt to breathe deeply, and he wondered how long the pain would last this way. He got paid with the others, standing in the grain line, being paid with a seru of rice that he took home and added to whatever his mother had brought.

He made it a point to do more than he was asked. A few months after he turned fourteen, Nari took him out of the cattle shed and put him to work in the kitchens. In the mornings he joined the others, sweeping the vaakili, scrubbing floors with metal brushes, chopping up firewood, running the boilers, milking the cows, slaughtering chickens or goats, carrying rice in from the granary, pounding maize into flour in the kitchen, turning up the lamps when dusk fell. Made all the beds. At harvesttime, if a field hand fell sick, he went out in the fields. Often he accompanied Surendra Deshmukh to the city. He never complained, never tired, always obeyed. Each night he came home to the palm grove, to sleep, and then left again at the crack of dawn.

But no matter how hard he worked, he knew it was only a matter of time before it stopped escaping their notice that his brother could be put to work also. Only a matter of time before Krishna was summoned. But the summons did not come, which he still found distressing.

Then one afternoon in September, his mother was finally asked to come to the gadi. Afterwards, they talked outside the cottage, out of Krishna's earshot, then went inside to tell him.

It was Surendra Deshmukh himself who'd talked to his mother. It would be such a waste, he'd said, that someone so good at school was going to be put to work in the fields. Krishna would grow old and die in the fields. "But you have my brother's extraordinary kindness to be grateful for," he said. "It isn't right, he says, for someone born with such a gifted mind to have a life of hard labor. Surely, it isn't what you want for him, is it?"

They wanted to send him away. They would allow Krishna to leave, sent to a school in Hyderabad City, a whole two hundred kilometers from Irumi. They'd even give them money for college after. Only there were conditions. The first was that Krishna could never return. Not for a day, not for a minute. Krishna would leave the day after Diwali, and they were to never set eyes on him again. The second was that Ranga could never leave. His mother accepted.


Diwali came in late October.

For the entire month preceding the festival day, everyone indentured to the Deshmukhs was put to hard, laborious work. Made to burnish every bit of the house—teak stripped and varnished, copper and silver buffed with tamarind concoctions, floors scrubbed, grout in the Chettinad tile re-done with cotton wads. The exterior walls received a coat of white limewash so blinding that it hurt to look at the gadi in the afternoon. The delicious tang of turpentine and stripped iron emanated off every doorway, every window frame. The gadi was full with the annual arrival of close, and distant, Deshmukh relatives. The kitchens were not sufficient to handle the meals of so many people, and parts of the orchard were cleared of shrubs, outdoor cooking fires set up.

Ranga was indispensable; they needed him to keep the fires hot, to manage the water boilers, to milk the buffaloes, to stand over the hot oil, fry heaps of puffed golden puris. Not a moment to spare. He'd even been given that task entrusted to no one under the age of twenty because the temptation to steal would be too great. To haul in the wooden crates delivered from Sivakasi. Filled with firecrackers. The crates were never kept open, their contents hidden out of sight. One of the Deshmukh relatives, a thickset man, had looked at him and said, by way of praise, what was better than a boy who could do a man's work.

On the morning of Diwali, Ranga was out in the lemon grove. There was a half-full wicker basket at his feet. He was wondering if he had enough lemons when he spotted Krishna through the trees. He was coming around the stepwell.

All these months he and his mother had kept him at home, afraid of what would happen should the Deshmukhs encounter him somewhere and change their minds. He picked up the basket and hurried towards Krishna with the intention of asking him what he was doing here, today of all days. To order him home.

As he approached, he observed Krishna bending over something—his schoolbag, it had remained hidden behind the stepwell—brushing dust and dead leaves off of it. He was a few paces away when he realized, and he knew Krishna also realized, that Vijaya was there too.

They had both failed to spot her straightaway because of how silent and unmoving she was, sitting on the earth behind the stepwell like a graven, copper-skinned sculpture. Like one accustomed to existing without being heard or seen. In the dappled light of the banyan tree, she was nearly invisible. He grasped that she must have been coming here all this time, perhaps waiting for the day Krishna would show. Holding vigil. He recalled what the others who did housework at the gadi whispered about Vijaya; that now she spoke so rarely that it was easy to miss her presence in a room. They'd be startled after several minutes of speaking their minds aloud—gossiping, chitchatting, saying things they mustn't—thinking they were alone in their cleaning, only to find her sitting in a chair with a book in her lap, or sitting on a window ledge looking out.

Seeing Vijaya, it was as though the anguish and guilt Krishna carried everywhere on him like a mask, one that even Ranga had been unable to pry away, was a mask yet. And like a mask, it could be lifted and placed aside for a moment. Krishna seemed transformed in this fundamental way when he saw her. It made Ranga recognize his brother: it was Krishna once again, headed home with him at sunset, cutting through the wheat fields, telling him to watch out for lark eggs in the ground, reminding him not to take any.

For a few moments, neither of them said anything. Then Krishna placed his bag on the ground, took a step forward, knelt in front of Vijaya and put his arms around her. Slowly, he drew her close. Ranga looked away. He didn't want to see.

When they parted, Krishna took something out of his pocket, placed it on the ground. There was so much reluctance in him, as though every strand of his being was protesting against walking away from her. But he did it.

Once Ranga could no longer see Krishna, he put the basket of lemons on the ground, came towards the stepwell. She was crying, she did not hear him approach. Ranga looked at what Krishna had left behind. She was holding it.

Ranga wanted to seize that trinket they'd made together—shatter it, throw the broken pieces into the stepwell. Then he remembered how carefully his brother had treated it, hiding it in his bedding, making sure never to sleep on the spot where it was nestled. He couldn't do it.

Vijaya looked up and saw him. For a split second, there was expectation on her features; she thought Krishna had returned. Then she stood up, looking afraid.

Ranga closed the distance between them. He reached out and wrapped his fingers around her neck. She didn't shout. She didn't scream. She shut her eyes and tried not to struggle. In complete silence, he pressed and pressed, feeling the soft, delicate rings of her larynx sliding under his palm. "Stay away from him. Do you hear me? Stay away from my brother."

She gave neither assent nor dissent. She did not nod. She did not let go of the kaleidoscope. She said nothing. She simply stood there, eyes shut, unmoving, allowing him to strangle her.

He forced himself to let her go. He went back into the grove, picked up the basket and returned to the kitchens.


In the evening, Ranga along with the others was sent home early. At nightfall, the villagers would gather at the base of the hillock, wait for the spectacular display of fireworks to explode above the gadi's roofline. There was a spot, a clearing near the tanning settlement, from where a good view of the gadi and the vaakili could be had. Adults and children, burning through mounds of firecrackers, faces lit by the dim orange lights of oil lamps, pinwheels, ground spinners, fountains, sparklers, the violent hues of bottle rockets tucked in sand.

In the clearing, he and Krishna sat next to each other on the fallen trunk of a neem tree. "Look," he said, placing a hand on Krishna's shoulder, "look what I got."

He opened his palm. Two long-stemmed sparklers: wire-thin metal rods coated in a gray layer of gunpowder.

"Where did you get them?" Krishna whispered.

Ranga touched the back of his neck. It had become a tic, stroking the edges of the thick, coiling ropes of healed skin.

"Tell me!" Krishna said. He wouldn't touch the sparklers. "Tell me! Tell me you did not steal."

"I didn't steal."

"Then where did you get them?"

"Saroja-dorasani gave them to me."

Krishna's face relaxed. This was not hard to believe.

He told Krishna to hold still while he worked on lighting them.

He and his mother would wake Krishna together, early tomorrow, after everything was ready. Krishna's few belongings: clothes packed into a cotton sack, a small tin filled with a meal, a few coins to get him through the day-and-a-half's journey to Hyderabad City. They would walk together, for the last time as a family, to that place outside Irumi where the district bus stopped, smelling of diesel fumes, alive with fowl, livestock, villagers carrying wicker baskets full of household possessions. Krishna will not cry. He'll want to be strong for them, and as the bus slowly gathered speed and moved away from them, their mother will remain standing, her face stricken, her lips pressed together, upturned like a young girl's. But he, Ranga, will jog a short distance and keep up with the bus, keep Krishna in his sight for a minute longer; see his face pressed against the window bars, watching him remain in the place his brother could never again call home.

It took a while to light the sparklers. They had been soaking in the sweat of his palm. He and Krishna each had only a close approximation of how to light a sparkler, how long to hold the lit match against the sparkler's edge, but soon enough they started burning, miniature stars erupted from the tips, glowed orange, and disappeared into wisps of smoke. He watched the look of joy spreading across Krishna's face. He tried to remember his brother's face the way it was now, so clean, so happy. Much too quickly, before they could properly remember how it felt like to hold a burning sparkler, the metal rods warped and went dark. But the scent of gunpowder hung in the air for longer. He wrapped his arm around Krishna's shoulders and drew him close, kissed the side of his head. Together, they watched the night sky explode with fireworks.

# PART TWO

## 1965

# A CADRE OF REVOLUTIONARY COMMUNISTS

———◆———

This winter there had been too much fog. It descended from the ghats and flooded Irumi with such conviction that for anyone walking on the dirt roads on the outer reaches of the village, near where the jungle began, it was like moving through thickly hung spider-webs, cool strands stretching against one's cheeks and ankles, feeling simultaneously soft and threatening.

A twenty-six-year-old sharecropper named Suma was walking along such a dirt road, unable to see more than three feet ahead of her. The sweater she wore underneath her sari was full of moth holes, her teeth were chattering, the cold hurt her cheeks, but she did not slow down or stop. The road was deserted, the ground moist, impressed with the paw prints of jungle cats and sinuous channels made by snakes fleeing into the undergrowth. Suma was leaving Irumi to join a dalam—a cadre of revolutionary communists deep in the jungles of the Nallamala.

She stopped and looked back at the way she'd come. Then she knelt down, pinched the earth between her thumb and forefinger and wiped it across her forehead, from temple to temple. It was a gesture of parting—what she thought of as an irreversible parting—because Suma did not know that she would return to Irumi. That as Comrade Suma, she'd stand alongside her dalam in the orchard behind the gadi; her rifle slung over her shoulder, her camouflage fatigues smelling of gunpowder. That she would bear witness to the People's verdict being pronounced over the Deshmukhs.

As if this inexorable providence for Suma echoed in the hills, there was a split second of silence, arising from the thick jungle surrounding Suma; a lull in which the bullfrogs stopped croaking, the insects in tree hollows stopped trilling, a sloth bear digging out termites in a high tree branch paused and turned, as immobile as a large brown bird's nest. As if someone screamed it for all of Irumi to hear. For Satish to hear.

*Be quick Suma*, Satish had said before leaving their hut this morning. As he did every morning of the winter planting season for the ten years that Suma had lived in Irumi.

He was at their field now, her husband, waiting for her, letting a foot of muddy water rise in the field, ankles buried in the wet mud. They cultivated paddy, starting the seedbeds in the dirt behind their hut, and as soon as the winter planting season came, they raced to transplant. They owned neither bullocks nor implements, borrowed both from the saukar, and worked as hard and as quickly as their bodies allowed, desperate to give the paddy as much time as possible to burrow roots before the monsoon hit, so the crop could survive the twenty inches of rainfall that slammed down on Irumi each year.

They had both continued to refer to it as "our field" even though it belonged to the Deshmukhs. It was an old habit because this was the same bit of land of which they had once been owners. It was one square acre, and it had been like the very blood in their veins.

The year they married, the crop failed. The rain had come too heavy, too early. The river overflowed, and they stood side by side in the pouring rain and watched it drown the crop. Satish had walked up the hillock, stood with his footwear tucked under his arm, and touched the dirt at Surendra Deshmukh's feet. He'd placed an ink-stained thumb on a blank piece of stamp paper and there it was, a stack of currency, readily handed to him. The debt was deep. The mithi was twenty-five percent. "Will you be able to pay it back or not?" Surendra Deshmukh had said. "Ne banchan dora," Satish replied, touching the dirt at his feet once more. "Where shall we go?"

And they planted cotton instead of rice in order to pay back the debt and still have enough to eat, but the cotton attracted weevils, and no matter what they did to stop them, the weevils ate through the lobes of the plants with a ferocity until nothing was left of the crop. The bolls shriveled before they turned fat enough or white enough to pick, there was nothing left but a field of dead leaves, quietly ruffling in the hot sun.

The zamindari collected on their debt. That land, their one true family, was taken. It had seemed impossible to believe that the earth that they'd tilled, watched over and cared for, the red soil they could rub between their thumb and forefinger, did not belong to them anymore. So, Satish did the only thing that made sense. He walked up the hillock again, to the zamindari again, placed again an ink-stained thumb on a blank piece of stamp paper and asked to have loaned to them the very same piece of land and there they were, feet resting on the very same soil, borrowed iron tillers on their shoulders, sharecroppers in permanent, irreversible debt.

*Be quick Suma.* In the decade of their marriage, those words were the only words that Satish uttered while still meeting her eyes. It made her cheeks fill with shame every time he did this; her shoulders deaden with guilt; her back prickle with fright, cold, cold fear. She had been fifteen when they married. Sixteen when they became sharecroppers. *Be quick Suma*—he'd first said this when Suma, as the wife of a sharecropper, was summoned to the timber card house behind the Deshmukh gadi. They had guests, she was told. She had felt her feet glue to the mud floors when she was sent for. *Be quick Suma*, Satish said as she left, his face turned away. And when she did return, he pried her fingers open and extracted the bit of gold clutched in her damp fist.

Suma went back to the Deshmukh gadi. Every year, in the dry summers when there was no field work, no harvest, no grain, no food. She worked as a seamstress those months, exclusively for the Deshmukhs, who asked for embroidered pillowcases or bodice cloths or hems of silk saris to be finished by hand. She'd imagine a world where there was a need for embroidered pillowcases while pushing her needle through the lush plumage of a peacock, or the eye of a fish, or the rim of a decorative silver bowl, and she'd prick her finger. She'd drop the silk and suck her bloody fingertip, careful not to let even a speck of her blood ruin such beautiful fabric.

She stood, summer after summer, in their hot vaakili, flagstones burning the soles of her feet, waiting for that girl who lived there with them—the one with the Russian name—Katya, to take the fabric inside the gadi, to be appraised, paid only if the work was so undeniably laborious that it likely ruined Suma's eyes for good. Sometimes Katya came back saying that there was a broken thread somewhere, a seam that had come undone, or that the embroidery was far too spaced out to look beautiful, that she'd ruined their silk, that the fabric smelled like livestock, that it stank of her mud floor. They wouldn't pay her. Instead, Katya would give her a bottle of grain alcohol. Walking down the hillock, clutching the bottle to her hip, she'd find an old tree to weep under. Then she'd wipe her face and return home, hand Satish the bottle.

Six months ago, Suma saw the young communists arrive in Irumi. There had been a cholera outbreak in the village. Suma had gone next door where her friend Gita's son lay sick. The child's name was Badri, he was four years old.

Every so often, Badri had the habit of wandering into her hut and Suma always found something to give him; a treat, usually cut up pieces of sugarcane that he ate sitting cross-legged on the mud floor, his round black eyes on Suma's face, teeth chomping furiously. Suma would crouch on the balls of her feet and gaze at him, her chin balanced on the heel of her hand, simply, simply for the pleasure of watching Badri eat sugarcane without a care in the world.

At Badri's age, she had been placed in an army camp near Akkanapalli, a tiny hamlet along the Krishna River. It had been one of those hamlets that the Razakars raided during the annexation of Hyderabad, one of those hamlets where the Razakars urinated on the deities inside temples, burned the men alive, committed mass rape. She remembered hiding in a well with the other children until the army came, sitting near her mother in camp, shoving mouthfuls of hot rice past her mother's clenched teeth. Afterwards, they were given a buffalo and a small sum of money and re-settled back in Akkanapalli. There was never enough to eat. She was twelve when a man showed up at their door. He offered two rupees and a kunche full of rice in exchange for Suma. He said that Suma was beautiful and her beauty meant that she could be sold to a gadi as an adabapa. Her mother said yes, took the rice and shoved Suma towards the man. Then, when the man held Suma's hand and began dragging her out of their hut, she said no and gave the rice back. It's not enough, she remembered her mother saying. That was a lie, because even at twelve she knew that a kunche of rice was plenty, two rupees was plenty. Plenty.

The next morning, her mother drowned herself in the river.

When she heard Badri was ill, she went without telling Satish. She expected Gita alone with Badri, instead she found most of the village crowding the mouth of Gita's hut, peering in on the dying child; each asking the other, is it cholera, is it typhoid, what is it, this time. They had all come to see.

Badri lay on the ground. Gita was rubbing her son's feet, whispering and kissing each of his toes in turn, tears streaking down her dirty cheeks. She placed a hand on Gita's shoulder but withdrew it, realizing that her presence had gone unnoticed. Gita's face was feverish, her eyes were wide and fearful, her lips were chewed up, broken and bleeding at the edges. Badri coughed and threw up blood. Gita trembled as she wiped his lips. The villagers watched them in silence.

As Suma gazed on Badri, a strange feeling came over her; she felt as though she were leaving her body behind and becoming Badri, lying flat on the mud floor, the one dying in that repressive, overbreathed air. For the first time in her life, she knew what she desired: she wanted to take Badri's place, trade her life for his. After all, isn't that why there was a god? To allow this trading of lives—to not permit children to die.

But Badri heaved, his breath caught, and his eyes became still.

The following week, cholera came for them. The worst of the outbreak lasted for nearly six months and in that period, nobody from the village was allowed to the mouth of the river, past the hillock where the Deshmukhs lived, where the water was clean. No one from the village was allowed to enter their vaakili, and it was only their army of vetti who were allowed off the hillock, into the village and back, only to deal with farm produce, tradespeople, to herd the manual scavengers armed with stained wicker baskets and reed brooms, tasked with cleaning the soiled mud under their lavatories. Those who did vetti were, they told the villagers later, sprayed down with antiseptic soap and cold water before being allowed to set foot in the vaakili, and if they had to actually step inside the walls of the gadi, to enter the rooms, to clean, they had to dip their hands in aluminum bowls filled with Dettol, which they were told killed the cholera.

The pyre keeper of Irumi was at work every day during those six months, sometimes having no choice but to burn without extracting his fees, and a sickening stench hung over Irumi; the black odor of burning skin, sinew, and bone. It made Suma want to retch all day. She stayed prone on the floor for days at a time, in a state of catatonia, afraid of everything. All day, she sucked on a piece of chalk and tried not to hear. Stepping outside meant stepping into the filth overflowing through the open drains, it meant hearing the squeals of penned animals because no one took them out to pasture, all those wasted lives.

The entire world had forsaken them. Even Poleramma, before whose shrine the potter had cut a healthy goat's neck, had forsaken them. Only the communists hadn't. The faces of the young communists bore signs of education and nutrition. They brought soap, rice, fever medicine, ORS powder, mosquito nets, told them to boil water, to separate the sick from the well.

Afterwards, those in the village that survived emerged from their sickbeds hollowed out: ranks of ornamental bones, mere skeletons covered in skin as frail as kite paper. They immediately went to work in the neglected fields because the monsoon was coming, that wall of water that thundered down on the valley, and there was paddy, corn, oilseeds, wheat, cotton, jowar, pulses to be planted, vegetables and flowers to be harvested, debts to be re-paid. Satish did too. But Suma did not. Instead, she went to the meetings. She went to the night school. Because she could read and write, they gave her Gorky's *Mother*. "Meet us at the clearing across the river at daybreak, Comrade."

The sun was rising, the fog was clearing. The bullfrogs croaked again, the insects trilled, the sloth bear continued to dig for termites. Suma straightened up and began walking again.

She entered the forest. The trees were sparse, and at first she could still smell the village—the scent of woodstoves, burning firewood, the insistent ringing of the temple bell. Later, she could only smell dew and forest sumac. They walked for hours. Someone was clearing the path in front of her, hacking at tree branches, slashing overhanging vines with a curved, short-handled blade. Leaves grazed her cheeks. The falling undergrowth made rustling noises like the wings of birds. As she walked deeper, the forest grew thick and lush, tree trunks became wider, grew so high and so close together that light dimmed, morning became twilight, the screams of birds deadened, and the taste of sap filled her mouth.

The first morning Comrade Suma awoke in the training camp, she felt the entire forest waking with her, she felt the world tip and pitch her against its soft green walls. In training, she stood shoulder to shoulder with her dalam. She crawled under barbed wire, learned how to conceal land mines, pack gunpowder, wrap cordtex wires around detonators. At night, she stayed crouched on her toes for hours on end reading Marxist literature. She was not merely a little girl who hid in the well as her village burned to the ground. Not merely a girl who could not recognize her mother's drowned, bloated body as it floated downriver. Nor merely a sixteen-year-old girl summoned to the timber card house behind the Deshmukh gadi; the laughter, when she said no, when she asked to go home. Not the one who had to dig a grave small enough to bury Badri.

In the forests of the Nallamala, it would be the spring of 1967—two whole years—before she could stop telling herself these things. Two years before she recognized that, amongst the members of her dalam, she carried a .303 rifle over her shoulder, a bore gun and two hand grenades. She was a comrade.

# THE GIRL IN THE MIRROR

———◆———

As soon as Sree heard the school bell, the percussive *twang-twang-twang-twang* of the hammer hitting the iron block, signaling the end of classes, she darted out of the classroom. Before anyone attempted to stall her. Delay her. The fair, the fair, she reminded herself. She mustn't be late.

Today was the last day—there was a play being put up, air guns to shoot, a dancing bear, a children's circus, a photographer's studio, even a carousel. She and Tara and Vijaya were going. They'd never been allowed before. Every year, when it was put up, their uncle would say that it wasn't a place for "dignified girls" to go. Or her mother would say that the flashing lights and the loud noises would bring on her headaches, or that walking there would strain her back. But she'd caught her father within a short window of time after he returned from the makta, when he was alone in the library, before her mother got the tea served, before her uncle came and they'd move into the drawing room and talk business until dusk fell. Within that window of time, she caught him and he said she could go, but only if Tara and Vijaya went along.

It had taken a few tries to catch him out like that; sometimes she was too late and he'd already be in the drawing room with her uncle, the doors shut, an argument raging inside. It seemed like all anyone could talk about at home was the land. The land! How it was being unjustly seized by the government! (Her uncle.) How the vetti refused to come!

(Her mother.) How the peasants were squatting on their land! (Her uncle.) How the fountain and the vaakili needed to be scrubbed with metal wire brushes but no one came to do it! (Her mother.) But she found it all so thrilling, because her uncle made her sign the "land papers" last week, and she didn't yet have a signature. She had to make one up and experienced the original joy of feeling the nib of the ink pen swish between her thumb and forefinger, the ink flowing out to make the bauble under the *S* for Sreelakshmi; the big loopy *D* for Deshmukh.

Once she was out of the school grounds, she took a deep breath. Even without a real reason to hurry away from school like she did today, she often did. What she wanted to do, all day long, was to leave school and run past the open fields that hugged the mountain range, then run up the low hillock on which her home sat. Even though it was a vague and distant memory, she could still remember running.

All day long, as the schoolmasters droned on about quadratic formulae, molecular weights, atomic numbers, integrals, differentials, prose and criticism, geography, sepoy mutinies, imperialism and the enlarged diagrams of amoeba and paramecium, this is what she imagined: that she was out of breath from running up the hillock, that she'd caught sight of the stained glass windows of the gadi, luminous in afternoon sunlight, those beacons of her existence. That was where she liked herself best, where she was liked best. Her classmates, their stained smocks and soiled collars, their dirty feet and snotty noses, the way they stared at her all day long—when she got up from her desk and stood up, especially, especially when she walked—it was as if she were a thing put on show. Sree was older than all of them, yet she was the smallest, the frailest. At her age, she knew that Vijaya was already in junior college, going to town every day, whereas she was still finishing ninth form. On the level ground of the schoolyard, her family name meant little, and she had the sense that with each passing year, it was meaning even less. They hissed things. Lame girl. Scar girl. Cursed girl. Freak.

Her classmates all uniformly repulsed her. It was like her father said when she complained. Small village, small minds. One more year and at the end of tenth form, the last grade taught at Irumi's school, she would be done. Done. And later, she could go somewhere else. Somewhere big, with big minds. A town school, junior college, like Vijaya. That was what she truly wanted, to leave Irumi, to go somewhere big and far. Anywhere that was not Irumi.

She always took the same route home. A dirt road that cut through the rice fields, with the ghats rising beyond the fields on her left, the village and its hilltop temple on her right. Her mother insisted on having Katya accompany her to school and back, but she'd appealed to her father; he'd agreed that she should be allowed to be on her own.

The road was empty, quiet except for the gravel crunching loudly under her feet. She kicked at a loose pebble and watched it land a few feet ahead of her. When she reached the pebble again, she kicked it once more. It was a habit she had, kicking a pebble all the way home. It gave her a sensation of time pausing, of staying in that realm between leaving and arriving.

There was a slight chill in the air, it made her suspect rain. She began to hurry, but paused to watch a bird hovering above her. It was an eagle.

The eagle dove. For a second, she had the instinct to duck. But as the eagle fell through the sky in a graceful arc, a peculiar feeling of déjà vu came over her. She needn't duck; the eagle wouldn't pounce on her. She knew this. It was as though she'd already lived this day, but from a slight distance, with maybe her eyes scrunched up, tightly enough to sharpen and blur at the same time. She lifted a finger and felt under her jawline from ear to ear, around which a scar of long-healed sutures sat. It was a tic, stroking that long scar. Often, she claimed to remember getting this scar, and the other one, the thick and deep one, running up her shin all the way up her thigh, that made her leg "just a little lazy"—this was a joke that Katya made when no one was around to hear it, especially her mother.

In truth, the memory she had of getting the scar was vaguely tailored around what her mother had told her; that it had been raining and she had slipped and fallen on some jagged rocks near the river. I was so small, four or five, yet I remember it so well; it hurt so much—she always said whenever a new schoolmate asked her why she walked funny. The river threw me back out, she said, and enjoyed the stares; stares colored for a second by astonishment rather than revulsion. What she actually remembered were her own fingers, pressing urgently against wet rocks. The spindly rustle of thunder. No more.

The fair, she reminded herself. The fair. The fair. Again, she hurried forward. But again, she stopped.

A green scrub was growing a short way from the path. She'd come across it once, a few months ago, and had looked for it every day since. It was a mimosa plant: short, bright green, growing in between two rocks shaped like the tops of rabbit ears. Although they were fairly common in those parts and she was sure that there were many more of them growing deeper in the mountains and forests beyond, in the wild, this was the first time she had found one on her own. Katya sometimes brought her a whole stem to play with.

The mimosa had green, ferny leaves set close together in tightly spaced rows, each leaf the exact shape and size of a grain of wheat. Despite the rain that felt more and more likely to fall—she heard rumbling, thunder, a flash of lightning out of the corner of her eye—she left the path and made her way to the mimosa.

Sree knelt down and brushed the tip of her index finger along a tendril. A single decisive stroke. The cluster of leaves moved. They shuddered at her touch, shrank, and folded over. She exclaimed loudly and ran her finger again and again, down each row of tightly spaced leaves, along every tendril, and they all moved, shrank, and closed in on themselves, until the entire bush plainly hid its face from her, the ferny leaves now anemic and ragged-looking.

Looking around, she gathered a dozen even-sized pebbles, and placed them in a tight zigzagging pattern around the base of the mimosa, stood up and hurried back to the path.

It began to rain. Within minutes, she was drenched, soaking wet and out of breath. She walked up the incline of the hillock as fast as she could, ignoring the sharp stabs of pain running up her leg and arriving in her spine, so intense it was as if she were being stabbed again and again with a blade. The pain pierced her, it agonized her, she cried out, but she refused to slow down. She passed the stepwell, the overflowing water fountain, its stone animals covered in a thick layer of moss. Finally, she reached the doors of the gadi.

The front house was empty of all staff; the accountants, bookkeepers, farmers, laborers, vetti, and miscellaneous way-people that stopped by. Through the exposed section of the roof, rain was pouring in, swirling joyfully in the pool, smashing against the intricately patterned tiles. Inside the gadi, the clatter of rain was hollowed out, condensed; like drumbeats against the windowpanes, against the exterior beams, against upturned metal buckets, filling empty pots and cisterns scattered in the courtyard.

She whipped the tips of her fingers, shook water out of her braid, wiped her face with her hands, and took a deep breath. On the way up to her room, she paused at the library. Although the doors of the library were closed, she could hear voices inside. Vijaya's and their father's.

Sree hesitated, then drew close to the door.

Through the gap between the double doors, she could see a sliver of the room inside. Her father didn't like anyone going into the library, and she couldn't remember the last time she was there. The library was in disarray. Behind her father, the wall looked bare, all the books had been taken out; they were standing in short stacks spread across the floor, across the desk. This disarray carried to his desk—he had a ledger book open in front of him, and around it were scattered pencils, a stapler, paperweights, loose sheets with scribbles, what looked like legal stamp papers, an empty inkpot with its lid open. The gramophone, which normally sat on a low table in the corner of the room, was on top of the desk, its gold ear curving around his elbow. The only thing that looked to be in order was the three-pen stand with the ink pens all angled in the same direction, like the tail wings of an endangered flock.

When she was little, in the dead heat of the afternoons when everyone napped, when she too was supposed to be napping, she used to sneak in there. She sat on her father's desk, touched the tips of the three ink pens, pressed her cheek against the glossy wood of the desk, shut one eye and looked through the glass paperweight, watched the world swirl.

Vijaya was speaking.

She could only see a part of her father's face, the part not obscured by Vijaya, the pleats of Vijaya's orange sari. She noticed the material, how wispy it was, how it reflected the yellow light of the library, almost seemed to absorb it. She was sure she had something too, in that material, in that color, but why couldn't it look this good on her?

"Can we afford it?" Vijaya was saying. "With the way things are . . ."

*Afford.* It had never occurred to her that there were things they couldn't.

"If we can, I want to leave," Vijaya said. "I cannot stay here anymore."

"Did you speak to your mother?" their father said.

Vijaya shook her head. Her waist-length hair was loose, and she tucked a strand behind her ear.

"I can't send you abroad, like I went. Do you understand? It has to be somewhere close."

Vijaya said something that she couldn't catch.

"It can't be Osmania, Vijaya."

"Why?"

"Because your uncle will never permit it."

"But he went there. Why won't he permit it?"

"You are young, but you will learn that sometimes in life it is best to let some things lie."

"I don't understand."

"If your uncle wants to speak to you about this, don't mention a thing about Osmania or any other college in Hyderabad. Just say that you will go anywhere. I'll take care of the rest."

"Do you think he'll want to speak to me?" she said, her voice expectant. "Will he?"

"I think he regrets the distance between you. But . . ." He shook his head. "Why not go to Madras? It is far enough."

Vijaya said nothing for a moment, then muttered, "Far enough from what?"

"*Here*, Vijaya. Far enough from here. But you have to help me understand why you need this. Your mother . . . think of how she is going to react. How difficult she is going to make this. Is this about last week?"

Last week. What happened last week? Sree had had one of her headaches, she was in bed the whole week, and there arose a vague memory of her mother shouting at Vijaya just out of her view.

"She asked me why I didn't die," Vijaya said, her words thick, as though they were being wrung out of her by force.

Her father leaned forwards, and now Sree could see his face clearly. His hands were joined together, supporting his chin. He was looking at Vijaya with kindness, as though watching someone weep.

When Sree was younger, on coming home from school like this, she would have thrown her book bag on the floor, gone up to him and linked her arms around his neck. Now she only had a vague memory of how it felt to embrace her father.

"Vijaya," he said, "your mother, she doesn't mean it. When she's angry, she cannot control herself. She never has been able to."

Then, Vijaya said something, so quietly that Sree had to draw closer in order to hear.

"I need to be untethered from Sree. I need to know what it is like to exist away from her pain and her suffering. To not be responsible for her, for once."

Sree drew back from the door and went upstairs to her room.


"How did you manage it?" Vijaya said, coming into her room.

Sree didn't turn around. She was standing in front of the mirror in her room, trying, unsuccessfully, to pick out an eyelash that had fallen into her right eye. This happened often; her lashes were thick and prone to shedding. She shut both eyes and blinked furiously even though it hurt. She shook her head, took a deep breath, and tried again. She made out the edge of the lash lodged underneath the fleshy pink rim of her eye. Carefully, she pinched the skin there and managed to pull it out. She blinked again, with relief this time, and Vijaya's reflection slowly came into view, standing over her shoulder.

Vijaya was wearing her old earrings; delicate, made of gold wire and strung with oyster-colored pearls, they accentuated the already rounded features of her face, softening the high planes of her cheeks and even the tip of her nose. Against the copper undertones in her skin, the pearls appeared lighter in color than they really were. Her own skin was pale and milky, almost white. She avoided wearing pearls because they made her look even paler. There was an incandescence to Vijaya's skin now, newly acquired through the habit of sitting in very sunny spots in the open courtyards of the gadi. "Soon, you will be the color of crow," their mother would mutter, walking past. But their mother's criticism only seemed to please Vijaya, and after finishing junior college, she spent all her free hours, every day, reading in patches of sunlight she could find within the unyielding confines of the gadi, flittering like yellow butterflies as day passed from morning, to midday, to afternoon, to evening.

"And why do you need me?" Vijaya said. "You and Tara always seem to be together . . ."

She and Tara had recently become friends. Even though Tara was Vijaya's age, it was her Tara chose to be with. And Tara and she looked similar. So similar to each other that nearly everyone at family gatherings, those relatives far and near, even the maids and cooks and jeethas expressed surprise, again and again, how strange it was that Vijaya and Sree did not look alike despite being sisters but how strange it was that Tara and she did look alike despite not being sisters. "Suddenly I'd see one and think the other," their own mother would sometimes affirm, hands thrown up into the air, chuckling amiably and proudly. It never seemed to escape Vijaya's attention how much this pleased her. Each time that phrase, or a variation of it, was uttered, it deliciously omitted Vijaya from their family; even in that vague light cast by the idle observations of outsiders.

When the three of them were together, Tara often took the lead in treating Vijaya with as much regard as they showed a broken mirror, and in this too, she knew Vijaya took pleasure. That face she made, like a martyr. But she alone knew that Vijaya took pleasure in the insults and the disregards, because they allowed her to return to the solitude of her room and the solitude of being by herself in the sunny, butterfly-shaped patches of the gadi. It grated at her, that Vijaya never looked truly sad.

She no longer slept in Vijaya's room. She had her own; it was next door to Vijaya's. She heard her through their shared wall, Vijaya throwing crumpled papers against the wall or having Katya sit on the floor holding a book of poetry, staring at the cover, while she recited "I Wandered Lonely as a Cloud." Then *she'd* call Katya. Provide an escape. And Katya would always come to her because she was always the priority. Then *she'd* have Katya sit on the floor holding her science textbook. Recite the first thirty elements in the periodic table along with their atomic weights and Latin names. Over the years, Vijaya had made no changes to her room; the windows still opened up to the tree line of the Nallamala forest under the hillock, the lemon grove, the old stepwell, her writing desk against them all: all of it unchanged, clear and sweet as molten sugar. The only change was the addition of a long mirror against the opposite wall, next to the teak closet. Even though she had a mirror of her own, she longed to look at herself in Vijaya's mirror.

Katya nudged the door open and came in. Vijaya stepped aside. Katya spread a green silk skirt and a magenta pink voni on her bed. "Dorasani asked you to wear this," she muttered under her breath, addressing Vijaya. Katya still had that air about her; a huffy silence at the ends of her sentences—as though she'd only just received a scolding, even though it had been weeks now.

Katya had ripped out page after page from Vijaya's physics notebook the day before her final exam. She'd used the pages to apply polish to the little silver lamps that their mother used for her prayers. The book did not look old, or like something she'd found in the scrap pile in the library, as Katya had claimed. Sree didn't tell anyone that she'd warned Katya, when she came across her sitting on the kitchen floor, the bottle of polish at her feet, crumpled pages strewn about her. She did not want to make matters worse.

"Put it in my room," Vijaya said, and Katya turned back, gathered up the clothes as though resisting the urge to crumple them.

Vijaya looked like she wanted to say something, and it was in her power to punish Katya for the constant insolence she displayed in her attitude towards her, but she never did. With Sree, Katya never hid her dislike for Vijaya. She did not remember how it started, Katya's silent, almost imperceptible disobedience towards Vijaya. The longer it went on, the more acceptable it became, even to their mother. Now, years later, it was too late to muddy those waters.

Katya and Sree, they were insiders it seemed. Except for that strange day when Katya had accosted her in the front room, and for no apparent reason demanded Sree tell her what her uncle and her father were talking about in the library. Sree had said, very truthfully, that she didn't know. "They are hiding land," Katya replied, very angrily. "They are hiding it in your name. Your sister's name. Your mother's name. In the names of all the women of this house."

A shadow of malevolence passed Katya's face. And as soon as it passed, Katya fussed over her like it never happened, taking her schoolbag and asking her to wash her feet. Talk came up, often, of finding a husband for Katya, but bringing the groom to work in the gadi instead of sending her away because Katya had become beloved, like her name.

"Do you want me along, or not?" Vijaya said now.

"Whatever you like," she said.

After Vijaya left, she combed and braided her hair, a single braid beginning high at the top of her head, curling around her shoulder and trailing down to her waist. She ran the comb through the ends. From the jewelry box in her closet, she added a hairpin, a thin gold band, shaped like a half-moon and tipped with tiny emeralds.

When she came downstairs, she found Tara and Vijaya waiting by the main door for her.

Tara was a delight to be around. There was an ease about her, the way she filled the air around her with delightful noises; chatter, giggles, fascination towards all objects pretty: mainly clothes and jewelry.

"You're wearing green too!" Tara exclaimed, crumpling her lips in mock sadness, looking her silk skirt up and down, eyes lingering on the foot-wide gold zari.

"Katya picked it," she said.

"Pichamma is getting careless these days," Tara said, turning her this way and that. "See how badly she had ironed the silk. Mine too. Full of creases. It's *silk*, not some coarse piece of country cotton."

"She has far too many things to iron now, Tara, too many things to wash. We have too many clothes," Vijaya said.

Tara gave her a withering look, raised a quick eyebrow at Sree as though sharing a snide remark, pushed the door open and went out. She followed, falling in step with Tara. Vijaya behind them.

Walking down the hillock, Vijaya continued trailing behind. Tara linked her arm around Sree's. For the first few paces, Vijaya tried to catch up with them. Once or twice, she fell into step, but Tara steered her, now quickening her pace, now slowing down, intent on outpacing Vijaya. Vijaya stopped trying to keep up with them and fell back. Tara winked at her, and she felt Vijaya's eyes boring into the back of her head.

The fairgrounds were by the river, on cleared forestlands between the hills and the riverbank. Each year, a single monsoon brought the forest cover back, and it came ferociously, overtaking pickaxes and grass blades before being fought back again. They heard the fair before they saw it: the din of happy laughter and chattering voices, bright shouts of children spinning on the wooden horses of the carousel, hooves of nervous ponies tied up in the paddock, air rifles pinging off their marks, corn silk snapping exasperatedly over hot coals, the rhyming anklets of folk dancers striking in unison at turned, brilliant red earth.

When they reached the fair, they stopped for a few minutes on its edge to take it all in. It rose over them. It was much larger than they had imagined, only having looked at the fair from the windows of the gadi each year. She realized now that it was filled with people from beyond Irumi, from all over the district, the crowd so large that their going there was a matter of no consequence to the people who attended. It seemed willing to grant them a degree of anonymity.

But she was wrong, because as soon as they entered, heads turned, people parted way for them, studying their faces and clothes with frank curiosity. Sree fixed her sights on the blurred hues of the carousel spinning in the far distance, on a large knot of people just ahead of them, standing in a circle, their collective attention fixed on something at its center. They started walking more briskly.

"Shall we go see?" she asked, pointing at the gathered crowd.

"No," Tara replied, moving past the knot. "It's some poor animal. Monkey or something, made to dance and clap. Let's get on the carousel first."

"She will get sick on them," Vijaya said at once.

"She'll be fine," Tara said, dragging Sree, doll-like, on her linked arm.

They worked their way through the crowd, Vijaya still tailing. Despite what Tara said about the performing animals, they still stopped at the large group. It wasn't an animal performing. It was a child.

A small child. A little dark girl. She was being whipped round and round in the air by only her feet, pieces of her gaudily colored circus clothes flapping in the breeze. People clapped, and the child was spun faster. Watching the child was making her feel sick. "Sree, look away," Vijaya said.

After the set ended, the child was brought around, eyes held shut by her handler, a bare arm outstretched at the crowd. People brought out coins. She wasn't carrying any money; it hadn't occurred to her that she should. The child passed her. Tara and Vijaya looked too shocked to fish out coins from their purses.

Next, a tree bear was being brought out, its neck wrapped in a metal chain. Its back: ropes of fur clearly burnt off, by a lash or a poker.

"Let's leave," Vijaya said. Tara agreed.

Even after they left the crowd behind, they could hear the clapping of a pair of brass cymbals, the anklets on the bear's feet chiming. It was obviously dancing; raising a leg and lowering it every time it heard the cymbals crash together.

They made it to the carousel. Vijaya said again that Sree shouldn't go on it.

"I won't allow it," Vijaya said.

"I'm going, okay?" she said.

The round was starting and the ticket collector was looking at them. "One spot left," he said. "One of you can get on, then the others."

Tara looked at them. "Go," Vijaya said. Tara left, secured herself on a yellow horse. Sitting sidesaddle she waved at Sree, her mouth open in delight.

"You're not going," Vijaya said.

"What's it to you? Why are you suddenly all bothered."

"Sree, I don't want the flashing lights to trigger another one of your migraines. Remember last time? You were in bed for a week. Remember?"

"I know what I can or cannot do. You don't get to tell me."

"I think I do. Our father sent me so—"

"You're leaving!"

The wooden horses began to spin. Slowly at first, then a little faster. Around and around, their painted bodies blending with the fair's yellow lights in a whir so liquid, that scarlet, and green, and yellow became a sheet of light and laughter; the horses galloped at her, the music went in and out of focus. Vijaya's fingertips pressed into her wrist, her skin burned. "Sree," Vijaya said, her voice shivering, as though she were on the verge of tears.

"You're leaving. You get to leave. What about me?" Her vision was going blurry. She wiped her face with her sleeve.

"Sree. Please don't cry. I'll be back soon."

"Who cares? Who cares if you are back or not. Who cares? I don't. You can go to Madras and stay there and never show your face here again for all I care."

"Sree, I'll miss you too."

"I won't! You aren't worth missing. Who do you think you are?"

Someone bumped into Vijaya. She dropped her purse. It was a man. He was wearing polished brown shoes. He was apologizing to Vijaya, handing her the purse back. Vijaya let go of her wrist.

The man's voice was mellow, and he spoke in the diction of someone from the city; a smooth manner of speaking that could arise only from two places she was aware of—inside the gadi or outside Irumi. She looked up from his shoes.

He was tall, narrowly built, with a handsome face and striking, jet-black eyes. He stood out strangely, in his pressed white shirt and brown trousers, out of place amongst the villagers in their dhotis and turbans and bare feet. There was a warmth to his skin that was just like Vijaya's. His face was utterly recognizable. It was familiar, almost familial, but she could not place it.

He was standing very close to them, looking at Vijaya even though Vijaya had taken her purse and turned away from him. He raised his hand and opened his mouth as though about to say something. But it was as if he did say something, because Vijaya stopped speaking and turned again to look at him. "Krishna," Vijaya said.

The carousel was slowing down. He looked past Vijaya and met Sree's eyes. He lowered his hand. Sree looked into his face. His lashes were like hers, thick and dark. His hair fell across his forehead in waves. The crowd getting off the carousel came in between them. Sree turned and walked away, letting the crowd swallow her.

She was so rattled she found it difficult to concentrate on where she was going, but she kept walking. She tried to remember what it was like before the carousel, when she did not feel so wrung out. She tried to return her mind to that moment. She tried to calm down. Her leg began to ache once again, radiating up her spine in thick waves. It wasn't a good sign that she'd allowed it to hurt this much, twice, in a single day. Her mother would say she was being irresponsible, Katya too. But she didn't care, pain was her one constant companion.

She only stopped once she reached the edge of the fairgrounds. In the semi-darkness where the bright lights of the fair barely reached, she sat down and shut her eyes. Again and again, Vijaya's hurt expression invaded her mind. Again and again, the man's face invaded her mind. "Krishna," Vijaya had said, "you've returned."

# KRISHNA'S HOMECOMING

———————◆———————

At Osmania University, Krishna stood silhouetted against the windows at the very back of the Rooms. Lit orange by the setting sun and packed wall to wall with students, it was stifling inside. Half a dozen ceiling fans were creaking and thudding in unison overhead, winnowing, throwing again and again sheets of tropic heat, like hot water, into everybody's faces. In his hand was a glass tumbler of Assam chai; Krishna blew on the hot tea and steam wafted back at him, leaving pinpricks of perspiration all along the length of his nose. A burning cigarette dangled loosely between the fingers of his left hand, as it did in the hands of anyone able to find a spot near the windows, occasionally craning their necks to blow smoke out of the sides of their faces, occasionally leaning over Krishna to tap the ends of their cigarettes into a small flowerpot on the windowsill; the plant long dead, the soil flecked with dying ash, cigarette butts furrowed like yellow-brown seedlings.

Although referred to as the Rooms, the student union was, in fact, a long and narrow section with checkered floors, no wider than a hallway, on the fifth floor of the arts building at Osmania. Backed by plate glass windows, it overlooked a grassy, diamond-shaped quad, enclosed within which was an oblong pool that reflected, upside down, the entirety of the granite prewar building; an exquisite, rippling illustration far more romantic than its object.

The quad was empty and desolate now, because nearly the entire student body was crammed into the Rooms, waiting for Gagan Gupta to begin speaking. Gagan was standing at the podium on the other side of the room, and through the haze of cigarette smoke, Krishna watched him shuffle a stack of papers before him, waiting for the indistinct mumbling in the room to die down. Scattered here and there on the floor, he could spot the pamphlets that Gagan had distributed around the quad the day before: "To be Hindu is to be Indian—shaking loose the fallacy of secularism as precondition for nation-building."

Krishna touched his pocket. In it was the train ticket he had been carrying around with him for weeks. The ticket was blue, the color of summer skies in Irumi. He checked his watch. His train left at six, now it was four. Today, for the first time in ten years, he was going home.

Even though he would have preferred to go to the railway station and wait for the train, he came to the Rooms at the union because Gagan had insisted. In the years since leaving Irumi, Gagan was the sole person he had considered family. This was because, all through his school years, and through his graduation from City College with a degree in mathematics, his mother and Ranga hadn't permitted him to return to Irumi. Nor did they visit him. It was as if Krishna was purposefully orphaned; as if they believed that in this state of orphancy lay his safety, his future, his otherness from them. It was how they'd chosen to love him.

Now, in the safety of his position at Osmania, with his doctoral scholarship and his stipend and the ability to pay his own way through life and not beholden to the small sums of money that his mother had miraculously managed to send him over his school and undergraduate years, he'd written to tell them he was coming. He hadn't asked for permission.

And the way Krishna had managed to survive this orphancy was by separating himself; by becoming capable of isolating and confining that part of his memory in which his mother and Ranga lived. Where Irumi lived, where Vijaya lived.

Also confined there were the reasons for his leaving, the ruins he'd left behind—because remembering would splinter him, break him, with regret, with longing, with the threatening, menacing possibilities of *what if*. He never permitted his mind to go there.

But now, waiting for Gagan to start, with the ticket in his pocket and the hour ticking close, Krishna had a moment of lucidity. Suddenly, he felt flooded—by the delicious green hue of the palm grove in which his home continued to stand. He saw Ranga, he saw his mother; he heard his mother's laughter. Felt Ranga's knee resting against his; they were sitting side by side, the earthen floors of their veranda smooth and cool against his ankles, the green tops of palm trees rustling and swaying like so many paintbrushes against Irumi's hot blue sky, the sound of coals crackling in the ash pile outside their door. He saw Vijaya; her brown eyes, her pockets full of the almonds she stole for him; capturing all his green marbles; asking if he wanted a story; standing over him, Irumi and the forest beyond spreading underneath her feet like a grand, beautiful carpet. And then, just as suddenly, the mirage, so liquid and sharp, vanished and he was once again surrounded by the din of the Rooms of the student union.

Gagan cleared his throat. He placed the stack of papers in front of him with the air of being ready to start. At once, the room fell silent.

Gagan always wore white khadi shirts for his public events, and standing at the podium, he had the habit of drawing himself to full height and placing his hands on either edge of the podium. Although not as tall as Krishna, Gagan was powerfully built. Broad-shouldered and square-jawed, he commanded the attention of any room he walked into. A blinding white triangle underneath a square jaw, Gagan was a spectacularly gifted orator. One could lose days listening to him speak, feel the little hairs behind their ears stand on end, hear their hearts thump. Gagan's voice radiated with the hypnotic conviction of his beliefs, and Krishna imagined a pulpit forming under Gagan's feet when he began speaking; the polished floors rising underneath him, lifting his stocky, pugilistic figure above the heads of his rapt listeners. Gagan began:

"Often, I find myself celebrating when a communist dalam bombs a government building. There is a part of me that feels true joy. In fact, one would be hard-pressed to find a single college campus in the entire country where there aren't students just like us moving towards revolutionary communism. The cause is impossible to ignore. I understand their rage, because it is our rage, my rage: anger towards this nation that wrongs its citizens, one that victimizes its weakest, turns citizens into squatters on their own ancestral lands, and the corruption—the corruption of our daily lives—this stink that will stay with us till our dying day and follow us into our next lives. This is a failing nation. The communists believe that it must be destroyed and re-built. It is hard to disagree . . ."

Here, Gagan raised his hand, asking for quiet because applause had broken out. He continued:

"But I find myself asking, what *is* this nation—other than merely a sum of its faults? What is it the communists are so intent on destroying? What is the image of the thing they wish to re-build once this proposed destruction is complete? When we think of 'nation' what are the markers that emerge in our mind's eye?

"History, perhaps. Those posts in the moving sands of time, written and re-written by the victorious. We as a people are fated to be prey; conquered again and again and again because we are—in Marx's own words—an unresisting, divided people. The final conqueror—the English conqueror—was successful in robbing and razing to the ground so thoroughly all that was worthy it is impossible to see beyond the devastation. No, not history. We look away from our history because our pain lives there.

"Is it land, then? The places we own, share, draw our heritage from: streets, cities, towns, villages, fields, forests. What of them? Who owns them? Does it belong only to some of us, or do we all have an equal right to own, and therefore an equal right to destroy, free will to do as we please? No, not land—its allegiance shifts, that is its nature.

"I think it is much less complicated. In this country, where the differences between its citizenry are so great that we have no single word under which to group ourselves, call ourselves, that we call ourselves by a name given to us by outsiders—Indians—the only thing that unifies us is simply the way we live; the animals and trees we worship; the gods we revere; the ancient carved rocks in our temples that shore up grief and joy and stay immovable century after century as only rocks can . . ."

At the podium, Gagan paused to take a sip of water, wipe his brow with his blue handkerchief. Krishna glanced around at the rapt, attentive faces around him.

There were many students at Osmania who were like him, the children of agricultural laborers or tenant farmers or those who did vetti—those who'd managed, like himself, to scale what were inviolable barriers in order to be here. Those who had as much to lose as he did by getting involved in campus politics. Krishna avoided their company. He even went as far as not acknowledging they existed and did not associate himself with them in any capacity.

Even with the others in his general circle of friends at Osmania, he sidestepped direct questions, while giving enough description of his homelife that allowed the drawing of a vague but true portrait, but without actually revealing the whole truth that his mother was a washerwoman. He did this because he'd learned the hard way that he mustn't hide his provenance completely. In his early years in Hyderabad, he had made the mistake of not revealing himself before befriending a boy, Mahesh Iyer, at public school. It was a mistake that stood out clearly in his mind, an upright pole on which he could hang the exact beginning of his life outside Irumi.

He had been invited to come along with Mahesh to his home. He was then thirteen, entering ninth grade, and had assumed that the rules he had grown up with applied only and only to Irumi, that outside existed a kind of freedom.

Mahesh's grandmother was sitting on their stoop when they arrived, shelling peas into a wide brass bowl. She looked up and smiled at him. Krishna's arm was around Mahesh's shoulders. Mahesh crossed over the stoop and beckoned him to come along, and his grandmother said, "Is this your friend, chinna?"

"Yes, Granny," Mahesh replied, beckoning Krishna more vigorously.

"Are you good at school?" his grandma asked Krishna, smiling widely, still holding him in her sights. Mahesh walked around and came back to stand with Krishna. "He's the best," Mahesh replied, thumping Krishna's shoulder. "He got a double promotion from seventh grade. He's two years younger than I am."

Mahesh's grandma opened her mouth in surprise, her face coloring with admiration, making that gesture that old women made; a thumb resting on her chin, index finger extending to her cheek, head tilted slightly, smiling mouth agape. "Our boy is not so smart as you are," she said, shaking her head and going back to shelling peas, but finding that she was finished already.

Groaning slightly, limbs crackling like bits of old paper, she heaved and stood up, holding the brass bowl to her waist. "Will you stay to eat, Krishna?" she asked kindly, and Mahesh nodded, adding, "My granny is the best cook in the whole world!" Then, Mahesh took a few steps forward and threw his arms around the old woman's waist in a familiar gesture, as though it were a thing he did at the end of each day.

Watching them, he felt strangely emotional, as though there was something fluttering and liquid in his chest, a pleasant buzzing in his ears. He muttered, "I have food at the boys' hostel."

For the first time, doubt entered her eyes. "Hostel?" she said, sharply. "Your parents live far away then?"

Krishna nodded, not looking directly at her, unwilling to be questioned, unsure even of what he was trying to hide.

"Which hostel?" she asked.

"Government hostel," he mumbled.

"Where?"

He told her the area. There was only one there: the state-sponsored, developmental social justice program funded under the third five-year plan; the government hostel for boys of scheduled castes, scheduled tribes, and other backward castes—what it said on the curved blue board over the entrance.

"Come!" Mahesh said, motioning for Krishna to cross over. "My uncle brought me a model car from Madras, with moving wheels. I want to show it to you."

Krishna moved towards the door, but Mahesh's grandma blocked his way.

"But we are going out," she said, throwing a fierce look that silenced Mahesh at once. She repeated herself, in a mechanical way, twice, until Krishna understood that he was not welcome now. His ears burned, he felt embarrassed, the back of his neck was prickly and hot and inexplicable tears threatened to fall out of his eyes. He did not want to be rude, so he forced himself to say in a cheery, high voice, while looking at his toes, "I must be going now. I think Mahesh needs to get ready. I'm late too."

Without a backward glance, he walked out of their gate and onto the street, but not before he heard the old woman's ringing whisper, the order she gave Mahesh: "Don't you ever bring him here again!"

He walked away quickly, stopping only to wipe the tears that were dampening his collar. It took him a long time to stop crying, to compose his features into an everyday face, straighten his school tie, brush hair out of his eyes, confine this memory.

Gagan put the water glass down, straightened his notes and continued speaking:

"Yes, the communists wish to rescue our nation; from corruption, from poverty, from having to bear witness to the unimaginable pain inflicted by the zamindars on the rural peasantry, protect our collective national morality, salvage our conscience, to tear down and re-build. Our turn to communism, then, is a solution to many, many ills—of caste, surely; that malignant, many-headed bastard born out of the most base of human impulses: to simply be born superior.

"The communist promise is to erase our differences, to make us equal to one another. If there is no religion, then, there is no caste, no god, no desire for individual wealth. We are entirely and perfectly equal. A nation of entirely, perfectly equal citizens. A faultless goal. But communism is an ideology we are embracing not *because* of its appeal or its beliefs. It is one we are embracing because it is a reaction to hard times. Because it promises an immediate solution to more immediate problems. But it is also one whose consequences will eventually outweigh its expressed ideals. Communism promises to build our nation, but it comes wrapped up with the promise of secularism, and we accept it because we have convinced ourselves that secularism is the building block of a nation. We accept it because, once again, we do not wish to look inwards; we, a nation of divided, unresisting people wish only to measure ourselves against a scale given to us by our conquerors."

As he watched Gagan, Krishna thought of one exact point in time when he had known a different version of Gagan. But only a slightly different version, like a slant rhyme. They had met for the first time, at sixteen or seventeen, as undergraduates, in the mess halls at City College.

Gagan was standing in the mess line behind him. As soon as Gagan joined his line, Saravanan, the head cook, motioned for him to move up the line. Krishna had turned around to see at whom Saravanan was motioning. Gagan was wearing cricket whites, soiled at the knees with dirt as they would be after a long, jovial game, his hair cut in the short, military style of the armed forces. Gagan did not appear to Krishna, at once, as one who merely came from old money or old-fashioned education; but both, generations of it, those invisible markers he recognized because he had grown up around them in Irumi.

Gagan hadn't understood and Saravanan motioned more vigorously.

"He's asking you to move ahead of me," Krishna had said, turning around so he could properly face Gagan, "and use a different plate."

"Different plate?" Gagan repeated, sounding puzzled. "Why?"

Gagan refused to move. Saravanan frowned at him.

Krishna knew that Saravanan was using one of his cryptic skills at deciphering the social standing of those occasional thrill seekers at the mess halls. Their dinner plates were made of dried isthari leaves, ashen green, sewn together with wood splinters, which sometimes dislodged and entered their mouths and had to be fished out before piercing their tongues. Though the mess hall came equipped with racks of steel plates, Saravanan did not permit their use. People like Krishna ate there because they couldn't afford to eat anywhere else.

Saravanan was the head cook and the disperser of each and every meal that Krishna had eaten for three arduous years at the welfare mess hall. In the heat of the mess, Saravanan's skin turned pink. Standing at the head of the hall, bare-chested, limbs caked in reams and reams of holy ash, his plump stomach spilling over the waistband of his dhoti, fingering the yellowed, aging, sacred thread running in a loop diagonally across his chest; over one shoulder and under the other; he had an intense way of staring at the hostelers, as though resentful of having to handle their food, as though accusing them of the crime of eating in front of him.

Mostly, they avoided looking at Saravanan around mealtimes. Because it was important to follow Saravanan's directions, to do exactly as he said, to not look directly at him or betray in the twitch of a neck, the curling edge of a lip even a shred of insolence if one did not want to starve that day, that night or the whole week or month; for it was possible for

Saravanan to make this happen if he so pleased. He had a long memory, and never missed an opportunity to deny someone food. The prospect of a hungry night made sure there was no one brave enough to question Saravanan or interrogate his methods.

But for all his righteousness, Saravanan was no purer of blood than a common thief. He received a combination of funds and subsidized rations from the state government—jute sacks bursting with polished white rice, cans of peanut oil, spices, dried nuts and fruit, lentils and peanuts and money for fresh vegetables. Despite this, over the years, Krishna had forgotten what a real vegetable tasted like; couldn't remember whether a nub of cauliflower tasted sweet when cooked with peas; if it was possible for rice to exist without reeking of limewash or flecked with smooth black pebbles; or if lentils ever tasted like anything but yellow water and dead grain beetles. It was a habit amongst the students who had no choice but to eat at the welfare mess hall to eat around their adulterants, without looking at Saravanan or meeting his eyes. "Even the shadow of a corpse burner or latrine cleaner mustn't touch me," Saravanan declared often in a carrying voice. "And my tongue," he'd add to the two servers with the tone of conspiracy, touching a finger to his lip, "reads the sacred Vedas each morning and its power mustn't be sullied for any reason."

True, they weren't allowed to cross him; in the very meaning of the word, they were not allowed to walk across Saravanan or face him directly. If he walked your way, you walked the other, especially when he entered in the morning after his prayers. It was their duty to protect Saravanan's purity because to him, those of Krishna's birth were inauspicious portents, the equivalents of black cats and young widows.

In his years at City College, all three meals, every day at the mess hall, Krishna had bitten into more stone than rice, fished out more than a dozen button-sized cockroaches from his lentil stews. That the rations disappeared, food was adulterated and vegetables purchased were the cheapest kind; the ones sold off in the markets in large rotting heaps. Then there were the unexplained disappearances when Saravanan ran out of even the adulterated rations, shutting the kitchens and the mess hall without explanation, till the money came in for the next month. Those days, Krishna starved, subsisting on salt biscuits and jugs of water.

He learned later that it was the first time Gagan ate at the mess, arriving there on a whim; usually he ate where he fancied, driving across the city on his motorbike after classes, coursing the blank canvas on which afternoon streets simmered, day laborers transported bricks, schoolchildren crammed into buses, stopping only to refuel, drifting, drifting, until night drew close.

"I'm Gagan," he said afterwards, choosing the seat next to Krishna. He saw that Gagan was eating from an isthari plate, like him.

"What's your name?"

"Krishna."

Krishna watched with interest, the grimace that appeared on Gagan's face as he began eating. After a few minutes he gave up, pushing the plate away from him in disgust. "How are you eating this?" Gagan said, outraged. "This is a state-funded mess hall, they have money, they are *given* money, it's part of the national budget and this isn't food meant for humans!"

He said again: "How can you stand this."

Krishna did not know what to tell Gagan. True, at a point in time, long ago, he might have had a vaguely similar reaction. Now, he was accustomed.

Gagan was still speaking to him, his square features inscribed with fury, but it was as though Krishna wasn't even there.

Gagan strode over to Saravanan and began shouting at him. The dinner line behind him was backed up, and the students seemed angry with Gagan. "Go and eat in a five-star hotel if you have such high demands!" someone shouted from back in the line "Someone push him out." Saravanan, encouraged by the students, screamed back at Gagan and finally came around the serving table and physically shoved Gagan away.

"Why don't you say anything? Why don't you demand for the things that you have a right to?" Gagan asked the room at large. Most students avoided meeting Gagan's eye, making it clear to Saravanan that they were not to be associated with him.

Gagan returned to their table and said again, "Why don't you say anything?"

"Be quiet," Krishna muttered, noticing that Saravanan was staring at him now, eyes widened, "or he will throw me out of the mess hall for as long as he wants. Some of us have nowhere else to eat."

"Starve then."

"I'm sure that is an easy thing for you to say," he snapped.

Krishna frowned at his plate hoping that Gagan would leave him alone. When he looked up from his plate, Gagan was gone.

Nearly a week afterwards, he arrived at the mess hall one morning to find the shutters drawn and a large steel padlock clamped over the bolt. After his classes, he returned to his room feeling light-headed and sick. He could hear his blood, pounding in and out of his veins, in and out of his eardrums, a stitch in his stomach, his palms cold, his grip shaky, an odd, distant hammering inside his skull, louder each passing hour. He made sure that the water jug in his room was filled, and prepared himself for the twelve hours that lay ahead of him: papers, lectures, classwork, the heat of the afternoons and the night.

To his dismay, the mess was closed the next day. It had never been closed two days in a row. But then it was closed a third day as well. Krishna, unable to do anything else, surrendered his last coin at the tea shop, eagerly gulping down a glass of bland, milky tea, wishing for his coin back. He felt nauseated with hunger. He tried to reach the last dregs in his glass. For three whole days, the mess was closed. On the fourth, to his enormous relief, it was open.

Krishna entered. He swallowed and bit the inside of his cheek. The fragrance of the prepared meals was overpowering: steel buckets of lentils cooked with spiced tomatoes, pillowy heaps of white rice, crisp papads dripping with peanut oil, sliced eggplants fried and then simmered in a sesame and tomato gravy. He had never, in all his years there, remembered smelling anything so delicious.

Gagan appeared behind him, and Krishna returned a tight-lipped smile.

To Krishna's surprise, Saravanan did not look up as they approached. In fact, Krishna had the distinct impression that Saravanan was avoiding

looking at Gagan directly. As they drew closer to him, he heard Saravanan muttering under his breath. "*Rat . . . that rat . . .* just let me catch
him . . . I will have him thrown out of the university. Just you wait . . .
underestimating my influence . . . the provost is my brother-in-law . . .
*wring him by the neck . . .* !" He banged his steel ladle against the lentil
bucket in his anger. Gagan looked amused.

It emerged, while they ate, that someone—here, Krishna had a good
idea who—had gotten into the kitchens when it was closed the first day,
stolen all the kitchen supplies, rations, dumped it into a pile on the stoop
of Saravanan's house, doused with gas oil and lit on fire.

There was a police investigation that yielded no culprits, but rather
an inquiry into Saravanan's finances, and into the contract he held for
the mess hall, into the state of the mess hall, seeing as the kitchens were
closed when they were never supposed to be closed. Saravanan was in
a lot of trouble, with potentially a civil prosecution, and no chance of
winning the tender the following year. There were to be spot checks and
surprise inspections.

"Leave," Krishna whispered across the table, through hurried mouthfuls, barely stopping to breathe. "He will know it's you."

"I'm not hiding," Gagan said, and Krishna remembered thinking how
he had never, in his life, met anyone who spoke with such conviction in
their voice.

They had never agreed on meeting again, but soon afterwards, Gagan showed up at Krishna's hostel room. It was a narrow, cement-walled
room with a zinc roof on the topmost floor of the hostel building. In the
summers, the heat was sticky and unbearable. It was early evening and
his room was filling with the scent of wet earth. It was raining outside,
droplets of water were drumming against the roof, the windowpanes, its
melancholy rhythm shattering when Gagan strode into the room, paying
no attention to Krishna sprawled on his cot amongst a jumble of class
notes, ink bottles and empty tea glasses.

Pulling on a Wills Navy Cut with his head at an angle, Gagan drew
out the chair from under the wooden desk, threw open the window and
sat down. He blew smoke out of the corner of his mouth and said: "So.
This is where you live."

Had he not met Gagan, he would never have been at Osmania now. Although Osmania was a state institution, there existed intricately woven layers of bureaucracy—all thin crisscrossing strings continually snapping and re-spooling—between it and its day-to-day running. Public contracts and tenders were awarded each year for the handling of everything from grain distribution in the mess halls to the glue binding of exam sheets to thesis grants to scholarship dispersals. It was only because of Gagan, and Gagan's ability to navigate those complicated waters with equal measures of wit, connections, charm and bribe money, that Krishna was even here. This trip home was owed to Gagan.

The first time he'd received a pay order, made out to his name, he had stared at it for two whole minutes. He sent his mother money, nearly all of his stipend; but despite that, if it were a choice between skipping a meal every day for an entire week and purchasing a new pair of shoes, he would choose the latter. Because even as an adult, he took great care of his clothing. Painstakingly ironed his shirts and trousers each morning, and paid to have a washerwoman—while ignoring the irony of this—starch them, sew any missing buttons, replacing them entirely if he ever found a sleeve frayed or a collar even slightly distressed. Amongst his small family of possessions in his new hostel room: two sharp blades for his razor, a bar of red Cinthol soap, an HMT quartz wristwatch with a steel band, two pairs of leather shoes, six long-sleeve premium cotton shirts, a blue striped tie, a smart black jacket and four pairs of tailored pants because clothes were important; clothes were markers; clothes were disguise.

Only Gagan knew everything. He was the exception to Krishna's disguise.

Just a week after he and Gagan arrived at Osmania, Gagan founded the Progressive Hindu Democratic Front, and decided to contest in the student union elections. The last person to put himself up for candidacy without the backing of the ruling party, like Gagan, was discovered with a crumpled suicide letter amidst a jumble of his own broken teeth; shattered and strewn across the stone pavement after having apparently thrown himself, face-first, from the fifth floor of the astronomy building at ten in the morning, just as classes began. It was a dangerous thing to do, and no amount of dire warnings or vehement pleading from Krishna, asking Gagan not to do it, had made a difference. Gagan had made up his mind.

Gagan was approaching the end of his prepared remarks. Krishna was startled to see Samuel standing a few feet away from him, watching Gagan with distaste.

Samuel was the current student union president, associated with the Marxist Progressive Student Front. Knowing what came in the next section of Gagan's speech, Krishna felt anxious and nervous, wishing that Gagan had changed parts of it since last night.

He knew the whole speech beforehand because it was always Krishna on whom Gagan practiced. In the evenings and late into the nights while Krishna worked on his midterm papers in his hostel room. Gagan strode in without knocking, collapsed into a chair, put his feet up on the desk and lit a cigarette before saying anything. Krishna hardly ever looked up from his work, used as he was to Gagan's cyclonic entrances.

Krishna had never wanted to be directly involved in campus politics, but being Gagan's friend made that task impossible. No matter where he went on campus, he felt as if Gagan was always standing next to him, he was known by association. And because he couldn't extricate himself from Gagan's politics without extricating himself from Gagan's life—*this* he couldn't ever imagine doing—Krishna gave in: he went to the meetings at the union and stood wordlessly in the back; he allowed Gagan to practice his union speeches on him, while also maintaining what distance he could—by never participating directly, never contributing, and never having an opinion.

"Listen," Gagan had said last night, drawing close to Krishna, looking at him seriously. "Communism—this red wave sweeping our country, it is antithesis to all that makes our nation a nation."

When Krishna did not respond, Gagan drew from his cigarette, blew smoke out of the window, stuck the cigarette back between his lips, raised both hands and said, "Anyway, you have to hear this. For tomorrow. I'm going to read the last section aloud."

He flipped to the end of his notes. "Hear this part," he said: "Communism cannot exist in India. Just as secularism cannot exist in India. Is it possible to imagine an Indian conscience without its beliefs? An atheist India? Our way of life is as old as civilization itself. And despite the fact that we have veered so far away from our roots, this is still India in the small ways we live; to survive in this universe without doing harm, to never attack for personal gain; to understand, truly, the fluidity of human existence, to understand that our existence in this universe is insignificant, *must* remain insignificant. If the communists are successful, what will remain of India is a body without its soul, a prop.

"This conversion of our youth, to violent, extremist communism, in order to establish a just society will mark the beginning of India's vanishment from this world. We will go the way of indigenous peoples, the way of Hellenics and Bactrians. A thing that the English empire could not do, tried as they might for two hundred years. A thing that the Islamic invaders could not do, tried as they might for five centuries. We will be doing to ourselves. The only true fact is that India is no country without its way of life, without its religion, and that religion is not communism, it is Hinduism. To understand this, we must not judge ourselves while looking into a mirror given to us by our conquerors, or fogged up by the ideals of the West. The truth is that if you call yourself an Indian, no matter what god you worship, you are calling yourself a Hindu. And a social revolution that results in loss of identity, religion—erasing these markers that make us who we are—would be a grave mistake. To be communist is to erase ourselves; to be Hindu is to dissent, to be united in our plurality. We cannot build our nation by burning our roots, but only by returning to them."

Gagan had asked, "Krishna, what do you think? Is it outrageous? Will they call me an ethnonationalist? A Hindutva fascist?"

"Do you *want* to be called a Hindutva fascist?"

Gagan grinned. "It absolutely cannot hurt."

He threw the stack of notes across his desk and kneaded his temples with the tips of his fingers. The notes, Krishna observed, were filled with rows of Gagan's neat cursive. No matter what Gagan said or did not say, his handwriting gave him away; that smooth, lettered cursive of private education, of expensive fountain pens, crested school uniforms, high mountains, cricket whites, horse riding lessons, polished black breeches, money.

Gagan never spoke of his family or where he was from. He maintained a strained, perplexing silence over the matter.

When Gagan finished speaking, the applause was shrill, rebounding and crashing upon itself in the narrow space. It was impossible to distinguish one face from the other. After the applause died down, there was once again the indistinct mumbling of people, chairs scraping floors, students milling around the exits, chatter about where to go for tea or tiffin.

The rim of his tea glass was cold and sticky. Krishna tilted it and drained the last dregs, drew one last time from his cigarette, pushed the butt into the flowerpot, and began fighting his way towards the door. It was a quarter to five. He'd go back to the hostel to get his trunk and head to the station.

He was surprised to find that Gagan had disentangled himself from the throngs of people who came up to talk to him afterwards, and joined him before he reached the bottom of the staircase. He thumped Gagan's shoulder.

"Where are you going?" Gagan demanded.

"The hostel. My train is at six."

"Come with me to the tea stall first."

Krishna checked his watch again.

"You have time. The station is only ten minutes away. Don't be paranoid, you won't miss the train," Gagan said.

The tea stall was across from the men's hostel. A brown awning covered the stoves, with wooden benches for tea drinkers scattered underneath it. Noticing them approach, the stall owner, Suri, lit his stove. In the mornings, Suri served breakfast for those who chose not to go to the mess halls; idlies, dosas and Mysore bondas. In the evenings, he stuffed large, sweetish green chilies with tamarind paste and fried them in a flour batter. Their tea arrived, and Suri placed a plate of mirchi bajjis next to them, waving his hand at Gagan and saying, "You don't pay, Gagan," when he fished in his pocket for change.

Krishna sipped his tea. He looked up at the overcast sky, wondering if it would rain. He liked Osmania best when it rained, when the thin film of dust that habitually coated every surface—the buildings, classrooms, libraries—was washed away and he saw his surroundings with sudden, shocking clarity, the enormity of him even being there, the opportunities within his grasp.

"So," Gagan began, "how are you feeling? About going home."

Krishna took a sip of his tea, resisting the urge to touch his pocket, check his watch.

"They should have let you come home before. Or visited you, at least. I don't understand why they never did."

Krishna shrugged.

"Do you have to go back to the house? The Deshmukhs' house?"

"I think so," he said. "I think my mother will make me, surely she will make me."

"Don't be afraid," Gagan said. He leaned over and gripped Krishna's shoulder. "Remember who you are, Krishna. Who you are *here*."

Gagan sat back and added, "Also, there is something I wanted to tell you before you left. Krishna, I'm planning on leaving Osmania."

Krishna thought he might have misheard.

"The state elections are coming up, and—"

"What does the state election have to do with you leaving Osmania?"

Gagan took a deep breath. "I'm planning on leaving the university because I want to contest in the state election."

"You mean you want to quit college and contest in the outside world? That's absurd, Gagan."

"It makes perfect sense, actually."

"Are you joking?"

Gagan's face was serious.

"Why?" Krishna asked, suppressing the edge of desperation that was creeping into his voice. He waited to see if Gagan would burst out in laughter, saying it was a trick. But Gagan merely looked at him.

"Gagan, don't!"

Gagan didn't say anything. Two students sat down on a nearby bench. One of them held up two fingers at Suri, who again busied himself at the stove, boiling milk, taking chilies out of oil. Krishna looked away.

"Don't be afraid. Remember who you are," Gagan said again, in a soft voice. "What time is it? Go get your trunk. I'll borrow someone's motorbike and take you to the station."


On the overnight train, Krishna couldn't sleep. He kept waking up to check the station boards every time the train made a stop, mentally calculating how much time he had before he arrived. The anticipation made his stomach ache.

It was afternoon the next day by the time he arrived in Irumi. Ranga and his mother were both waiting for him, standing on either side of the door of the timber cottage.

The palm grove had remained exactly as he had left it. Long, rippling shadows in the sunny afternoon, cheerful birdcalls, insect trills. His mother too, had remained, exactly as he had left her. Other than the few locks of hair graying alongside her temples, the imperceptible lines around her eyes and cheeks, a slight rounding of her jaw, nothing else about her had changed, not even the countless piercings and earrings she still wore all around the rims of her ears. But the tall stranger with bronze, sunbeaten skin next to her, wearing a white dhoti, standing with his bare feet apart and his arms folded across his chest could have been anyone except that he had his brother's light brown eyes.

As he drew closer, Ranga gazed at him with a peculiar expression; his brows drawn together, his eyes strangely alight, as though he were watching a building burn. But with pride.

They both wordlessly embraced him. They touched his cheeks as though trying to believe. *How tall you have become. How big. How old. How handsome.* His throat hurt. He wiped his wet cheeks with the back of his hand, and his eyes fell on a kite leaning against the wall.

"Ranga made it for you," his mother said, noticing him looking. She pointed at the roll of manja next to it. "And Ranga ground up the glass for the kite string himself. He had thin cuts all over his fingers for days afterward," she added, smiling, proudly holding up Ranga's hands for him to examine.

He was twenty-two years old, and they had made him a child's present. But Krishna felt an absurd joy looking at the kite, a pale pink diamond leaning against the timber wall of their home, two decorative blue circles pasted on its panes like the eyes of a majestic snake. He heard it ripple in the breeze.

In the evening, his mother took him to the gadi. As the familiar childhood landmark loomed closer, it felt less familiar, removed like a distant cousin.

The water fountain was empty, and Krishna saw thick salt flakes floating on its bottom as he walked past. The vaakili was no longer gray and clean-scrubbed, it had taken on the appearance of aged, dirty stone, and where rainwater dripped down the stone columns in the gadi's façade, across the corbels and the carved figures atop them, mildew gathered, moss curled, in great fat stripes of green and black along the edges and corners. But the lemon grove was unchanged, full of thick, rubbery leaves, and beyond it, underneath the banyan, hidden slightly by boulder and brush, was the stepwell.

As they drew closer, he felt inexplicably cold and afraid. He told himself, again and again, that he was no longer a child, that he was a doctoral student in mathematics at Osmania, a gold medalist from City College. That he was twenty-two, not twelve. He thought all of this again and again as though it was a talisman, as though it was armor. But the thought of seeing Surendra Deshmukh made his stomach clench in terror. It was as though he could still hear the sounds of his boots, the dry leaves in the orchard crunching underneath them. Ranga saying *ne banchen dora*.

And Vijaya? He was so afraid of seeing her that it made him wish he hadn't returned.

As they stepped inside the doorway, it was as though his mother heard his thoughts. She said, "Only Mahendra-dora will be home now. Don't forget to touch his feet when we go in."

Saroja-dorasani smiled at him. And he found himself breaking through every resistance and searching her face for all the things Vijaya will have inherited as an adult; the blurred child-version he'd be able to recognize underneath. Then he was afraid of how much he wanted to see her.

"You have become so tall. Hasn't he, Pichamma?" Saroja-dorasani said.

"Yes, Dorasani," his mother said. "Taller than our Ranga now."

"Your mother said you have a gold medal," Mahendra Deshmukh said, looking up at him from his easy chair.

Krishna knelt down and touched Mahendra Deshmukh's feet, the tips of his fingers brushing his toes. "Dora," he said, in a tone that meant yes, bowing his head a little.

The brass curved ear of the gramophone was still there, a large radio next to it. The sun was setting, and the holy basil in the Deshmukh courtyard was in shadow.

"Take good care of your mother," Mahendra Deshmukh said. "She has only you."


Ranga was now working as a line supervisor at the Deshmukhs' new sugar factory, and at the end of the day when he sat next to Krishna, they did not talk very much.

It became obvious to him that something was lost between them; the camaraderie; the old bond; the ability to know what the other was thinking. And then there was the inability to know what to say alongside the pressure of constantly wanting to say something. He was now slightly taller than Ranga, yet he had the inexplicable feeling of turning into a child when he spoke to him.

Ranga and his mother treated him with a discomfiting mixture of reverence and familiarity; a beloved, venerated stranger in their home; a fragile outsider. His mother refused to allow him to help her cook or clean or chop up firewood or do her ironing. She wanted him to sit, just so. And whenever she sensed that he was setting out of the house, she'd say, "Sit awhile Krishna. Let me look at you."

On the rare occasions Krishna managed to venture into the village, he attempted to ignore the signs of change, the signs of want inscribed on every face he saw, the smell of draining starch, ribs pressing against tanned skins, distended bellies of boys, the things that he had never noticed while he lived there. Harder to miss were the disappearing youth, both men and women, and whispers; whispers about "the inside": guerilla camps established by the revolutionary communists in the Nallamala jungles surrounding Irumi, absorbing the young and able; and looming over it all, the gadi's façade, as grand and terrible as ever, but only from a distance.

In the ten days since his arrival, he hadn't told them about the scholarship he had to Osmania, or even that he'd begun the program already. But it was as if they sensed that he was holding something back, as if they were waiting. Eventually, the day before he was to return to Hyderabad, he told them. Ranga squeezed his shoulder. His mother was lost for words. It depressed him that they were so thrilled for him to have reason to leave again, reason to live away from them. All these years he had waited to return, to this place, so familiar, the only place he would be wanted, and yet, they willingly embraced the fact that he would never again return to live with them. He accepted their happiness, hid his sadness.

His mother asked him when he was going back. He said that his train was in the morning.

"And I haven't been letting you go anywhere," she said. The way she said it was as if he'd never again have the opportunity to see Irumi. She told him he should go out, see something of the village before he left, maybe the fair.

At the fair, Krishna wandered.

He watched the circus performers, the spinning child, the dancing tree bear. He heard air guns going off, the loud, carrying voice of the burrakatha storytellers in the distance, music from the play. The noises of screaming children, the anklets of folk dancers, the whirr of light and color and the scent of roasting corn.

At the carousels, he bumped into a girl in an orange sari. He apologized. She turned to look at him, and it was as if time stopped.

How could Vijaya still look the same?

After all this time. The same immensely brown eyes. The same coppery skin. All he wanted to do was close the space between them. To touch her. Her cheeks, her hair, the yellow pearls dangling from her ears, the tips of her fingers, to see how she could exist outside his imagination.

Before he could gather himself, she turned away, and tried to hold a pale girl by the shoulders, saying something, speaking but as though from a great distance. The pale girl pulled away from Vijaya and looked straight at him.

He felt blood rush to his head. There Sree too was: stroking the needles on the lemon tree; making the drumming noise before Vijaya began her stories; the bright and silvery edge in her voice when she called out Vijaya's name; all that cream from the custard apples gumming up her hair. Dying in Ranga's arms, pale and bloodless like a ruined porcelain doll.

Something was wrong with Sree. Something not quite right. And it wasn't the thick, ruinous scar running alongside her jawline. There was an unreal quality to her, as if he was only looking at a reflection of her in a mirror in front of him, not the original.

Vijaya turned away from Sree, a stunned expression dawning on her face. She recognized him. She said his name. She asked if it really was him, if he'd returned. Her voice was radiant—like his mother's, like Ranga's—as though she'd known all this time that he'd come back, and now he had and she didn't blame him.

He couldn't stand it. Couldn't stand to remember how he had left her there. Her and Ranga and Sree. They had all paid a price for what happened, while he'd gotten away. All these years, he'd never once looked back, never allowed himself to remember because he was afraid of what he'd see there.

He reached out and touched her face. The warmth of her cheek was so utterly familiar that it too was like coming home. He tried to speak. Say how sorry he was. Say everything, anything. He couldn't.

He turned and left, indiscriminately bumping into people. He walked fast, he walked away, he went straight home to the palm grove.

He pulled the cottage door open. "Ranga?" he shouted.

It took all he had to not allow his voice to break, to not sound like a child. There was no answer, no one was home. All these years, he had survived by not returning to that day. But now, shards of that day rained down upon him.

He was here, in this very cottage, shivering from cold and fright as he washed the mud off his face, as he scrubbed it out of his hair, from between his toes. The mud was everywhere; how did it get everywhere? How light Sree was in their arms. Like air, like water, like nothing. His heart was beating in his ears. He cleaned the floors, all the mud he'd tracked inside so that his mother wouldn't know. *Don't tell anyone you were with us.* Ranga had made him promise. The three of them at the top of the hillock. Ranga stopping and turning to make sure he wasn't following. *Go home!* But his mother didn't come home. Ranga didn't either. The tremors that racked his stomach when he thought of what was happening to Ranga made him double over and retch. He waited all evening. He waited until nightfall. Then Ranga came, his body flayed open.

How did his mother live like this? Seeing Sree every day. Seeing Ranga every day. How did Ranga live like this? How painful it had been to leave, but he'd done it. Was this what his mother was afraid of? That he'd see Vijaya and never be able to leave again? Did she know? Did they all know?

But, when Ranga and his mother came home that night, he said that he hadn't gone to the fair after all. He kept it all to himself.

In the morning, Ranga walked with him to the bus depot. It was the same place where he'd boarded the bus all those years ago. It took him to the junction, from where he took the overnight train back to Hyderabad.

Ranga loosened the length of red fabric tied around his head like a turban, and it fell around his shoulders.

"Will you stop working at the factory? Will they allow it?" Krishna asked.

The question had been eating at him. He sensed that there were parts to Ranga that were closed off to him. That the only thing that had kept him here, the task of educating Krishna, the bargain they had made in childhood, that trade in fates, was accomplished.

Ranga continued walking quietly by his side, the veins of his forearm straining under the weight of Krishna's trunk, which he had insisted on carrying. Slowly, he nodded.

"Work hard," Ranga said. "Concentrate on your studies and *do nothing else*. Don't get involved in campus politics at your university. To become an educated man, to never return here again. That is your destiny. This is all that I want for you."

"I want to come back."

They arrived at the bus stand. Ranga stopped walking, put down Krishna's trunk and faced him. "Krishna, you will never come back. Promise me."

He did not immediately respond. He chewed his tongue. Finally, "But will you visit me, Ranga?" he said, feeling childish, emotional, as though those words were wrung out of him by force. What he meant to ask was: *But do you still love me? Will you ever forgive me?*

"Ranga, come to Hyderabad. Come to see Osmania—"

"I've seen it," Ranga said, adding that he'd visited Hyderabad many times. With Surendra Deshmukh.

"Why didn't you ever come see me?" he said, stunned. "Not even once."

When the bus rounded the corner, Krishna looked out of the window. Ranga was watching him leave, he was tying up his turban again, bare feet apart.

"I promise," he whispered, and looked away.


The night he arrived back at Osmania, Krishna walked to the post office on the northern edge of campus and bought a stamp for fifteen paise. Noticing neither the stamp—a green, embossed image of an Assamese tea-plucker— nor the fact that an inland letter did not need postage, he attached it to the letter and wrote out her full name, Vijayalakshmi Deshmukh, above the address: a women's boarding house in Madras city.

He'd asked his mother before leaving, small questions without raising suspicion, about Sree, about Vijaya. He walked to the red postbox. The metal was warm from the day. He had written the letter on the train, he had written without pausing. He did not strike things out, he did not re-write. He wrote recklessly. Now, in this moment, he grew aware of the fact that this letter leaving his hands would breach the boundaries he had set up around himself, and perhaps ones she had too. Time had built those boundaries. Regret had built those boundaries. Guilt had built those boundaries. And the transgression he was committing now would destroy them, raze them, and he knew that it was a transgression he would never be able to stop himself from committing again, that it may fate him to yearn for her as long as he lived.

He placed the letter inside the flap and waited, seeing how long he could hold it without letting go. He sensed someone walking up to the postbox behind him. He let go, and heard the soft flutter of the letter falling inside, the mouth of the postbox scraping shut. He turned around, it was merely someone passing by, not even noticing him.

# LIKE SUGAR THAT BURNS

———◆———

I f not for the smell of sugar, she'd have missed Ranga. It was that scent, like fresh-cut sugarcane just put through a mill, that gave him away. It made Katya double back.

Ranga was sitting on a boulder on the side of the road, his elbows resting on his knees. He straightened up when he saw her, letting that length of cloth he always wore around his neck fall away. His reddish hair was brushed back tidily, his clothes were clean and dry. He was barefooted as always, just like she was.

Katya crossed the road towards him. They were on the path that wound away from the village and went towards the bus depot, passing by the school. They used to not be able to hear the village through the thickets before, but now they could—there was chatter from those returning from the fields, cowbells, children, the lone singsong voice of a woman drawing water from a well.

"Did your brother leave? Your mother said he was leaving this morning," she said.

He did not reply. He seemed agitated.

"This road goes all the way to the bus depot, doesn't it?" she said.

"He left," Ranga said.

"Have you been here all day? It's almost sunset."

His gaze lingered on her face. It was as if he recognized something fond in it. He wanted her to stay, she sensed.

Katya sat on the ground next to him, balancing herself on the soles of her feet. She pulled out the knot at the base of her neck, shook out her hair and gathered up the strands again, twisting it back into a knot. "I was in the village," she said. "That girl who used to seamstress for us— Suma was her name—did you know her? Dorasani sent me to fetch her."

"Is that why you seem so agitated?" he said.

She added quickly, "She's run away with someone else, no doubt. Where else would someone like her go?"

"Is that so?"

They looked at each other in silence for a moment.

"Will *you* ever leave them?" Ranga said.

"Whom?" she said, though she knew perfectly well what he meant. But she decided to humor him. "Why would I?"

"Why would you, because they treat you well? Think of you like family? Like their own daughter?"

"They *are* my family," she said. "I've known no other."

He looked agitated again. Abruptly he said, "How old is she now? Thirteen? Fourteen?"

"Who?" Katya said. He didn't seem to miss the ominous note in her voice. But she couldn't understand why it should make him smile.

"We're the same, Katya," he said.

"Is that so?"

"*It is* so. The people we love, Katya, we love so intensely we'd do anything for them. We'd take the very bones out of our bodies and use them to pave their paths in life. Yet, even for their sake, we cannot forgive."

"I'm going now," she said. But she couldn't move. He smiled at her, and it wasn't like the face she'd seen all these years, working around the gadi; doing exactly as asked; never, ever, stepping out of line, the solemn youth. "My brother's path in life is paved, Katya. He'll be all right. And *I* made that happen. He gave me his word that he won't return here. He's free of this place. And after today, I'll never see him."

"Why do you look so happy about that?" she said.

"Do I?" he said. "I don't know what my face looks like when I'm happy. Tell me, Katya. What's it like?"

"I'm going," she said again. But she did not leave.

"Do you know what Surendra-dora said to me one night, a few years after Krishna left? He'd had too much to drink, and I was standing by the door of his study, seeing if he wanted anything else. All day we'd been out together, every muscle in my body ached but I did not show it. Suddenly he turns to me and says in a voice full of regret, 'How were you born there?' I look to where he's pointing—at the village below us. 'It is a mistake,' he says. '*What a mistake!* You should have been born here, in this house. How I loved her, Ranga. If she'd been alive and we'd have had another child, it would be just like you. It would have been so grand.'"

Ranga laughed. It was so harsh and violent, his laughter. "And I felt it too, Katya, felt exactly what he meant. If only I was his son. A Deshmukh. Imagine that.

"But he didn't stop there. He says, 'But then there's two of you! Two aberrations! Two who do not fit into the molds that were created for them. One? One can be broken, sanded down, made to fit. But two? Two's too many, Ranga. What to do then? Break them both? No. It won't work. No, what you do is break one and make the other one watch. Sever what binds them. That's how you get them to fit. Tell me, Ranga, didn't I do the right thing?'"

Ranga didn't look agitated anymore, nor happy, exactly. He said, "Do you know what a prisoner feels like, Katya? When he's finally free?"

"Why would I know that?"

"*He wants to go back*," Ranga said in an awestruck voice. "And how to go back? Wait all day for the right person to show up, one who can take him back."

Now she stood up, but Ranga gripped her arm. "Let go," she said.

"Ask me where I'm going tonight, Katya. What I'm going to do. Ask me and I'll tell you."

"What business of mine is that?"

"You will smell it in the air tonight, it will be like sugar that burns."

Ranga stood up, still not letting go of her. "Ask me!"

She'd quite forgotten, all these years, how frightening Ranga was, how even as a child his laughter used to have such inexplicable wildness in it. Only she hadn't known he could hide it so well. "No," she stammered. "Move out of my way. Let go."

"You aren't afraid of me, Katya," he said, letting go of her arm. "You are only afraid of what they'll do to you for simply knowing the truth. It's all right, you don't want to ask me? Don't. But, Katya, you have to face your own truth someday, you must! All your life you have been standing in that passage to the kitchens: servant on one side, offspring on the other. Now look at me, Katya. Look at me when I say this—"

"Enough!" she said. "Move out of my way. Move now." She walked around him and did not turn back.

He called after her, "Who's your father, Katya? I'll tell you. But you know already."

# UNGRATEFUL CHILD

———◆———

Only a slow rail line existed between Irumi and Madras. The journey took three days, and Vijaya insisted on going alone.

On the train, she dwelled on her father's parting words at the station, wishing her all the luck in the world, stroking her hair once. Sree stood biting her lip. "Say goodbye to your sister," their father had said, nudging Sree's shoulder. Sree said goodbye but did not come any closer. She'd found her uncle's restraint while avoiding her eye far more upsetting than if he had shouted at her or ordered her or flatly told her she would not be allowed to go. "Please take care of yourself, Uncle," she'd said. "Watch your diabetes," she'd said. But he hadn't replied. Yet, despite the disaster at their sugar factory, he'd made it a point to come to the station to see her leave. Her mother hadn't done even that. And she'd overheard him berate her father on why he was allowing her to travel alone. If she had enough money on her, enough books, enough clothes, enough everything.

To travel alone was a request that her father acquiesced to, but one she regretted almost immediately. Unaccustomed to going anywhere alone, Vijaya felt jumpy and threatened whenever the train stopped at a station. She chained her trunk to her seat and ventured onto the platform only when it was absolutely unavoidable. Even hot tea, she bought from the tea vendors through the bars of the compartment windows, sipping the tea so quickly that it burned her tongue, just so she could return the glass without getting out of the train.

It was a lonely journey, punctuated by memories of her mother's fury in the months before her leaving. She'd scream, that Vijaya had no right to change her mind about leaving Irumi, that she was violating their decade-old promise, that she was a selfish and ungrateful child who cared for no one except herself and that it was how Vijaya had been ever since she was born, that no amount of good pedigree or motherly efforts could remove some people from their base natures, that it would be a terrible scandal amongst the Deshmukh relatives, and that she had no idea how a daughter of hers could have inherited such a terrible character, such selfishness; over each single meal, over every passing encounter in their home, again and again and again until Vijaya felt her mother's hatred seeping through her door and suffocating her in her bed like some noxious gas.

"Can't you do this one thing for me? I'll never ask you for anything else," her mother had said, in her final attempt. "When you finished junior college, I thought we were done, I thought we could get you married and you'd belong to someplace, someone else. Not our headache anymore. Why must you prolong this? Prolong your connection to us."

When she said nothing, her mother said: "Ungrateful child. I don't know how you are mine."

An endless series of towns passed her window, each town stranger than the last. Soon, the yellow station boards began announcing the town names in a florid script Vijaya did not recognize. At first it puzzled her, then it dawned on her that the train had crossed the state border. Her first feeling was of enormous relief. Of having successfully escaped her mother. It was like taking a deep breath above water.

What remained the same and cheered her was the flashing countryside between stations. Slowly, the hills fell away and it steadily grew greener, flatter, hectares and hectares of coconut trees erupted into view. Uncultivated pasturelands, orchards, rice fields, canals. Occasionally there were small towns, jumbled messes of cement roofs and thatched roofs, shop boards, streets aglow with lampposts and scooters. Once in a while, she would spot an elephant, bathing leisurely alongside a river as though it had all the time in the world.

All around her in the bogie sat villagers from places just like Irumi, peasants or farmers wearing grim expressions and sitting awkwardly on their berths, the soles of their feet flat against their seats, walking sticks laid between their feet. Although they all spoke to one another as though belonging to the same extended family, they did not speak to Vijaya. They snuck glances at her, furtively stealing looks at the zari of her silk skirt or the thin strand of gold and pearl around her neck, the diamonds in her ears, the suppleness of her brown leather satchel. She rummaged in her trunk and extracted a small package of orange candies, and that, having attracted their flocks of children, warmed them up to her.

"Not from around here?" or "Going to college?" or "Whose child are you?" they repeated in a series of languages, chins jutted out, friendly smiling teeth stained red with tobacco or gutka or paan, until they hit upon one she understood. She talked to them, asked them where they were going, how many children they had, or how many days of journey they had left on the train. Three days, she replied herself.

For lunch, she bought idlies from the vendor threading his way through the aisle of the crowded compartment, lugging along a steel dispenser filled with sambar, carrying on his shoulder a jar of coconut chutney wrapped in a cotton towel. She marveled with them at how only the Tamils knew how to make proper idlies; white as snow, melting the second it touched their tongues, sambar so sweet and sour that its aroma awoke sleeping men. "But no chai here," they'd tell her, crestfallen, shaking their heads, "these people only drink coffee!" A most grave error in judgment that immediately reversed any admiration they had for the Tamilians' idly-making abilities.

At night, Vijaya lifted up her seat and stretched out on her berth. She couldn't sleep. As she watched the single yellow bulb until it went out, the swinging shadows it cast across the compartment windows, she found herself acknowledging something for the first time since it happened. She hadn't dared; not while walking back from the fair after finding Sree; not later, at home, where there never was any room for her to feel what she did— lightness, absolute lightness at what felt like the very center of her soul.

For as long as she could remember, Krishna had lived within her, like a melody she was born with but could neither sing nor forget. She counted the ten years it had been since they'd last seen each other, the day they'd parted at the stepwell, the life they'd both lived in the interlude. That one day he would return was a secret she held against the knowledge that she was unwanted by everyone in the place she was born. Now he had returned, he'd held her, said her name. He'd come bearing all the marks of an outsider. The polished brown shoes, the starched white shirt, the wristwatch, the way his dark hair fell across his forehead in waves. But underneath all of that it was still Krishna in the way his face softened when he caught sight of her. Now she was old enough to name the expression on his face—ardent, that's what it was. Ardent, like what he saw was beloved. Even when they were children it had been the same. If it was to be another ten years before he'd return again, to the only place they'd known together, she'd still wait.

The light in the compartment went out, and there was only the music of the railway track, the somnolent hammering of steel lines against train wheels washing over her like water.

Arriving at the station in Madras, Vijaya met the ayah who was to take her to the boarding house. The ayah left her at the gates of the ladies' boarding house and not knowing the etiquette, Vijaya erred on the side of caution, peeled out of her satchel a small wad of rupees and gave it to the old lady. The ayah looked simply astounded on receiving the tip, gave her a gap-toothed smile and walked off into the night.

The boarding house was a whitewashed building. It had three floors and against the night sky, it looked like a giant seashell. The courtyard inside was bathed with the fragrance of flowering plants; she smelled damask roses, ylang-ylang blossoms, and was even able to make out the scent of a jasmine vine lurking underneath it all. The middle-aged woman who ran the boarding house met her in the courtyard and took her to the third floor of the building, where her assigned room was. *Deshmukh* read a small, neat sign by her door.

The woman spoke very little Telugu and Vijaya had to ask her to repeat everything, twice, and even then, she had to strain her ears and concentrate on her moving lips, trying to decipher the exact meaning of her words. All she got at the end, other than the steel padlock and key for her room, was that the woman preferred to be addressed as *warden-*

*ma'am* or *ma'am*, and not by her given name. Although she had begun finding Tamil shrill and unmusical, she decided that it was probably the speaker's manner of delivery that mattered. She had three years to spend here, she'd have to learn.

Alone, she shut the double doors and looked around—it was a narrow single, wedged between the stairway to the terrace and a large iron-grilled window overlooking the courtyard below. The room, although small, gave off an impression of extreme orderliness and cleanliness. A boy had brought up her trunk, it was heavy and she dragged it, slowly, until it sat next to the window like an old guard. She extracted a sheet and a pillowcase from her trunk, then spent a good ten minutes making sure it fit correctly on the mattress.

She felt grimy and even though her freshly made bed looked soft and inviting, she desperately wanted a bath. She took a towel, fresh clothes, and went in search of the bathrooms. There were two, one on each end of the wide corridor and she realized with a jolt that even though it was dark, she could hear the sea from her floor, and if she concentrated, she could even hear it approaching, then hurling itself against the shoreline, faintly, in the quiet of the night.

She could not remember the last time she felt this buoyant, this full of good cheer, energy, optimism.

In the morning she unpacked her trunk. There was a narrow closet behind the door, with just four shelves, and Vijaya was glad she packed very little, few clothes, almost no jewelry. From amongst all the jewelry she owned, the only piece she'd brought with her was a thin chain, hung with a heavy gold pendant the shape and size of a ripe kumquat. It was engraved with the image of the goddess Lakshmi, with a small bloodred ruby at the base of the lotus she sat on. It was the oldest thing she owned. Although it had been made for her on her first birthday, imagining decades of use for it her mother had the goldsmith add a pin on its back, so that it could be detached and worn in her hair, at the top of her braid. Except for the pendant, she put everything she brought in the closet, leaving the velvet jewelry box in her trunk.

She dressed carefully, picking a flowy, Mysore silk sari, green the color of jungle moss, with a thin border of gold and pink zari. She used a hand mirror to line her eyes and draw a perfect dot of red high between her eyebrows. She checked her reflection thrice. Outside, she put the padlock on the door and put the key in her satchel. She was almost at the stairs when she hesitated and went back. She opened her trunk again and extracted the gold chain. She put it around her neck and held the hand mirror at an angle; the pendant glowed bright and yellow, a tiny sun against the green of her sari.

She was to wait for Warden-ma'am downstairs, in the courtyard with the other newly arrived girls. In daylight, the courtyard was bright, square, laid with white stone pavers, windows of the rooms above overlooking it on all sides. It gave off the same impression of extreme orderliness and cleanliness that her room did. There were potted plants and rosebushes all along the sides, and the jasmine vine she'd smelled the night before was young, climbing the building on its own, floor by floor.

There were about twenty other girls, roughly her age, standing in the courtyard. A girl standing close to her turned and gave her a cheerful smile. Her name was Deepthi, she said, and where was Vijaya from?

"Irumi," she replied.

"Telugu?"

Deepthi had a round face, with dimples that fell like needles into her doughy cheeks. She was Telugu as well, she said, but from an area bordering the Tamil region so that she spoke Tamil well and Telugu poorly, with a heavy accent and without conviction. She asked Vijaya a lot of questions within a short span of time, one after the other in rapid succession, a new question at the ready as soon as an answer for the last was out of Vijaya's mouth—where exactly Irumi was—an exclamation when she realized who her uncle was—did she have any siblings? Which program she was in at Presidency; what year was she born; had she ever stayed in a boarding house before?

Deepthi's head barely reached the top of Vijaya's shoulder. And Deepthi had a way of speaking where she lowered her chin and spoke in half whispers, and Vijaya had to lean forward, dip her neck a bit to hear her. Deepthi was standing very, very close to Vijaya. If Vijaya drew back,

Deepthi moved a few inches closer. This happened a few times before it occurred to her that Deepthi wanted to make sure she was not overheard, even though it would be impossible for anyone to overhear their conversation, even if they stood shoulder to shoulder with them. Vijaya felt interrogated at every turn.

"I already know all the bus routes here, actually," Deepthi was saying. "I'll show you. I just wanted to meet the other first-year girls so I came. There aren't many of us this year. Fewer than last year as far as I can tell. You know this boarding house is brand-new, less than five years old? That's why it's so white, because the rain and heat haven't yet had the chance to age this place. But I heard the warden has it whitewashed each year for no reason. Don't you love the rosebushes? Apparently we aren't allowed to pluck any flowers—hah, what use is it to have flower plants just for decoration? You know suddenly, there is a big surge of women going to college now, it's like the latest fashion trend. There weren't so many before. In my mother's time, they were married off by fifteen or sixteen at most, children, then on and on. Oh, Vijaya, see over there, the warden is coming, let's be quiet!" and Deepthi placed a finger on her lips, raised and dropped her shoulders once. Vijaya massaged the back of her neck as inconspicuously as she could.

The warden arrived.

"Hey, you know what?" Deepthi murmured. "There is one girl in our boarding house who is a repeater. Second year but will sit with us in class. Her name is Asha. I mean, why bother? You know it isn't like we *have to* get college degrees. Our life doesn't depend on them."

Vijaya hoped that no one could really hear them. Deepthi gave a small giggle, the edges of her lips dipping with mock sadness. As the warden began speaking, Deepthi coiled her arm around Vijaya's.

"Mail is delivered every day," the warden said. In her fatigue, Vijaya hadn't noticed the previous night how severe the warden's tone was. "It will be sent to your rooms as long as it comes under your name. There is a postbox at the end of the street for your outgoing mail. There is a telephone in my flat on the ground floor. You will be allowed to make trunk calls but only in case of emergencies and after hours. No local calls, use the phone booth for that. Bills are paid at the beginning of the year, I will send notice when it is time."

The warden held up a stack of white cards. "I will distribute the bus schedules. All of you are at Presidency and so you will have the same route. You must always take the ladies' special bus, you are new here and I don't want you to go on the general buses." She held up the cards but did not distribute them. Vijaya had the feeling that the warden was pausing for effect.

"This boarding house is my home," the warden said, in a still more severe tone. "I think of it as my home, and I only permit girls from good, respectable families to live in my home. Properly raised. Your parents trust me, they have sent you so far away from home only because they know you are under *my* supervision. Their trust in me is everything, and I will go to any lengths to keep it. Those of you who are here will all make good, respectable marriages in the near future. And so, I do not tolerate any funny business in my home. If I ever spot a man waiting for you out on the street, if I even hear that you were seen in the company of a man outside college, I will write your parents, I will remove you from my home. Be warned. Follow my rules. We will not have any problems."

"I really like your necklace, by the way," Deepthi said. Her dimples were showing again. They were walking towards the bus stop together. It was very close to the boarding house, one quiet street over. Most of the homes in the neighborhood were single-story bungalows and cottages painted in vivid pastels. Here and there were young banyans, lone coconut trees.

By the time they arrived on campus at Presidency College on Kamarajar Salai, Deepthi amassed around herself a small group of girls that included Vijaya. They chattered incessantly and Vijaya had trouble keeping up with the many simultaneous conversations. She had never been around so many women her age. She was finding the experience thrilling, watched them with interest, curiosity; the way they fussed with their saris, swung their long braids over their shoulders, threw their heads from side to side when agreeing or disagreeing. She noticed also that even though none of them wore clothes that were particularly expensive or remarkable, they were very fashionable.

"Did you prepare in advance for classes before coming here? I heard the econ program here is extremely selective, very difficult to get through,"

Shivani, a girl in a mustard-colored sari, asked, falling into step beside her. The entire group, except for Vijaya and Deepthi, were in the early education program.

"Anything is tough if you think it's tough," Deepthi interjected before Vijaya could respond, bodily emerging between them. "My thought is that if it's too bad, we'll just switch into another program," she added, speaking directly to Vijaya and angling her body in such a way that she cut off Shivani entirely. Shivani hesitated for an awkward second before taking a step back and falling into conversation with the others.

They parted ways with the others at the econ building. Entering the first-year classroom, Vijaya realized they were the only women in a class of nearly thirty. It was a large, oval room, with benches of threes, rising step by step, spaced evenly from front to back like a small amphitheater. Deepthi walked ahead of her, slipping into a bench immediately next to the entryway, nearly at the door. Vijaya sat down next to her. She hadn't prepared for her classes in advance, she'd barely glanced at the textbooks. The only reason she'd chosen economics was because only a program that involved some kind of serious study—finance, economics, mathematics—could justify her leaving Irumi and going so far.

Now it dawned on her, sitting next to Deepthi in that large and oval college classroom, that she'd done it. She'd gotten away. She'd woken up this morning, and for the first time in her life, she had not crossed paths with her mother. She had not been tasked this morning with carrying the terrible, nameless, and yet omnipresent burdens for which her mother thought her as both the cause and the source. The derision and the contempt in every single act of every single minute of every single day. The weight her mother placed upon her was like the breath in her lungs, always there, noticeable only when absent.

The foreignness of her surroundings began to seep into her. Everything felt touched by humor and happiness, spreading across her skin, coloring her. Like the momentary buoyancy she experienced the night before, hearing the ocean hurl against the shore. The foreignness and lightness had a name: possibility. That was what it was, possibility, like riffling through blank pages. Her room must be standing empty now. Sree, what was she doing now? Sree's face erupted into her mind, and then, she felt the humor ebbing away. Was Sree at school? Was she at home? Was she in her room? Today, she'd begun the day without having crossed paths with her mother, but also not having seen Sree.

Sree had overheard her conversation with their father in the library, and her heart ached when she thought of how much of it she might have overheard.

After twenty minutes, Vijaya began to feel self-conscious. Her neck prickled when she imagined the eyes of those sitting behind them on her. She and Deepthi did not speak, did not turn around to look at who else was in class with them. Suddenly, she was glad she had Deepthi, that she wasn't entirely alone.

The door opened and another girl entered. She was light-skinned, had dark eyes, with an almost fragile quality to her face. Vijaya moved a little to make room on their bench, and the girl took the spot next to Vijaya. Her resemblance to Sree was so striking, right down to the color of the thin veins running up the side of her neck that Vijaya could not help but stare. She waited to catch the girl's eye, so she could tell her how much she resembled her sister. She opened her mouth to say hello, but the girl did not glance at her or Deepthi, and instead turned around and started chatting across the room with a few male students in the back row she apparently knew, because they spoke to her with great familiarity.

One of them threw a paper rocket at her. Vijaya watched, as the girl caught its sharp edge, deftly between two fingers, threw her head back, laughed, and launched it back at them. Deepthi pressed a finger against Vijaya's shoulder and leaned into her ear. "That's Asha," she whispered. Deepthi lowered her voice further, drew so close that Vijaya felt her hot breath against her earlobe. "Don't tell anyone I told you, but I heard that she has had an abortion. Her parents threw her out."

Asha turned back around and faced the blackboard, neither looking at them nor attempting to make conversation. She placed her fountain pen on the desktop and struck the nib, watching it whir round and round.

The first professor who entered the classroom did an exaggerated, comical double take at their bench. "So many of you!" he exclaimed, swinging his head from side to side across their bench like an old dog. As he introduced the subject, he added, over their heads in a genial, fatherly tone, "Now, boys, we have to be careful how we speak in this class. We must keep our manners and remember that there are ladies here."

This professor's subject was microeconomics. He began his lecture. "A demand curve is a theoretical tool that uses the price of a commodity and the quantity of the commodity. In representation, price appears on the y-axis and quantity on the x-axis."

Here, he plotted a map with axes of price against quantity.

"Demand will decrease, as a response to an increase in price"—he drew a neat downward curve in the graph—"and will increase in response to a decrease in price"—here an upward curve cutting across the first one. "The behavior of a consumer in a competitive market is, therefore—" The professor stopped speaking.

He'd spotted Deepthi whispering into her ear. She met his gaze and realized too late that she shouldn't have, she was supposed to have lowered her eyes and not have looked straight at him.

"You," he said, pointing at Vijaya. "When I say 'price' of a commodity, how is this calculated?"

He said, "Stand up when I ask you a question."

Vijaya stood up as he asked, thoroughly conscious of the eyes of the entire class trained on her.

"With quantity, there can be reliable metrics. For instance, we can measure how many quintals of a particular grain or raw material have been processed through a manufacturing plant or factory, but price varies from place to place. In a predominantly informal market such as India, this variation can be very large. For example, if we consider only the wholesale price measured in a particular city or town, won't the resulting demand curve be unreliable?" he said.

Vijaya wasn't sure if he was continuing his lesson, or if he was prompting her for an answer by giving her more information, or if he'd excused her and it was okay to sit back down. She felt a bead of sweat roll down her back.

The professor continued speaking, looking at the class at large. "For example: If we are plotting the demand curve for, say, onions, which are sold wholesale in, say, Maharashtra, would this metric be reliable for the entire state of Maharashtra, or a particular district, say, Solan District, or for all the downstream markets in that district?" Then suddenly he looked at her again, as though remembering that she was still standing.

"How is the price of onion as a commodity calculated, miss?"

Vijaya stared at her tabletop. She was aware that she was biting the inside of her cheek. Then, a snide voice from the back of the classroom. "Why don't you go buy us some onions and let us know."

A few snickers erupted across the class. The professor gave a dry chuckle, then waved a hand in her direction. "There is no need for you to come to college if all you want to do is chitchat." He turned away and faced the blackboard again.

Vijaya sat back down and stared at her fingertips.

Deepthi stopped whispering in her ear for the remainder of the hour. She wondered if she was imagining it, but she felt as though Deepthi was slowly, but steadily angling her body away from her, as though detaching herself from Vijaya's hip. Asha glanced her way once, but with an expression she recognized as sympathy.

When classes ended, it was late afternoon.

On the walk back to the bus stop, they rejoined the other girls. Deepthi talked, but Vijaya had stopped listening. Soon, Deepthi outpaced her and fell in with the other girls. She could spot Shivani amongst the group. And within a few minutes, Vijaya found herself walking alone, trailing the rest of them.

At the bus stop, it began to rain. The bus had no shelter and large drops struck her cheeks, splashed across her green silk sari. Vijaya covered her shoulders and her head with the end of her sari. They crowded together under the spare branches of a neem tree close by. The bus was running late.

Soon, more people arrived at the stop, gathered under the neem tree. It was becoming crowded, the air was sticky and humid. Vijaya touched her hair and was stunned by how the texture felt—like sandpaper, as though the sea air had been coating it with new layers of salt with each passing minute.

Nearly an hour passed. Still, the ladies' special bus did not come. Her feet hurt, she leaned against the trunk of the neem tree and flexed her knees. The crowd grew larger and larger, as did the chatter and the rain. It was extremely uncomfortable to be simultaneously drenched by both rain and sweat. There were three months of summer left still, and Vijaya shuddered to think how awful traveling to and from college in the heat would be. Each time a general bus pulled into the stop and departed, she felt a longing to get on it, finally sit down and rest her legs, close her eyes and process the day. She tapped her foot, kicked at a small stone, feeling hot, impatient, tired, drowsy. Finally, after another twenty minutes passed, the ladies' special rounded the corner.

When the bus pulled into the stop, it was utter chaos. She felt elbows and hips and feet knocking into her as the women waiting underneath the tree with her staggered forward all at once. Everyone tried to get into the bus through its narrow single door at the same time. She had never been this close, this pressed up against so many strangers at once, and she too attempted to scramble onto the bus like the others, feeling as though her entire body was being squeezed through a metal tube.

Before she could react, take in what was happening, Vijaya found herself shoved every which way, then summarily deposited on the footboard of the bus. She could not see Deepthi or any other girls from Presidency. The bus began pulling out of the stop with many women still attempting to get on it. They would have to get off the footboard and wait for the next ladies' special.

She had managed to get herself lodged somewhere in the middle of the bus when it pulled out of the stop. Wet saris soaked her face, spongy bodies pressed on all sides. She lifted up her neck and looked at the roof of the bus, the rail in its ceiling. With great difficulty she was able to remain standing, held up like a doll between the other women, hand gripping the metal rail, unable to breathe freely.

For a few minutes it felt novel, comical even. But after thirty minutes, her feet were numb and she could no longer feel the metal fasteners of her sandals digging into her ankles. The windows of the bus were kept closed to keep rain out, they began going foggy. There was no part of her body that wasn't revolting pressed up against another. The stale air, the smell of diesel and sweat and wet clothes was overwhelming, it made her want to retch.

Feeling light-headed, she took deep breaths, tried to suppress her nausea. Her leather satchel was out of sight, but she felt its strap cutting into the side of her neck. Someone's wiry hair was pressing against her cheek, someone else's watch strap was pressing into her hip.

Every time the driver braked, and it happened often, those precariously balanced were thrown a few feet forward, then backward again when the bus sped up. When someone needed to get off the bus, they shoved everyone aside in their campaign toward the door and people would allow themselves to be shoved without protest. Through all of this, it felt as though she was the only person who looked utterly bewildered. Everyone else appeared to her jovial, laughing, carrying on conversations only momentarily interrupted by the braking bus. Those who managed to secure seats were crammed four to seats of three, sharing boiled peanuts to snack on, asking one another about how far away their stops were, how terribly hot it was inside the bus, this rain, it always came when one didn't want it.

Finally, the bus arrived at her stop, braking just as violently as it had many times before. She began fighting her way to the door.

She was finding it difficult to shove people out of her way, and instead she began asking. "Excuse me!" she said, again and again, asking them to move aside. "My stop is here." Most did not hear her and she had to repeat herself. She was too far away from the door, and by the time she made even a few feet of progress, the bus gave an almighty lurch and sped away from the stop. Vijaya was thrown off-balance and fell.

"Stop the bus!" she said in a shrill, panicked voice, scrambling to get up, gathering her satchel. No one heard her. Out of the window, she caught a glimpse of Deepthi and the other girls, who had had no trouble getting off from the rear exit, walking away from the stop in the direction of the boarding house.

"Stop the bus. I need to get off!" she shouted again. Someone heard her and repeated her request. Out of pity for her, the crowd seemed to part. "Go, go, go fast and ask the driver to stop," someone said.

"Ask quickly, he may or may not stop," said another.

The driver's seat was separated from the passengers by a steel frame. The driver looked haggard, his khaki uniform had moist patches of sweat all across it. He was chewing something in a tired way. Tobacco, she guessed from the vile odor. The pastel bungalows of the only street she knew in Madras were swiftly falling away. "Excuse me, excuse me," she said, trying to not panic. The driver pretended not to hear her, stepped on the accelerator as though to spite her.

Soon, older buildings and shop fronts flashed past. They were entering a busy area, and traffic came up to the bus on all sides, heaps of scooters, rickshaws, vans, dump trucks, paper vans. They were approaching an overpass and not slowing down.

"Driver!" Vijaya said in a louder voice. The overpass came closer. "I missed my stop. Driver. Let me off the bus." The driver did not look at her. Instead, leaning out the window, he spat out a thin stream of tobacco spittle.

On the overpass, the bus bounced over every metal joint, and with each jerk she was thrown this way and that. Her fingers were raw and red from clutching the driver's metal frame. The women standing around her watched curiously as she asked the driver to stop again and again. Her voice began shaking. She was trying not to cry. They crossed the overpass and approached a busy junction. The signal turned red and the bus screeched to a halt.

She was unsure if she was allowed to get off a bus stopped in traffic.

"What are you waiting for?" a girl behind her said. "Hurry. He is not going to stop. The next stop is very far away and you cannot walk back from there. Go, before the signal turns."

Vijaya hurried out of the bus door. Thankful to be on firm, steady ground again, she nearly ran into a stopped rickshaw. She threaded her way through traffic and reached the other side of the road and turned around to look at the bus.

It was not raining in this part of town. It was nearly sunset, the light was turning deep red and she felt conspicuous in her damp clothes. The signal had changed, the bus was moving away, its many passengers pressed up against the glass like colorful balloons. Her silk sari was rumpled, wet, stained with sweat and rainwater. She felt soiled, bruised, dirty. Her head was throbbing.

She was fairly certain that the bus hadn't taken any turns. She had to walk straight back until she reached the overpass, and after crossing the overpass it would be a short walk to the stop she was supposed to have gotten off at. She guessed.

This was a commercial area, so busy that people bumped into her from every direction. The sidewalk was dirty, splashed in bright red paan spit every few feet, smelling of urine and stray dogs. Traffic blared. There were repair shops, junk metal dealers, cafés, stalls, hawkers, paperboys. She covered her nose with the end of her sari and walked quickly, trying not to sprint.

Vijaya heard someone on her right make a noise, a prolonged whistle. "Hey, you. You in the green sari!"

She made the mistake of turning around and looking. It was an auto repair shop. The shop was closed, and a thin man was leaning against the metal shutters. He had an elongated face, like that of a hunting dog. On seeing her turn his way, he gave a start, puckered his lips and kissed the air, then he stuck his tongue out and leered, staring unblinkingly at her in an obscene way. Disgusted, she looked away, picked up her pace.

She was afraid to consider what would happen if she were to be lost there at nightfall. Already, it was beginning to get dark. What if the bus had taken a sharp turn and she hadn't noticed? In her panic, she was blanking on the name of her boarding house. The harder she tried to remember, the worse her recollection became. Now she couldn't even ask a kind stranger to point her in a particular direction. It is a white building—maybe she could describe it? Maybe she could ask for directions to the railway station instead, ask a woman, someone who looked friendly, and then from the railway station she could trace her way to the boarding house? The way the ayah had led her? Would she remember? Maybe, maybe.

The shops fell behind and she saw the overpass again.

She felt relief wash over her. The bridge was there. She was on the right path. She would be back at the boarding house soon.

But when she reached the bridge, she sensed someone walking close behind her. She turned around and realized that it was the same man from the auto repair shop who had whistled at her. He was following her, still leering in the same obscene way. He smiled at her, and his smile made the small hairs on her arms stand on end. She felt soiled simply by the way he was looking at her.

She hurried away, and every few paces she noticed that he was walking faster to keep up with her. Within a few minutes, he was within an arm's reach of her. So close that he could touch her if he wanted to.

"Darling, look here once more, I know you want to," he said, his voice menacing, closer and closer. He kissed the air again, but in shorter, quicker bursts. The overpass was deserted. Vijaya tripped over a large pebble on the ground, stumbled a little but kept walking, as fast as she could without actually running. She was afraid to run.

"Green sari, turn around. What's with the attitude? If you don't want me to follow, why are you wearing such pretty clothes?"

Vijaya kept walking.

"What a piece. Look at you. Whore. How much?"

Vijaya stopped walking.

In that moment, her mother's words came back to her. When she was little, her mother used to be fond of saying that she had inherited so much of her uncle. He had a particular way of glaring at the vetti, the jeethas, the laborers, the sharecroppers, the villagers. A glare that made them feel as though he'd stepped on their throats and stood there. He needn't even speak. Her mother would say, "You have your uncle's *face*, Vijaya," and she'd say it simply, without spite or accusation, but with satisfaction. "You have your uncle in you, it's in your blood. Blood is blood."

The earliest memory she had of her uncle was from when she was five or six. This age she guessed simply because Sree did not figure in it, which meant that either she wasn't born yet or she was a small baby under a year old. She remembered she was playing in the courtyard by herself, twirling around each stone column, humming, round and round each column, one after the other after the other. She was wearing a pink skirt.

A sharecropper and his son had come to speak to her uncle. They were standing a few feet from her. Her uncle was sitting in an easy chair next to the gramophone.

"What are you looking at?" her uncle said. She turned to look. The sharecropper's son was looking at her, spinning there in her bright pink skirt.

If one looked at this boy closely, they'd know that something was not quite right with him; there was a vacantness in his eyes, a dullness in his speech, a sluggishness in his gait. "That girl over there," the boy said, raising a finger and pointing at Vijaya, but only he didn't quite say *girl*. He said *pori*. A coarse word he must have picked up from the adults in the village.

The sharecropper panicked, pulled his son by the neck and slapped him hard across his cheek, then said to her uncle in a hurried voice, "Dora, his mind is not quite right. He doesn't know what he says most of the time, I'll give him a good thrashing myself."

But her uncle had gotten that look in his eye, the same look she had now on the overpass. He asked for the sharecropper to fetch his whip and had proceeded to beat the boy, right there in their courtyard, until the boy's back turned raw, pink like the skin of a scaled fish.

She had watched, transfixed, until her mother hurried over and covered her eyes. Incredibly, her mother had been angry with her. "What are you doing? Close your eyes! Don't you know you aren't supposed to see such things!" she'd said, dragging her inside. As she left, she heard her uncle tell the sharecropper to take the whip back and oil it again.

Then, as though it were the next picture in a series of connected images, there was Ranga. His ankles fastened to the tamarind tree. Blood dripping down his back. Pleading with her uncle to stop. That he couldn't bear it anymore. Ranga, his hands around her throat. A fog filled her head. Sree's screams on the nights when the pain was at its worst. Sree being sedated. Her blood turned cold. *Stop*, Vijaya told herself. Helping Sree walk again. *Stop. Stop! Don't go there.*

On the overpass, Vijaya turned around and looked at the man, the leering man. She glared at him feeling such venom, rage, anger, that she could scarcely remember where she was. She gave the man her uncle's *face*. "Come near me and I will push you off this bridge," she said.

Her voice was calm, collected, just like her uncle's. She meant it. She had no doubt in her mind that should he come any closer, even say another word, she would push him over, watch his head shatter under the wheel of an oncoming lorry, watch his blood pool, his face split open, his tongue pulverize, and she'd feel nothing. What was really true was that she had never been disrespected in her life. It had never been permitted.

The man hesitated, turned around and walked away from her.

Soon, the busy neighborhood was far behind her and the bungalows and cottage homes swam into view. She passed the green bungalow she recognized from the night before, walking from the train station. She noticed that there was a gum tree in front of it. She was firmly back in the good neighborhood.

She arrived at the bus stop feeling very calm. Vijaya placed a palm on her chest, massaged her neck. Taking a deep breath, she expected her fingers to feel the familiar—the round pendant with its engraving, the sharp facets of the ruby, the grooves of the lotus. But she only felt the texture of her sari. The pendant, and the gold chain it hung on, were both missing.

She looked at the ground around her, then she walked back the way she came, doubling over now and then, looking at every patch of earth, each blade of trodden grass. Already she knew she needn't look as closely. If the chain had really fallen alongside the footpath, it would be unmissable, it would gleam; the chain bright and thin like a stream in sunlight, the pendant, fat and yellow, dazzling as though it had absorbed the very sunset.

At the green bungalow again, she stopped. She could not get her feet to move, walk all the way to the traffic junction where the bus left her, across the overpass. She was afraid to leave this neighborhood again. She walked back to the bus stop, palm still on her chest, not quite sure what to do.

She deserved this. She had abandoned Sree. She had left, and this was what was happening; it was right. She felt miserable. Not caring if anyone saw her, what they would think of her, she held her head in between her hands and sat down on the dirty bench in the bus shelter. She felt sticky from the humidity, damp and smelly from the rain, and her regret was making her so physically ill that her forehead and shoulders and cheeks were sweating. Then, once again, she felt someone standing very close to her.

A small child, of five or six, was touching her shoulder. He was bare-chested. Here and there, his face was covered in pale spots. His legs were thin, and the corners of his dry lips had white patches, small rips in the skin.

"Sister," the boy said, raising the tips of his fingers to his lips, then lowering them into an open palm, "can you give ten paisa? I'm so hungry."

The boy waited. He was so close to her that she could focus on nothing except the jet-black line of grime underneath his fingernails. There was a roll of banknotes in her satchel amounting to nearly a hundred rupees. By the time Vijaya collected herself and extracted a twenty-rupee note from it, he had already walked away from her, ambling across the street in the manner of someone very old and very tired.

There, across the street, he approached another woman. He pulled on the end of her sari, repeated his request for ten paisa. The woman extracted a coin from her purse and gave it to the boy. Vijaya still held the note in her hands, but the boy did not turn back. He pocketed the coin he was given and walked away in his tired manner, disappearing into a side street.

The woman across the street was looking at her. It was Asha. She crossed the street and came up to her.

"Are you all right?" she said.

Vijaya did not reply. She looked away, shoved the note back into her satchel and stood up. She felt ashamed. She did not even know how to give.

"Why are you sitting here alone?" Asha said.

"I lost my chain," she said, wiping her face, aware of a tremor in her voice.

"Was it real gold?"

She nodded.

"Did you look around the stop?"

"Yes."

"You didn't find it?"

"No."

She took a deep breath and added, "I got off at another stop. I don't know where I lost it, if it fell on the ground or on the bus or somewhere else. I don't know. I noticed it only now . . ."

"Did you take the ladies' bus?"

Vijaya nodded.

"They are so horribly crowded. I never go on those. Whether you lost it on the bus or on the street, you won't ever find it. Lost gold is lost gold."

Somehow, Vijaya felt relieved hearing this. It meant she didn't have to walk back to the overpass again. It meant she didn't have to look for it. She could simply give up on it.

"See, you have to be careful on those buses," Asha said, walking away. "They are so crowded and you never know whose hands are going where. People lose things all the time."

Asha stopped and said, "Come on, let's go. There are chain snatchers, pickpockets, conductors who insist you haven't bought a ticket and make you buy again. Don't feel bad though; everyone loses something on the bus. I lost my purse from inside my bag, and the clasp wasn't even left open. They sneaked it out without my knowing. They are very skilled at this, and really, any jewelry that isn't physically attached to you, like earrings, can be lost. Finding a seat and sitting is safer than standing though. Anyway, was it very expensive?"

Vijaya didn't know how much it cost. "I don't know."

"It happens. It happens. Don't feel too bad. Stolen gold brings bad luck, it will come back to you another way."

"Maybe I can ask the bus driver tomorrow if he's seen it?"

Asha looked at her with surprise, made a face, crumpled her nose, as though Vijaya was the naivest person she had seen in a long time. "Of course, you can try. Who knows?"

"How do you come back from college, if not in the ladies' bus?" she asked.

"General bus. They are very frequent and rarely crowded. If I find one that's crowded I just take the next. I'll take anything over that mass crushing." Asha held her throat as though choking.

"The warden said we aren't to go on the general bus."

"That warden, always barking something. Don't pay attention to her."

Vijaya suspected animosity in Asha's tone, but she didn't ask why. They arrived at the whitewashed façade of the boarding house, crossed the courtyard and parted ways on the second floor.

"Take a bath and feel better, Vijaya," Asha said, patting her shoulder.

The dining hall was on the terrace. It was a slab supported by painted concrete columns, open on all four sides to views of city and sea. Vijaya arrived there after taking a long, hot bath. She smelled of talcum powder. She felt calm. Now and then, the missing pendant pricked at her conscience. At least she wouldn't have to tell her mother immediately. At a later time, when she was back in Irumi for the holidays, she would express surprise at having discovered it missing. That would be that.

She filled her plate with food and the hollow eyes of the beggar child came back to her.

"Not hungry?" Asha asked. She had a spoon in one hand, a fat novel in her other. She opened the novel carefully to the middle, laid the spoon across the binding to keep it propped open. Soon, Deepthi arrived, along with the other first-year girls. One by one, the tables filled up. Deepthi came over to where she was sitting.

"Where were you? Did you miss the bus? Oh my god, it was so crowded I thought I'd die!"

"I missed the stop," she said.

"Oh no! How did you walk back? You don't even know the city here . . ."

"It was just a straight road. I just walked back."

"Oh good, you know this place better than me now, don't you?" Deepthi said, laughing. Quickly, her eyes darted toward Asha, as though asking Vijaya wordlessly what was going on with her. Asha paid no attention. She was eating, her eyes on the pages of the novel, like she was alone.

"Come sit with us," Deepthi mouthed at her, pointing a thumb at her table.

"Later," Vijaya replied, her voice perfectly audible. Deepthi's smile faltered, she walked away.

"What dessert did you get?" Asha asked, looking at Vijaya's plate. "I got semiya. They make it every Monday, it's very good. Try some from my plate if you like."

Vijaya took some.

"Have you been to the beach?"

"No. I just got here last night," Vijaya said.

"You must have seen it from a distance, at least?"

"No."

"What do you mean? Marina Beach is across the street from Presidency."

"Really?"

"Yes, really!"

"Do you want to go after dinner?" Vijaya asked.

"Yes. Good idea. Shame if you don't go to the beach on your first day. We'll go. We'll have some tutti-frutti ice cream, we will sit on the beach and you will forget all about your missing necklace."

After dinner, Vijaya came back to her room to get her purse. Asha was going to meet her in the courtyard. There was a knock on her door. It was Deepthi.

"Are you angry with me for something?"

"No," she replied.

"Sure?"

"Yes. I'm sure."

"Okay. Listen. I've decided that I'll switch to the teaching program and be with the other girls. Even one day in that horrible econ class I found impossible. I cannot stand it for three whole years. I wanted to let you know, since you were the only other girl there, you might want to switch with me."

"Asha is in our class."

"Yes, but . . ." Deepthi said, turning up her hand as though Asha couldn't be counted.

"So, you will switch with me, right?"

Vijaya shook her head.

"No?" Deepthi exclaimed, her tone unbelieving, smiling as though Vijaya were joking.

She shook her head again and did not smile. Deepthi waited for her to elaborate, but she said nothing more, continued to look at her without expression. Spotting the purse over her shoulder, Deepthi asked, "Where are you going?"

"Marina Beach," she said, "with Asha."

Deepthi stopped smiling, dimples vanishing.

In the courtyard downstairs, she waited for Asha. The warden came out of her room and handed Vijaya a letter.

"Why did they put a stamp on an inland letter?" she demanded.

Vijaya took the letter, looked at the offending stamp. A tea-plucker in profile. The letter was addressed to her full name: Vijayalakshmi Deshmukh, not Vijaya. Who called her that? Nobody.

"But you just got here," the warden added, looking as though she was on the verge of demanding that Vijaya open the letter and show her who it was from.

"I don't know," Vijaya said truthfully. She turned it over in order to check the return address.

"Shall we go?" Asha said. She and the warden exchanged what Vijaya thought was a charged glance, and then the warden left.

"Psychotic woman," Asha muttered. Vijaya put the letter in her bag.


At the beach, a full five hundred kilometers from Irumi, Vijaya savored the townscape: the squeals of seagulls, the shrill cries of children racing on the sandy beach, noisy hawkers selling puffed rice, green coconuts, whole roasted peanuts. She watched fishing boats land and leave; brilliant, knife-shaped streaks of red or green or yellow, appearing and disappearing against the blue horizon as though by magic.

Asha asked her if she wanted tutti-frutti ice cream. She said yes. Waiting for Asha, Vijaya fished the letter the warden had given her out of her bag.

She was surprised to see that it was postmarked nearly two weeks ago. The handwriting was neat, slanted, trained. She turned it over and stared at the return address. It was a post office in Hyderabad. The postmark said Osmania University.

Dear Vijaya,

You might think it utterly rash of me to write you like this. I don't expect a reply. My mother told me where you were. I hope I won't get her into trouble. I'm hoping I got your address right. If not, well.

My mother tells me that Sree has terrible headaches now, that she is a cripple. She tells me because she doesn't know that I was there too. She blames Ranga, like everyone else did. You and Ranga. If I was brave, I would have told her the truth. If I was brave, I wouldn't have let Ranga take the punishment in my place that day. I left. And it was all my fault. And I could never admit it.

I cost Ranga the ability to live his life the way he wanted, I cost Sree the same. And I left you behind. I was never punished for it. Guilt is an unbearable burden. It is torment. You can never be free of it. As time passes, the cage it builds around you only becomes stronger, smaller, denser. Doesn't it?

The night we met, I was not brave. I went home.

All of this is to say that time has passed. That I wish to believe that it is possible for me to be absolved of my sins. That it is possible to stop carrying this regret, this guilt, this open wound. And I want the same for you. Forgive me, Vijaya, for all the pain I caused you.

I've enclosed my address, but I'm not naive enough to expect a reply from you. You are, after all, a Deshmukh. I simply wanted to have my say.

Krishna

Vijaya smoothed the creases of Krishna's letter. She stroked the sharp line that divided the letter in half. She read the letter once more. Her heart was beating in her ears. Her fingertips were cold.

The letter's age was showing, the blue ink had run on its long journey across the country to her. She sat back and studied Krishna's handwriting. It was a practiced, slanted cursive. She went over all the places he had written her name. The *j* had a swoop. It felt so familiar, his writing, like catching sight of an old friend in a crowd. Then it occurred to her that it was familiar because it was just like hers. Always had been. That old book in which they used to write together.

She summoned the memory of the Krishna she once knew. Dark-eyed, thin-limbed, in his neat blue school uniform, waiting by the step-well every day after school. But Vijaya didn't think of the day they went into the jungle, or even the after. What arose in her mind was a different memory.

She's eleven years old, standing in her mother's closet, trying to choose the right silk sari to cut up. Her braids, after a day of staying tightly wound up with red ribbon, were falling down, spilling around her shoulders. A pair of brass tailor's shears was lying at her feet. She pulled out drawer after drawer, until she found one that wouldn't budge. She used both hands and pulled. The draw grated loudly, and she paused, waiting for the noise to die down, waiting to see if anyone had heard. Then, gently, she wiggled and cajoled and eased the drawer open.

In it was a bright red sari. The silk was glossy, soft, velvety to touch. All across it were little paisleys woven in with gold and silver thread. Zari work that some weaver must have spent months, possibly a year on. She wiped her hands against the inside of her pinafore where the fabric was clean. She eased the sari out. Very carefully, she laid it on the floor, a little gold-and-red rectangle. She was sure it was a sari that her mother wouldn't look for frequently because it looked like a thing that could have been part of her bridal trousseau, bound up in memories of being a newlywed, the priest, the holy fire. She laid it on the floor. Gently, gently. She opened it up quarter by quarter. That way, she could cut out a strip from the inside and fold it back up the same way, following the same folding marks, so it wouldn't be discovered for a good long while. She memorized the order in which she opened each fold. She picked up the shears, lifted one section of the sari, slipped it between the blades. She began to cut. The shears were sharp, and the cut section began to fall away from the main body. It wasn't like cutting paper—there was no crinkling, no rustling, no satisfying snap when the blades met. Cutting silk was a quiet job, the sound it made was like hushing. She pulled away the cut section and laid it aside. She folded the sari back up, following the folding marks the same way. She slipped it back in the drawer and pushed it close.

Who was that girl? She didn't know.


Back in her room at the boarding house, Vijaya took off her slippers, got into bed and pulled the sheets up to her chin. From this angle, a sliver of the street outside was visible, the white stripes of the road divider in the dull, flickering light of the streetlamp. She got up and shut the window, cutting off what little breeze there was.

When morning came, she got out of bed and opened the window. It wasn't daybreak yet, the light was cool and blue. It must have rained in the night, the leaves of the jasmine vine were wet. In the courtyard below, the furry rows of moss that grew between the white stone pavers were an emerald green. The gardener had arrived, he was trimming the rosebushes, a beedi tucked behind his ear. In the distance, she could hear the chorus of the street sweepers, their reed brooms scraping cement pavements. Soon, the girls would all be up, running between the bathrooms and the mess hall. Soon, she'd meet Asha and take the bus to Presidency. Soon, the day would turn out to be like any other day.

Vijaya drew the cap of her pen, pulled out a fresh inland letter from the stack she brought from home and wrote without sitting down, afraid that she might change her mind.

She went downstairs, walked up the empty street as quickly as she could, and dropped the letter in the postbox across from their bus stop.

"I saw you," Asha said at breakfast. "Whom did you need to write so early?"

"My sister," Vijaya lied.

How long had it been since she'd told a lie? Maybe she did know that girl after all.

# THOSE WHO LEAVE

———◆———

"Krishnanna! Krishnanna! Krishnanna!"

It was a childish yet decidedly business-like voice from outside Krishna's door. Half-asleep, Krishna heard vague footsteps, fellow hostelers moving outside, smoking their first cigarettes of the day, drinking their first teas. Matchsticks striking, birds waking.

The first impulse Krishna resisted, as he awoke, was to read Vijaya's letter again. In the week since it arrived, he'd lost count of how many times he'd re-read it. How astonished he was that she'd written him back. He wrote her again straightaway. Then sent another letter by the evening post even before she replied.

Vijaya's letter was in his desk drawer, and whenever he was in his room—between classes—between his thesis meetings—between the volunteer work he was doing for Gagan at the union—waking up, falling asleep—he couldn't help but re-read it. It was a short letter, only a few sentences long, restrained, equal parts intimate and elusive. But each time he read it, he glimpsed something new; the curious, unselfconscious slant there now was to her loopy cursive, the small baubles she made instead of dots over the *i*'s, the places where he was sure she hesitated, resisting, like him, the impulse to strike things out. It made him feel strangely breathless. It was like encountering a piece of long-forgotten music, the bars soaring; now lilting, now strident; striking him tangibly, almost physically.

He also felt a tender sense of ownership towards her. There was and there could be no one else who understood this part of her like he did.

"Krishnanna!" The voice was louder, this time accompanied by three sharp raps on his door. "Don't you want your chai today?"

"I'm coming," Krishna said. He got off his cot and opened the door. His hostel room was so narrow that it took him only one step from cot to door. It was Chinna, the tea-seller Suri's son.

Each morning, Suri sent his son to the men's hostel for tea deliveries before school. Seven years old, tall for his age, Chinna had small white teeth; parrot teeth—his father was fond of saying—and a smile so open and so frank that it stretched across every single feature of his face, the kind of smile it was impossible not to return. It was barely quarter past six in the morning and already Chinna looked as though he was in the middle of his workday; his thin arm was straining from the weight of the tea carrier he was holding, sweat was pouring down his face.

Krishna squinted. The sky over the hostel building was streaked in delicate shades of orange and pink. "Aren't you late for school?"

"It's the annual day," Chinna replied, handing Krishna his tea, holding the glass by its rim. "No classes. Just a song-and-dance function for the children and sweets afterwards. My father said I didn't need to go."

Krishna pushed a fifteen-paisa coin into the front pocket of Chinna's shirt, and Chinna hurried away, knocking on the next door down the corridor before Krishna could ask another question. He wanted to ask Chinna more about his school, about how much he scored on his arithmetic quarterlies—Krishna had tutored him—but he sensed the weight of the tea crate, the urgency to deliver before the tea dropped no more than two degrees in temperature. If the chai Suri sent up did not threaten to excise the taste buds off the drinker's tongues, Chinna would get an earful from the residents of the hostel. Already he'd lost precious time repeatedly knocking on Krishna's door.

Before Krishna took more than a few sips of tea, and before he could gain his bearings, he was accosted by Samuel coming down the narrow corridor.

"Morning, Krishna! Did you just wake up? What are your plans for today?" Samuel said, rocking lightly on the balls of his feet. His face was eager, awake; much like Chinna's.

"Classes, as usual." Krishna kept his tone friendly.

Samuel had taken to befriending Krishna whenever the opportunity presented itself. "A group of us are going to a meeting this evening, at the library. Will you come?" he said.

Krishna noticed that the cuffs of his pajamas were growing damp. There was an inch of standing water in the corridor. "What do you say? We are doing a reading of *Mother*," Samuel said.

Gagan had won the student union elections, defeating Samuel by a significant margin. No one had been allowed to win the union elections in the past eight years, since Samuel himself had been a newly enrolled student like themselves. First he was backed by the ruling party, and now by the Marxists. Though he looked the part of a college student, Samuel was in his forties, keeping up his enrollment as a research scholar with an ABD, interfering with university administration, herding and shoving students into polling booths without having a detectable hand in any of it. Samuel was also responsible for the business of providing the mass of university students able to march in protests on behalf of whoever had his allegiance; their solemn faces and placards plastered across the evening papers, and when required, to rally against the opposition, burning buses, garlanding effigies with rubber slippers, beating up shopkeepers, calling bandhs, and breaking glass façades of office buildings when asked to do so.

Before arriving at Osmania, Krishna hadn't known that student union president was a position of power or real-world consequence. Gagan had explained to him how it was both: at Osmania, like any other public university in the country, student political movements were married to the politics of the outside world. The student union belonged to a system of intricate balances wrung together by the power exerted on it by the ruling party currently in office, through the union president. Every year until now, there had been only one candidate—Samuel—running unopposed using a combination of money, threatened violence, and actual violence. With Gagan's intention to run in the state assembly elections now, it seemed like the scale of things Gagan was standing on had continued to grow so large, so crucial, that it seemed important that Krishna not do anything to hurt his chances.

Krishna stepped back into his room, trying to shake the water off his pajamas. "Well, it is a Wednesday today, isn't it?" Samuel said, following him inside before Krishna could block the doorway.

It would seem an odd thing to say, but on Wednesdays, the staff of their hostel building—the watchman and his wife—washed the corridors and the stairs. This involved standing at the top of the third-floor stairway, where Krishna's room was, and pouring buckets of water from the overhead tank, flooding the corridors, then using reed brooms to push the water down, floor by floor. It was an inefficient system of cleaning, made a racket in the early mornings, and the stairs and corridors remained sopping wet, new hostelers slipped often, falling face-first into standing pools of water, cracking knees and ankles.

"I will," Krishna said, because it didn't look like Samuel would leave if he said no.

Samuel, now seated on Krishna's cot, looking around his desk, smiled, and said he would wait for Chinna to come around again. "I hope people won't think I'm breaking up the dynamic duo, Gagan and Krishna," he said, stretching his arms over his head jovially. "By asking you to a meeting, you know?"

By the time Krishna got rid of Samuel, a line was already forming for the bathroom at the end of the corridor. He hurried, fetched his toothbrush, his towel, and joined the queue himself. People ahead of him were brushing, then leaning over the parapet wall and spitting foam into the garden below.

They all called it a garden even though it wasn't much of a garden. It was a small group of hawthorn bushes that the watchman's wife painstakingly cultivated. Krishna would observe her watering the plants and clearing the soil around them of tossed cigarette butts, saunf wrappers and all manner of trash at the end of each day. This was even though she kept vigil over her precious flower bushes throughout the day, glaring at anyone who looked like they might be carrying a piece of lint in their pockets, grumbling curses under her breath. But in the morning, when the hostelers stood in the corridor—most of them bare-chested, wrapped only in cotton towels—she didn't keep vigil. And the hostelers took this opportunity to antagonize her just for the fun of it. The hawthorn leaves would be splattered in patches of white toothpaste foam afterwards, and they'd hear her screaming curses from downstairs and exchange smirks.

Later that morning, as was his routine, he sat outside the arts building reading the morning papers.

The grass was an intense, springy green, it had been trimmed and watered recently, and he made sure to choose a dry location underneath a sprawling mahogany tree overlooking the quad, a view of the arts build-ing in the distance.

In the morning time, he liked to simply look at it awhile. It was a soothing presence, in it was a quiet beauty that never failed to give him pause. The first time he encountered the arts building, back when he'd first arrived at Osmania, Krishna had stood transfixed for an entire min-ute, then spent a good ten minutes simply walking around it. It was a blend of flat and curved faces, a cross between palace and fort. A group of undergraduate students from the architecture department had come to sketch the building, and Krishna had once overheard what their instruc-tor told them. It was built in the neo-Mughal style, the instructor had said, and the architect had done away with the excesses of the Mughal style—no dome, no minarets, no ornate, excessive fretwork of florals and calligraphy. Only the shell remained, a massive rectangular block of pink granite protruding thirty feet into the sky, two arms alongside it, turning at right angles and running the depth of the building. This imposing façade was softened, with balconies hewn into its face in the shape of tra-ditional, double-tipped leaves, each load-bearing lintel embedded with sparse meshes of flower vines, honeycombs. Over the entryway stood a vaulted gateway, a stalactite standing guard between heaven and earth.

He suspected that his fascination for the arts building had something to do with the Deshmukh gadi. It too was a grand thing that stood all by itself, amidst the profound neglect of everything else around it.

He did not spot Gagan successfully locate him across the quad, weave through students chatting, lying on their backs in groups of threes or fours. Absorbed in the newspaper, he only noticed Gagan when he sat down on the grass next to him.

"What classes do you have today?" Gagan said, collapsing on the grass beside him, checking his watch.

"Topology," Krishna said, not looking up from his paper. "And you? Have *you* been to any of your classes yesterday?" Krishna said, looking up from the paper.

"No," Gagan said, pulling the paper out of Krishna's grip. He took the sports section out and handed the paper back to Krishna. Gagan followed the cricket games, local or national, with a religiosity bordering on reverence. He lay back on the grass and held the paper over his face.

"How about last week?" Krishna insisted. "Did you go to any last week?"

Krishna hadn't been able to dissuade Gagan from his plan to run in the state elections. Now he was planning a protest against the chief minister, T. K. Pillai, and the MLA of the Hyderabad constituency, Hasan Omar Rizvi, whose seat Gagan would be contesting if he ran. The subject of the protest would be the failure of the state government in enforcing the land ceiling laws, the land reforms of '56. How there hadn't been any significant change in landownership in the decade since the act had passed.

Gagan did not reply. Krishna looked up just in time to catch Gagan shrugging.

"Are you coming to the Rooms after?" Gagan said.

"I have a meeting with Dr. Ramaswamy," he replied, "but I'll come afterwards."

Dr. Ramaswamy was Krishna's thesis supervisor. He had asked Krishna to come to his office. The timing was odd. Krishna had just submitted his proposal, and Dr. Ramaswamy hadn't approved it. This meeting, he was dreading.

Gagan lowered the sports paper and looked at him, temporarily distracted from the cricket scores. The Indian national team was in the second innings of a three-match test series in Leeds, England. "I wonder what he wants," Gagan said. "Tell me what he says."

Krishna turned over the front page. The first item was a piece about the revolutionary communists, the violent Marxist-Leninist faction that had broken away from the Communist Party. They were now calling themselves Naxalites. It was a name fashioned after a place called Naxalbari, a tiny hamlet in the state of West Bengal, where the M-Ls had staged a revolt against the region's landlord. He thought it a strange word—*Naxalite*—sharp-edged, vaguely alien, threatening. The movement was spreading across the countryside, reaching the densely forested regions of Telangana.

Was that who Ranga was now? A "Naxalite."

"Have you heard from your brother?" Gagan asked, as though following Krishna's train of thought.

"No," Krishna said.

This was how Gagan asked after Ranga, and how Krishna always left it. They discussed it delicately, deliberately, neither expressing what they each simply knew to be true.

Soon after Krishna had returned from Irumi, he received a letter from his mother. Ranga was gone.

In fact, the last time his mother had seen Ranga was when he'd offered to walk Krishna to the bus depot. He'd simply never returned home afterwards. She'd waited all night, she said. Then she told him things about Ranga.

To Krishna, what she said felt incoherent. It was as though she were speaking of a different person, an imposter, one half of a puzzle that refused to fit with the other half; the half that Krishna carried in his heart.

Ranga had worked at the sugar factory belonging to the Deshmukhs for a year now. Workers were employed from the village, and because Surendra Deshmukh needed someone trustworthy to watch over the labor, watch over the ton or two of sugarcane that came through the factory each day, put through industrial crushers and processed within twenty-four hours, Ranga was chosen. It was Ranga's job to make sure that the workers arrived on time, did not slack off, did not steal either sugar or sugarcane, did not take too many breaks, left before the day ended, met their quotas. Ranga was the only one entrusted with the money that changed hands when the sugar dealers came to pick up shipments, the factory keys.

But the night that Ranga disappeared, the sugar factory burned down. The money was gone. His mother was interrogated by the police about Ranga's whereabouts. When they wanted to take her to the station, Mahendra Deshmukh had intervened.

He had disappeared before, she told him. There had been several unexplained absences, long blank periods in which she waited and waited for Ranga to come home, and he did come, emerging in the dead of the night, covered in bruises, brambles, as though he'd been traveling in the forest for days. He would eat ravenously. But this time she said it was different. That the factory burning down had something to do with Ranga did not need spelling out. If Ranga disappeared, Krishna knew, as his mother surely did, that it could only mean one thing—Ranga had joined the Naxalites. Ranga *was* a Naxalite.

Each morning since reading his mother's letter, whenever Krishna read the papers, his palms turned cold, he trembled. Because the next time he would see Ranga's face, if he did at all, would be in the papers. There would be no court, no trial. There would be a police encounter. There would be a photograph. A swollen dead body laid alongside his comrades; alongside a catchment of recovered rifles, rounds of ammunition, Semtex, land mines, trip wires, machetes. His brother's name would be printed under an alias. What would it mean that even in death no one would call his brother by the name that Krishna had known him.

Each morning like this, Ranga's adult face never came to Krishna; what came always was the Ranga of his childhood—long, gangly locks of copper-streaked hair, calloused hands and bare feet, towering over him, drawing him close and kissing the side of his head. That impression Ranga always gave, even as a child, of knowing everything, capable of anything. Ranga, that specter of a powerful, all-knowing brother.

"Krishna, maybe he will come back. Don't worry," Gagan said.

"Do you have to contest in the state elections?" Krishna said, feeling suddenly infuriated. "Why can't you let things be?"

"Let things be?" Gagan said, putting down the paper. He sat up and looked straight at Krishna. "Let things be?" he repeated.

Krishna regretted saying it. He knew, by now, that the only way to be Gagan's friend was by not opposing his beliefs—by never having an opinion; by maintaining a steadfast silence, but thinking about Ranga had made him forget.

"I don't understand how you, Krishna—*you*, of all people—how can *you* say, 'let things be.' How *you* can be unmoved?"

Krishna said nothing.

"It has a name," Gagan said, looking squarely at him. "That pole to which the vetti are tied, whipped mercilessly in the villages. It is called a *gunja*—do you know this, Krishna?"

Krishna looked away. He stared at the paper in front of him.

"Imagine it having a name, Krishna. You lived in this world, your family did—does, even now. Even *I* can understand your brother's choice. How can you, Krishna, of all people, be unmoved? It has been ten years— more than ten years—since the land reforms," Gagan said. "And nothing has changed. We cannot 'let things be.'"

Krishna read the same word over and over again. *Naxalites.* He resisted the urge to crumple the paper.

Gagan said, "People like your Deshmukhs in Irumi—landownership continues to be concentrated in the hands of people just like them, the old zamindari families. And this isn't the first time this so-called red wave touched us, is it? The last time it came to Telangana was back in forty-six—the Telangana peasant rebellion. It was exactly like the Naxalite movement. What happened then? Did that change anything?"

"Gagan—" Krishna murmured, in a low voice, unsure of even what he wanted to say. But Gagan talked over him.

"These communists. First it was about opposing the Nizam, joining the Indian union instead of Pakistan, resisting the atrocities of the Razakars. Then, after the annexation, the movement fractured. On one side, the Razakars disbanded and formed the All India MIM. The other side, the rebel leadership, they too disbanded and formed the People's Democratic Front.

"And what happened to the Telangana peasants? Once again, without any real, long-lasting changes, the old practices came back—the vetti system—the not wearing of white clothes—the footwear held in

hands—wives of sharecroppers used as entertainment for the landlords' guests—the countless 'taxes' for births, marriages, even for death.
Imagine paying someone in order to die, Krishna. The social capital the
landlords hold in this country—the power—that is simply derived from
owning land. Land is every kind of wealth.

"Who do you think is leading these 'Naxalites'? Again it's the upper-
class, college-educated men, who will again, once this round of bloodbath
is over, abandon the peasants and return to democratic institutions. Because only the power won through democratic institutions lasts. So, no. I
cannot 'let things be.' Like you."

Krishna put the paper down and stood up. He muttered that he was
late to class. A look of regret crossed Gagan's face; he opened his mouth
to speak, and Krishna knew it would be something conciliatory, regret-
ful. He didn't want to hear it. He walked away from Gagan.

He hadn't been sure, up until then, if he would tell Gagan about
Vijaya. Now he decided that he wouldn't.

Surely Gagan would consider it a betrayal. Vijaya, after all, belonged
to the class of people that Gagan was basing his entire campaign on—
how damaging would it be, if Samuel found out, for instance? Krishna
was known everywhere Gagan was known. They'd make him out to look
like a fraud. Or maybe it was easier to think all this, rather than wonder
why else he wanted to keep her a secret.


After class, Krishna headed toward the pure sciences building, a dilapi-
dated brick structure with flaking limewash that caught on shirtsleeves,
and a crack in the foundation that habitually let out groundwater in the
rainy season, flooding entire classrooms on that level. He was running
late for Dr. Ramaswamy.

A breeze blew something into his eye and he squinted, rubbed his
eye as he walked across campus, but by the time he made it to the pure
sciences building, his eye turned red and he could hardly bear to keep it
open, it hurt to even blink. At the washbasins on the end of the hall, he
groaned, blinking furiously, splashing tap water into his eye.

He was more than fifteen minutes late, his sleeve and collar were damp, but when he arrived outside Dr. Ramaswamy's office, he saw that there was already someone inside, a young woman. The door was ajar, and Dr. Ramaswamy saw him and motioned him inside. "Come in, Krishna," he said.

Krishna went in, but looked around awkwardly as he waited for them to finish their conversation. The office was old and decrepit, just like the rest of pure sciences. It smelled musty, as though the room had seen its fair share of yellowed newspapers and solitary meals. The blue paint on the walls was peeling, exposing an older, orange-tinted shade underneath. Krishna could smell moisture in the walls, telltale signs of a leak deep inside the bricks, a broken plumbing line somewhere.

"It was such a pleasure seeing you again, Uncle," the woman was saying. "It's been years. When will you come and visit us again? Papa asked me to make you promise that you'll come in the summer."

Her voice was delicate, like that of a radio announcer. Though she was speaking in Hindi, he thought she looked like a foreigner; strikingly pale, her hair a color whose name he did not know, just that it was not black. Dr. Ramaswamy held her hand in both of his. "My dear, dear Ada," he said, "I promise."

As she left, the woman nodded at him and said, "He's all yours." Krishna smiled back politely.

Dr. Ramaswamy sighed, as though her leaving had saddened him.

Krishna always felt a mixture of fear and respect in Dr. Ramaswamy's presence. He was in his late sixties, but easily looked a decade older. He had a friendly face, sparse white hair and red spectacles that hung around his neck on a lanyard. He had the habit of wearing the spectacles at the end of his nose when he had to read something, then immediately taking them off, so they always swung around his neck like a set of friendly red butterflies.

Dr. Ramaswamy was a wonderful teacher. Though he never had any favorites, Krishna always suspected that he himself was his favorite, or perhaps that was how each of his students felt. Krishna spotted his proposal lying facedown on the cluttered desk.

"Good afternoon, Krishna," Dr. Ramaswamy said.

"Is there something wrong with the proposal, sir?" Krishna replied without preamble, sitting down.

"Why? No. Nothing is wrong." He picked up the papers, placed his spectacles on the end of his nose and continued, "On the contrary, I asked you here so I can tell you that your work has tremendous potential."

He took off his glasses again, and looked up at Krishna. "You have a lot of fresh ground to cover here. Your theory on the specific real-world applications of topological data sets is a brilliant start—not just in traffic flow patterns and city planning in your outline here—but even further, I think. This is just simply splendid."

He paused, then added, "I called you here because I wanted to speak to you about a related matter."

Dr. Ramaswamy made a gesture then, the typical one he made before the beginning of each of his lectures—chin tilted inwards, voice slightly raised. Krishna frowned. Even before he had time to process Dr. Ramaswamy's compliment, he was already moving on. Krishna tried to remember some of the words. *Tremendous potential*, he'd said. *Impressive*, he'd said. *Splendid*. He felt gleeful, like a child.

"I want you to consider—really take the time to consider—leaving Osmania."

Krishna wasn't sure he'd heard correctly.

He blurted, "What did you say, sir?"

Dr. Ramaswamy nodded, as though he'd expected this reaction and was prepared for it.

"I want you to consider leaving Osmania. I have never spoken to a student this way, but in your case I'm making an exception."

Krishna stared.

"I'm finding it difficult to say nothing, Krishna. I'm aware that as someone not related to you, I have no authority over you, but I implore you to listen."

Krishna waited. He was utterly confused, taken aback by the turn this conversation had taken.

"I know that you and Gagan are close."

Krishna felt too stunned to say anything. Dr. Ramaswamy, of all people, was talking about Gagan. Krishna tried not to express the surprise he felt. He listened.

"Certainly, Gagan is exceedingly bright, intelligent. Also, from simply life experience, I know that Gagan is the kind of person who will survive in the world outside, thrive even. Doors will open for him, people he barely knows will do anything to help him. It will all appear to be good luck."

Again, Dr. Ramaswamy paused, looked into Krishna's face to make sure he was listening. "In other words, he is different from you, Krishna. Different from those of us who have to fight tooth and nail to get half the opportunities that he will be simply given. Gagan comes from money, Krishna. Are you understanding what I'm saying?"

"Not quite, sir."

"This is about you. You need this degree because your whole life depends on it. Your future, your everything. If you are not careful, all that you aspire to, your family—I assume—aspires to, will disappear in a second. I won't be surprised if Samuel takes a special interest in you, and finds a way to harm you to get at Gagan; he won't hesitate to use you as a tool, Krishna. He has enormous influence over the administration, even if Gagan is the union president now. He's been here a lot longer than Gagan, he is clever and cunning, he can find a way to get you thrown out of the university if it benefits him in some way. I'm sorry to say that I have seen it happen too many times before."

"Sir, I don't think Gagan—"

"Gagan can do as he likes, Krishna. You on the other hand, cannot. I'm being very frank, Krishna. I fear—no, not fear—I'm fairly certain that your association with Gagan will destroy your opportunities in life.

"Already, I've heard talk on campus that Gagan is set to leave Osmania, and—I couldn't believe it when I heard—he is going to contest in the state elections here next term. You must know how dangerous that is. People are murdered over such matters. Associates get murdered over such matters. It is all goondas and rowdy-sheeters. Politics is a dirty business, Krishna, there is no room for ideology. I'm asking you to separate yourself from Gagan, to distance yourself, to not be seen with him in public, during his public meetings, and especially do not go to that protest he is planning. It is tantamount to announcing his intention to contest.

"Krishna, worry about no one and nothing except yourself, your own prospects. Act in your self-interest. You have so much more to lose than Gagan."

Krishna sat frozen. He felt as though Dr. Ramaswamy's addressee wasn't him, this careless, thoughtless person squandering away the only opportunity he would ever get in his life, squander the enormous sacrifices that Ranga had made for him. Ranga. Who'd made him promise that he'd work hard, study, to do nothing else. Ranga. Who had to stay. *Krishna, you will never come back. Promise me.* What would his mother say, if he was thrown out of Osmania, if he went back to live in Irumi?

"As long as you are at Osmania, you cannot escape Gagan. Please take my advice. Let me help you. I have an acquaintance, an old college mate who is the dean at the University of Bombay—Ada's father, the girl who was just here before you. It is as far away from here as you can get. I'm happy to write you a recommendation. Krishna, I highly doubt if Dr. Godrej won't see what I see in your work. You understand what I'm saying? He will take you on, you can be assured of it. I want you to finish out your doctorate there, under him, away from here. From Bombay you could go anywhere, Krishna. Imagine. Try to imagine. Anywhere in the world."

Krishna headed back to the hostel. He felt like being alone with his thoughts, to extricate the truth of what he was feeling from the confused mixture of guilt, fear, trepidation. It had never occurred to him that his association with Gagan could harm him. He had never thought of Gagan that way because all he had for Gagan was affection. Gagan was his family.

It had never occurred to him either, that he could leave everything behind. He, who had never traveled more than two hundred kilometers from the place of his birth. But Dr. Ramaswamy had spoken of it as though it were not only plausible, but possible. As if the only thing that mattered was the choice he made.

He walked back to the hostel. Suri's tea shop was closed, wooden benches were strewn about its mouth. Midway up the stairs to his room, he stopped. He remembered his promise to Gagan. He turned back and re-traced his steps across campus, towards the Rooms, past the science hall, past the arts quad. He cut through the grass field. It was getting dark, there was dew on the grass, clumps of fireflies glittering low, appearing for only a fleeting second before disappearing.

Outside the arts building, he stopped and looked up. The windows of the student union rooms blazed yellow. The windows were open, and he could hear the din of conversation drift from above. Streetlights beyond the field flickered into life. All of a sudden, he felt removed from his surroundings, as though he were flying away, yet he felt strangely close, an odd feeling, something like nostalgia towards a place from which he wasn't even distant. He felt close to the city, to the university, as though it were a living being with whom it was possible to experience intimacy. Hyderabad was like this. A beating heart. Here, on the east, where Krishna stood, was Osmania, and on the west were the four minarets of the Charminar, the mecca masjid, and between them ran the Musi River, cleaving the city in two; the old city from the new; its past and its future. But when he stood very, very still, like he did now, everything would stop, the night would cool, a slight breeze would play, maybe a drizzle of rain, yellow streetlights, same as anywhere else.

Reaching the third floor, he noticed that his shoes were coated in bits of cut grass. He scraped the soles of his shoes against the top stair and entered.

The Rooms were crowded as usual. A record of a recent film tune was playing. Students were talking in loud, untroubled voices, clouds of cigarette smoke drifted above. Krishna squinted, trying to locate Gagan. He recognized most of the students there, they waved at him as he threaded his way through. He knew some of their names; there was Sriram, Prashant, Ramesh, Raja; all of them from physics—Gagan's department—but he was certain that, if pressed, he couldn't put the right name to the right person, except for Shireen—the lone girl he knew from Gagan's circle. But they all knew who Krishna was. Gagan had always been the one link he had to the world at large. Here and there he paused to talk, asked how he could help. Gagan was nowhere.

Krishna spent most of the night working with the other volunteers, preparing for the protest—banners, cardboard placards, cutouts, writing slogans with brushes dipped in pots of red ink and black ink. At the end of the night, he returned to his hostel room without having run into Gagan. His clothes smelled of ink and turpentine, his right hand was cramped, the back of his neck ached, his knuckles smarted. Still, he went to his desk and pulled Vijaya's letter out. He read it once more.

Krishna,

I don't blame you. You don't need my forgiveness. Yes, Deshmukh is my last name. But one does not choose the house one is born into. One does not choose one's burdens.

At the fair, I wish we had more time.

Vijaya

This wasn't about Gagan, after all. Or protecting his possibilities in life. Or even that he did not wish to leave this city, the home of his adulthood. This wasn't even about what Dr. Ramaswamy wanted for him, what his mother wanted for him, what Ranga wanted for him, the duty or promise Ranga had extracted from him. None of that mattered. This was only about *his* deepest, most ardent desire. What *he* has wanted his whole life—Vijaya. Going to Bombay meant the possibility of a life that could be lived away from everything he and Vijaya had ever known; from everyone who knew the people they came from, their blood, their histories, their language. They could be orphans together. And was that what it meant, to love? The ability to be orphans together in a place where they were free to carve out a togetherness. Forge new identities and never again look at what was past.

He took out a sheaf of paper from his desk and wrote to her. It was a short, determined letter. He asked to see her. And it took him no time to realize why he wanted to go, what it was that he couldn't put in writing.

# THE HIBISCUS BOX
# OF LETTERS

———————

O n the first Thursday of every month, Vijaya received letters from Irumi. She imagined her father waiting for the postman outside the gadi. It would be warm, early afternoon, when the postman came. Her father would hand him the stack of letters and wait awhile, watch him get on his bicycle and ride downhill and disappear. Three letters came each month—one from her father, one from her mother, and one from Sree.

On Thursdays, after classes and dinner, she sat at her desk to read. She'd gotten into the habit of chewing fennel seeds while reading. Afterwards, after the letters were read and put away, she liked that their green, watery aroma remained in her room. She'd purchased a box at the stationery shop the week before. It was cream-colored, made of wax-coated cardboard, and hand-painted with an illustration of pink hibiscus flowers. She'd bought the box expressly for the purpose of storing those letters that she had no intention of throwing away. So far it contained only letters from Sree, and from Krishna.

Her mother had begun writing to her after a month of complete silence, and now, four months after Vijaya had first arrived in Madras, she wrote and wrote, even before Vijaya had the opportunity to respond to her last. Even though the letters were full of admonishments, emphasized her various faults, she felt an unexpected warmth spreading through her whenever she encountered her name written in her mother's hand. She'd let her eyes linger on the rounded Telugu alphabets, the circle over the *vi*, the little horn attached to the *ja*, and feel as though she were being hugged by her mother.

Her mother's letters were rich in detail, containing things that her father omitted. Buried amongst all the complaints and grumbles and petty grievances was the real picture of how things were in Irumi, how quickly things had deteriorated. Her mother always began with a list of things that were going badly and only managed to scratch a sentence into the very borders of the inland letter, the words addressed solely to Vijaya, things like *take care* or *eat well*.

I hope you are in good health. We are excellent, don't worry about us. I think your hostel food is likely dreadful, the water worse, the weather I shudder to imagine. I am sure you have grown to look as dark as those Madras people, but you were always a little too dark though, so it may not be as noticeable. I remember the comments from your grand-aunts when you were born: "Wherever did this color come from?" they all said. "And where, my god, did she get those brown cat eyes." Did you know that when I was little, we never allowed anyone with brown eyes to play with us? Anyway, it is very hot here too. Rains have failed third year in a row. Our orchard is dead. There has not been a single fruit there this past season. Nor a single flower, not even a lousy marigold forget about jasmine. And during summer there was hail, and when hail comes down you know how it knocks all the baby mangoes off the branches, what little was left is gone now. No mangoes. It makes me so sad to look at the orchard. When I'm in the kitchen, I don't raise my eyes, I'm afraid of catching a glimpse of those dead trunks and dead leaves. If you look up, you will see that the branches are covered in red bugs. Clumps and clumps and clumps of them. Even when I don't look, I can hear them trilling so loudly I feel the air move. It makes my skin crawl. What used to be so green, so lush, so many flowers, Vijaya, you remember? The colors could blind you. But every day, before the sun goes out, I look. Because my heart is madly hopeful, that I might catch a little green plant blooming amidst the dead ones. But of course, I am wrong. Your father says that we should burn it down, to make the bugs leave, start over. I said no. I cannot bear it.

Sree doesn't listen to me. She is trying to be like you, I think. She always asks to be left in the sun, like you, even with her headaches, which as you know are much, much worse when she spends too much time outside. What to do? Why don't you try to tell her? She will listen to her big sister. I worry so much about her headaches that I'm afraid to leave her alone for even a minute. They come on suddenly, without warning, as you know. It starts when she feels dizzy, and as you know, she won't tell us, she pretends to be okay and continues playing pachis with Katya or shelling peas with Katya. Last week, she was downstairs and suddenly she fell off her chair, scattering her papers and her pencils everywhere. We carried her upstairs to bed. I had to cover her windows and keep a cool towel on her forehead. She stayed there in the darkened room for a few days the sweet, poor darling. I can only trust Katya with her and no one else. Katya notices the flush in her cheeks and knows before it is about to happen. They are getting worse, Vijaya, more frequent, more intense. Sometimes it is days before she can sit up again. Vijaya, I'm scared. I'm so scared something might happen to her.

Last week there were vandals. The villagers we have known all our lives are dying or leaving. Their children do not respect us. They hate us. They boycott work in the gadi. They want to be paid with money. With money! There were days when the vetti were tied up to that old tamarind tree in the orchard and whipped with a vine for merely speaking the wrong thing. Remember what happened to Ranga, Vijaya? Remember?

A group came to the gadi at night last week, when Surendranna and your father were away in Hyderabad. It was only us at home. Katya too. We locked all the doors and waited till they went away. Those kinds of people are making our kinds of people afraid, imagine, imagine, how the times have changed. Anyway, why talk of that? Nothing can reverse time. They brought pickaxes and broke the carved stone fountain, the sculptures, and hacked down trees in the lemon orchard.

Whatever did the poor lemon trees do to them? It is good that you are away, safe, isn't it? I hid Sree upstairs in the closet in your room. Anyway, they damaged all the tilework. All the old handmade tile from Chettinad is gone. Your father told me that such tile is no longer made. Nobody is afraid of us. But why talk of all that. You must be busy with your own life.

Vijaya saw it as clearly as if she had really been there: a group of men holding hammers and pickaxes, marching up the hillock, through their courtyard while Sree hid upstairs, breaking the ornate water fountain piece by piece. She felt far too agitated to continue reading but the letter would not stop.

. . . these lands were ours since your great-great-grandfather's time, before independence he was the raja of this samsthanam. First they reduced us from royal titleholders to zamindars. Now, they say we have no right over what is ours. How is it fair? Your uncle says we will never give up the land, he says we will fight it in the courts till the end of time. I want to believe him but things are not looking good. Anyway, soon you will be married, you will leave us and our problems will be none of your bother. You are a daughter after all, and not a son who has to stay and worry.

Sree says she wants to get a college degree also. Being the younger sister, she wishes to do everything you do. Still like a child. I don't say anything but your father, he is reckless, he encourages her. How can he? He leaves that job to me, the job of breaking her heart. Nobody can tell her that she can't go anywhere, she can't do anything. Where will she go? With her condition, her leg, her headaches. She will be with us forever. But I will not live forever. Then what? Who will look after my poor darling? She was perfect once, do you remember those days, Vijaya? Who better to remember them than you; you were there.

Every time I think of that day I always wish it could have been different. You could have made different choices and none of this would have happened. You may feel bad when I speak like this but am I wrong to wish it, as her mother?

But who cares for my opinion in this house? My legs hurt from housework in the gadi, my age is catching. The vetti have become unreliable. Even when we pay them more than ever, they no longer want to work here, they refuse to work and are so brave they say it even to my face. Even the barber refuses to come, the potter refuses to sell to us, the smiths refuse to mend tools, what next, the pyre-keepers will refuse to burn our bodies? They say the old kamminist sangham is leading the boycott. But the sangham isn't made of peasants, it is and always was made of the petty landowners and the lower-caste landowners, those who pretend to be our victims so as to occupy our lands in the name of this or that upliftment. They give nothing to the peasants anyway. Your father is a kind man, isn't he? And your uncle, he isn't like one of those Deshmukhs in Visnur or Jangam, where they used to make the laborers work in the fields for sixteen hours a day. Babies used to die because their mothers were in the fields, not allowed to leave to even nurse them. The mothers used to be given mud saucers to squeeze out the milk from their breasts, right there in the fields, and beaten viciously if they dared to protest! But you know that things were never like that in Irumi, and yet these people want to treat us the same. Is it fair?

Most days Katya and I do all the cooking ourselves, and sometimes the vaakili remains unswept, full of dead leaves and dead fronds, the gray stone covered in dirt. Pichamma is the only one who comes every day without fail; she refuses money. You remember her and bring something for her from Madras, maybe a sari. Her son, you remember him, he is a mathematics gold medalist at Osmania. She is very proud, talks of that medal every day. She gave it to me for safekeeping, the medal. I put it in the safe, someone might steal it from her hut because everyone in the village knows her son has a gold medal. She is a lucky woman to have a son like that. At least one son like that. The other one, Ranga, has disappeared. There is talk that he has gone inside, into the jungles to become a Naxalite. That he was responsible for the sugar factory burning down. This, after all these years of being fed at our hand. This is how these people are; no loyalty; no morality.

Remember when the two of them were little I used to have them sit on the floor and give them each a handful of roasted peanuts? Now one is a gold medalist and the other is a Naxalite. Such is time. Don't roam outside too much, Vijaya, take care, eat well. Be my darling girl, don't become thin.

Your beloved mother

The fennel seeds were chewed out. She re-read the last words: *take care, eat well, darling*. She found all the *Vijaya*s.

It wasn't hotter than it was when she'd started reading the letter, but now her blouse was sticking to her back. She felt unable to breathe.

She never had to see Ranga all these past years. He was a presence, a specter, somewhere out in Irumi. And her mother had never brought it up, no one ever brought it up—the day they went into the jungle, the night, how it began, how it ended—in all these years, not even once. They only said "accident," especially because no one wanted Sree to overhear the specifics. There wasn't a discussion, they all simply agreed without talking that it would be better for her to not know anything. Then, intentionally, unintentionally, it had morphed into this secret; kept from Sree, and also a way to pretend that Vijaya wasn't to blame.

But now, her mother wrote it. She also wrote his name. It felt malicious, as if she was purposely bringing it up in order to punish Vijaya for leaving. Even this far from Irumi, she had retained her ability to punish Vijaya. She stared at Ranga's name in the letter. It was as bad as catching sight of his coppery hair. She felt terror, even if she was too far away for him to touch her, to lay hands on her again.

Most of all, she wished her mother hadn't mentioned Krishna. Ranga had become a Naxalite, then, if her mother was to be believed. Did Krishna know? If he did, he didn't tell her.

She stood up and cracked the window over her desk open. The night was warm. The boarding house was silent except for the grumbling of crickets, interrupted now and then by the hollow ticking of a nightjar. The jasmine vine in the courtyard was in bloom. Ever since she got here, the vine had doggedly tried to get into her room. She nudged the woody branch off the windowsill and made a mental note to borrow shears from the gardener.

She turned away from the window and crumpled her mother's letter. She dropped it into the rubbish bin under her desk.

It had taken some time for Madras to stop feeling strangely disappointing, for it to feel like home. Still, every now and then, particularly on the mornings after she got letters from Irumi, she'd wake up imagining Katya calling for her from downstairs, telling her that the hot water for her bath was ready, telling Sree to hold still while she braided her hair. Before she opened her eyes she'd imagine the lemon grove outside her window, the stone fountain in the vaakili, the blue mountains, the stepwell, the banyan, the branches of the guava tree in the orchard thick with parrots. The loudness of the orchard. It was impossible to picture it dead, she refused to believe it.

Most other correspondence she had from Irumi centered on people disappearing from the village, jeethas refusing to show up for work, lack of rain, lack of rice, lack of cotton, lack of oilseeds, the talk of Naxalites everywhere. The seizing of debtors' lands for defaults was going badly, her mother wrote once. The sharecroppers were refusing to pay them for the use of land, tilling and sowing where they pleased, harvesting and selling as they pleased, newly unafraid of the name Deshmukh. The old order of things was slipping and falling, breaking, crashing like that old stone fountain in their vaakili, and no one could stop it.

Even though she knew Sree hadn't written this week, she looked through her mail again. She always read her mother's letters first and then followed it with her sister's to rinse out the bad taste. Sree's letters were very long, always. They were extremely detailed reports of the most innocuous happenings in Irumi; everyday life in the gadi from the vantage point of Sree's room. Things like what Katya said on Monday morning, how she sat at the foot of Sree's bed and massaged her ankles because they hurt, how the lemon pickle had turned out to be too sour and had to be given away to the jeethas, how fat and yellow the two papayas cut up for breakfast had been, the army of black ants marching up her windowsill, a single granule of sugar between them. Sree made note of the angle of light in the afternoon, the smell of wet trees when it rained, that it made the river look like a satin ribbon if she squinted and tilted her head that way.

She pulled a sheaf at random from the hibiscus box. This letter she suspected Sree wrote in bed, when she had one of her headaches and could only see out of her window and hear the goings-on outside her room. The details were so fine that Vijaya felt as if she were tucked in bed alongside Sree, head resting on her shoulder.

And Katya keeps cutting up carrots into small pieces, or grating and mixing it in my sambar. As if I don't notice. She thinks she's so smart. Same with radish too, she grates it into my yogurt. Still, I ate without making faces last week because she stands on tiptoes by the door, peeking, waiting to see if I can make it out. I feel bad for her. You know I was in bed all last week and I just didn't feel like fighting with her. She sits on the floor next to me all day long, sewing or darning. What are you doing? Do you have any friends there? Wish I could go somewhere like you. Wish I could go far from here.

Vijaya put Sree's letter away.

She began refilling ink in her pen with the intention of writing her mother back, when her eyes fell on the inland letter sticking out from underneath Sree's. She'd saved all of Krishna's letters. After the first time, they'd simply never stopped. She imagined him making this time for her, only her, between the pressing things of ordinary life.

Her mother's words were still echoing inside her, and she pulled out the stack and riffled through them, picking out Krishna's, reading them out of order, at random; a sentence in one letter, a paragraph in another.

Vijaya, do you blame yourself? You shouldn't.

I remember it like it was yesterday, sitting with you behind the step-well, watching bird after bird dive into the valley below. Burying the almonds. The good parts. Do you think a tree ever grew there?

Even now, when I think of you, in my mind's eye I see the girl with the large, brown eyes, whispering into my ear. The wild stories of adventures and fairy tales and tigers. Isn't it important to remember the good parts? A whole life cannot just be about the bad parts. You, Vijaya, are the only one who makes me want to remember.

When Ranga and I were little, Ranga stole a mango from your orchard. Your uncle caught him and gave him a terrible beating. I still remember the sound of his boots, the crunch of dry leaves as he walked up to us, the terror of being found out by him. Ranga made me hide. It was only a mango. But for your uncle, it was the principle of the thing. Dora, ne banchan. It is a phrase that sits on the tip of my tongue at merely a passing thought of your uncle. Even now. Even though I haven't lived in Irumi since I was twelve. Ranga, I imagine, had to say that all the time. I am your slave. I am your slave, master. Now it seems like a bizarre dream, that things like that were said once, said every day. Said even now, perhaps. Isn't it repulsive?

I say "I imagine" because Ranga does not write me. He made me promise never to return to Irumi. To never think of Irumi as my home. At Osmania, because everyone is from someplace else, when someone asks me where I'm from, I hesitate. Where is my home? To whom should I belong?

It is true, one does not choose the house in which they are born. But I suppose they can choose where they live. They can choose with whom.

I have a friend here. His name is Gagan. He is the student president at Osmania. I don't think you'd like him very much, the way he talks of the zamindars (but maybe you will?). In October, he's planning a protest against the zamindars and the CM.

Have you ever been to Hyderabad? Have you seen Osmania?

Do you not want me to write you? Tell me and I will never.

Can you tell me about your life in Madras? What is Presidency like? Tell me, is it a women's college?

There aren't many women in the mathematics program here either, but I haven't looked hard to find one. Are the boys all madly in love with you? I want to know everything you did in the last ten years.

Gagan is almost exactly like Ranga, but also so entirely different it makes absolutely no sense. Fearless, adventurous, a presence. I never hear from Ranga at all. My mother tells me nothing about him. Is it odd for you, writing to me? Am I a stranger to you? You aren't, to me.

Have you heard about Naxalites in Irumi? I don't think there is any other reaction other than a revolutionary reaction to the way things are in the countryside, Vijaya. The violent faction of the Communist Party is extremely popular at Osmania too. Even though Hyderabad isn't Calcutta, there are some who've joined from the cities, the educated ones, the engineers who now wear turbans and country cloth and write songs for the cultural wings, but still it isn't like Calcutta; police stations being lit on fire, CRPF troops being murdered and pipe bombs being made in university hostels and so on. I'm afraid saying "Communist" and "Naxalite" is one and the same nowadays.

Gagan isn't a communist, though. People say he is a Hindu nationalist and Gagan says "Excellent. That is exactly what I am."

Am I an awful person for not wanting to get involved? To simply graduate and get a job somewhere far away. I don't say all this to Gagan of course. I go to all his meetings and support him whenever he wants me to support him but the truth is, I will admit only to you, Vijaya, that I do not care. I don't. Does that make me ungrateful? To Gagan, to the world? I can tell you the truth.

Because I'm from Irumi, Gagan asks me if it is true that the zamindars are finding every single loophole there is to find in the land ceiling laws. That they are splitting holdings between family members to stay under the ceiling, that they are happily ignoring legislation that makes it unlawful to extract vetti, that they accept the money the government offers to give up wet land, but they keep both money and wet land. They give up the useless land that runs off the hills, or between bridges, that the surveys are cheated every day. But some landlords are giving up excess land voluntarily. I suppose, that is my roundabout way of asking what your uncle is doing. It is hard to imagine him giving up anything.

And the only one that she hadn't answered, even though it was months since he'd sent it to her.

I am desperate to see you, Vijaya. Do you want to see me? Tell me, and I will come.

It had been only the second letter she'd gotten from him, and it had stunned her. But she understood what he meant, it had felt like he was speaking for the both of them. He hadn't asked again, and she knew he wouldn't. What was it that she thought would happen if Krishna came to Madras? If they saw each other in a place that wasn't Irumi. She wanted to say yes right away. But she didn't.

"Why don't we go to the beach?"

She and Asha were walking out of Presidency together. It was late in the afternoon.

"Not Marina, somewhere else," Asha said.

Vijaya checked her watch.

"You seem so quiet these days. Is something the matter, Vijaya?"

"Yes."

"What is it?" Asha said.

"Let's go to the beach, I mean."

After waiting for ten minutes at the stop, they got on the bus that took them to the Madras beach. On the bus, Vijaya sat at the window, Asha took the aisle seat next to her. The breeze from the open window made their saris flutter, she could smell the vetiver in Asha's perfume.

The bus was empty except for a group of young boys in the back. Despite the many vacant seats, they were all crowding the rear entrance of the bus, standing on the footboard, joking, laughing, watching traffic pass, once in a while sticking their heads out and letting the wind run through their hair. The bus made its usual abrupt stops and abrupt takeoffs, winding its way through motorists and scooters, rattling at the hinges whenever its tires bounced in and out of a pothole.

The conductor came up to them, steadying himself against the metal rail set into the floor of the bus. His khaki uniform was greasy, patches of sweat across his shoulders and arms. "Ticket," he muttered without looking at their faces, retrieving the ticket dispenser slung around his neck.

"Two for ECR Beach," Asha said, not looking at his face either. She handed him the money and waited for him to make change. The conductor licked his index finger, flicked through a stack of tickets, and plucked them out of the dispenser. Asha, as was her habit, crumpled up the tickets the minute they were in her hand. The conductor began walking away when Asha turned and said, "Where's my change?"

Vijaya caught the conductor raise his eyebrows. He looked Asha over.

He had a sullen face. His skin was broken in two or three places alongside his jawline, as though he regularly nicked himself while shaving. Vijaya could detect the remnants of a night spent drinking. Asha again asked for change. He made a show of looking in his change bag. They heard the distinct rustle of small coins.

"I don't have change," he said.

"Okay, give us our money back then," Asha challenged. "I'll give you exact change."

"What a nuisance," he grumbled.

"Nuisance?" Asha's voice rose. "Do you want me to make a written complaint—"

"Asha," she interrupted, "let it go."

"Why? He's thieving."

That was the wrong word to use.

"How dare you call me a thief!" the conductor screamed, and he came towards them. He stood a little too close. His leg was touching Asha's knee.

"You'll make a complaint is it? Go make a complaint. Go right now. Hey"—he yelled over his shoulder at the driver—"make a stop here. We will drop these fancy ladies in the middle of the road."

"Fine, stop the bus," Asha said, unfazed. She did not draw back, even though Vijaya hooked her arm through hers and tugged. "Watch me. I'll make sure you lose your job."

"Asha," she hissed, "stop it. It is only a few rupees."

"Why are you acting like I'm embarrassing you?" Asha said, turning to her. "He's the one—"

"I don't want to walk all the way to the beach, okay? Let it go.

"Brother," she said, turning to the conductor, talking over Asha. Asha glared at her. "Why make a big fuss with complaints and whatnot? Keep the change."

"Keep the change?" the conductor screamed, drawing even closer, looking angrier than ever. "What am I, a beggar you think? Big fancy lady with diamonds in her ears and pearls around her neck thinks the rest of us are beggars?" He withdrew a few coins at random from his bag and tossed them at her feet. A coin struck her little toe. It stung.

"Suresh! Stop the bus!" he shouted at the driver. The bus braked and ground to a halt, throwing them all forwards.


"Serves you right," Asha said.

They were standing on the side of the road.

"Leave it be," she replied.

"The labor class is the labor class," Asha continued. "Give them a drop of power—even as a lowly bus conductor—and they will dance on your head. They think the world owes them simply because they don't have."

Vijaya didn't want to argue. Their stop was two kilometers away. Not a single taxi passed them by. She wasn't wearing shoes meant for walking.

"Did you look at his face? Must be Koy or Gond or some other chillar hill tribe—"

*"Asha!"*

"What? These are the same people who would be too afraid to meet our eyes, not even be allowed to cross us on the street back home. Who'd wash the clothes in our houses for a seru of grain. Put them in a big city, they join some union and think they are all big shots. They think they are our equals. Fucking communists."

A taxi was coming up the street. Vijaya waved. The taxi did not stop.

By now, she knew Asha well enough, she had to let her talk herself down. She looked up and down the street. Traffic was light but the roads were terrible on this route: tar roads sporadically missing large sections, drain holes missing covers, cement speed breakers so high they seemed to scrape the undersides of passing vehicles. Aging city buses groaned and whined up and down the street. None would stop for them. The street had a stink, of drains and dogs.

"Let's just take a taxi back to the hostel," Asha said.

"There are no taxis."

They began walking.

The hot sun was prickling Vijaya's back, and sweat was beading down her face. She felt the dust and black smoke from passing vehicles in her eyes. "Forget about that conductor Asha," she said. "We'll be there in no time."

They smelled the sea before they saw it. The horizon dipped and fell away into the sea, and in the September light, its waters shimmered.

No matter how many times Vijaya came here, no matter how many evenings she spent sitting in the sand, the vastness of the open waters still took her breath away as if she were encountering it for the very first time. For a brief moment, it was as though she could only see—and all the life around her, the shrieks of seagulls and the protestations of ships and freighters and screaming children did not exist. It was her and the immense, glittering blue sea.

They made their way towards a shaded spot underneath a coconut tree. The tree's trunk was bent nearly double. Trained by the wind, its green fronds hung over its trunk in a graceful arc, like the neck of a tea-kettle. It was low tide, and here and there, brown sandbars and gray rock formations showed. All around them, children ran, screaming at one an-other, kicking up sand. There was the crushed-ice vendor ringing his bell, the sugar syrups in his cart sitting like bottled rainbows. There was the roasted-corn vendor sitting with the wicker basket at his feet, waiting for the day to cool down enough to light his coals.

Vijaya drew her knees up to her chin. She picked a fistful of sand and let it stream out, from in between her knuckles, over her wrist. The sand was hot. Often, Krishna wrote her twice in a single day, by the morning post and the evening post, even before she had the opportunity to respond to his last. The hibiscus box was getting too full.

Her uncle made her sign the land papers before she left. Vijaya did not ask him what they were for, but she knew. He was splitting their land-holdings so they escaped the surveys. When the Bhoodan people came to ask for voluntary relinquishment of land, her uncle received them, he was magnanimous even, turning over to them nearly a hundred acres for distribution amongst the landless peasants. It was printed in the papers, his magnanimity. But she knew it was fallow land of such terrible quality—unsettled, rocky, sandy, unirrigated—that it couldn't even be used to graze cattle. She did not tell Krishna this. What she did tell him was that ten years passed her by like it were one year. Time collapsed, as it did when every day was exactly the same. How her mother did not speak to her for months; looking through Vijaya as if she wasn't even there; as if she were dead. How she'd never let Vijaya forget. She'd go hungry for days, and eventually it would be Katya, despite her obvious dislike for Vijaya, who'd bring her a plate and ask her to eat and say that starving herself wouldn't help Sree. How Sree used to scream at night, how it used to fill her with blind panic, how she used to be drenched in sweat without even moving. But she'd pretend to be happy and cheerful, and tell Sree that she was going to be all right. How difficult it was to get away to come to Madras, how she could breathe here, but how this breath too felt tinged with the guilt of having left Sree behind. That Krishna was the only one with whom she could talk to; about this; about anything; and with him alone she could share this weight she carried everywhere. Her stomach clenched at the thought of seeing him again. It should comfort her, shouldn't it? It should be solace. Seeing him. It should be pleasure. Then why did it terrify her?

Her attention was drawn by a group of boys at the edge of the water.

Vijaya recognized them, they were the ones who'd stood on the footboard of their bus. They were racing one another into the water. The group targeted one amongst them, a skinny one whose eyes looked like he'd just taken off his glasses. They piled onto him and submerged him into the crashing waves. He disappeared, and re-emerged moments later, guffawing, shoving his friends away, his wet hair plastered against his forehead.

Asha laughed. The boy looked over at Asha, pushed hair out of his eyes and waved, returning a cheerful smile.

"Hey, is that Deepthi?" Asha said.

Vijaya looked. It was. Deepthi was, astonishingly, sitting by herself. She looked forlorn, she was staring at her feet.

"How odd," Asha said. She wondered if they should call Deepthi over. Vijaya said no.

She did not want to tell Asha that it wasn't merely the annoyance of Deepthi's presence. She had, over the months, thought of telling Asha about how, on their very first day of class, in an attempt to ingratiate herself to the other girls with a juicy bit of gossip, she'd started that terrible rumor about Asha. None of the other girls accepted Asha's invitations to go anywhere with her, and everything she said and did was viewed with suspicion, colored with the perceived looseness of her character. Asha tried to hide it, but Vijaya knew that she was bothered by it. What Deepthi did was unforgivable.

"Why not? She's going to annoy us of course, but she looks terribly sad."

"No. Let her be. I hope she doesn't see us."

"No one speaks to her nowadays, did you notice? They treat her worse than they treat me. Whatever did she do?"

This too Vijaya knew. After the first month or so, Deepthi had seen a girl from the boarding house at a matinee show with someone. She'd hurried over to the warden with this information, making all sorts of accusations. The girl protested, but the warden took Deepthi's word over hers and summoned the girl's parents.

Deepthi was wrong. The girl had been at the movie with a cousin, and the parents had brought him along with them. They gave the warden an earful. And the girl, angry, had slapped Deepthi in front of the warden and called her hateful, that she was out to make accusations simply to make herself seem important. After that, Deepthi no longer had any friends at the boarding house. Having nowhere to turn, she'd taken to spending more and more time with the warden. Vijaya often caught the two of them eating breakfast together in the dining hall. Sometimes, as though to prove to everyone else that she was one of them, Deepthi would approach one of the girls; to tell them that the strap of their slip was showing, or to discreetly pull up a sleeve or adjust a neckline or ask to borrow a fresh pad when she was on her period, with the smile and the expression of being one of them, an insider. Still, it was as though in everyone's eyes she and the warden had become interchangeable, only Deepthi still had her glorious dimples.

"Deepthi!" Asha shouted, waving. Deepthi did not hear her.

"Hush! Don't," Vijaya said.

"Why are you being so mean?" Asha asked.

"I'm not mean," she said. "You don't know what she says about you."

Asha looked away from Deepthi and stared at her. "What do you mean?"

"Nothing."

"You meant something. Tell me."

"Nothing. Call her over if you want, I don't care."

"Tell me, Vijaya. Or else."

Vijaya did, hesitatingly. She hated the words coming out of her mouth but she repeated the bit about Deepthi telling everyone that Asha had had an abortion. That her parents had thrown her out of the house. Asha's face was expressionless.

"I wonder how she knew," she said after a while.

Deepthi was standing up. She dusted the sand off the hem of her sari and started walking towards the bus stop across from the beach.

"I suppose we have to head back too."

"We can take the next bus," Vijaya said, too afraid to comment on anything else.

"Don't you want to know?" Asha asked.

She said nothing.

"You look very disappointed."

"I do not."

"You don't lie very well, you know. You didn't believe it till just now, till I confirmed it. You try, but you can't lie, Viji." Asha paused. "Is that why you don't have any other friends here? Because you are seen with me?"

"I don't want any other friends."

"Well, that's another lie."

Asha pursed her lips and stared at the water.

"You know, Vijaya, I always thought I was going to marry him. There was nothing wrong with him. My parents arranged the match, they knew his family. But I changed my mind. And he got very angry. He warned me, he told me what was going to happen if I continued to say no. I didn't believe him."

Vijaya looked away from the water.

"He did as he promised and see, even Deepthi, a girl with whom I have absolutely no connection has heard it. I suppose he thought I'd have no other choice."

"What did your parents do?" Vijaya asked.

"They told me that now I had no choice in the matter anyway. It was all my own doing. That I should have been more careful, more sensible. I should marry him."

"You still said no?"

"What do you think?"

"Where is he now?"

"Oh, you know. Back home. Married. Three kids. Happy."

"Your parents?"

"To them, I am no longer alive. My father made it a point to perform death rites in my name, a way to wash off the shame you see? And be welcomed back into society having done the virtuous thing even though fate had dealt them a blow. They are on speaking terms with him, though. They have a need to be apologetic, about me. That I ruined his life and my life for no good reason."

"That's disgusting!" she said, and Asha looked at her as if she'd uttered something astonishing.

She listened as Asha described how she'd threatened to take the warden to the courts on grounds of discrimination if she refused to allow her to live there anymore. How her grandmother, despite belonging to a generation even more conservative than her parents', had been the only one who'd supported her, emotionally and financially, and when her ajji passed, she'd left Asha an inheritance.

She put her arm around Asha and they stayed like that for a while without saying anything. The boys were gathering their things, waving in their direction as they left.

"You look like my sister," Vijaya said, "exactly like her. Have I told you this before?"

"Only about a hundred times," Asha said, smiling a little.

"Well, you do."

"What is she like?" Asha said. "I'd like to meet her."

She said that Sree was bright, that she was an absolute delight to be around. Asha would adore her.

"I wish I had a sibling," Asha said. "Someone with whom I could grow up, with whom I'd share all my childhood memories. I'd have them even if I didn't have my parents. It must be such a tender thing, to be able to share the same history."

Asha leaned her head on Vijaya's shoulder. Vijaya looked out at the water again. She could say that Asha was as good as a sibling to her, and she'd have Vijaya even if there was no one else. It was true. It would make Asha happy. But she didn't say it. Sree wouldn't have liked her saying that. But Sree didn't share the same history as she did. Couldn't, because Vijaya had made a mistake so grave that it had taken away all of Sree's abilities, not just the ability to be her sibling. What Vijaya had were the pieces of a sister she was meant to have. Only Krishna remembered the good parts. She didn't. Couldn't.


In October, the jasmine vine stopped blooming, stopped trying to get in her room. The weather cooled, and they began keeping their windows shut to keep out the chill. The semester drew to a close. They were in Asha's room. Vijaya was sitting on Asha's bed with a book open in front of her, Asha was at her desk reading the week's edition of *Swathi*.

Vijaya was going home to Irumi for the holidays. Tara was getting married. The thought of returning home had filled her with a dread she'd felt too ashamed to express. She had asked to stay back, saying that she had to prepare for her finals, but her mother called the warden, had the trunk call held until Vijaya rushed downstairs. "You *are* coming home, Vijaya. What do you think? We won't mind going without seeing you for such an important occasion? The whole family has to be here. That means you too." Her mother's voice came back to her over the crackle in the line, the demand in her tone, as if she possessed Vijaya whole. "And your uncle won't hear of it."

"When is your train tomorrow?" Asha asked, turning around.

She hadn't turned the page in more than an hour.

"Will you tell me what the matter is, Viji?" Asha said, putting the magazine down.

Vijaya saw her fold the corner down on what looked like a film review.

"Hello? Where is this Vijaya-dorasani? Scion of the illustrious Deshmukh family? Can she hear me?"

"What?"

The playfulness in Asha's tone dropped away. "I've noticed this change in you since that day we were at the beach. Do you not want to be friends with me anymore? Because of what I told you . . ."

"No. I don't," she replied sarcastically, shaking her head and returning to the book she wasn't reading. "That's why I'm sitting here. What better way to tell the world.

"Don't insult me, Asha," she added.

"Then why are you so quiet? What is happening with you? Won't you tell me?"

Vijaya hesitated. Partly because she did not want Asha to think that she was pulling away from her, and partly because she sensed how good it would feel to confide in someone, she told Asha about Krishna. The question she'd been unable to stop pondering all these months; whether she should allow him to come to Madras to see her.

Asha's face was expressionless.

"Do you want to marry him?" Asha said.

"What?"

"You heard me. Do you want to marry him?"

He wouldn't want that. Why would he want that.

She must have said it out loud, because Asha said, "You mean why would he want *you*."

The change in Asha's tone was so sudden it caught her off guard. She swallowed, looked at the page in front of her again. It had been a mistake to tell Asha, she understood now.

"Why *wouldn't* he. What does he have, Vijaya? Nothing. Where does he come from? Dirt poverty. That's where."

Asha stood up. "You don't see it, do you? You never see yourself the way others see you. You don't allow it. Why else would he come here? What other reason is there? He's obsessed with you, and from what you've told me, he always has been.

"Do you think, for a single minute, that any amount of education, or even money, can wipe away the stains of one's birth? The position of one's family? It will be a disgrace, Vijaya. Your family will be disgusted with you. They will hate you. He has everything to gain from you. Tell me, Vijaya, what is it that you will gain? Your parents will become like my parents, unable to show their faces anywhere. But worse, because you will be happy, and they'll know that you're happy.

"Your uncle. Your mother. Even your father wouldn't forgive you this. Think of everything you would be giving up. Do you think it is easy, to live like I do? Alone. Never part of the only people who remember the person you used to be? Do you think they will let you return home? Let you see your sister again? You are throwing everything away—look at me, Vijaya. If I could turn back time, don't you think I would have wanted a different life for myself? That more than once I've thought about how different everything would have been, if I'd never said no."

"I'm not you, Asha," she said quietly.

"What is that supposed to mean?"

Vijaya said, "Please don't raise your voice at me."

Asha turned away. "I think you should go back to your room."

"Please don't be angry with me," she said. "There are things you don't know."

Asha did not turn around.

Vijaya picked up her book. At the door she hesitated, turned. "Asha," she said. Asha did not turn around. Vijaya knew she was crying.

Once she was back in her room, Vijaya lay down on top of her covers and stared at the ceiling. She did not turn on her lamp, and in the darkness she watched small lights flit across the ceiling; the headlights of passing vehicles, streetlamps sputtering in and out of life, silhouettes of people crossing the courtyard. Her window was open and a breeze was playing at her feet. She turned to her side.

Abruptly, she got out of bed and switched on the lamp on her desk. She pulled out a fresh inland letter. As she copied down his address at Osmania on the front, she remembered that the protest he and his friend were planning was tomorrow. It was possible that he wouldn't receive her letter, or read it, right away. She kept her response as simple and straightforward as his question had been. She asked him to come. In the morning, before she got on the train back to Irumi, she posted it.

# BULLET

On the morning of the protest, Krishna showed up on the arts quad at the appointed time and found it completely empty. A gardener was trimming the tops of bushes in the distance, and the metallic *clop-clop* of his shears could be heard. Yellow sunlight was pouring into the empty quad, into the water pool underneath the arts building. The day was already hot and clear.

Gagan was standing at the edge of the grass field, the place overlooking the quad where Krishna normally read his morning papers. His hair was neatly brushed, and he was dressed in a white linen shirt, brown khakis, polished black shoes. Gagan had asked the demonstrators to follow a dress code: white clothes.

"Who has ever shown up on time in this country," Gagan exclaimed across the field, throwing up his hands. "They will come!" Gagan's voice swam across the field like a large, waking bird.

"I didn't see you all day yesterday," Krishna said on reaching him. "Where were you?"

"Paperwork. I made doubly sure that every bit of it is allowed today, legal. I want everything to go smoothly." He looked a little nervous.

Gagan had mapped out a route that went north to south, starting at Osmania, then along the banks of the Musi River, passing the quarantine hospital, the Imblibun bus station, the museum, and ending at the gymkhana parade grounds, across the street from the red minarets of the high court of Hyderabad. Gagan would speak at the parade grounds.

It was supposed to begin at nine. But it wasn't until a quarter past eleven, and after three overly sweetened tumblers of milky chai, that thirty or so people gathered on the quad, carrying between them stacks of cardboard signs and rolled-up sheets painted with black, bold letters.

He hung back at the tea stall while Gagan went to speak to them. The sun had settled into its midday position, heat was prickling the back of Krishna's neck. Raja or Ramesh waved in Krishna's direction. Shireen was kneeling on the grass, unrolling a sign that needed to be held up by three people. When the group migrated towards the water pool underneath the arts building, Gagan gestured in his direction and Krishna followed.

About an hour later, the number of protesters doubled, then tripled, until the quad was swathed in placard-holding students, dressed similarly in white like Gagan, but in traditional kurtas and matching white caps. "How many?" Gagan asked him, waving at the people he recognized.

Krishna climbed on the edge of the pool. Too many to count. He couldn't spot a single person wearing regular clothes; like himself. Even though Gagan had made no comment, it made him feel conspicuous. "Two hundred?" he guessed. Getting down, Krishna thought of Dr. Ramaswamy's advice to not be seen with Gagan. Being here felt like disloyalty: a betrayal of Dr. Ramaswamy, how his concern for Krishna's future had compelled him to cross a professional boundary. A betrayal also of his friendship with Gagan; not confiding in him what Dr. Ramaswamy had said, the offer he'd already decided to accept—this betrayal felt worse, it felt treacherous. Even his having that conversation with Dr. Ramaswamy was because of Gagan. Krishna was glad for the two hundred, the large number comforted him. It granted him anonymity, he could even say he wasn't there. He wished he had acquiesced and worn white.

There was supposed to be a microphone set up at the top of the stairs of the arts building, but it seemed that someone had misplaced it. "I'll go look," Krishna said, but he found that his progress back into the building was slow and halting; people he had no memory of ever meeting stopped him to demand what the delay was, when was Gagan going to speak, what the route was. Some even asked why they were here. But they all seemed to know Krishna's role—which was what? He shrugged noncommittally, politely, but by the time he made it to the top of the stairs, he could already hear Gagan shouting the answers. He turned around.

From his position at the top of the stairs, it was an arresting sight. Krishna could see the top of Gagan's head—he was standing on the edge of the pool now, his back turned—and beyond the quad, he could see all the way to the perimeters of the grass field, the traffic slowing at the intersection that bisected the field before it dipped out of sight. Everywhere he looked he saw protesters dressed in white; small groups sitting on the ground, on the stairs, on the edge of the field under the mahogany tree, under the awnings of the tea shop, the thick knot of people in whose center Gagan was speaking. Everywhere. The number he'd pegged at two hundred just minutes ago was clearly wrong, it had to be close to three hundred.

He wondered if anyone noticed the distinct hum that seemed to rise up over the quad and the field; the blurred chatter of so many people, but stamped with the type of nervous, purposeful energy that, he supposed, came from so many people standing shoulder to shoulder in a single place in service of a single principle. The very ground underneath him seemed to tremble expectantly. Here and there, he spotted—with relief and recognition—lone students dressed in ordinary colors like himself, instead of white, attempting to weave their way out of the quad, some watching warily from the entryway to the pure sciences building; Krishna averted his gaze.

He didn't want to lose track of Gagan in the milieu, so he took the stairs two at a time, fought his way back towards the pool again. "Time to start," Gagan said, spotting Krishna returning, turning on a megaphone. "Mic testing," he said. Krishna shut his ears. The noise was shrill. Gagan lowered the volume and spoke into it again. Krishna raised his thumb and said it was loud enough.

Gagan addressed the crowd. He insisted again and again that they had the absolute right—an enshrined democratic right—to protest; but *only* to a peaceful protest. That every single person who'd made the choice to come here today was also accepting one rule: to remain calm, no matter what happened. Then the megaphone feedback began jumbling up his words, and Krishna couldn't make out the rest of Gagan's short address. Gagan spoke for a few more moments with a finger plugged into his ear, but looking irritated, he lowered the megaphone and motioned with his hand towards the edge of the field; he planned to lead the way from there.

When they reached the edge of the field Gagan re-checked the megaphone again. "It sounds all right now," Krishna said. "Don't increase the volume Gagan, keep it there. Maybe it's the volume that's the problem."

"Rows of twenty. Twenty! Leave one hand's distance!" Gagan shouted. More than anything, it reminded Krishna of prayers at assembly, the march-pasts for Independence Day, when they were split up by grade and organized in neat rows of threes, columns of twenty. Move only when the people in front of you move. Don't break formation.

Into the megaphone, Gagan demanded the chief minister's resignation, and his phrasing was chorused exactly by a line of twenty students on his and Krishna's either side, and the section right behind them, the phrasing radiating backwards, section by section, until they heard the last repetition, and Gagan would say it again; the same phrase or a variation of it: the injustices committed against the sharecroppers, the inhumanity of the zamindars, the plight of the landless. When Gagan was satisfied, he motioned to move out of the university grounds.

Clenching and unclenching his fists, Gagan gripped Krishna's shoulder, released it. "Stay by me, Krishna," he said.

Krishna stopped glancing over his shoulder to peg a number; he was losing track, without a vantage point he couldn't see far back enough. Once they filtered into the narrow alleys outside the university, the line of twenty on his and Gagan's either side became a line of ten. But it remained organized, the formation unbroken, Gagan's phrasing still being echoed in the same manner, but the last chorus now reached them faintly. Housewives paused while hanging out their drying, holding up their toddlers, pointing at them.

It was maybe an hour after they exited the alleys and emerged onto the main junction that it became apparent to Krishna that they were no longer leading. Their university group had disintegrated; but not intentionally. They'd picked up new people into their ranks—not students dressed in white—but general public, though only men and not women. It made him nervous. "Who are these people, Gagan?" he said. But Gagan didn't seemed to mind, he looked thrilled. They were supposed to take a break at two in the afternoon, that was the plan, but they didn't stop. Krishna felt parched, wished for some water. They reached the main road.

The traffic on the main road— covered rickshaws, scooters, city buses, jhatkas—slowed at first and then came to a complete and resolute halt around them. Only those on bicycles were still filtering through their midst. Around him he saw Osmania students dressed in white, standing, looking around—on footpaths, on stray boulders—mingled almost with an equal number of men in regular clothes; he saw one of them climb onto the top of a parked city bus, the driver yelling. They'd certainly stopped following that route Gagan had so painstakingly mapped out. How did it happen? There was a large bird shop nearby, and the earsplitting screeches of caged parakeets soared over even the din of everything. From its shop board, he made out that they were in the Siddiamber bazaar.

"We don't have permission to demonstrate here, right?" Krishna shouted at Gagan.

"It's all right," Gagan replied, though he didn't seem so sure now.

Krishna had no idea whose voice it was, screaming over their heads, chanting a variation of Gagan's original phrase, but seemingly targeting just one person—Rizvi—the MLA whose seat Gagan was planning to contest. Indeed, when he turned to look at the commotion right behind them, he saw a haphazard mass of people among the stalled vehicles, into whose midst an effigy was brought forth. Clearly, based on the skullcap, the effigy was meant to be Rizvi. He felt himself being shoved aside passionately by people he did not recognize, almost none of them seemed to be college age; none he recognized; they were all uniformly older. The effigy was garlanded with rubber slippers, then doused in kerosene, then lit on fire. A press corp photographer asked him roughly to move out of the way—when did the press arrive?—but he spotted two more, taking pictures of the burning effigy, the people standing over it. Krishna thought it was grotesque, and certainly not something Gagan would have planned or endorsed. He turned to say these things, but Gagan was nowhere.

"Gagan!" he shouted, but wherever he looked, there were only stalled vehicles. People screaming. Diesel fumes. Engines thrumming. "Gagan!" he yelled. "Were we even supposed to take this path?" he said. No longer seeing anyone he recognized, Krishna fought his way towards the footpath, shoving people out of his way as roughly as he was being shoved. His progress was slow and uneven. Every few feet, he had to stop completely, wait for an opening. It was the fleeting details he noticed on the people he encountered; the smell of talcum powder on the neck of one man, a thick burn scar on the forearm of another, red string tied around the neck like a talisman, clothes that gave off the distinct smell of rancid oil. None in the conspicuous white clothes of Osmania students. Where were they? There were so many who'd started with them.

When Krishna reached the pavement, he saw a music shop owner hurry forward and roll down the metal shutter over his glass display of ornately painted sitars. He glanced once at Krishna, made sure the lock latched correctly and fled. It was a strange feeling, to have someone look so afraid of him. The sun overhead was fierce now; his shirt was sticking to him, and his throat felt dry and scratchy. The top of his head felt as though baked, even his hair was burning-hot to touch. He felt confused, panicked, but he just stood there trying to decide what to do next. He considered going back to Osmania, but where was Gagan? He stood on the pavement, trying to gain his bearings, trying to spot Gagan, anyone he recognized. "Shireen!" he shouted, spotting her hurrying in the opposite direction. He got off the pavement, trying and failing to part his way through the crowd. But there was no room to go anywhere, no room to breathe; the crush of bodies felt immense. He wiped his forehead, tried to return to the pavement, but before he made any progress, Krishna felt someone coming up behind him. "Gagan," he said, turning around, but instead he came face-to-face with a large man in a red kurta towering over him. Three others standing just behind with what looked like hockey sticks in their hands. Before Krishna reacted, the man roughly held him by the collar, then just as quickly shoved him aside. He fell face-first onto the tar road. His cheek scraped and bled. Someone stepped on his ear but withdrew their foot, stepped over him. He picked himself up. He touched his cheek, gingerly sponged the blood off with this shirt cuff. He had the horrible suspicion that they were looking for Gagan.

Nearly all the shopkeepers had downed their shutters now; street-sellers and panicked motorists were fleeing on foot. Krishna saw, as if in slow motion, a single rock fly through the air before him. He traced its clean trajectory before it fell against the glass display case of a sweet shop, shattering it. After that, it was chaos; every single storefront on the street was being smashed. Burning bottles of kerosene flying through the air. Indistinct screaming. Stone pelting. Krishna smelled blood. He tried to push through the horde. He saw a woman dragging a child by the arm, another smaller baby at her hip. The boy was holding a paper fan. He moved aside to let them pass. The paper fan fell out of the boy's hand. The boy stooped to pick it up, letting go of his mother's hand.

If it weren't for Krishna, the boy would have been crushed to death. Krishna retrieved the paper fan, held the boy by the other hand, tried to locate the mother. Couldn't. "There," Krishna said, handing the fan over. "What's your name?" he asked. The boy looked petrified, his face was as though frozen. His shirt was green, so neatly pressed that the crease marks on his sleeves were still visible. On his breath, Krishna smelled orange candy. The boy held his paper fan, clutched Krishna's leg. "Come!" Krishna said to the boy. Making him let go of his leg, Krishna picked him up. He fought his way down the street; he was certain that was the way the mother had gone. He cast around. Where was she? The boy was clutching Krishna's neck, his palms were clammy. Everywhere he looked there was only warped metal, smoldering public buses, broken shop fronts, orphaned footwear, torn banners, a litter of spare rocks and burning rubber tires. Everything smelled like petrol.

"What's your name?" Krishna said. The boy began to cry. Then began to scream. Krishna tried to ease the boy's grip around his neck. "How old are you?"

He heard an explosion behind him. He turned to see a city bus burst into flames, its glass windows shattering like crystal. He felt himself move a few feet backward, instinctively, bumping into someone, then being shoved out of the way, the boy still in his arms.

The boy was fighting him, trying to leap out of his arms, when Krishna spotted the man in the red kurta again, with the same three men behind him. They were gathered together around something, someone, across the street. Krishna tried to tighten his grip on the boy, tried to see. "Stop it," he told the boy. "You'll fall. You'll be crushed. See how many people there are!" He craned his neck, easing the boy's grip on it, tried to spot the man in the red kurta across the street again. Then two things happened in quick succession; the boy escaped his grip, fell out of his hands; and the man in the red kurta moved aside. Krishna saw the dark hair, the white linen shirt.

Krishna did not know if the boy made it safely, nor did he know if the person the men were gathered around was indeed Gagan, because no matter how much he tried, Krishna couldn't fight against the tide of panicking crowd fleeing in the opposite direction. Why were they fleeing? It took him several moments of attempting to fight his way through, to realize that it was the effect of the CRPF trucks rolling down the street; a half dozen of them. Riot police—rubber-tipped batons—water hoses. An announcement on the megaphone that live rounds were going to be fired. To disperse immediately.

The streets were systematically cleared, he was told, at the Irani café he found himself in, blending into the tables of tea drinkers, trying to catch his breath. A three-day curfew. Osmania students were special targets, Shireen told him; there was blood running down her shirt, and he realized that it was running down his own too. Their white clothes identified them, she said, and they were hosed down and mercilessly beaten. Loaded into police vans and processed at overflowing stations. There were those severely injured, their bones fractured in multiple places, crushed at the joints, pulverized, with head injuries and facial lacerations, admitted to local hospitals, stitched up, limbs set in plaster casts. Amongst their number was Gagan, possibly the worst injured. "How did you escape?" Shireen asked him. Krishna said he didn't know. "How did you?" Shireen didn't know either.

What happened that day was covered by every newspaper in not just Hyderabad City but the entire state. Gagan's photograph, caught mid-cry as he stood in front of the initial group that started at Osmania, graced the cover of every morning and evening broadsheet. If one looked closely at this photograph, in each and every one of them, Krishna appeared, just by Gagan's shoulder. Two days later, Krishna visited Gagan at the university hospital.

Gagan was unconscious. His right eye was injured, from baton or water hose it wasn't possible to know. His face was puffy, a bandage covered most of it. Partly visible underneath the gauze were deep gouges, long sutures snaking their way around his jaw, across his cheek. Gagan's leg was broken in four places. Ugly purple cuts and blotches ran up the length of his arms and chest.

When he looked into Gagan's face, he felt sick, as though he'd had too many cups of tea and too many of Gagan's cigarettes, too fast. Even though all the blood was wiped off, it was as though Krishna could still see Gagan's face covered in it, spreading across the hospital pillows, running like ink.

A nurse came over and stopped by the head of Gagan's hospital bed. She checked on his drip bag.

"What's wrong with him?" Krishna asked.

"There's fluid in his brain. He will be kept asleep till the swelling reduces," she said, adding, "he will recover. Lucky man. Three people were shot dead, more than fifty injured."

"Has the doctor finished his rounds?" Krishna asked, trying not to imagine Gagan being shot.

"Yes, but he comes back around nine in the evening again."

"Where there any children?"

"Children?" she said.

He turned to look at her.

"No," she said. "No children."

After the nurse left, Krishna leaned closer and, not knowing what else to do, smoothed Gagan's pillow. It was white, not scarlet, he told himself. He took in Gagan's ruined face. He wanted Gagan to wake, to be himself again, to push his hostel door open with his shoulder, clicking a lighter as he did so.

It had been the same with Ranga, watching over Ranga all those long years ago. It was unbearable. Who cared what the zamindars did? Who cared if sharecroppers hung themselves from the rafters, who cared if they sold their kidneys for money? Gagan had everything, why couldn't he simply be? He resented Gagan the waste he was laying on his life. He leaned forward and clasped Gagan's hand between his own. His palm was warm, but his fingertips were cold. He kissed Gagan's hand.

He stayed awhile, then got up and went back to his hostel room.

During the period of Gagan's convalescence, Krishna went to his classes. After his classes he went to the mess hall, ate dinner, and spent the rest of the evening sitting in a hard wooden chair by Gagan's hospital bed. All day long people came by, newspaper reporters, people from the protest, the many supporters he had gathered along the way. In all that time, Krishna waited to see who else would come for Gagan. One single family member, a man or woman bearing Gagan's demeanor, an identical nose, a sister with the same shape of his eyes. But no one came outside of the populace of Osmania.

A fortnight later, when Krishna arrived there with his books after dinner, he found Gagan sitting up in bed, spooning buttermilk rice into his mouth with his left hand. Krishna reached across Gagan and embraced him. "How are you feeling?"

"Good as new," Gagan said. His voice was thin, cracked. His face had a shrunken quality to it, an emptiness in his eyes. Still, he thumped Krishna's shoulder in a gesture familiar to both of them.

Within an hour, people poured into Gagan's hospital room. Someone shoved a garland of orange marigolds around his neck. Another added a jasmine-and-rose one. Krishna stood on the periphery, he wondered if Gagan had the chance to finish his rice.

There was a commotion outside the door and people fell quiet. Silently, they parted way for the new arrival.

It was Hasan Rizvi, the Hyderabad constituency MLA. People whispered in low voices, parted way for him. Two security guards in safari suits, armed with AKs, stayed outside the door. A few newspapermen with cameras filtered into the room alongside Rizvi. Shireen came to stand by Krishna.

Krishna was surprised to note that Rizvi was young, only in his forties. He had a trimmed black beard and wore a burgundy sherwani with a matching embroidered cap, a man who would not look out of place at a ghazal performance. Rizvi stood by Gagan's bed and shook his hand warmly, holding it between both his palms and not letting go for close to a minute that he talked in a low voice, in cultured Urdu, asking after Gagan's well-being, how he was recovering, his eyes full of genuine concern.

"Where's the doctor?" Hasan Rizvi said over his shoulder, still not letting go of Gagan's hands from between his own.

Someone went to fetch the doctor and the doctor appeared, hurriedly jamming an arm into his lab coat. It was a junior doctor, he looked like he had fallen asleep, perhaps after a long shift and had just been mercilessly jolted awake. The doctor was shoved into Rizvi's presence, whereupon he was subjected to rude questioning about "the patient's" well-being, as though the doctor himself was thoroughly responsible for Gagan's current state.

He and Shireen exchanged a look. They were, along with everyone else in the room, witness to an extraordinary performance by a seasoned politician. Whether it was Samuel, acting on behalf of the PDF, or the ruling party, or Rizvi, whose seat Gagan had all but announced he'd contest—*who* was responsible for the infiltrators at the protest or for Gagan's injuries seemed beside the point. Either could just as easily claim it was the other one; no one would be prosecuted, much less accused; Gagan certainly wouldn't.

The press corps photographers took more pictures. Then, after the doctor was allowed to leave, Rizvi handed Gagan a bouquet of pink roses.

Gagan received them gracefully, posed for the picture: Gagan propped up on pillows on the hospital bed, face torn up, and Rizvi next to him, their hands clasping.

"Gagan is never going to back down now," Shireen muttered. "Mark my words, Krishna. He won't rest until he wins Rizvi's seat."

Shortly afterwards, Gagan left Osmania for good. He left without ceremony, did not even stop by Krishna's room to say goodbye.

For Krishna, this meant that the campus suddenly became a lonely place. He saw less and less of the people he knew, declining any invitation that came his way. He never went to the Rooms now. More and more often, Samuel came by Krishna's hostel room, and Krishna went to great lengths to avoid him, hiding out in the library until late in the night until the library closed and he had no choice but to return.

Vijaya had stopped writing him. Now, it was more than a month since her last. He felt crushed by her rejection. He turned over in his mind all the reckless things he'd said to her. He regretted it all. Each evening he stopped by the watchman's room to see if anything came for him. Then he walked up the stairs slowly, slower if it was Wednesday.

By now, the hawthorn bushes that the watchman's wife had so hopefully planted had wilted. No one plucked the flowers but they had fallen off and never re-bloomed, the bit of soil there looked worn, forlorn. Every morning he'd see her trying to revive it, see what else she could plant there. She was a woman from the countryside, he could tell. She plowed, watered, sowed, but the soil reaped nothing. Perhaps she was promised a small bit of earth when she married, had imagined growing a patch of flowers there, some yellow marigolds she could use for prayers, or crossandras she could wear in her hair year-round.

Krishna went by the mess hall either at opening or closing, so he usually ate by himself. The rest of the time he was either in pure sciences, or the library. It occurred to him that in ten or twenty years he would come to resemble Dr. Ramaswamy exactly, he too would have a set of red spectacles hanging around his neck. All the same, Krishna avoided Dr. Ramaswamy.

When Dr. Ramaswamy broached the subject again, he said something hesitantly, noncommittally, and Dr. Ramaswamy insisted that he take his time to decide, said that it was a good omen that Gagan had left Osmania.

One evening, he was in his room when his eyes fell on the corner of an inland letter sticking out from underneath his cot. Its blue edge was so distinctive, he was surprised that he hadn't spotted it before. It must have been shoved underneath his door and spun all the way across, landing underneath the bed. He bent down and pulled it out, surprised to see that it was postmarked a month ago, from around the time he'd last written Vijaya.

She was going home to Irumi for the holidays, she said. But after she came back, she wanted him to come to Madras.

His heart pounded. His fingers were shaking. He picked up his pen and composed his reply. He said he was sorry, that he hadn't gotten her letter in time. He asked if he could come right away. *I'm coming to see you, Vijaya*, he wrote.

He'd just finished re-reading it when there was a knock on his door. He left the letter open on his desk and went to answer it. It was Gagan.

The last time he had seen Gagan was a week or two after he was discharged from the hospital, when he'd come to Osmania to drop his enrollment and collect his university transfer certificate.

"Krishna!" Gagan cried, throwing his arms around Krishna's shoulders and drawing him into a hug. "How have you been?" he said, not letting go of his shoulders, looking at his face sideways. Krishna grinned, feeling utter joy, elation, genuine pleasure. Before he could say much, "What is this!" Gagan said, striding past Krishna into his room.

Suddenly the room felt full, each inch of it smaller in Gagan's presence, like every room Gagan entered. "It is too neat. Like a lonely, lonely bachelor's loneliest home."

"It looks the same as usual."

"Hmm . . ." Gagan rubbed his chin, turned around to face him. "We have to go out. No. We are going out," he said, "to have some good fun."

He took Krishna by the shoulders and shook him.

Krishna did not like to drink. But he still followed Gagan downstairs. There was a motorbike parked there. A blood-red Royal Enfield Bullet 500. The name *Royal Enfield* was emblazed on the fuel tank in gold lettering. The effect of gold against scarlet was grand.

"Isn't it great?" Gagan said.

"It's yours?"

"Got it last week."

"Wow, Gagan. Did you take it to the temple yet?"

"What for?"

"What do you mean, what for?"

Gagan looked genuinely puzzled.

"It's tradition."

"What is?"

"Taking a new vehicle to the temple."

"Why?" Gagan shrugged.

"Well, they will read verses over it, break a coconut, dab some turmeric and some sandalwood . . ." Krishna went on, "so you will not have any accidents. Really Gagan, you don't know this?"

"I'll go tomorrow. Anyway, do you want to drive it?"

Krishna shook his head. "Don't know how."

"You don't know how to drive a bike?"

"No."

"I should teach you sometime."

Gagan swung his leg over the bike and kick-started it. The Royal Enfield roared into life, its deep metallic thrumming resounding across the darkened hostel blocks.

They passed Suri's tea shop. It was extremely cold. Osmania had so much greenery, so many trees growing against every available surface, large tracks of land covered in thickets so overgrown and undeveloped that students cut paths across it to traverse the campus quickly; trails recalled by memory, it was easily possible to get lost. Krishna shivered. The temperature rose once they exited campus.

Outside, the streets were deserted. It was half past eleven. A few shops were still open, but the sounds of rolling metal shutters and other lockup ceremonies could be heard every few feet. On the sidewalks, rows of men were settling down for the night, wrapping themselves in thin jute blankets, dousing wood fires.

Driving down the highway, yellow streetlamps flashed past. Krishna felt the wind in his hair. "What's even open this time of the day?" Krishna asked, leaning forwards, over Gagan's shoulder, speaking loudly enough to make sure his voice was heard over the noise of both roaring engine and rushing wind.

The drinking establishment did not have a name. It was a strange-looking place, a small room, semi-dark, large enough to fit six cramped tables, all except one in the leftmost corner occupied. It was a permit room at the back of a closed restaurant, a known place if one knew it already.

Despite this appearance, it served the very best, what Gagan wanted. Imported single malt scotch: a 1945 bottle of Glenfarclas. The excise duty on imported goods was one hundred percent, and Krishna could not imagine how much this would cost.

The servers all seemed to recognize Gagan, and Krishna observed that there was a little competition between the four servers there on who got to serve their table, Gagan's table.

"Cheers," Gagan said, as they clinked glasses. Krishna did not enjoy drinking. There was something about the scent of alcohol, of any kind, that made him somewhat fearful. It was hard for him to reason why, but he suspected it had to do with his mother, how she never allowed him or Ranga to go anywhere near the places in the village where men drank. This, despite the fact that her husband, their father, had been a toddy tapper by profession.

Krishna took a sip from his glass, a small, almost imperceptible sip. The scotch tickled the tip of his tongue, and all at once he had the sensation of pressing his tongue against toasted wood, against an exotic tree in a boggy place; howling winds; cold waters, everything crashing against a jagged coastline somewhere.

"Good, isn't it?" Gagan was smiling. He was watching Krishna.

Krishna nodded. He didn't think this drink belonged in the indelicate glasses of the permit room. Every time he took a sip, a small explosion of warmth and flavors occurred, spreading to his throat, pausing there, then repeating all over again. He couldn't quite place what came afterwards but it was wonderful. It warmed his ears, his face. He felt simultaneously cheerful and melancholy.

"My father was a toddy tapper," Krishna said suddenly. He felt like saying this. A specific thing he hadn't had reason to tell anyone before, not even Gagan.

If Gagan was surprised by this, he did not show it. It would be a thing he assumed made one fall in estimation, but Gagan simply looked at Krishna.

"He died when I was four."

"Do you remember him?" Gagan's voice was quiet, impassive.

"I don't know. But I know Ranga does. Wish I could." His brother never talked about their father, neither did his mother. "Sometimes I've heard them remembering, you know. Fond things: that he had this way of sitting in the doorway so he could watch my mother cook and Ranga play at the same time, then he'd duck outside, every once in a while, to take a pull from a beedi he kept burning on the porch."

Gagan looked away.

"And you know, Gagan?" Krishna continued. "She never dressed as a widow, my mother. She felt it better to not draw attention to that fact. We lived a little bit off from the main village, and it worked. If we lived with everyone else, at the center of it, with neighbors and such, it would have been different. No one lets you forget over there."

Although Gagan looked away, Krishna knew he was listening. "Then it mattered that she was favored in the Deshmukh household, people were afraid of the consequences of hurting her in any away. She was like a lesser family member to them. I was too. They paid for my education, you know, all of it. Mahendra Deshmukh did, Vijaya's father."

"Who is Vijaya?"

Krishna ignored the question and continued, "But I realize now that being a widow with small children would have made her so vulnerable. She didn't want her sons to think of her that way."

"She sounds like a wonderful woman," Gagan said.

Gagan's glass was empty already. He poured himself another.

"What about your father? What did he do?" Krishna asked in a voice so low that Gagan could have pretended not to have heard the question. He felt overwhelming curiosity, very aware of the fact that he was broaching a subject that Gagan did not discuss.

Gagan put his glass down. Then he picked it up again and swallowed slowly. He was silent for a long time. "It isn't some great mystery. People always think it is. It isn't."

Krishna waited.

"My father was an army colonel. I look exactly like him."

"Where is he now?"

"They are dead."

"You're an orphan then," Krishna said.

Something flitted across Gagan's face.

The words had escaped him. He didn't know how to explain what he really meant. "Sorry. Gagan. I didn't mean it like that. Sorry."

Gagan gave him a wry smile. "I am though," he said. "My parents and my sister are dead. I don't have any family, and I suppose that makes one an orphan."

Krishna said nothing. He hadn't expected this. A part of him wished he hadn't broached the subject at all; a part of him wanted to know more.

"They were driving up a ghat road in pouring rain," Gagan said, answering the question Krishna hadn't asked.

"You don't need to tell me. I'm sorry. I shouldn't have asked."

"The gardener told me afterwards that my sister insisted on the trip even though the weather was bad. She wanted to come see me, you see. She was eight. What did she know?"

Krishna leaned forward, put his glass down, picked it up again. He looked away, focused on a table on the far edge, where three men were bent forward, discussing something in low voices.

"My father should have known better," Gagan said. There was a startling bitterness in his voice.

"Don't say that," Krishna said. "You mustn't blame the dead. Much less your father. It's wrong."

"I can, though. I never really knew him, never really knew any of them, at all, to be honest."

"You don't really mean that."

"I didn't grow up at home, Krishna. I really never knew him, or them. They were all three of them people I visited over the holidays. Their deaths meant nothing to me."

Gagan told Krishna that he'd grown up at military school, on the southeastern edge of the country. The King George's Royal Indian Military School, set within a nature preserve, amid pine forests, at the feet of the Himalayas, home to deer and pheasant.

Krishna tried to imagine Gagan, miniature but much the same, walking towards the school's high-altitude cricket pitch; set atop a nearby hill, oval, green, surrounded by a ring of Himalayan cedar beyond whose drooping leaves lay blue skies, a precipitous drop into the valley beyond. He tried to imagine the grand buildings there; of red brick and gray stone; a dormitory beyond whose windows lay manicured grounds; a dining annex where dinner dress was required; an assembly hall where the national pledge was read out in a chorus of ardent, boyish voices. *India is my country, I am proud of its rich and varied heritage, I shall always strive to be worthy of it.* Gagan in a navy blazer, trudging through snow in winter, mud in monsoon, grass and daffodils in summer, his shirtsleeve snagging on the thorny vines of Gulmarg roses that grew around the physics laboratory. Gagan in his final minute of childhood, sitting in the library, his tie ironed like bond paper, watching raindrops pound against the windowpanes, striking so hard, so loud, that it sounded like pebbles, percussion. The principal had come himself. The ghat road was a helix, there were no guardrails, the visibility was poor, a bus had come from the opposite direction.

"My father was an excellent driver. He had known it was dangerous, that they shouldn't have come at all. But he never said no to her, my sister. She was eight. What did she know. He killed her. He killed my mother. They were both his responsibility."

"Don't say that," Krishna said. He'd said it loud enough that people from the nearby tables paused, looked over at them. He didn't know why he felt so angry. Then people looked away, returned to their own conversations. A few minutes of complete silence passed.

"But it would have been so simple to just say no," Gagan said, leaning forward, as though trying to bargain. "Why didn't he say no? It's his fault they are all dead."

"Gagan, please. Stop it," Krishna whispered. "You shouldn't blame him like that. It's wrong. Just don't."

"No?"

"No. You cannot. It's not his fault, it's—"

"Then whose fault is it? Mine?"

"That's not what I meant. You know that's not what I mean. I was going to say it's no one's fault."

"You know everything, don't you? The smart, intelligent, mature, level-headed Krishna, the villager, son of a toddy tapper."

For a while, they were silent. Then Gagan said, "Your glass is empty."

He picked up the bottle of Glenfarclas and refilled Krishna's glass, then his own. Despite it being only Krishna's second drink, the bottle was nearly empty. The tables around them were vacated, one after the other. Night was passing. Gagan motioned the server over and asked for another bottle. An inexplicable gulf had opened up between them.

"I'm sorry. About what I said." Gagan gave him an apologetic smile. "It wasn't supposed to go like this; today, I mean. Today was supposed to be about something else."

"About what?"

Gagan shrugged. "Never mind that now."

Two hours later, the same server sidled up to them again. It was closing time. Krishna assumed that it was a habit, because Gagan was expecting this. He told the server to get himself a glass and poured out a drink for him. This was what the scuffle between the servers had been about. The server held his glass like a tea glass, just between thumb and forefinger, and downed his drink in one go, smacked his lips. Gagan poured him another.

"Are you brothers?" the server asked, downing his second, even faster this time.

"What's that?" Gagan said.

"Are you both brothers?" the server repeated.

Gagan grinned. "Of course we are." He leaned over the table and clasped Krishna's shoulder. "Come here," he said, pulling him forward.

Jowl to jowl next to Krishna, Gagan said, "Can't you see the family resemblance?"

The server nodded vehemently, extending his glass to Gagan again. "Yes, yes, the same eyes. And nose also." Gagan gave him the rest of the unfinished bottle to take home.

They were the last ones to leave. The permit room had been kept open late only for them. Outside, the streets were abandoned, all the nearby shops were shuttered. There was no noise of traffic. It was well past three in the morning.

Krishna felt very tipsy. He'd had just enough to make the world move slower than usual. But Gagan was more than just tipsy. Krishna tried again, pressed him a few more times about what he'd meant earlier about this night being about something else. But Gagan only shrugged, waving a hand in his direction, telling him to not bother.

Walking back to the Bullet, Gagan scratched his nose and muttered something indistinct, sometimes quickly, sometimes slowly, stretching vowels as far as they would go. It could have been *insurrection*, but also could have been *resurrection* or *predilection*. It took him three tries to get the key into the ignition, but he kick-started the motorbike in a single try. Again, the Bullet thundered awake. He took a deep breath, squinted at the road ahead.

"Well," he said, pausing, rubbing a spot of stubble on his chin, "as your brother, I should teach you how to drive."

"Okay, Gagan."

He looked at Krishna. "Now, I mean." He got off the bike and held it by the handlebars. "Get on."

"Now? No."

"Get on. I'll teach you."

"I was joking. I can't drive now. I'll kill us both."

"Well I can't drive either. I'll put us both in a divider."

"No."

"Don't be scared, you'll be fine. Let's go."

They argued for a bit, and then, with great reluctance, Krishna got on.

Gagan sat behind him. "Now," he said, "hold down both the brake and the clutch. Put your foot on the gear pedal, and your hand around the accelerator. Ready?"

"Wait! What gear is this?"

"It's in neutral now. Hit it once, that's first gear. Hit it again, second. Then third. Then neutral again. Good. Every time you press it with your foot, it cycles into higher gear. But the bike will not move, remember this. It will only move when you let go of the clutch and the brake. One after the other. Slowly. Ready?"

Krishna said nothing. He felt terrified.

"Let go of the clutch, then the brake next. Slowly. Then turn up the accelerator."

The Bullet lurched forward, almost throwing them both off-balance. Then it stalled.

"Too fast," Gagan said. "You have to let go of the clutch slowly, very slowly. The engine dies otherwise. Try again."

The second time, Krishna was more successful. They reached the end of the street when Gagan told him to switch to second gear. The engine stalled again there, directly under a streetlight. "Too fast," Gagan said. He was slurring his words again. The moment of clarity that had come with his first instruction was quickly evaporating. When they started back again, Krishna was afraid to blink, he kept his attention on the road. His few drinks had vanished, his mind was clear and focused. It didn't take him very long to learn.

Once they reached the highway, Krishna learned to recognize the smooth click of the second gear, then the third gear. He began to enjoy the blank echo of wind rushing through his hair, cool air whistling past his ears and his ankles, the yellow beam of the Bullet's headlight, the warm thrum of its engine underneath.

"Don't fall asleep," he said over his shoulder. "Are you awake?"

There was no response.

"Gagan!" he said again.

Gagan was swaying.

Krishna felt him slump forwards, on him, quite clearly asleep. Krishna lifted one hand off the handlebars and threw it behind him, held Gagan by the shoulders. He slowed down, afraid that Gagan would fall off. He was finding it difficult to steer the Bullet with only one hand. He'd decelerated too quickly, the gear failed and the engine stalled once more.

Krishna rolled to a stop very carefully, bracing his feet against the road for several feet before they came to a stop.

There was a loud honk and Krishna looked up. A yellow sand lorry was coming towards them in the opposite direction. It was driving towards them in the wrong lane. Krishna cursed. This was unfortunate but unsurprising. So often at nighttime, lorry drivers, in order to avoid wasting petrol on U-turns, drove up the wrong lanes, honking people out of the way.

Still astride the stalled motorbike, still with only one hand on the handlebars, he walked it over to the edge of the highway, as far out of the lorry's way as possible. The bike began tipping over with Gagan's weight.

Krishna managed to balance it, pull it back up just in time. Gagan awoke. He opened his eyes.

"Is it morning?" he said in what Krishna guessed was annoyance, then got off the bike and walked directly into the street. Krishna let go of the bike and lunged forward. He heard the bike fall behind him with an almighty crash.

The lorry driver honked loudly as he passed them, blowing dust and small speckles of grainy sand into their eyes and nostrils. The lorry had passed within a hair's breadth of both him and Gagan.

Gagan turned around as if to thank Krishna, but his eyes fell on the upturned motorbike. The Bullet lay on its side; a sad, fallen horse, an ugly scratch, deep and silver, on the scarlet fuel tank.

"No!" Gagan exclaimed. Walking towards the bike, he knelt down by its side, placed his palms across its chassis as though it really was a fallen horse, and bowed his head. Then Gagan began singing, humming something, so poorly and so badly out of tune that it took Krishna some moments to realize that it was the national anthem.

Krishna felt bewildered, then he burst out laughing. Gagan looked up at him, a hurt expression on his face, but Krishna found it hard to stop laughing.

Still laughing, Krishna darted forward and pulled Gagan away from the Bullet. He was in danger of burning himself on the exhaust pipe.

In his hostel room, "Krishna, Krishna," Gagan said.

"Yes, Gagan?"

"I feel like eating double ka meetha. Will you get me some?"

"I could," Krishna replied, spreading out a thin blanket on the floor, wondering where he'd find that elaborate dessert at this time of the night.

"It was Preethi's favorite."

Gagan fell asleep on his cot before he looked up.

"Krishnanna! Krishnanna! Krishnanna!"

Again the same cheerful, childish, business-like voice. Three sharp raps in quick succession. Krishna struggled. He got off the floor and felt unsteady. He crossed over to his door and threw it open. He held onto the doorway just to have something to hold.

"You are opening late every day!" Chinna complained. "I'll take the money later." Before Krishna could react, Chinna was off, journeying down the corridor door by door.

Krishna's vision felt blurry, his stomach was burning. There was a breeze coming in, so he left the door open. Gagan was sleeping, his face was turned towards the wall, his arm dangled off the cot.

In the corridor Krishna ran into Samuel. "Krishna, I came by your room last night. Where were you?"

"Out," Krishna said, massaging his temples.

"I heard Gagan is here."

Krishna nodded.

"Drinking?" Samuel said with an expression of great distaste. Krishna said nothing, continued to massage his temples and waited for Samuel to leave.

By the time he came back from his bath, Gagan was awake. Krishna felt only slightly better, his stomach was still churning, and it felt as if the scotch that he had enjoyed so much the night before was oozing out of the pores of his skin.

Gagan was sitting on the bed. He was talking while running both hands through his hair at once. Chinna had come back, presumably to bring Gagan a fresh glass of tea. He was sitting on the chair by Krishna's desk, feet dangling off the floor, looking a little awkward at being treated like an adult. Chinna's face was animated, they were deep in conversation. Gagan nodded in his direction. "Do you know Krishna, this fellow here scored a ninety-five on the quarterlies. Ninety-five! First in class." Chinna grinned, looking utterly pleased with himself.

"Really?" Krishna said.

"And if that father of yours ever says anything about making you leave school, you come to me. Yes?"

"Yes, Gagananna," Chinna said, getting up, bobbing his head from side to side. Looking simply delighted at the prospect of telling on his father, he darted out with his empty tea crate.

"Want to go for some tiffin?" Krishna asked. He hoped breakfast would fix his stomach.

"I want to talk first. Before we go."

Krishna hung his wet towel on the open door and turned around. He took the seat that Chinna had vacated. "What?" he said, pulling on his shoes.

"What yesterday was supposed to be about. The reason I came here."

Krishna stopped tying his shoelaces and looked up.

"Since I've left Osmania, I've been thinking. Krishna, will you join me? Leave Osmania, that is. Help me with my campaign, be by my side. You are in the papers already. People know who you are."

Krishna shook his head, went back to tying his shoelaces. Then he let out a hollow laugh.

"I have never expressed any interest in getting involved in any of this. You know that already. I have no sides, except that I want to graduate from here, leave, get a job. That is all I want."

"Krishna, don't you see? You and I together, we can effect real change. Don't you care?"

He couldn't believe it. It was their old argument, resurfacing again.

"Why are you asking me? Someone who has any real interest; there are many, many people more qualified, more fit. Any one of those who'd shown up week after week to hear you talk. All those people at the hospital."

"I can't ask anyone else. There is no one I can—"

"Control?" Krishna said with dawning comprehension. "Control completely, Gagan? You need a puppet, you mean."

"For once in your life, Krishna, look up. Look up from your books, your wants, your needs—look at the world around you. Look at the needs of the world. Consider, for once, what is larger than you. Consider why you are on this earth. What is your purpose? Why are you alive? Do you think that is your purpose—to go to Bombay—run away, not think of who you leave behind as long as you get what you want? Is that your purpose in life?"

Gagan was looking at him without expression, without affection.

Krishna felt enraged. "How long have you known? Was this why you left without even saying goodbye?"

"When were you going to tell me?" Gagan said.

"I don't need your permission."

"I think you do. You can't leave, Krishna. I need you here."

"But you don't. What you want, Gagan, isn't really me. What you want is my story. Where I'm from. How I came to be here. What you want is my *lack* of privilege, that is the prize. What you want, Gagan, is how my presence next to you wrings into balance all the opportunities you've had in your life, how it equalizes us. Do you know what it is like to go hungry for days at a time because there is no other choice? Do you know what it is like to have your family give up everything just so you can be the survivor, to carry the weight of all their sacrifice, their expectations on your shoulders? What burden that is? What duty that is? Do you have any idea what it is that you are asking me to give up?"

Gagan frowned before saying, "Yes. So what?"

"So what?! This is all about power for you, Gagan. This has nothing to do with what you say you believe, nothing at all. This is all about power! And the only reason you think you can demand this of me is because of your power over me, because I wouldn't even be here without you. You think I owe you and therefore you own me."

"Don't imagine yourself as someone who isn't attracted to people with power. Of course this is about power Krishna. Don't be naive."

Krishna stared.

"Yes, this is about power. I do need you for your lack of privilege. I do think I can ask this of you, you do owe me. So what? Why does that mean it isn't about the things that I believe in? Why does that mean I don't love you like I would my own brother? Beliefs, Krishna, are irrelevant when it isn't accompanied by authority. Because nothing—no single belief, no single truth, or justice, or duty, or morality, or ethics; nothing, I mean *nothing* matters unless you have power. Real power. Power over others. People with power exist above everything. And they are the only ones who can effect any kind of change. This is the way of the world and there is no use pretending otherwise."

Gagan took a deep breath and lowered his voice. He tousled his hair as though annoyed with himself and stood up.

"I'm asking you. Give me your answer."

Krishna noticed that Gagan was standing in his doorway now. He would leave. Exit his life and never return.

All he had to do was say no, and his and Gagan's paths would diverge here. Some years later, maybe they'd write each other. Or maybe they wouldn't. And instead a passing thought would occur to him every once in a while; a wistfulness, a bittersweet regret in remembering a friend he had once known, owed, parted from what could have been lifelong. It would sadden him, surely, but it would also make sense. If Gagan left, there would be a life within his reach. A different one, an aspirational one, a marvelous one, away from the very things that he had spent his whole life attempting to leave behind.

One that could include Vijaya. To be with her, he would give up anything, even Gagan.

The words were nearly out of Krishna, when once again he had that feeling of separation from his surroundings. He felt unaware, of Gagan standing there, the hard wooden chair underneath him, the babble of voices up and down the corridor outside, the hostel, the university, the city beyond. He felt himself returning, and Gagan was still there, waiting for his answer.

Krishna took his time. He finished tying his shoelaces. Then he said no.

# THE SHORE TEMPLE

K rishna was arriving tomorrow.

It was to be a Sunday, and on Sundays everyone at the boarding house stayed in late. It would be noon by the time anyone ventured out, mostly for matinee shows at the Minerva, or at the Globe where the British council screened English-language films. Then for coffee and tiffin at one of the eateries on Pycrofts Road. It was a routine that Vijaya herself had with Asha. They ate medu vadas or dosas off plantain leaves at Kalinga Lodge, where the proprietress recognized them by sight, choosing for them the best out of the four or five tables spread out underneath the drumstick tree. She wanted to show Krishna all the places she loved, but in all these places there was a good chance of running into someone from either the boarding house or from Presidency. All these places she was to avoid.

He was staying for only a day and she didn't want him anywhere near the boarding house. If she were seen with Krishna—even if no one in Madras would know who he really was—it was not hard to imagine what her mother would do. What her uncle would do.

She asked Krishna to meet her at the bus shelter at six in the morning. Even if anyone saw her there, there wasn't anything suspicious about taking an early-morning bus, it was easily explained: a walk on the beach, a temple visit. Krishna had never seen the sea, and she wanted to be the one to show it to him.

Sunday morning broke dark and quiet. Vijaya awoke, checked her watch. It was early, only five. Still, she got out of bed and began dressing, there would be no point lying in bed now that she knew sleep wouldn't come. She dressed quietly, careful not to pick out clothes that were too nice, too pretty, too out of place on a leisurely Sunday. She settled on a navy-blue sari; cotton, unstarched, embroidered with pink rosebuds. She'd get there early.

Outside her room, the corridors were empty. The floor lights were still on, a smattering of dead moths around the bulbs. In Irumi, she remembered, the jeethas would collect the bugs and take them home, to be fried up and eaten as a snack. "Do well on your finals," her father had told her the day before she returned to Madras. "It is important that you do well. So that you may continue." What did he mean, she'd asked; why *wouldn't* she continue? "Well, things may be different after you come back," he said, "after your finals." This part—she realized with dawning comprehension, meant that he suspected a marriage alliance was making its way towards her, and he wasn't allowed to tell her; it was all her mother's maneuvering.

It made Vijaya realize that her mother's insistence on her presence at Tara's wedding was less because she was an important member of their family and more because it was an opportunity to let Vijaya be seen, by relatives who knew relatives who knew someone that was a good match for her. And there had been that one woman to whom her mother introduced her, adjusting the ruby necklace Vijaya had worn so it wasn't off-center. And her uncle had come too, shaken hands with the woman's son, a young man as tall as her uncle, a whole foot more than her, with a broad, open face and hair that sat in thick curls close to his head. Vijaya was studying economics at Presidency, her uncle told the man. He said it in a tone of such unvarnished pride that she'd scarcely paid any attention to how the woman was looking at her—the furtive assessing expression. Where's your father? her uncle had asked her in an undertone, as if it were an everyday thing, his talking to her. She seized the opportunity to look at him directly, all the lines in his face, the mustache streaked generously with white, the darkened, sunken skin beneath his eyes that was either the result of sleepless nights or the diabetes that Sree told her was uncontrollable except through insulin injections. Sree's doctor did them too. Vijaya didn't even remember the young man's name, smiling politely at her, introducing himself. Only that he was a surgeon. What kind? her uncle asked him, in that tone she was so familiar with; the ring of authority that lived within it like something caged.

And after she returned, Asha had shown up at her room. She waited at the door for Vijaya to gather her things so they could set out to college together. She didn't broach the subject of their last meeting; neither did Vijaya. Vijaya said she was cold, and Asha lent her a sweater—a cashmere one in the same shade of pink as the rosebuds on her sari, she realized now. Vijaya went back into her room, pulled it on, closed the door behind her once again. Downstairs, crossing the courtyard, slipping out of the gate, she did not run into anyone.

Despite the sweater, it was chilly out. By the time she reached the tree-lined street where the bus shelter was, it was half past five. Dawn was breaking, but the street was still foggy, mist was rising off treetops, and dew sat idly on the few blades of grass sprouting between the pavers in the sidewalk. Her teeth were chattering, her palms were clammy and cold, her nails nearly blue. She took a deep breath and began walking towards the bus shelter.

After a few paces, she came across a street sweeper holding a reed broom. They were just beginning and Vijaya became aware of the smooth chorus of reed brooms striking pavements and pathways on neighboring streets. The woman was expansive, she wore a khaki sweeper's vest, and as Vijaya passed, she stared at her, her eyes traversing the length of Vijaya's face, her sweater, and finally her shoes. Vijaya ignored her and kept walking.

She'd given Krishna the location of the bus stop and two landmarks nearby—the gum tree and the green bungalow a few yards from it. Walking up the street she found herself unable to remember if she'd told him to wait at the bus shelter or at the gum tree or outside the bungalow. She'd miss him, and his trip all that way from Hyderabad for her would go to waste because she was careless enough to forget where she'd told him to meet her. Maybe they'd circle each other in that vast city and she'd never get to see him.

She had the sudden impulse to turn around and leave. Maybe that would be for the best; she could go back to the boarding house and go back to bed and pretend none of it happened, it would be so easy, so simple and so uncomplicated. She stopped walking a little ways from the gum tree because Krishna was already there, waiting for her. It took her breath.

At the fair, their meeting had been so unexpected, she hadn't the chance to see him clearly. But now she could. Krishna was sitting on a large boulder underneath the gum tree, elbows resting on his knees. He had a narrow frame, with long and gangly legs that were out of proportion with the rest of his body. He had the same handsome face he'd possessed as a child; the same almond-shaped eyes, the same toffee-colored skin, black hair that fell across his forehead in waves. He'd dressed carefully, she noticed, in pressed trousers, a starched blue shirt, polished leather shoes. If there was one thing that had remained absolute, unchanged from when they were children, it wasn't the way he looked or the way he kept his clothes so neat. It was the way his eyes were on the fallen leaves of the gum tree, littered all around him. He was looking at them as though the chance patterns the yellow leaves made against the damp earth were meant to be divined, studied, pondered over with utmost concentration, the way he used to study the leaves of the banyan outside her window.

She wondered what would happen if she did turn around and leave. Surely, he would wait for her, an hour, a day. Then he'd leave. There it was, an easy universe within her grasp, if and only if she turned around and walked away unnoticed. Everything Asha said to her was resounding in her ears. She hadn't allowed herself to think of it in the same way she hadn't allowed herself to think of the day she'd met him at the fair; held the lightness as far from her for as long as possible. Most of all, what Asha said about the purpose of Krishna's visit here. *Why else would he come? What other reason could he have? Worse, Vijaya, because you will be happy. Do you want to marry him?* No. It was absurd—the possibility of happiness was absurd. *Things will be different the next time you come home.* What her father wasn't allowed to say. Her mother adjusting her ruby necklace. Her uncle shaking hands with the curly-haired surgeon, all that pride in his voice when he introduced her, how she longed for corrections in her relationship with her uncle. That was reality, a future moving towards her so unalterably that it never occurred to her to step out of its way. Then why had she asked Krishna to come?

When she reached him, she touched his shoulder. Krishna stood up. He said her name.

And there it was, the reason she'd asked him to come—that ardent expression that appeared on his face, now, then, and on every day of their lives they'd crossed paths with each other. She'd known, ever since he told her that Ranga made him promise never to return to Irumi, that she'd never see him again. She'd wanted the chance to hold a moment with him in both hands, like a thing alive, warm and golden like the almonds they buried in the earth behind the stepwell. To lie back, her hands splayed, her eyes closed, as if she could hear the tree growing.

The shore temple was a place Vijaya chose for its distance from the boarding house, and because it was where tourists went, not locals. Except for a little gray-haired woman with a wicker basket full of chickens in her lap, the bus was empty. Vijaya could hear the birds ruffling their feathers whenever the bus went over a bumpy patch in the road, the rattle of the windowpanes, the drum-drumming of the engine underfoot. The woman with the chickens was falling asleep with the basket in her lap. Krishna looked nervous, but also delighted. He turned to look at the chickens in the basket whenever they clucked. The sky was so clear and so powdery that she felt as though she could reach out and pick up a fistful of it.

Her heart was beating so fast that she felt out of breath. A little jolt passed through her every time she realized that the tall, handsome stranger on the bus next to her was Krishna. Now and then she felt his eyes on her face. She could hear his breath; air going in and out of his lungs forcefully, stridently, like a sleeping child's. She felt it impossible to stop listening to him breathe.

She took off Asha's sweater, folded it and laid it in her lap just to have something to look at, to fiddle with.

She could see that she was wrong—although his face was the same, there was something else. He was so much older now; older in the way he looked out of the window, at the sheets of sea that appeared between buildings and shops, bracing himself by holding the rail when the bus took a sharp turn. Such adultness, unlike her, because Krishna had lived most of his life in a world that was so much bigger than hers. An unsheltered life that had allowed him to start over, hardening him in ways hers hadn't.

Krishna turned to meet her gaze. His hand was open in his lap. On the surreal public bus with no one, while the chickens clucked and the windowpanes rattled, he moved his hand, so that his thumb rested on her wrist. As if he was holding back the urge to touch her, yet also attempting to make sure that she was real. She slipped her hand into his. She could feel all the grooves in his palm, the ones bisecting his fingers, the ones cutting across the base of his wrist. His thumb resting on her wrist. She shifted her hand slightly so their palms matched up. He tightened his grip. For a moment, they simply looked at each other in disbelief. Then he smiled. Such pleasure, such unvarnished delight. When was the last time she saw anyone smile at her like that?

She noticed his teeth. The ones that sat on either sides of his incisors jutted out slightly. Canines? Was that what they were called? His canines turned outwards at an angle, away from the neat row of the rest of his upper teeth. There was something that the faulty teeth added to his smile; it made it seem juvenile, innocent, sweet. Guileless. That's what it was. His smile was guileless. When he kissed her, his breath against her lips was so familiar, it was almost recognizable.

When the bus pulled into the stop, they were the only ones that got off. She and Krishna watched the bus pull away, watched it round the corner and disappear, still holding hands.

Across the street was the shore temple. It was a large complex made entirely of stone. Ornately carved, multistoried, pyramidal structures resting atop the deity's shrines—there were two temples: a larger one, and a small one tucked right next to it. At least sixty feet tall, the temples stood right on the shore, almost in the sand, solidly gray against the blue waters of the Bay of Bengal. It was a strange and haunting sight, the presence of such opulent structures on a sandy beach seemed unintentional, accidental, as though a giant hand hauled them out of the very earth at a moment's notice. The water was rough, agitated, loud, wave after wave crashing against the shoreline, slapping the stone with so much violence it was as if the sea held a grudge. It was surrounded—littered—it seemed, by the ruins of a boundary wall, the ruins of a stepped water tank, the ruins of a sacrificial altar.

They crossed the street. There was a battered plaque at the entrance. The paint on it was peeling, and here and there letters were missing. They stopped to read.

SHORE TEMPLE. BUILT BY THE PALLAVA KING NARASIMHAVAR-MAN-II (RAJASIMHA) (AD 700–728). CARVED OUT OF BEDROCK, THE SHORE TEMPLE IS BEING AFFECTED BY THE ROUGH SEA AND SALT-LADEN WINDS. ARCHEOLOGICAL SURVEY OF INDIA IS UNDERTAKING CONSTRUCTION OF A GROYNE WALL TO CHECK THIS EFFECT.

NO PICNICKING. RESPECT INDIA'S HERITAGE.

A number of tourists were milling about the entrance. There was a short queue leading up to the ticket booth. She and Krishna joined it. They were standing right behind a small family. The father was carrying his son on his shoulders, the mother held a smaller baby in her arms. She was looking at the baby's soft hair when the mother turned to look at her and Krishna. From the woman's gawking, Vijaya knew that she was mistaking her and Krishna for newlyweds. Vijaya didn't let go of Krishna's hand. How pleasurable it felt to imagine a stranger's mistake.

The family collected their tickets and moved away. Krishna withdrew his wallet and asked for two tickets, handing over a five-rupee note before she had a chance to protest. Written in Tamil and English, the board above the ticket counter said: MANAGED BY THE ARCHEOLOGICAL SURVEY OF INDIA. ENTRANCE FEES COMPULSORY. FOR INDIANS—2 RUPEES. FOR FOREIGNERS—10 RUPEES.

Krishna collected their tickets, folded them neatly in half and slipped them into his shirt pocket.

Entering the temple complex, they paused. Close up, the temples were an even more extraordinary sight. Massive, wonderous. She could make out that once upon a time, they had been intricately carved; in the rising stone columns sat the impressions of flower vines, grand chariots, musical instruments, perfectly scaled figures of elephants and dancers. In the reliefs across the base sat the women, the soldiers, the calves, the cavalry, the horsemen.

But they were only impressions. Time had robbed it of all rich detail. The salt and the sea air had been at work, sanding down the surface, patiently, little by little each passing day for the twelve hundred years the two temples had been standing. It saddened her that time had passed. And the people who'd built this grand thing, brought their prayers there, worshipped their gods there, were all gone.

Brushing past them, someone bumped her shoulder. "Watch it," Krishna said indignantly. It was a guide, following the family that had been ahead of them in the ticket line. Another guide materialized in front of them. He was short, polite. A neat line of vermillion sat on his forehead.

"Look at the Chinese people here," he said, pointing to a particular section in the stone pillars, where figures of men stood in rows, horses by their sides, "and the Arabs too. All these traders used to come here once upon a time to sell horses. Can you imagine?" he asked with such genuine amazement on his face that Vijaya could have believed he was speaking of it for the very first time.

Then the guide muttered in a low voice, "Sir—madam—I can take you inside the temples. You aren't allowed to enter, of course. Strictly speaking, the ASI won't let tourists in on account of damage and all that stuff, but I know the security fellow, I can manage it." He held up his hand, his fingers bent, and made a cutting motion.

"No," Krishna said, waving politely, glancing at her to confirm.

The guide caught this exchange. Now he began addressing only Vijaya. "Madam—how about the dance pavilion in the far end? Look over there—"

"No," she said noncommittally, but looking in the direction the guide was pointing. It was a raised pavilion a short distance from the main temples. It was in a state of complete disarray, surrounded by a pell-mell jumble of fallen pillars and damaged reliefs of various animals and various gods, all stuck with orange labels and string tags.

"That doesn't look like a dance pavilion," Krishna countered. "It doesn't look like anything at all."

The family was haggling nearby. "Too much!" the father proclaimed, waving away the other guide; who also didn't give up, and was trailing them, cooing at the baby on the mother's hip.

She and Krishna stepped around him, but their guide didn't give up. He followed them, keeping up with their pace. "But that's where the queen used to perform!" he insisted, latching on Krishna's response; anything but the word *no* seemed to excite him. "She performed only for the members of the royal family, you see. I'll show you."

They tried to step around him again, but he blocked their path, grinning good-naturedly.

Vijaya laughed. The guide's manner was so easygoing and self-aware that he seemed to expect, even want her to laugh at him, then hire him. It made Vijaya feel as though she and Krishna were nothing but tourists here, like everyone else. The anonymity was wonderful. Krishna grinned at her, her laughter seemed to please him. "What do you think?" he asked her, as though it was a foregone conclusion. "Should we hire him?"

Vijaya made a polite, noncommittal sound that may have sounded like assent.

"Yes, of course. Madam will like it," the guide interjected.

In the end, they found themselves walking towards the dance pavilion, the guide leading the way. Krishna took her hand again. She threaded her fingers through his. It was so easy.

The pavilion was weathered. A large crack ran across its face, nearly severing it into two, the halves seemingly held up by bits of sand and seagrass. Its back was to the sea, as if the sea were a spectacular stage background. It did not seem to attract any other visitors, it turned out. They were the only ones there.

The guide bent low and showed them little hooks, carved into the stone, running across the base. The sea was so loud that the guide had to raise his voice to be heard. "Meant to tie up the cloth screens, you see," he shouted, "so that no common man may look at the queen while she danced. It is said that she was of prodigious skill in Bharatanatyam, and

she performed to mark the beginning of the Tamil month of Margazhi."
He jabbed a finger toward the sky, pointing at an imaginary full moon.

Vijaya wondered if they were being taken in. What proof was there
that this was even used as a dance pavilion? Let alone the specific recital
that the queen supposedly performed. This cracked, grassy thing could
have been anything. What was history. What was memory.

After fifteen minutes or so, the guide left them, but only after repeating
his offer of allowing them to go into the temples. They declined. They saw
the other guide going inside the bigger temple, the one dedicated to Shiva,
with the family, while the security guard pretended not to see them.

Vijaya moved towards the pavilion and sat on its edge. The stone was
cold. She could feel it through the fabric of her sari.

A couple of college girls were walking towards them, their arms were
linked. The girls stopped at the pavilion. "What do you think this is?"
Vijaya overheard one of them say. The other shrugged. "Maybe a dining
hall for the poor? Hard to say. It's too ruined."

"Vijaya, where's your sweater?" Krishna said.

Then she remembered. She'd left it on the bus. She touched her forehead with her fingertips. "I forgot it on the bus!" she said. "And it was
Asha's—my friend's."

Krishna grimaced, sitting down next to her. "There's no chance of
getting it back. Will she be upset?"

If Asha knew where she was, whom she was with, it wasn't the loss
of the sweater that would upset her. "I'll get Asha a new one," she said,
lowering her hand.

"Why did you want a guide?"

She turned to look at him, met his eyes. How impossibly black they
were, she'd quite forgotten. "I didn't," she said.

Krishna laughed. "I didn't either."

She shrugged. "I don't know. I thought you might want to see something worthwhile in Madras—that's why I chose this place, I'd never
seen it before either, I thought you'd like it. You've never seen the sea."

"Why would I want a guide when I have only a day to spend with you?
I didn't come here to sightsee, Vijaya."

All of a sudden, she felt melancholic. The sun was high and bright. In no time at all, he was going to ask her. Yet again, she'd cause him pain. Yet again, she'd been selfish, ungrateful, cruel, all the things that her mother said she was.

"You look upset," Krishna said. "What did I say?"

He looked puzzled. He held her gaze. She looked away.

"Well," he said, "at least someone made money." He gestured in the direction the guide had gone; he was following a group of older women now. "Good on him."

She eased her hand out of his grip. She pulled up her feet and wrapped her arms around herself.

Krishna was watching her. He said, "It is strange, isn't it? How everything feels utterly familiar. To be near you"—he closed his fingers around hers—"to touch your skin?" He touched her cheek. "Everything. Even what you smell like, what your skin smells like, when you are close enough, what your breath smells like, like on the bus, like now." He kissed her again, slowly this time. He held her palm to his chest. "See? So utterly familiar."

She muttered, "It's absurd."

"Are you cold?" he said. "You're shivering."

"What do you think the queen might have looked like?" she said, withdrawing her hand again. She looked at the sea. "Performing exactly here, where we are sitting right now, at this time of year?"

She wondered if the commoners could see a shadow of the queen; her figure moving behind the cloth screens, hear her feet slapping against the stone, the music of the flute, the cymbals, the percussion of the mridangam, the hands of the musician moving across the veena's twenty-four frets. The note softly falling, gliding, as she pauses, shifting her stance. She tried to imagine the pavilion as it was a thousand years ago, untouched by the sea air, unsoiled by time. Clean. Perfect. Each detail vivid and dramatic. A roof over the pavilion, a crowd around it. The queen—standing there, dressed in her red-and-gold outfit, adjusting the heavy bronze anklets at her feet, walking across the pavilion, and with each step she took, her anklets chiming, the sea tossing.

"You can see it, can't you?" Krishna said. "You know exactly what she'd look like. What the music sounded like. You're *seeing* it. Aren't you?"

"How can you know that?"

"And if I asked you to make something up, you'd be able to. Right this minute. Won't you?"

"Make something up?"

"Some tale. You used to make them up all the time. Instantly. You had this gift—remember that story you had with the king and the horse that talks? How did it end again?"

He added, "Vijaya, are you cold? Tell me. Maybe there is a place we could buy you a shawl?" He stood up, looked towards the bus stop. Scanned the street.

"I don't remember," she said.

"What don't you remember?" He looked away from the bus stop.

"I don't remember it. Anything. The story."

"How can you not remember? You must. Sree must, wouldn't she?"

"I don't know."

He seemed to hesitate, and she knew what he was going to ask her next. The last time they'd seen it together. "Do you still have the kaleidoscope?"

The college girls came around again, and one of them looked at her curiously. What was on her face, she wondered, that they'd avert their gazes, walk away. What did strangers do when they came across a grown woman looking frightened, ashamed, in a ruined, beautiful place?

"Do you think of Ranga?" she said.

A shadow crossed Krishna's face. He looked away, then back at her.

"Sometimes," he said, sitting down beside her again. His eyes were on her, but she didn't turn to face him, she looked at the sea. "By accident, really. When I read a piece on the Naxalites in the newspaper, for example. But that's how I am. I learned to survive that way. And I think I can live without ever looking back. Never thinking about what has passed, most of the time. Do you think that makes me a terrible person?"

"It is because of me, isn't it?" she said.

She'd destroyed an essential piece of him. This thing he was saying, about never looking back, was her fault. Her doing. What she had done to his sense of family. What she had done to her own family, to Sree? To Ranga? She was the source of everyone's pain, everyone's suffering.

Ranga had been right, hadn't he? Even all those years ago, he told her to leave Krishna alone. Ranga was the one who truly loved Krishna, not her.

"Vijaya," Krishna said. He touched her cheek, gently turned her face towards him, as though he could see into her mind, hear her thoughts. "It wasn't your fault."

"But it was."

"Vijaya, let me ask you: Suppose, *I* said no. Suppose, *I* said that it was too dangerous and *I* refused to come. Would you and Sree have gone by yourselves? Think. Would you?"

She didn't say anything.

"No. You wouldn't. Then, suppose I did agree, but I didn't bring Ranga, would we have found the ravine by ourselves?

"No. We'd have stayed at the stepwell, taken turns holding the gun, pretended to find the tiger, and then we'd have gone home. *Or*, we'd have gone into the jungle and would have turned around at the sight of the first rattlesnake skin. It would have terrified us. *Or*, we'd have gotten lost, but closer to the path and we'd have been found soon enough, scared, but safe and well.

"In each and every scenario, Vijaya, it was my decision that mattered. Not yours. It was my decision that changed the course of all our lives. Don't you see that? You and Sree were never allowed to leave the gadi. How would you know what was dangerous, what wasn't? I should have known. I *did* know. But I wanted to amaze you, Vijaya. I wanted to be the one you continued to look at with amazement. I couldn't bear the thought of you never coming to see me again. I thought that would happen if I said no. I'm to blame."

Krishna took a deep breath.

"Do you see it now? Do you see how long you have been carrying this burden as if it were yours alone to bear? It isn't, it's mine to bear, Vijaya. But I got to leave, I got to start again, and I have this inhuman ability, to live without looking back that has nothing to do with you. But you? You were the one who had to remain. To stay; watch Ranga suffer, watch Sree suffer.

"Ranga had me, as a reason and meaning for his sacrifice. He will do anything for me, and he accepted the things that came his way because it would benefit me. I know what it is like to see someone you love in pain, to suffer, on your account, without the ability to bear it away from them. I only had to do it for months, looking after Ranga, and you had to do it all your life. You are still doing it. And I left you."

Krishna's voice cracked, he leaned over and wiped his eyes.

"And through all this, you have remained a whole person, Vijaya. A whole person who still knows what kindness means, what forgiveness means, what compassion means. You can still see the beauty in everything. Do you know how extraordinary that is? You are extraordinary, Vijaya. And all my life, I've been in love with you. Even when I didn't know what that meant, what love meant. And I've come here today for one thing only. To ask you to marry me. This is my fate, Vijaya. To return, to arrive at a shore—your shore."

He stood up. When she didn't resist, he pulled her up to her feet and drew her close.

She'd forgotten, how it felt to be held by someone. How their body pressed up against hers, how it made her heart beat slower, how it made her want to shut her eyes, the comfort, the luxury of it. She could smell the iron on his clothes, the hot skin on his neck against her forehead, the clasp of his wristwatch against her waist, all of it so utterly comforting. "Vijaya," he said, "look at me." When she did, it was as though they could hear the silver anklets chime through the years, feel the kaleidoscope turn in their hands, and there Vijaya was, watching Krishna pull out strand after strand of saffron from the milk cakes she'd stolen for him. Krishna, gathering the strands and putting them all in his mouth. The bite marks on the cakes. "What does it taste like?" Krishna, perplexed, wanting to describe. "Like blood." And there they were again, that last time at the stepwell, Krishna holding Vijaya close, like now, like then, hearing her grief echoing inside her. How he alone could make it stop echoing. Make it so that she was allowed to possess a form of herself, a whole, unfractured self that no one else remembered. How he alone made her familiar, almost recognizable, to herself.

# KATYA OPENS THE
# VELVET BOX

———◆———

The postman arrived.

Katya collected the mail. But before she went back inside the gadi, she heard her name being called, with that bent, stretched-out *e* before it; meaning it was one of the jeethas who tended the animal sheds. Yadaiah, she guessed when he called again. He must have heard the postman's bell and known she was out of doors, being the only one who was permitted to collect the mail.

She went in the direction of the sheds, separating out Mahendra Deshmukh's mail as she went. Another stack for dora. Then there were two other letters: one for Sree, from Tara. The other for Saroja-dorasani— this one wasn't inland, it was stamped mail. Formally addressed, and not from someone who wrote them frequently. It was from the woman who ran Vijaya's boarding house. Stepping through the gate that went into the sheds, she slit the letter open.

"Can you stay with the foal?" Yadaiah said.

"Why?" she said. When he didn't answer, she looked up.

Yadaiah looked worried. "Don't tell dora yet," he said, "but it is a little sleepy. I'm going to get it some jaggery. Maybe it bit on something it mustn't. I haven't left its side, I swear."

She looked beyond him. The old stables were all empty except for the little black foal. From here, she couldn't see it. "If it groans, put your fingers in its mouth," Yadaiah said. No one but him was allowed to touch the foal. "Rub its tongue down." He mimed the motion as he left.

Ever since the foal was brought into the sheds, Katya hadn't wanted to come here at all, much less be left alone with it. Now she went, entered the stable. She put the stack of letters on the ground and knelt in front of the foal. It was in discomfort, she could see. It raised its head to look at her, then lay back down. How black it was. How delicate and shiny its belly was, rising and falling with every rapid breath.

It was curious. All the time she used to go into the sheds before, ever since she was little. In odd hours too, without meaning or reason—in the middle of the day on sultry afternoons, or deep into the night, when the whole family was sleeping. She'd bring a jute mat, lay it in the middle of the hay pile and sleep there, listening to the goats and the chickens and the cows. On those mornings, when Sree asked her why she smelled like hay, she'd say she didn't know. But now, since the new foal arrived, she'd avoided the place. Surendra-dora had brought it soon after they'd heard from the doctor's family—that boy they were all trying to get for Vijaya. They had said yes, and they wanted to arrange a proper meeting between the families when Vijaya came home after her exams.

"Why the foal?" Mahendra-dora had asked. There hadn't been a horse at the gadi in years. Who rides horses anymore? It's a nuisance. Instead of answering his brother, he'd said to Katya, "Make sure Yadaiah is giving it the alfalfa." And every moment he encountered Katya, he made her go to the sheds, to bring him a full report on the foal's well-being.

It wasn't his old passion for horses, Katya knew. No. The foal was a way to ensure that Vijaya returned to Irumi all the time, even though she'd be married to someone who lived in the city, and whatever else her life included that would take her as far as possible from Irumi. Surendra Deshmukh couldn't bear it, she knew. He'd wanted a solid, living reason for Vijaya to return constantly. He was a stubborn, unyielding man who'd go to all these great lengths to love Vijaya from afar in ways that no one in the family had ever loved her.

She averted her eyes from the foal. She gathered the letters and sat back, pulling up her feet and leaning against the wall. She drew the pages out from the envelope.

She read most of Saroja-dorasani's letters out loud to her. She knew how to read, which was unusual, and she was proud of this. It was Mahendra Deshmukh himself who'd taught her; something that wasn't seen as a privilege; it wasn't like she was sent to school. But to her, it *was*, because neither Vijaya, nor even Sree, had been taught by him. The trick was to read the letter beforehand, instead of stumbling on unfamiliar words and betraying herself. She'd pause, sound out the consonants in a low voice. It was pleasure, or something like pride—the expression she'd note on dorasani's face when she read briskly.

Katya read the warden's letter, quickly once, slowly a second time.

Though the language was simple, the words were more than usually complicated. It was diplomatic, respectful, even a little fearful. It was a coded letter; everything seemed to echo with hidden meaning, unexpected turns at the ends of sentences. A lot of repetition, and insistence, that this was in no way an accusation. That, of course, there must be a valid explanation as to why Vijaya was seen with someone at a tourist site outside Madras city, a place called the Shore Temple.

There were no direct accusations—the woman seemed keen to insist on this—but merely the wish to prove diligence: she'd *never* presume to say that the man Vijaya was seen with, by friends of a girl called Deepthi who was Vijaya's classmate, wasn't someone known to them already. He was tall, and they seemed to be "familiar" with each other. There was one last thing the warden wrote. Katya grasped the meaning of the sentence, underneath all the politely insisting language. It meant that she feared Vijaya could be planning on running away, likely with the person she was seen with, likely after her finals. *But*, the letter went on to insist, *never* would such an accusation be made against someone who bore the Deshmukh family name.

Instantly, Katya knew who it was. Krishna. Pichamma's other son. All these long years, and they still wouldn't leave each other alone.

Outside the stables, she heard voices. She was so startled she dropped the pages.

Coarse language. Inane conversation. Mirth. Katya stayed still, made sure she was well hidden behind the stable walls. The foal seemed to be asleep. She knew who these people outside were. Some of them were murderers. Thieves. Former dacoits. Hired criminals, all of them. She'd helped carry the crates of grain alcohol they were given every three days. They were a new addition to the gadi: paid to protect, stand guard. Goondas—Saroja-dorasani called them. But no amount of needling disapproval could convince her husband or her brother-in-law to dismiss them, not even on festival days. The least she got was that they weren't allowed to step across the threshold—any threshold. They ate outside too. And even in daylight Katya was never to allow any of them to catch a proper glimpse of her, much less find herself alone with them, like now. "You are too beautiful, Katya," Saroja-dorasani said. As if that was what made her vulnerable.

Katya waited until the men left, and made her way back to the gadi. She didn't dare turn around to look at the foal again.

She went into the library, placed the stack for Mahendra Deshmukh on his desk, on his right-hand side, under the paperweight, the way he liked it. The larger stack for Surendra Deshmukh she left on the teapoy. He came here in the evenings to talk to his brother.

She checked to make sure there was no one outside the library doors, which were ajar. Whatever she was allowed, above and beyond what the vetti or the jeethas were allowed, she knew she wasn't supposed to close the library doors while alone inside. She read the warden's letter a third time.

"Katya!"

It was Saroja-dorasani, calling her from upstairs.

Saroja clutched the sides of her temples and shut her eyes. "Katya!" she called again.

"Coming, dorasani," she heard Katya call back.

Tomorrow it was Diwali, and even though they didn't celebrate as grandly as they used to in the old days, Saroja still wanted to get the gadi ready as if they did. The goldsmith had just sent over the velvet boxes, and she'd been looking over them. One by one, she shut the boxes. She'd begun acquiring jewelry for Vijaya's wedding because—with her impending return home—the day would be nearly upon them.

His name was Ravindra. He was a doctor, a house surgeon at Gandhi Medical in Hyderabad. He was an only child too, and he was so even-tempered, good-natured, good-looking, intelligent. What else could one want? In fact, her heart was so set on Ravindra, she wanted to make sure it all happened quickly, before anyone else had the opportunity to snatch him up. She'd wanted to arrange for Ravindra and his family to see Vijaya when she was home for Tara's wedding; that was the original reason she insisted on Vijaya not staying in Madras. But Mahendra had said no, let her finish the year. But she'd still managed a brief meeting, and because of that the whole thing was all but guaranteed. And when Vijaya came home, they'd settle everything. Vijaya would return to Madras—if she did, that would be up to Ravindra—a married woman. Not her problem.

Ravindra and his family wanted a proper visit, but all that was a for-mality, of course; who would ever refuse to forge a relationship with them? They'd talk over the dowry: All the jewelry she already had ready; wet land; dry land, at least twenty kilograms of silver—platters, bowls, plates, tableware. Cash amounts that would be negotiated between just the men. But, before all that, before they arrived to see Vijaya, the house had to be re-painted, the banisters stripped and re-varnished, the bro-ken pieces of the Chettinad tile replaced, re-grouted, the fountain in the vaakili cleaned. The Fiats had to be parked out front. Because a wedding was a symbol. Everyone understood that.

She went out of the room and stood in the gallery. They were burning sambrani in the courtyard below. The resin smoked, a thick cloud of it, rich, fragrant, billowed up, reaching her on the floor above. It smelled sweet, like wood, balsam, musk. It perfumed the gadi. The fragrance would linger on the walls for weeks. Sambrani was burned during festi-vals, weddings, during births. It was a good luck. Good energy. Then she felt something else. What was it? That burning.

Rage. That was what it was. Rage, but an extinguished version of it, like a fire that was dampened by rain, wet smoke rising. A memory. Memories got dulled by time, but one only had to have the right trig-ger—a smell, a sound, and it would all come rushing right back. They'd burned sambrani in the house when Vijaya was born. They'd burned it every single morning for three months. They burned it in the courtyard, in the nursery where she tilted her head over the brass smoker so that it would perfume her hair.

Katya was coming up the stairs. Katya had the look of youth. That phase when youth itself was the source of beauty. She was older than Vijaya by a year. Saroja stepped back into her room. She needed a few clean breaths. Escape the smell that was everywhere.

A wedding was a symbol. This is what her own father had told her, when she asked why Lachi was being sent with her. A wedding is a symbol darling, he said, and so there will be an adabapa sent with you. Lachi is part of the dowry. An adabapa, Lachi was likely one of the very last bound to that practice.

She hadn't wanted Lachi to come with her. But Lachi did, because a wedding was a symbol. So it was Lachi who'd dressed her in the beginning months of her marriage, her life in Irumi. Lachi was the one who burned the sambrani in her room, perfumed her hair.

Lachi was the one who'd fallen pregnant, after scarcely a month in Irumi.

"How much did my father buy you for?" she'd asked Lachi once. She asked this one morning, lying in bed, a novel open in front of her. She let her eyes go over Lachi's figure, the large round belly that everyone pretended not to notice. She was only a few weeks away from giving birth, they told her.

Rage. That was what was coming on now. Rage that began at the base of her spine, and curled upwards, like a snake, invading her body, her mind, until that was all she could feel.

She lay down on her bed, turned to her side and shut her eyes.

Katya knocked and came in.

Kind Katya, loyal Katya, beautiful Katya. It was true. Katya was beautiful. Even if she did not apply the low standards set aside for housemaids and servants, she was objectively beautiful. Her skin was pale, her hair thick and dark. Even the bad clothes and the dirt in her fingernails seemed to not subtract enough. Just like Lachi. Katya was wearing Vijaya's old clothes, just like Lachi used to wear hers. A faded violet skirt, a pink blouse. But unlike Katya, Lachi used to mend them, darning rips, patching tears discreetly, skillfully. The other maids asked her if Lachi was being given new clothes, that's how well Lachi used to mend old clothes.

It amused her in the beginning, like the vanity of a small child preening in front of a mirror in her mother's jewelry. She encouraged it even. She was the young, beautiful new bride. A chinna dorasani. Lachi was the adabapa. The slave.

"Two rupees, dorasani," Lachi replied, her voice all quiet, her neck bent, her eyes on her toes, "that was what they got me for. And a kunche full of rice for my father."

She'd summoned the trap cart that very day. An order she'd made from bed. Put her in it. Send her back where she came from. Where did she come from? Some nameless hamlet where she'd lived as a child. Did she even know the name? The cart driver had stared in the direction of the window, seeming to be struggling with the order. She could read his thoughts. A woman about to give birth mustn't sit in a trap cart, shaken about on a journey that would last weeks, through rough lands, on a route famed for two things: banyan trees and dacoits. All this seemed to be posed to her, in the look of the cart driver, the way he looked at the open window, then at his two large dirty feet. But no one objected. Not even Mahendra. Whose child was it? The one inside Lachi's large round belly, pushing and jostling and sucking its little thumb.

Lachi stood where Katya was standing now, then she left, closing the door softly behind her, all those years ago. The last and final time. She'd pleaded, falling to her knees and trying to touch her feet. Please, dorasani. She might have relented, except Lachi did something. An unconscious movement: She raised her hand to her belly and rubbed a spot, caressed it.

She'd caught Lachi in front of the mirror once, one of her silk saris thrown over her shoulder; a gold-and-orange one, it sat against her pale complexion and her round belly like a river in sunlight. But I'm freeing you, aren't I? she'd said. You are free. Go. Free to be beautiful. Free from the job of looking after me, dressing me each morning, undressing me each night, folding up the yards of saris and putting away my jewelry. Go.

The trap cart had done its job. Lachi gave birth at the side of the road. The baby lived. Lachi did not. A wedding was a symbol.

"What's that in your hand?" she asked Katya now.

"It's a letter for Sree-dorasani."

"From Tara?"

"Yes, dorasani."

"Nothing from Vijaya?"

"No, dorasani."

"Give it to me. I have to go downstairs anyway, I have to tell them to stop burning the sambrani, I have to check on how they are stringing the marigolds and the mango leaves on the doorways. Why must I do everything?"

"I can do it, dorasani."

"No. Give it to me."

Katya handed over Sree's letter. The other one, about Vijaya, was tucked into her waistband.

"And Katya, put away the jewelry."

Putting things away, locking up.

Only she was charged with this. Only she'd remember which emerald or ruby or uncut diamond necklace would go best with which outfit, for Sree or Saroja-dorasani or Tara. For Vijaya too. On Diwali every year—like tomorrow—she was given new clothes, but she was never given jewelry.

Katya began stacking the boxes, velvet on velvet. But when she came across the smallest velvet box, she paused. She cast a glance at the doorway and opened it.

Inside were tiger claws.

Two of them, the tips facing outwards, their roots fastened together with a band of gold. It was a pendant. She'd seen one just like it before. It had been part of Tara's wedding trousseau. She remembered Saroja-dorasani telling her that the pendant was for the future firstborn child, to be strung on a gold chain and placed around the neck of the newborn on its naming ceremony.

The claws had come from the same tiger whose head was mounted in Surendra Deshmukh's study. She remembered Saroja-dorasani telling her that there were enough good claws—long, tapered ones—to make three pendants, one for each girl that was to marry out of this house, one for each girl with the last name of Deshmukh. This was for Vijaya, then, the oldest Deshmukh girl.

She went out of the room and looked in on the gallery. Saroja-dorasani was talking to the jeetha.

"Dorasani, shall I burn more?" the jeetha said, the brass smoker in his hand, chunks of the dried-up resin sitting in it like almonds.

It was the sambrani; it did this to her, drudging up all that muck from the bottom of her mind. She could never be exorcised of it. Never.

Saroja said: "Enough."

The jeetha must have misheard her. Or she must have misspoken. Because he went back to burning some more. The sambrani was highly combustible, a little spark and it would billow up clouds and then disappear. They'd burned it the same way every single day for three months after Vijaya was born. When Vijaya's entire body would fit into the crook of her arm; toenail to hair end. A pink, tiny, wrinkled thing; a miniature old woman; gummy, toothless, leaking drool. She wailed like an old woman too, a tinny, high-pitched scream, a shriek, a drawn-out cry that made sweat bead on her forehead, break across her upper lip, drip down her back like oil. The crying made her aware of her own blood pulsing, whooshing in her ears. Rage. The feeling she had when Vijaya used to wail like that. Rage. Rage. Rage. It made her so angry that she wanted to pick up Vijaya from her cradle and hurl her against the nursery wall.

She didn't. She didn't tell anyone she wanted to do that either. That she wanted to do that was a thing she dwelled on like a delicious secret. Would the baby bleed? she'd wonder. Would its blood splash spectacularly on the wall? Would its head crack? It was so soft, that skull.

They were stringing up marigolds in the courtyard. Someone had thought of dropping rose petals in the water pool. It looked so beautiful, the pink rose petals floating in the foot or so of the water, the blue sky over the courtyard, the white lattices over the galleries all around the second floor. The smell of sambrani was making her head pound. She began going back up the stairs. She had this chair. In the nursery. It was a rocking chair, and it looked out onto the orchard behind the gadi. Back then, the orchard did not seem to have borders. It spread, jungle-like, whichever way it liked, down the gentle slope of the hillock, into the mouth of the river. How old had she been? Twenty, at the most. Vijaya was born in July, and in July the river rose. It was all so wet. It was all so green. A bright, wet, green light shot into the nursery each and every morning. Each and every morning used to begin the same way. Full of light. Full of hope. An extreme sense of happiness. So much energy she felt she could combust, that it would shoot out of her mouth like a thing with wings. Those were the few hours in the morning that Vijaya did not wail. She waved her fists around—a slow, uncoordinated, drunken kind of movement, like a thing that did not yet know it had hands. She'd be filled with love. After all, what was not to love in a happy, well-dressed baby in a cradle in a nursery that was full of wet, green light, the smell of sambrani perfuming its walls. An hour would pass. Two. The morning light would become noon light. Yellow, orange—not green, and she'd be overcome by a sense of defeat, a deflating sensation that would take over her body. A pit would form in her stomach and she would fall into it, waves upon waves of blissful sleep crashing and dragging her under. She couldn't wake. The nurse would stand over her, nudge her gently at first and then jab her with the tip of her index finger, then pinch her, because Vijaya was hungry. It's all right, the nurse said. "Pink milk won't hurt the baby." It would dribble down the sides of Vijaya's lips and the nurse would wipe it away.

She began sleeping in the nursery. She *wasn't* unfit. If she fell asleep, she'd still be right there, near the cradle. The light from the orchard hurt her eyes, so she began drawing the curtains, made them hang thicker curtains that would extinguish all light. So they began taking Vijaya out of the nursery each morning. And the nursery became her room. Then it was over, wave after wave of sleep would crash over her and she would fall into a dreamless sleep.

Now they were stringing the mango leaves. She'd come back downstairs. She must look so busy, hurrying up and down, shouting orders, buzzing with energy.

"String them tight," she ordered. I mustn't see the stringing thread, she ordered. Only thick green bunches of leaves. This home must explode with color, with celebration.

After all this time, it felt like yesterday. There was a wren outside the nursery window. It was building a nest. Twig after twig, reed after reed, it laid the nest, in the crook of the moringa tree. The wren was orange, its wings streaked here and there with fluorescent yellow. The wren came and went. Vijaya was in the cradle. The nurse wasn't there. She went to the cradle.

She looked at Vijaya. There were a few pillows on the bed. She went to the bed. The nurse made her bed every day, fluffed the pillows, pulled the sheets tight across the mattress. She sat down on the bed, picked up a pillow, fluffed it, put it against the headboard. She took another pillow. Stacked this one against the other.

Gingerly, she pulled up her legs, gritted her teeth and sank back against the pillows, Vijaya in the crook of her arm. It was dark, actually. Extinguish the light. It wasn't morning, it was night, and the wren wasn't there. Vijaya stirred, stretched out a thin spindly arm from her blanket. She had a curious sensation at this. She felt Vijaya move inside her, the same spindly arm pushing against her rib cage.

Then she thought: *This is how the baby will die.*

She had the sensation of falling. Sleep. Sleep was comfort. Sleep was velvet. When she came to, she was alone in bed, Vijaya wasn't in the crook of her arm. She called out for the nurse once, twice, three times before she spotted the cradle, a bundled baby in the cradle, fast asleep, chest rising and falling. Velvet, comfort.

There was a picture of Vijaya as a months-old baby. The nurse was holding her. A photographer—a camera even—was unusual in those days and Mahendra had one driven to them all the way from Hyderabad. She'd dressed that morning, full of determination, full of energy. *Today will be a good day. Today, there will be a photograph of me as a beautiful, young mother. Today I will be better.* She took a bath, had the nurse burn sambrani and perfume her hair. She rang out orders in her old manner. She was in charge. She was the chinna dorasani.

But by midday, when the photographer actually arrived, everything evaporated and she sank into bed, freshly clothed, perfumed. She told herself she wasn't going to sleep. She was only going to rest her eyes, just for a second. She leaned into the soft pillow and closed her eyes and lost the day.

They'd photographed the nurse holding Vijaya. Later, she'd heard the nurse whispering to the maid outside her door. She was having a lucid moment, when everything was in sharp focus: the chair by the window, the thick drapes, the bed, the pillows, the cradle. *Should we tell dora?*

Then came the news about Lachi's child. They'd written her from the nameless hamlet. Lachi's child was a girl. That girl was going to be a year old now. What did they want to do with it? If anything. What they were asking, was permission to give it away. What they would really do, was sell it.

She made Mahendra send a man to a hamlet. And dispatch a telegram even before the man set out. *Do not give the baby away.*

It had no name, the baby from the hamlet. Lachi's daughter. It had to have a name before it was brought inside the gadi, and she stood in the doorway while Mahendra named it. Katya. He'd taken the name out of one of his fat Russian novels. A slave girl's child with a Russian name, Katya was brought into the gadi.

Katya went back into the room.

And what was *her* last name? Everyone had one. Even the jeethas. But she had no last name. She was only Katya—kind Katya, loyal Katya, beautiful Katya.

She continued stacking the boxes. She considered. What would happen if she gave Saroja-dorasani the letter, read it out aloud?

They'd bring Vijaya home, immediately. At first they'd torment her. Then behave as if none of it happened, the way they did with Sree-papa. They'd keep it all quiet. Then they'd marry her off to that same doctor. Years would pass, the foal would become a grown horse, and none of them would ever once talk about it. They'd accomplish it, the way they could accomplish anything. They were the Deshmukhs.

And if she didn't tell them? Krishna was the only way for Vijaya to be truly and completely separated from the family. Her uncle would slit the throat of the foal, rather than let her step foot inside this house again. She'd be as good as dead. But she'd be happy, wouldn't she? Vijaya. It would mean that she'd have to let go of the promise she made to Vijaya all those years ago—to make her pay for what happened to Sree-papa. And nothing she did in that regard had ever mattered anyway, destroying books or clothes or dear things. She just bought new things.

You've been standing in that passage to the kitchens long enough, Ranga had said. Who's your father, Katya? Pick a side. Servant or sister.

Outside the room, she could hear Saroja-dorasani's footsteps.

Katya opened the velvet box, fished the pendant out. She tucked it into her blouse, shut the case, placed the boxes in the bureau, turned the key.

That night, after everyone was asleep, she went into the kitchen. She pulled the letter out of her waistband.

Sister or servant?

Katya lit the stove and burned the letter from the boarding house. The pendant was still inside her blouse, the gold was warm now, the tips of the tiger claws dug into her skin pleasantly. She hadn't stolen it. It was hers because Vijaya won't come back. Now, she was the oldest Deshmukh girl, she was the firstborn. She'd chosen a side.

# THE DESHMUKHS HAVE FORESIGHT

———◆———

At the district registrar's office in Velaire, Suma stood a little ways away and watched Comrade RK. He was their squad commander. There was a capture reward of two lakhs on him; if he was caught by the police, he would be shot without trial. And Suma knew his real name. Ranga.

Ranga approached the peon outside the revenue officer's room. He had an inheritance, Ranga said, a small patch of land—a palm grove— that had once belonged to his father. Despite the presence of a sibling and a mother, he needed the land deed transferred solely into his name, so that he may sell it off. "Here is my wife," he said, pointing at Suma. "She can be the witness and sign the affidavit that says they are both dead."

The peon looked at Suma. She took a step forward, nodded delicately, earnestly.

Ranga slipped a rolled-up banknote into the peon's shirt pocket. "Can it be managed?"

She was Ranga's wife. She would be, for the fortnight they were planning to watch the revenue officer and his family—what time the officer arrived, what time he left, where he lived, how many people were in his family, what times of the day they were alone. They were to not harm the peon, or the building's watchman—they were not the class enemies. Only the officer and his family.

Even after two years of underground life, how easily Suma had remembered that she needed ten pleats for the cotton sari she wore that morning, to stand a few steps behind Ranga when they arrived, to speak in a voice that wasn't shrill or startling. It was an unaccustomed sensation now, to walk without the weight of her rifle on her shoulder, without the cuffs of her green uniform rubbing against her wrists, the weight of boots on her feet. To look at herself in a mirror, sleep on a bed, hear the sounds of traffic. Not the sounds of a Naxal camp deep in the Nallamalla forests, protected by trip wires, land mines, patrol duty. How easily it all came back.

"That is all fine. Anything can be managed. But it will take more," the peon replied.

"What's your name?" Ranga asked.

"Ramesh."

"Ramesh, only you can help me."

She continued to watch Ranga, followed the path his hands made as he gestured, the green veins that ran up his wrists and into the sides of his neck. Now and then he glanced at her. His eyes were brown, in a shade so striking that every time she met them she felt a little startled.

It was a story, but only she knew that it was true, in parts. She alone knew the true parts because even though Ranga did not use his real name anymore, she'd recognized him the day she met him. He had only been the squad leader then. Their platoon commander had assigned them together on the execution squad that went to Wanaparthy; the Wanaparthy zamindars were a prominent, well-known family. Afterwards, on the walls outside the Wanaparthy gadi, they had drawn the party symbol—the hammer, sickle, and star over the words COMMUNIST PARTY OF INDIA MARXIST-LENINIST SERVES THE PEOPLE. Instead of paint, they used the landlord's blood. "The Wanaparthy massacre" was what the papers printed.

After that, Ranga had become commander. And like all the members of her cadre, he went by an alias. They told her that it was necessary, the forged names, to establish their new "inside identity" and also, to hide their real identities; protect families from persecution by the police because suspicion alone could lead to detention of family members, ruthless interrogations to reveal the cadre member's whereabouts. She had no one to protect, so she did not choose an alias. Even underground, she was Comrade Suma. It was possible that her and Ranga's paths crossed in Irumi, but she would have been unrecognizable to him. And after the Wanaparthy executions, in the weeks they had spent traveling together to Velaire, she watched him and watched him but did not tell him she knew, how much she knew.

Here were the true parts—Ranga did have a mother, the washer-woman Pichamma. He did have a sibling, a younger brother. Neither were dead. Particularly of Ranga's brother Krishna everyone in Irumi had known, because even though their mother did vetti for the Deshmukhs, Krishna had left to become a university gold medalist and never returned. It was all from before Suma had arrived in Irumi, and it was Gita who'd told her, years ago. When Badri was only a few months old, she'd go and sit with Gita in the evenings. "And there is something that no one knows," Gita had said. "Promise me you won't tell anyone."

Gita said the real reason for the Deshmukhs permitting Ranga's brother to leave—a piece of good fortune that no one in the village except the washerwoman was allowed to have—was because of Vijayalakshmi Deshmukh, the oldest Deshmukh girl. When Gita was little, she said, her father worked as a jeetha at the gadi, and sometimes she went to help him. "I saw them. Her and Krishna, meeting secretly by the stepwell, playing children's games. I saw them at it for months. Sometimes, the little girl—the younger girl—would be there too."

And one rainy night, Gita said her father came home looking fright-ened, sickened. They had gone missing, Vijaya and her younger sister, the little girl. When they were discovered, the little girl was near death, and Ranga was with them. And her father had witnessed what had followed: Ranga, subjected to a merciless whipping at the hands of Surendra Deshmukh, for hours, in full view of Pichamma and the jeethas and laborers who happened to be at the gadi at that hour, on that day. Even where whippings were commonplace occurrences, Ranga's was the one that remained in memory; it was cruel beyond what was cruel even for the Deshmukhs. Ranga was a child, and he had received the beating of an adult, and one that was designed to drive him to death—kill rather than maim. Ranga wasn't meant to survive. It *was* meant to remain in memory.

Gita said that the Deshmukhs had known that Krishna was there too, and that they'd all gone together willingly. Krishna was a handsome child, so undeniably clever that he'd been permitted to go to school; clearly destined for something more than what the rest of them were. It was Krishna whom they wanted to beat to death for his association with the Deshmukh girl. For being a handsome child, good at school, destined. But, it would have meant admitting that there *could* exist such an association—a world in which the Deshmukh girl could form an attachment with someone who was like them: less than human, born that way, destined to remain that way. They couldn't allow that to be the truth. And because Ranga survived, and the little girl survived, Krishna couldn't be allowed to grow up in the vicinity of Vijayalakshmi Deshmukh. They couldn't allow such a temptation of fate. And it was in their power to turn fate.

"The Deshmukhs have foresight," Gita had said wryly, looking over her shoulder. Badri was waking up, making that sucking sound with his mouth which meant he wanted milk.

Now, watching Ranga, Suma tried to find in him the child who didn't have to take his brother's place, didn't have to withstand death, wasn't separated from his brother, didn't become Comrade RK. Where would they all be if the Deshmukhs hadn't turned fate?

A bell dinged from inside the revenue officer's room and the peon jumped, placed his hand on the doorknob. "Come back tomorrow. But I'm telling you now, it will take weeks for your file to move across his desk. And it will take more . . ." Ramesh said again, patting his pocket as he disappeared inside.

"I will come back here every day, Ramesh," Ranga said. He waited until the door of the officer's room closed before letting the desperation from his manner disappear. He walked back to her, looking up the corridor behind them. It was noon, everyone had been cleared out of the building for the lunch hour and they had managed to be the last ones.

"There are three other rooms on this floor, one of them has to be the records room," Ranga muttered when he reached her. "I will go downstairs. Walk down the corridor and memorize what you see. If anyone stops you, tell them you were looking for the bathroom."

She waited until she heard the sound of his feet on the stairway fade. He had been standing so close to her that she felt as though he was still beside her. It seemed to her that it was a power Ranga had, to have his presence felt even when he wasn't there.

She began walking down the corridor. There were three rooms on her left, a wall of windows looking into the street on her right. She peered into the open door of the first room. It was a deep and narrow room, separated into two sections by a row of dusty bureaus and filing cabinets, with desks and chairs pushed all alongside the walls. At least a dozen office workers were chatting across battered-looking desks strewn with cardboard folders, stacks of documents weighed down by glass paperweights, staplers, paper punches and steel lunch boxes. The next room was identical to the first. She felt conspicuous but relieved that no one noticed her pass.

The third room had no windows and the door was shut. She looked up the corridor to make sure it was empty, then gently nudged the door open.

"Who are you? What are you doing here!"

She fell back. She caught a brief glimpse of the room before the man came out and roughly pushed her aside. The room had high ceilings, towering racks of files and folders.

"Who allowed you up here at this time?"

"I was looking for the bathroom."

"Bathroom? Do you think you are a queen or something? Looking for the bathroom on the staff floor! You people use the common one on the ground floor. Get out!" he said. He held her by her elbow and shoved her away from the room.

"Don't push me, I'm going," she said. He walked up to her, stared into her face, held her elbow and shoved her again.

Walking back down the corridor, she could still feel the tips of the man's fingers on her elbow. At the stairway she turned to look. The man was slipping a large brass lock on the door.

Ranga was waiting for her outside the gate. The watchman stared at her and said, "What were you doing inside, you—"

"She's my wife," Ranga said. She went to stand beside him, a step behind him. "When does the office open again?"

"Around three," the watchman replied. He took off his cap and tucked it underneath his arm. He wasn't paying Ranga any attention and was instead looking at Suma. She avoided meeting his eyes and looked at her feet.

"Does the officer stay long?" Ranga asked.

The watchman dug his little finger into his ear, wiggled it around and did not answer. He was still looking at her with brazen, lurid interest. "What business is it of yours? Get out and come back at three."

She and Ranga took one last look at the building before walking away.

An old, converted apartment building, the revenue office was not a grand building. Tucked between a row of residential homes no higher than two stories each, it looked decrepit. The limewash on the exterior walls was tinged with streaks of black mildew. The windows were large but so dirty that they were opaque and looked as if they were part of the walls. To anyone else, it would not seem like a place in need of such painstaking observation, strategy, planning.

While the revenue office was supposed to be an arm of the government that merely kept records, that enforced landholding ceiling laws and kept excess land out of feudal ownership and granted them to tenant farmers, it was instead an institution where ownership of land changed hands only to be quietly vanished, where a single person sitting behind a guarded door—at the end of a bureaucratic maze made up of sub-registrars and assistants and filing agents, peons and custodians and a network of corrupt government employees—became a king who had the authority to grant or take away what was life itself. The records room was where the land deeds were kept. Also where the passbooks were kept; hiding and disappearing good land, keeping it out of the grasp of the masses of desperate tenant farmers and landless peasants swarming the registrar's doors night and day.

They navigated the throngs outside the revenue building. The street was a makeshift village, helplessly and reluctantly dislodged into a large, urban town. They were all of them farmers from remote villages and hamlets all over the district, they were all of them older than average, illiterate, carrying walking sticks and coarse woolen blankets. The pavement was littered with bedding and crudely fashioned woodstoves because most of the farmers who arrived there had no choice but to live and sleep on the street for weeks, cajoling, bribing and begging anyone who could grant them their agricultural passbooks—green papers—emblematic proof that they owned the very land their families for generations had tilled and sowed and died on.

She and Ranga were staying at the safehouse arranged by Comrade Govind. It was a single room on the ground floor of a tenement apartment building, only three streets away from the revenue office. The only objects present in the room were a kerosene stove and a calendar.

In Wanaparthy too, Govind had been with them, his job had been to arrange the explosives. The son of a landlord himself, Govind had severed ties with his family to join the cause of the Naxalites. A former engineering student at Osmania, he was thin like a rail, with wispy hair that sat close to his head.

Pushing round silver-wire glasses up his nose, Govind had shown them a nearby bore well from which to get water, a small common bathroom behind the building, and when the landlady accosted him at the gate and demanded to know who he'd brought into her building, he said that Suma was his sister and Ranga was his brother-in-law. They were visiting him. When the landlady left, he winked at her.

"It was the third room on the left," Suma said now, shutting the door behind them. "I saw it. It was definitely the records room. It is kept locked."

Govind brought out a sheet of paper and a pencil. She and Ranga crouched down on the floor. "The first is the revenue officer's room," Govind said. "We cannot see inside it. But that is not important, you will find out where he lives."

"Here," Suma said, touching the paper with her finger. Govind drew two lines for the corridor, two rectangles on its left for the two office rooms she'd passed, a third rectangle for the records room.

"Did you see the revenue officer?" he asked.

"No," she said.

Ranga said, "This part you will do alone, Suma. They will not suspect a woman."

"Will you and Govind go for the explosives?" she said.

Still looking at the sheet, Ranga nodded.

"I'll find out where he lives," she said.

Before leaving, Govind offered Ranga a cigarette and some money. Ranga accepted the money and declined the cigarette. "Almost forgot," Govind added, before stepping out of the door, and handed Ranga a small package wrapped in newsprint.

Ranga unwrapped the package after Govind left. Inside was Ranga's tapancha, the single-shot country pistol he always had with him, and a curved dagger that could be used to cut rope, but sharp enough to slice the top off a raw coconut. She took the dagger.

For five days, Suma mingled with the farmers and loitered outside the revenue office.

Every day, around ten in the morning, the officer's car arrived—a cotton-white Ambassador with a driver and an attendant in the front. The revenue officer had a sallow face, wore horn-rimmed glasses that sat like a tent over his cheeks. The watchman stood up and saluted as he passed. After the officer went inside the building, the Ambassador left and returned again within the hour, idling outside the office till the end of the day when the officer went home. So far, she had been unable to follow the car home, or locate where he lived. She reported all of this to Ranga, and he would pass the information to Govind.

What she didn't tell him was that of the five days she'd watched the car arrive, the officer's son, a little boy, had come on three. That every day, the boy held his father's hand and went inside, and the watchman stooped and did a little mock salute for him too and the boy gave a loud, delighted chuckle in response.

She also didn't tell Ranga that at noon, around lunchtime usually, the car left to fetch the boy's mother, the officer's wife. When his mother took him home, the boy would cry; he'd twist his mouth as though grievously injured, raise both arms, scream, and ask to not be separated from his father. His mother would distract him, speak to him in a bright voice about toys and lemon candies, wipe the tears off his face, wipe his nose with an embroidered kerchief. His mother would put him in the back seat of the car and they'd be gone.

Badri had disappeared for her. When she tried to recall his face, all that came back to her was the red mound over his little grave. The smell of the sugarcane she used to give him. But she couldn't remember the shape of his face, his eyes, his mouth, his hair, all that was Badri.

"Don't lose the ability to see from the class perspective, Comrade," Ranga had said to her in Wanaparthy. "This is the class enemy, and the only way for our revolution to succeed is by the total and complete annihilation of the class enemy."

Wanaparthy was a village like Irumi. They had arrived in the middle of the night at a gadi that looked much like the Deshmukhs'. Only here, the family name was Chaudhary. The Chaudharys of Wanaparthy. She was given a long knife whose blade was as wide as her forearm.

The date of attack had been chosen to coincide with the naming ceremony being held for a newborn in the Chaudhary family. At first, the newborn was sleeping, and Suma remembered the mother—how she attempted to shield the baby, but a squad member had dragged her by the hair to the middle of the courtyard, then slashed her neck with a sickle. The landlord's eyes were gouged out, his blood was mixed with rice and forced into the mouth of an old woman, the landlord's mother, the baby's grandmother. Suma's hands were stained and wet, she didn't know who she'd killed. And all this time, while its family was being executed, the baby was wailing. It would stop wailing periodically, quiet for a few moments, then it would start again. She remembered picking the baby up. She bounced it, tried to quiet it. Her hands were slick and she was afraid of dropping it. Her squad looted the safe, burned land documents. And when it was time to leave, they doused the gadi in gas oil and set it on fire.

Ranga ordered her to throw the newborn into the fire.

Today, once again, the little boy arrived with his father. Around noon, the mother came too. Suma watched her come out of the revenue office with the boy in her arms. The mother waved the driver away.

"I'll walk," Suma heard her say.

The driver insisted, but the mother refused again. She put the boy down, straightened his shirt, held his hand, and began walking. Suma got up from her place on the footpath across the building and followed them home.

The mother was petite, well dressed, always beautiful. Her sari was a pale shade of blue, made of tissue silk and not of rough country cotton like Suma's. She held a small leather purse and a nylon umbrella in one hand, her son's hand clasped tightly in the other. She walked with the air of someone who did not have the need to walk; with the attitude of one who had at their call a car with a driver and was merely strolling to indulge in a novel experience. Suma watched her pause to open the nylon umbrella even though it wasn't a sunny day.

Soon, she was close enough to breathe on them. The little boy smelled of jam. What a curious little thing he was. She imagined the officer giving him jam to eat, spoonfuls of it up in his office on the second floor.

As it turned out, the officer's home was a bungalow only two streets over from his office. It was a tree-lined neighborhood filled with other bungalows, green lawns, working streetlights, wind chimes. Suma hadn't expected this. It was at a distance so short from the revenue office that she was sure it took longer to get in and out of the Ambassador, for its bulk to navigate the narrow, clogged-up streets than it did to walk. She hid behind a fig tree and watched them.

A gardener was watering the lawn. He dropped the hose to greet the boy and his mother. "Where are the ducks?" the boy asked.

"They flew away," the gardener said, flapping his arms wide like a bird.

"You need a nap," the mother said, scooping the boy into her arms before he had the chance to run across the lawn.

The bungalow's entryway had a row of yellow marigolds and mango leaves hung across the top. The tiled stoop had a pattern of red and green parrots on it. She watched the mother close the nylon umbrella and unlock the door. Suma caught a sliver of the room before the door swung shut behind them. The gardener picked up the hose again and resumed watering the lawn.

Suma walked past the bungalow and doubled back up, passing close enough that she could graze her fingers lightly against the concrete compound wall. She doubled back again and went past the bungalow a second time, again grazing her fingers lightly against the wall. She felt the gardener's eyes on her and she did not turn back a third time. Within minutes, she was back at her spot on the pavement outside the revenue office.

At the safehouse, the landlady accosted her. It was clear that she had been waiting for a while; she was a thin woman, with thick, graying hair and a frightening manner. "How many days are you staying?" she barked. "And where is your brother? I haven't seen him in days."

"He has been leaving early—"

"I wake up early. I haven't seen him!"

"You might have missed him. He is very quiet—"

"If I don't see him by tomorrow morning, I'm going to call the police. Locked doors. New faces. What's all this? Do you think I'm stupid? If you are married where are your toe rings? Where is that yellow thread round your neck?"

"But he is coming tonight," she protested. The landlady glared at her. She was muttering under her breath. Suma thought she caught the word *Naxals*.

Unsure what to do next, she walked past the landlady and unlocked the door, feeling the landlady's eyes boring into her back.

That night, she and Ranga sat on the floor of the room, eating dinner by the kerosene stove. They ate red rice alongside a pungent-smelling broth made of horse gram. Between them was a bowl of raw green chilies. Suma took one and bit into it, then followed it with a mouthful of rice and broth.

"Have you found out where he lives?" Ranga asked.

She chewed slowly. "No. Not yet," she lied.

They had fallen into a routine together as if their charade had really turned them into a married couple. It was a small room and after dinner, they slept next to each other. Ranga said that he and Govind had found a factory that made plastic mining explosives. They could steal gelignite.

They weren't going to use simple middle-grade bombs, those containing petrol and sulfuric acid cased in jute sheets of potassium chloride; those wet, slippery things would have been easy to obtain but they would not be enough to bomb the registrar's office.

After dinner, Ranga lay down on the floor a foot away from her. If she wanted to, she could reach out and touch him. She fell asleep remembering the texture of the concrete compound wall. It was coarse, strong; it had no faults.

Within what felt like minutes, Suma awoke to the sound of loud knocking. She opened her mouth to shout but before she could, Ranga covered her mouth with his hand. He was sitting up.

"OPEN THIS DOOR RIGHT NOW!"

She recognized the landlady's voice outside. The door was shaking on its hinges.

"WHAT ARE YOU DOING INSIDE MY HOUSE? GET OUT! GET OUT!"

She and Ranga listened together in the dark. The landlady knocked for almost half an hour before giving up.

"What if she calls the police?" Suma whispered, feeling the grooves in Ranga's palm against her lips.

"We won't be here that long," Ranga replied, lowering his hand.

"She is getting suspicious. She was asking about Govind today. She doesn't believe I'm his sister, or that we are married," she said.

"We need to know where the officer lives. Soon."

She could make out the shape of his face in the darkness. The copper tones in his hair in the dim light. Suma realized, all at once, that she wanted to push Ranga. To anger, to surprise. To anything. She wanted to make him react to her. She said, "I know who you are. You are from Irumi. You are Pichamma's oldest son."

The greenish veins that ran up the side of his neck stood out sharply. His jaw was clenched. Then she said, "Your brother's name is Krishna, isn't it?"

It was his brother's name that did it. A look of childish pleasure flitted across his face, appearing, disappearing, shadow-like, as if he'd been waiting for someone to say the name aloud. In his face was so much pride, so much longing.

It made her aware of the reason why she'd been observing him so keenly all this time, why she thought of the things Gita had told her, that turn of fate that brought them into each other's lives. They were a matched set, matched in having parts of themselves that would remain impenetrable. She reached out and touched his face, resting the tips of her fingers against his temple, against the side of his neck. She felt his pulse beat against her skin.

"Ranga," she said, simply for the sensation of having his real name on her lips, as if saying his name was like knowing what it would feel like for their bodies to press together, to feel the thick, rope-like scars on his back move underneath her fingertips, to have the insistent warmth of him push against her, the warmth of aloneness, of pleasure.

The next day, again around noon, Suma watched the mother arrive once more.

She looked different today. She was dressed as if to go out, in a brown tussar sari printed with tea roses, a thin gold chain around her neck, large gold hoops in her ears, a strand of fresh jasmine in her long, black braid.

Suma wondered what she would wear when her husband was dead. Would she dress in white, like a widow was supposed to? Would she be allowed to live in the bungalow with the marigolds on the doorway and the gardener and the ducks?

She watched her enter the building. The watchman stood up and touched the tips of his fingers to his forehead and said, "Madam," as she passed.

She waited, but the mother did not come out holding the boy in her arms like she usually did. Suma went to the tea stall and bought a cup of tea. On the footpath outside the building, she sat down next to an old farmer and sipped her tea. Today, there were fewer people waiting outside the revenue office, and she wondered if there was something she didn't know.

"On what work have you come?" the old farmer turned and asked. His face was sun-beaten, wrinkled, missing several front teeth. His lips snapped together like a doll's when he uttered the word *work*.

Before she could answer the farmer, the watchman spotted her and came towards her. He was carrying a short cane in his hand. She watched him come closer but did not move. He grinned at her, raised his baton and hit her across her thigh. He'd struck her hard, and her skin burned.

"Sit on the other side of the pavement!" He didn't ask the farmer sitting next to her to move. Only her.

"Why?" she said, resisting the need to touch her thigh where it hurt.

"Because I said so," he said. "Now shut your mouth, bitch, and move."

The watchman came and stood in front of her, his belly in line with her face. She looked up at him. He hit her across her thigh again, harder than the last time.

"Staring at me, are you?" he said.

Suma stood up but did not back away. Then she did something the watchman seemed not to expect. She smiled.

The watchman moved closer.

"Is the registrar going away?" she asked.

"No," he said.

He grabbed her belly and squeezed till it hurt. He did not let go. "Only madam is leaving. They are going away for a week to her mother's place, but the officer is staying. You want your husband's land work done, isn't it? Come back here tonight and I will make it happen. You will see how."

After a few minutes, the white Ambassador pulled out. Suma caught a brief glimpse of the little boy in the rear window.

Ranga wasn't home. She paced the small room while she waited.

After an hour, there was a knock on the door.

"Who is it?"

"It's us."

She opened the door and Ranga came in, followed by Comrade Govind. "I went by the landlady's room and showed her my face," Govind said.

Ranga said without preamble, "Have you found out where he lives?" He was carrying a jute rucksack over his shoulder. Suma watched him put it gingerly on the ground. He opened the top of the bag and Suma drew closer.

Inside the bag were a dozen sticks of gelignite. Green, soft, dough-like. Alongside the blasting jelly was a roll of cordtex, fuse detonators, steel ball bearings.

"Have you found out where he lives, Comrade?" he asked again.

She nodded. "We should do it tonight," she said, "he goes home early on Fridays. Around six. The driver leaves around then as well. The cook leaves at nine."

"What about the attendant?"

"He does not stay on Fridays. It will just be him."

"And what about his family, Comrade? Will they be home?" Ranga said.

"A wife and a son," Suma replied. "They will be home."

"Are you sure?" he said.

She saw the boy's tiny fist, the size of a sparrow, waving from the rear window of the Ambassador. Perhaps he was doing this now, running across his grandmother's green lawn, waving his fists, chasing pond ducks. She saw the newborn in the light of the fire burning in Wanaparthy. Its weight leaving her hands, soft and dense, when she threw it into the fire.

"Yes," she said, "I'm sure."

"Very good. Very good," Comrade Govind said. "We do it tonight then. We will leave in an hour. Help me with the detonators. We don't need bearings for the revenue office. It will be empty. We only need it for his house."

Suma crouched down and started unrolling the cordtex. She eased out the sticks of blasting jelly. The familiar, pliable texture, its green hue, its chemical, almond smell.

At nightfall, they arrived outside the revenue office.

The street was deserted. There were no tea carts or people milling outside its shut gates. The apartment buildings on either side were dark. The streetlamp in front of the office emitted a sickly yellow light. There were a few people sleeping on the footpath outside.

"Make these people move," Ranga told her. "We cannot hurt them. Govind and I will open the gate."

They scaled the building's gate and Suma nudged people on the pavement awake. She pulled at their thin blankets and told them to move. They saw her standing over them, the sound of the dead bolt screeching in the darkness and did not ask questions. They awoke and scattered.

Suma was about to scale the gate behind Ranga and Govind when she noticed a small blanket-covered figure right next to the gate. The light was so dim that she could easily have missed him. She nudged the man awake. It was the old farmer who'd spoken to her. Even in that state of semi-darkness and semi-wakefulness he recognized her. "Go away," he said, and pushed her.

"You need to leave," Suma replied, "we are burning the building."

"Then I will die," the man said, covering his head with the blanket again.

Suma drew her curved knife and pulled the blanket away from his face. She held the knife under his chin. "Move." He did not move, and Suma gripped his soft, frail arm. His bones seemed to move underneath his skin. She bodily dragged him across the street and away from the building. When she returned, the gate was open, creaking lightly on rusted hinges.

"Check the building," Ranga said, "clear out the watchman and any other grounds staff you find."

She watched Ranga and Govind go up the stairway to reach the records room. Then she made her way through the narrow gap between the building and its compound wall. Behind the building there was a one-room shed. As she drew closer, she watched the light turn on inside. The door opened.

"Who is it?" the watchman said, squinting in the light pouring out of his room. He was dressed only in a loose robe wrapped around his waist. She drew closer.

It took him no time to recognize her. He leaned against the doorframe and grinned at her.

"So, you have come."

"You need to leave," Suma said. She was supposed to identify herself. Tell him that the building would soon be razed to the ground. He was not the class enemy. Only the class enemy was to be punished for his crimes, annihilated.

But who was innocent anyway? Nobody. Except children. Newborns. Badri. Ranga before the Deshmukhs turned fate.

The watchman moved closer and stood right in front of her, breathing into her face. She was not supposed to harm innocents. It was her creed. But Suma raised her curved knife and sliced the vein on the side of his neck, right underneath his jawline. The watchman opened his mouth as though about to say something. Blood poured out of his neck. She pushed him inside the cottage, shut the door and bolted it close.

She could hear him. Gasping, thrashing, all quietly, just on the other side of the door.

Suma walked back to the front of the building and sat on the pavement. She waited for Ranga and Govind. A minute passed. The street was still deserted. The yellow streetlight blinked in and out of consciousness. The apartments next door remained dark. She realized that the knife in her hand was dripping.

A dog was crying somewhere. Suma grabbed a handful of her sari at her knee and wiped the knife clean. It was hard to say, in the flickering light of the streetlamps, whether the knife was still red.

Govind and Ranga returned.

"I will stay here," Govind said. "Check your watch. We detonate at the same time."

Ranga nodded once.

When they arrived at the officer's bungalow, there was no moonlight and the green lawn was dark. She and Ranga eased the gate of the bungalow open and went inside.

The compound wall, they'd decided, was too strong. She helped Ranga rig the glass windows. They placed the gelignite with the bearings and the charges all around its front door, its rear door.

Some distance from the bungalow, Ranga checked his watch. "Five minutes."

When they were a hundred yards away, Ranga detonated. The

explosion shook the ground under Suma. It reverberated through the soles of her feet like a wave, moving through her body, landing on a single spot between her eyes. The sensation was painful, otherworldly. A sheet of pure, molten red poured onto the bungalow. It burned and fell all at once. They fled, but Suma turned to look. She could still see the green lawn, the gate, the concrete compound wall she'd touched three times.

She waited, but Badri did not return to her. She did not feel his little face pressing against her shoulder as she carried him on her hip. She couldn't see Badri's round black eyes, catch a glimpse of her own humanity in them. In Wanaparthy, she'd lost it, in the fire into which she'd thrown the newborn.

# HEAT

GAGAN GUPTA SLATED TO WIN THE HYDERABAD CONSTITUENCY
by N. Varadharajulu (correspondent)

Exit polls predict that Gagan Gupta, 26, a former physics scholar
from Osmania University, is slated to win the Hyderabad seat in
the Andhra Pradesh Legislative Assembly election.

A virtually unknown first-time candidate, Mr. Gupta, an in-
dependent, has gained popularity in the aftermath of the riots
that followed the anti-government rally held in Hyderabad in
September this year. Mr. Gupta was seriously injured in the riot
and spent months in convalescence. Once dismissed by both the
ruling party and the Hyderabad MLA Mr. Hasan Omar Rizvi
as a "youthful flash in the pan," Mr. Gupta has since emerged as
a vocal opponent of both, labeling the current administration
"limbless and toothless." He has, since the riot, drawn swaths
of supporters and campaign volunteers from Osmania. Once
the EC releases the official results, speculation is rife that Mr.
Gupta will lean on Mr. Krishna, a PhD mathematics student
hailing from a remote Telangana hamlet called Irumi, and whose
family was subject to the brutal and illegal practice of vetti cha-
kiri by the region's zamindar. It is expected that Mr. Krishna will
run in Osmania's student union elections against a Mr. Samuel;

labeled by Mr. Gupta as "representing an organization that seeks
to sow the rot of communist ideology in India." Because of the
triumvirate forces of opposition he faces, this is a notably close
and beneficial association for Mr. Gupta, whose need for man-
power and volunteers drawn from Osmania's student body
cannot be understated. The significance of someone of such a
background as Mr. Krishna's in taking over Mr. Gupta's mantle is
not lost, particularly in the face of Mr. Rizvi's and Mr. Samuel's
attempts to portray Mr. Gupta not only as a Hindu nationalist but
also as one belonging to the "privileged, upper echelons of society" and as "a hill-station educated fellow who will always remain
an outsider in this country." An inquiry commission has recently
cleared Mr. Rizvi, who was widely accused of instigating the riot
that injured Mr. Gupta. The commission has cited lack of evidence
in the matter.

Krishna put the paper back on the desk.

He was stunned his name was mentioned. A reporter had called the
hostel's main line asking for him. He'd refused to make any comment
and hung up. He wondered how the paper got hold of all that information about him, where he was from, even the bit about the Deshmukhs.
He felt uneasy. He wondered if Gagan gave it to them. Of course, he was
not running for Osmania's presidency. He and Vijaya were going to be
married, and they were going to Bombay together.

The paper had that part wrong, he'd already gotten his transfer certificate to the University of Bombay, and he wondered again if Gagan gave
out that information. He and Gagan had arrived at a truce, once he told
Gagan about the marriage plan, about Vijaya.

Gagan asked to be present as a witness for the marriage at the registrar's, along with Dr. Ramaswamy. Vijaya was arriving in the morning.

Even though he knew that a small mention of his name was unlikely
to reach Irumi, he wished it had not been mentioned at all. This was
a city paper, and surely Surendra Deshmukh must have read it. What
would he make of it? What if Ranga read it.

He leaned back on his chair and rubbed his chin. He had to shave. It was too late in the night now, he'd do it in the morning.

He took out a pair of clean pajamas and a cotton towel from his closet. He walked down the corridor to the common bathrooms. The water buckets were all empty.

The pipes that fed the hostel building were all exposed, and after the heat of the day, the water that came out of the taps was boiling hot. Every morning, they filled the steel buckets with tap water and left them to cool until the end of the day. At night, after dinner, before bed, a bath with water from the cooled buckets was necessary if one was to fall asleep. Krishna had come too late, all the cold water had been used up. He undressed, opened the tap and filled an empty bucket. To his relief, the water, although warm, was not as murderously hot as he'd expected. But he still felt himself sweating, even underneath the soap and water. He dressed in clean pajamas, wrapped the wet towel around his neck and let it sit against his skin.

Back in his room, he turned on the tube light and collapsed on his cot. Sweat dripped down his back. Unable to bear the heat, he got up again and turned on the ceiling fan, which made the heat worse, and swirling gusts of hot air slammed his face. He put the wet towel over his face. It was so hot, he felt as though steam would rise out of his nostrils.

Dr. Ramaswamy had said that he was going on a short leave; he had needed a pacemaker for some time, and with the semester ending, he'd decided to have the procedure done in Vizag, where he had some family. He was staying until the wedding.

Krishna had rented a little cottage on the northern edge of campus. It used to be part of faculty guest housing, but the university had sold the cottage and nearly all other cottages along that street to private owners, most of whom did not live in Hyderabad. It was a small, white cottage, it had a blue gate that creaked, a porch with a cane swing, and a bright pink bougainvillea that covered most of the yard. He and Vijaya were to stay there for the ten days or so it took for the marriage certificate to be released, a kind of honeymoon, after which they could leave for Bombay.

He imagined making love to Vijaya there, and his stomach lurched, with expectation, anticipation.

Gagan entered his room without knocking. Krishna took the towel off his face. Gagan was covered in grime, there were patches of sweat seeping through his shirt. His face looked haggard and exhausted, his skin covered in a thin layer of dust from the streets. Even from the door, Krishna could detect the smell of whiskey.

Wordlessly, he collapsed in the chair. The ceiling fan swung madly overhead.

"God, this is unbearable," Gagan said, meaning the heat. He sat up and fished out a pack of cigarettes from his shirt pocket. He made to flick the lighter but stopped himself. "God, this heat," he said again. "God-damn this heat. It is unbearable."

"Have you been drinking again?" Krishna said.

"Stop being such a good boy. It is so goddamn irritating. Do you know that? How irritating it is to be around people who think they can do no wrong?"

"When did I say I can do no wrong?"

"It's just the way your face is. Like you can do no wrong."

"My face?"

"Yes, your face. Since you came back from Madras. Of all the world's problems, do you know how small your problems are?"

Krishna said nothing. Gagan, he knew, didn't mean a word of it. The drinking had been getting worse, and the worse it got, the worse he spoke, unloading on Krishna at the end of each day and apologizing for it in the morning or sometimes apologizing instantly.

"I'm sorry," he said now, his eyes full.

"Leave it, Gagan."

"No. No. You are so good to me, Krishna. No matter how awful I am. I don't deserve you at all."

"Stop it."

"And you are getting married tomorrow! God, I'm such an awful friend. Come here . . ." He came towards Krishna, drew him close and planted a kiss on the top of his head.

Krishna laughed, despite himself. "Don't be so dramatic."

"Let's go out, you and I!" he said, and suddenly, the haggard expression on Gagan's face drained away. He had that gleam in his eyes that Krishna was familiar with, the energy that was contagious. "Yes! Let us go. Tonight, the last night of your bachelorhood. You want to remember this, believe you me."

"It's late, Gagan."

Gagan added, temptingly, "The Bullet has a full tank. I'll let you drive . . ."

He said yes. Let's go.


Krishna pulled on a shirt and followed Gagan downstairs. It was past eleven, and most of the lights in the hostel rooms had been turned off.

Gagan was living in a small flat in Tarnaka, a neighborhood dense with trees and wild monkeys, some twenty minutes from campus. But whenever he was in Osmania, he slept in Krishna's room. Whenever Gagan was on campus, he was never alone, always surrounded by supporters or volunteers. Gagan said that it was unnecessary, but it seemed like no one wanted Gagan to be alone until the EC released the results; then, Gagan would be assigned a government security detail.

The Bullet was gleaming in the yellow light of the streetlamps. The long, jagged dent was still there. "I've been meaning to get it fixed," Gagan said, running his hand alongside the scrape.

The horticulture department had begun spending some time on the street behind the hostels. There were eucalyptus saplings planted alongside the footpath every few feet, and the line work had been put in for streetlamps, although none of the glass bulbs were yet functioning. It was very dark. The only light in the alley was whatever flickered through the windows of hostel rooms, those few hard at work at their desks late in the night. The cement road too had been newly laid, but it still had the look of neglect, strewn pebbles, bits of paper and remnants of burnt trash. The young eucalyptus saplings already looked withered and sad, as though complaining to passersby that the heat wave was to blame for their plight. The places not covered by dried-up grass were littered with cigarette butts. It was a favorite place for the residents of hostel block A to smoke.

Gagan swung his leg over the Bullet, but before kicking it into life he seemed to realize that he was still holding his lighter. "One before we hit the road," he said, fishing out a cigarette from the pack in his pocket, clicking the lighter.

Till his eyes adjusted to the darkness, Krishna could only see the orange tip of Gagan's lit cigarette. He offered one to Krishna, he said yes. Gagan leaned forward and clicked the lighter again. Gagan's face was jovial, cheerful, and as though his cheer was contagious, Krishna felt it too. In a matter of hours, he would see Vijaya.

"Did you read the exit polls today?"

"I did," Krishna said. He decided not to ask Gagan again about the information leaked to the paper. He didn't want to argue, it was too late for that anyway.

"Gagan," he said. Suddenly, he felt overcome. He took the cigarette out of his mouth. "Don't think that I'm not grateful to you. I am. For everything, I owe you. I think I must have done some great kindness in my previous life, to have you in this life. Please visit me in Bombay. You are my family—now onwards, my only family—*our* only family—and you are always, always, always welcome."

The streetlight began buzzing. Krishna looked up at it and frowned. There was another noise, of rumbling traffic in the distance. He saw the front lights of three scooters moving towards them; they were chetaks, Krishna knew, based on the grating noises they made as they moved closer. The scooters stopped a little away from them. Their headlights turned off. They heard footsteps, what sounded like three or four men.

"Gagan," he said.

He should have recognized it sooner. Gagan's eyes widened, the faint vapor on his breath became sharp. He dropped the cigarette and shouted, "Run."

Gagan grabbed his collar and pulled him out of the street. They began running back towards the hostel when the men caught up with them.

Krishna felt someone pull him down by his ankles. His head smacked against the edge of the cement pavement. Pain burst in his skull, so severe and disorienting that all thoughts, about where he was, who he was with, everything felt momentarily erased.

He heard Gagan's scream. His own voice was muffled by a large palm pressing against his mouth. There must be someone, there had to be someone who heard, who'd come for them. He struggled against the person holding him down, realizing that it was more than one person, the hands on his ankles and on the back of his neck were coarse, calloused, their breath stank of chewing tobacco and slaked lime. He flailed, and they pinned his arms in place. A hand reached him, held his head by a clump of hair and turned it sideways, towards Gagan. They wanted him to see.

Gagan was inches away from him.

Gagan looked utterly stunned, surprised, it hadn't yet dawned on him, the fact of what was about to happen. A man's foot was pressing all its weight against the side of Gagan's face.

Krishna felt tears pouring out of his eyes, tasted blood in his mouth.

*Quick*, one of them said.

There was a hiss. Then another. Another. No one heard him scream when blood spurted out of Gagan's neck, while his eyes faded, their gaze still on Krishna. He saw the way Gagan let go, let his eyes glaze over and lose their light. The hissing noises of steel daggers piercing Gagan's stomach was all he heard before blacking out.

# A MARRIAGE PLAN

———◆———

At the railway station in Hyderabad, Vijaya scanned the faces of the people on the platform. Her train had been late, though not by much. There was someone who was about Krishna's height, about Krishna's build, with hair just as black and wavy. She reached out and touched his shoulder. It wasn't him, his teeth were too perfect, his face was broader, and his hair wasn't really all that black. She apologized.

She overheard someone on the platform saying that all the trains on this line were running late—there was either a collision at a railroad crossing, or signal cables had been stolen and needed to be replaced, or there was dacoity on the overnight trains and railway police had to be brought on. Though the last part, she herself knew wasn't true; she'd come on the overnight train from Madras herself. Whatever it was, god help you, if you had a connection from here. When the Madras train departed, the platform was instantly deserted. The crush of passengers and visitors, the loud recognitions, the pleasant goodbyes; everything vanishing like rain that had suddenly stopped falling. And Vijaya was still there, looking.

It was very early. Though the sky was dark blue when she got off the train, it was already beginning to lighten. Soon, dawn would break. She imagined touching Krishna's face while the full sun shone down upon them. She remembered, the near delirium in which they'd returned from the shore temple, how she'd never wanted to let go of him again. It broke time, agreeing to be his wife. Now there was a before and an after.

The only people that remained on the platform now were an idly-seller leaning against a pillar a few feet from her, his khaki overcoat still crisp and unstained, and a small woman with a covered wicker basket between her feet. They were talking languidly. The woman's basket was full of fresh flowers—jasmine strands—Vijaya could smell them even from this distance. They were waiting for the next train to pull in. Where was Krishna?

Vijaya dragged her trunk to the iron bench and sat down. The platform did not have a shelter. She felt thirsty and parched from the journey, but she didn't want to go in search of water, she didn't want them to miss each other.

Her trunk was packed with all the clothes she'd brought with her to Madras, the hibiscus box of letters. She had all of Sree's letters, but now she wished she'd kept the ones from her father, from her mother. The only jewelry she had with her were her old pearl earrings. For an irrational ten minutes, she'd decided that she mustn't keep any jewelry from Irumi. She tried to take the earrings off, one after the other, but the clasp was screwed too tightly, her earlobes grew sore and she didn't want to be late for the train. Everything else she owned, she left behind at the boarding house. Krishna told her it was best to not tell even Asha; because Pichamma still lived in Irumi, they couldn't risk it. She could tell Asha later. The only people who knew were Krishna's friend Gagan and his professor, Dr. Ramaswamy.

The plan was a simple one. After her finals, her father had made the reservations for her, the overnight express train she had taken from Madras to Hyderabad. And then the connection to Irumi from here. He told her that the car would be waiting for her when she arrived at the station near Irumi. All she had to do was wait for Krishna in Hyderabad, and not get on the connecting train to Irumi. Once they were in Bombay, she'd write a letter addressed to her father, telling him that she was safe, she was well, she didn't want anything, and that she was never coming back.

A letter, because a phone call was more than she could bear to contemplate.

She pictured herself writing the letter now, pictured herself walking to the registrar's in the morning, pictured herself as Krishna's wife. She would have to change her last name, take his, ensure that they could never find her.

She heard footsteps and jumped to her feet.

It was a woman, another passenger; well dressed, about her mother's age, carrying a black leather satchel. Vijaya sat back down, and watched the woman make her way across the platform. The idly-seller and the flower seller stopped to look in her direction, then went back to conversing. The idly-seller was planning to send his son to a welfare hostel, but his wife was objecting. The woman sat on the iron bench next to Vijaya, smiled politely in her general direction. Vijaya returned it. The idly-seller said, "She'd rather her son remain uneducated than separated from her. Foolish woman!"

She tried not to panic. Krishna must have been delayed somehow, it was simply not possible that he wouldn't come for her.

The last time she had seen her own father was when she'd gone home for the holidays. Her father was sitting behind his desk in the study, telling her to work hard. How proud he was of her. She was to savor this period, he said, because life had so few of them, when it felt like the world was at one's feet, so full of possibilities and things that haven't yet been proven untrue. Her mother's manner too had been different over the holidays. The way she'd come into Vijaya's room, opened her closet, assessed the clothes she had, made a list of what she didn't have. Where did you put your gold anklets? was a type of question she'd spring upon Vijaya. And the way she said, "Vijaya, stand up," and measured her waist. "And don't you dare cut your hair."

There was a tenderness in her mother on this visit, a tenderness that seemed to arise now that—in her mother's mind—Vijaya would soon be married, belong to another. Her whole life, her mother had been preparing her to leave one day, but now it seemed almost as if she'd miss her. That she might want her back. One afternoon, she'd fallen asleep, and awoke to her mother running her hands through her hair. She kept her eyes shut and pretended to continue sleeping, so that she'd do it for longer.

When she'd been home for the holidays, she wished she'd known she wouldn't return. She would have known to say goodbye. She would have savored the lasts. Her stomach ached now, when she remembered how much time she spent shut away in her room by herself. How she'd allowed Sree to ignore her even though she knew full well that all Sree wanted was to be around her. How she hadn't bothered to break through the wall that Sree and Katya seemed to have erected around themselves, a realm they'd decided Vijaya wouldn't be allowed into, but one that she knew Sree craved for her to enter. Memories were treasures, she realized. And she'd been callous, she'd walked past it all as though they would always be there. Now it was over.

The stationmaster was walking towards them. He glanced at her and the older woman on the bench next to her, gave them a courteous shrug. "The train is going to be late," he said, assuming that Vijaya too was waiting for it. Vijaya glanced at the woman, and met her eyes for a split second longer than necessary.

"Where are you headed?" the woman asked her in English. "College holidays? Going home?" the woman added before Vijaya answered, switching to Telugu. "You look like a Telugu girl."

She didn't want to be rude, so she said yes.

"And where's your home?"

Vijaya hesitated, not wanting to say that she was waiting for someone. Never again could she say aloud that Irumi was her home. And what did it matter if she said so to this stranger. She allowed the word to fill her mouth, like something green and immortal. "Irumi," she said.

"Ah," the woman said, a look of recognition dawning on her face. "I know where it is."

Vijaya felt her heart sink, she hadn't expected this. She noticed the flower woman and the idly-seller stopping their conversation in order to listen in on theirs. She looked beyond the woman, at the entrance to the platform. She looked the other way, where there was only open track, curving away from her sharply, disappearing from sight, the urban buildings in the far distance. A mangy dog was picking its way across the track. It barked at something. She watched the dog, hoping that the conversation would not continue.

"The new dam project on the Krishna River is coming up there, isn't it?—my husband is the *executive* civil engineer in the irrigation department—and he had been going on site inspections, and once he stayed for a night in Irumi, at the home of the Deshmukh there. You must know them"—here, the woman cast half a glance at Vijaya's clothes, her earrings—"Surendra Deshmukh, pretty big landlord family. They are the doras there. Very old family, well known."

Vijaya felt cold fear flood her body, a prickly heat shoot up her spine, crack across her shoulders. She reminded herself that the woman was a stranger. A stranger, a stranger. And all Vijaya was doing, as far as the woman knew, was waiting for the train to Irumi. The plan was still a secret.

Lies. She must begin getting used to telling lies. To anyone who questioned her about her parents, her family, all the common first questions strangers asked. Neighbors asked. New friends asked. She must say no, if she was asked about siblings. She could never slip up like this again. And what did lying to a stranger mean, anyway? It meant nothing. She could even tell the truth. And what was home anyway? With this decision, she would never set sight on her home again, for as long as she was alive, her uncle, her father, her mother, Sree. Even Katya. Home was a particular melody. And it would recede from her, fade, become an unaccustomed melody, carry no weight.

"You must know them," the woman insisted, "if you are from there, you have to know them. Surendra Deshmukh. Do you know them?"

"That's my uncle," Vijaya found herself saying. She balled up her fists, dug her nails into her palms, trying to stop herself from speaking. Even to a stranger, she could not pretend to be an orphan.

The woman looked pleased. She gathered her satchel and moved closer. She continued to talk animatedly about her husband, how he'd stayed at a room in the Deshmukh gadi, how old and grand and beautiful it was, how it must have been like to grow up there.

Now, to her own surprise, Vijaya felt less fear, more nostalgia. She savored it, *the lasts* of a path in life from which she was turning away. She found herself talking to the woman enthusiastically, attempting to render into conversation what the view from her room was like. She wished once again that she'd known it was the last time she'd be setting eyes on what could no longer be home. It would be a longing she'd need to endure for the rest of her life. But she checked herself, remembered where she was, what she was doing, where she was headed. She took a deep breath and stood up.

She was still very thirsty, and realized that the sun was now really up. The heat was beginning to beat down, she could feel it on the part in her hair. "Can you watch my trunk?" she asked the woman.

"Do you need to use the bathroom?"

She said yes, and went towards the entrance of the platform. The ticket booth was closed. In fact, all the platform shops except for the newspaper stand were closed. She came out of the station and onto the street.

Even though it was late in the morning, the street was deserted, there was a tiffins hotel across the street with its shutters closed. It felt as if the city was on holiday. She stood at the entrance and looked, feeling anxious, feeling terrified.

On the way back to the platform, the newspaper fellow, likely mistaking the look on her face as an inquiring one, said, "bandh on this part of the city today." He said something else, something that sounded very much like murder, but she couldn't pay attention. She was trying not to panic. Trying not to shiver. Where was Krishna? Why didn't he come?

"Did you find the bathroom?" the woman asked.

She didn't know what she said, she must have said something, because the woman nodded. The woman brought out a steel water flask, unscrewed the lid and poured water into it, and drank without letting it touch her lips. She asked Vijaya if she wanted some. She said yes and accepted the cup, drank without letting it touch her lips either. She resisted the temptation to ask the woman if anyone came looking for her in the few minutes while she'd gone in search of the bathroom.

All throughout the afternoon, the shops on the platform remained closed. The gravel along the rail line began to give off the sweet mineral smell of rocks exposed to heat. When she saw the stationmaster leave on his lunch break, Vijaya checked her watch.

When had her train arrived? It was easily four hours now. No. Wrong. It couldn't be, she must be wrong, it couldn't have been four hours. The woman opened her bag and took out a round steel tiffin box, like the ones that Katya used to pack for her and Sree when they went to school. How long ago that felt.

"Here," the woman said. "I'm not hungry, you can have it."

Vijaya did not protest. She did not speak. She chewed, she swallowed and tried not to burst into tears. Her throat ached. It felt as though she was trying to swallow rocks. He'd told her that all his life he had loved her. He'd told her that she didn't need to be forgiven. He'd told her that she deserved happiness. She'd found all three things impossible to believe when he said them. After all, who could love her? Nobody.

"Do you have brothers and sisters?" the woman asked.

"A sister," Vijaya replied, wiping her chin with the edge of her sari.

"Little one or an older one?"

"She's my little sister."

She avoided the woman's eyes and looked at the track again. The dog was gone.

*Vijaya, did the king live?*

*Vijaya, I want to see elephants.*

"Ah, look, it must be coming now," the woman said.

She hadn't noticed the stationmaster return from lunch. He was standing expectantly on the platform, holding his green flag.

The train going to Irumi appeared on the track. She did not look its way, she shut her eyes, but she heard the loud horn, felt it enter her body, felt the earth vibrate, move through her very bones. She opened her eyes, and the train tore across the rails. The gust of wind sweeping the platform in its wake threw up pieces of litter into the air, candy wrappers, crumpled tickets. The scent from the flower seller's basket blew her way, the raw, honey-like smell of jasmine, even the coconut oil in the woman's knotted hair. The windows of the train were a blur at first, and as it slowed, she saw each window more distinctly. The thick glass fixed on the windows of the first-class bogie, followed by the iron rails of the second class and the third class.

It came to a standstill, filling her ears with the tinny, high-pitched squealing that the track emitted when the train slowed to a halt. The idly-seller and the flower seller moved towards the train; the descending passengers moved towards the platform. The woman gathered her satchel and went to the train door. Vijaya picked up her trunk and followed.

She wove her way through the crowd, feeling her shoulders brush against men, against women, against coolies with silver medallions strung around their sleeves, asking her if she wanted them to carry her trunk for her. She found the passenger list affixed near the entrance of the first-class bogie. All she wanted to do was to see her name. Her first name next to her family name, the person she was now. There it was—*Deshmukh, Vijayalakshmi*—next to the berth number she was assigned. "Is it there?" the woman asked her, checking for her own name.

And who would miss her? if she fell onto the tracks. Jumped.

She tried to imagine her mother's face on receiving news of her death. Her lament, the late realization that it was always true that she adored Vijaya, loved Vijaya, would always think of her as the newborn she'd cradled in her arms, how tender, how pink, how beautiful. She would continue to live that way, in memory, in the love of a mother. The only way to truly die was if she didn't go home, if she went to live a whole, unfractured life with Krishna. But Krishna didn't come. The pain she felt was excruciating. It flayed her. She was condemned to remain alive.

The woman was on the first class bogie too, she said, asking Vijaya why she wasn't getting on, what was wrong, why was she crying. Then the train's horn blew again, the engines were re-starting, it was going to leave. The woman said, "Don't you need to go home?"

And what was home? Home was the ruin that remained, the melody that would never become unaccustomed.

When the train pulled out of the station, Vijaya looked out of the glass windows of the first-class bogie. She watched the idly-seller lean against the pillar once more, the flower woman sink back to the floor, position the wicker basket between her feet. She watched them both turn around at the same time, look at someone addressing them. She leaned forward and pressed her fingers against the glass. It wasn't Krishna. It was an older man, with bright red spectacles hung on a chain around his neck. Vijaya shut her eyes and sank back into her seat. Butterfly-red— that would be how Sree would have described the color. And Sree's face came to her—her delicate smile; the chime of her silver anklets; the blankets they had to put on Sree's windows to keep out the light.

*Vijaya! Hold my hand! Why won't you hold my hand?*

He'd said that she deserved happiness. And what was happiness? Happiness was what could have been, if only. She deserved nothing. After all, who could love her? Nobody.

# A KIND OF HOMECOMING

The biology textbook was open to Sree's favorite page: parts of a leaf. It was a cross-sectional diagram, delicately illustrated in watercolor. All of the minutiae that made up a leaf were labeled with little black arrows; now straight, now squiggly. It was all so utterly fascinating, that all those parts had names. So many leaves she'd crushed in her lifetime without once realizing. All those veins, all those midribs, the axils, the venules. Petioles, laminas. "Stipules," she said aloud. What a funny word: "Sti-pules."

She was beginning the eleventh form at the end of the week. She'd bought a new schoolbag: a pastel pink canvas satchel with a secret pocket sewn into the lining.

She was finished with Irumi's village school now. Finally. The secondary school and junior college Vijaya had gone to—the closest one—was forty kilometers away. Her mother asked her if she really even wanted to go. She'd said yes straightaway. But her mother didn't believe her. She asked again, and again and again, as if that would get a different answer. Then, suddenly, what Sree had taken for granted became completely uncertain. The question of her continuing was broached as if anew, as if proposed for the very first time. You said I could go. I, we, never said that, her mother said. It isn't fair, she'd said. That she had to fight for the very thing that she had a right to—what Vijaya was allowed without question. The only thing that matters to me, her mother had said, is your health. Her mother reached out to touch her cheek. She'd pushed her away. She'd pleaded, begged. She'd nagged, grown angry.

They'd only relented when she refused to eat.

The car would take her, and Katya. The driver and the car and Katya would all wait outside until classes let out. But in between, she'd come out exactly at noon and have her lunch in the car without fail. Katya would oversee this. Her mother extracted another promise from her: If she felt ill, even ever so slightly ill, she'd tell them right away, she'd stay home. And if the car was needed elsewhere, or if Katya was needed elsewhere, then too she'd stay home. When her mother gave her this news, she'd whooped and thrown her arms around her, kissed her cheeks while making loud, smacking noises.

She had a week of holiday still left, and she began each day checking and re-checking the pink canvas bag, arranging her biology textbook and her geography and her civics textbook height-wise. She smelled the fresh glue on the bindings, drummed her fingers across the stiff spines of each book as though it were a pet that she had to contain, keep quiet. Each morning, unable to resist, she took them all out, laid them on the floor of her room, and repacked them in a different order. She opened them, but not fully. She'd only cracked the spine of one textbook. The civics textbook, because it had a photo on its cover—a bird's-eye view of the parliament house. From that height, it looked like a beautiful toy, a perfect ring hemmed-in by spindly columns, like a thing she could hold and lift and roll across the floor. The first page had the national pledge printed in an ornate font. Her father had taken the textbook from her and read the pledge with something like nostalgia, wistfulness on his face. "You know, Sree, it was originally composed in Telugu," he said.

"Hmm," she replied, nodding, resisting the urge to pull the book out of his hands. Then he gave the book back to her and walked away.

Visions formed. In her mind, she was finishing junior college, then entering real college, and living in a boarding house in Madras and attending Presidency, just like Vijaya. Walking to a bus stop on a busy road full of people and vehicles, cars, buses, rickshaws, pedestrians, hurrying along the footpath because she had places to be, things to see. From all the bits of information Vijaya gave her in her letters, she pieced together a fantastic collage: cinemas, restaurants, Presidency, buses, beaches. The friends she would make. The brilliance she would exhibit. Imagining that life was thrilling, like being inside a cart poised at the very top of the Ferris wheel, seeing for miles already, ready, ready.

Katya burst into her room, slamming the doorknob against the wall. "Sree-papa!" she said. "Vijaya-dorasani is coming home today. Did you know this?"

"Can you knock when you come into my room?" she said, looking up from her book. She'd stared at the cross-section for so long that Katya's face came at her from beyond the transparent outlines of the leaf, through the artist's cross-hatching.

Katya was carrying her breakfast tray in one hand.

"I mean it, Katya."

"Why's she coming?" Katya said.

"Is that for me?" she said, pointing at the breakfast tray.

Katya set down the tray on her desk a little too forcefully. "Is *she* really coming home?"

"What do you mean?" she said, realizing that Katya looked angry. Frighteningly angry.

Katya said, "Does she know the plan they have for her?"

"What plan?" she said.

She didn't. And she wasn't sure why Katya was treating the news of Vijaya coming home as if it were a surprise. Her college year was over, she was coming home. Some surprise.

Although there *was* a secret being kept around Vijaya's return, and it had quickly become obvious that it was only kept from her and from the household help. Her mother? She knew, of course, in the way she obviously hurried all over the gadi, shouting this or that order, or the way she pointedly stopped speaking to her father or her uncle, when Sree entered.

It infuriated her, how everyone still insisted on treating her like a child. When she really thought about it, she hit upon the realization that it was because of her smallness. She'd never been a tall child and wasn't, yet, as tall as Vijaya, and there was a slight elfishness in her features—in the small curve of her nose, her little hands and small feet. Even her teeth were small, as her mother constantly told her. She'd been told enough times to know that this demureness was a prized possession, a gift, and one that Vijaya did not possess. *Your hands are so fine, so slender, unlike your sister's. Your feet are tiny, unlike your sister's. Your face is so well shaped, not round, like your sister's. Your eyes are so black, unlike your sister's.* Whenever her mother said these things, it made her skin prickle, now with pride, now with guilt.

"Fine. Finish your tiffin," Katya snapped. On her plate was a crisp dosa, shaped into a cone just the way she liked, with the yellow potatoes hidden underneath.

Since Vijaya left, she ate breakfast in her room. Her father was out early, before she woke up, and her mother never ate breakfast. And it felt like a bother, to sit at the empty dining room table.

"Don't give me orders."

"Leave the book," Katya said, roughly pulling her biology textbook out of her hands. "You'll smear it."

The daily tablets were on the saucer with the pink roses, next to the glass of water. Their number had increased, steadily, until they began to need their own dish. She remembered the time when she only had two or three tablets to swallow each day, but that memory was growing distant. She couldn't remember if it was two or three. She couldn't remember their colors or shapes. Before she ate, as was her custom, she nudged the saucer so that it sat behind the water glass. That way, the contents of the saucer need not be tablets; the ghoulish tablets, orange, blue, fat, bitter, hurting her throat as they went down, always there, always ruining everything. But nudged behind the water glass, they were an optical illusion, a trick; she could angle her head and they'd come at her in their colors but now elongated, now spindly, now rippling, now rosy, a toy, a stolen paperweight hidden behind the pressed glass.

She began eating. Tearing a long strip of the dosa from the top of the cone with both hands, the way she wasn't supposed to, if she were eating at the dining table downstairs.

Katya said, now in a bargaining voice, "So much fuss she made to leave, Sree-papa. Is she really coming back?"

Katya only spoke this way about Vijaya when alone with her, without the customary dorasani abutting Vijaya's name. With her, Vijaya was a *she*—a *her*—a *your sister*.

"I said I don't know already!"

"Fine," Katya snapped. She strode out of the room, slamming the door behind her.

When Vijaya arrived, late in the night, Sree was in bed. She was asleep but the voices roused her, though not fully, so she heard everything in a state of semi-wakefulness. She was on the edge of a dream. She often had dreams. Dreams in which she and Vijaya were in the jungle together. Sometimes she'd even be alone, petrifyingly alone, unable to move, trapped in mud. When she awoke, she almost always remembered the dreams. But she only told Katya or her mother about them when they weren't as scary, otherwise her mother would insist on Katya sleeping in her room. Once, she dreamt that she was sitting in the middle of a forest clearing, alone, on a rock. That was it—the entire dream, she was just sitting.

In her head, the voices she heard conjured up the scene, the setting, the plot of the dream. Vijaya's room. Vijaya and their mother.

"No? What do you mean *no*?" her mother said.

"You will do as I say, you hear? You did something didn't you? Tell me now, what did you do? I knew we shouldn't have sent you there. I knew it. Liar. You were always a liar. What did you do?"

She heard a whimper. She heard the sound of skin striking skin. Their mother pulled at Vijaya's hair from the roots. Hitting Vijaya, indiscriminately at first and then more methodically, her cheek, her mouth, the side of her neck. Vijaya, on the floor, hands shielding her face, knees folded underneath while blows rained down on her. All the while keeping quiet.

"Then you shouldn't have come back here. At least that way, we could have thought you were dead. Then all this would be over. Did you think we needed you?"

She opened her eyes.

Silence. She was sweating. She threw off the covers, turned over, and fell asleep again.

In the morning, she decided not to tell them about the dream.

In fact, when Vijaya came downstairs for breakfast, their mother left the table and embraced her. Profusely. Now kissing her cheek, now kissing the part in her hair, the spot near her ear. Holding her by the hand, she led her to the dining chair, pulled the plate towards her. "You've grown so thin, Vijaya-bujji, you must eat well now that we've got you back. Katya!"

"Yes, dorasani?" Katya said, stepping forward.

"Get Vijaya fresh puris. Hot from the stove. These are cold already."

Katya moved to remove the offending plate.

"No. No. Leave this. I will eat today, I will eat the cold ones. Just get the hot ones for Vijaya."

Katya gave her a look, walking back towards the kitchens. A look meant only for Sree: As if. As if we believe this show between them. We don't, Sree-papa, do we?

Vijaya turned to her and said, "My sweet Sree," and held her chin between her thumb and forefinger. "I missed you so. Did you miss me?"

No, she didn't miss Vijaya. Vijaya could go wherever she liked and she wouldn't miss her, not even for a second. That is how Vijaya was, always consumed with her self-importance, her pretty brown eyes, her aspirations. As though the entire world revolved around Vijaya, as though she was the center of the very universe. Before she could act on the impulse to say something nasty, their mother interjected.

"Of course she missed you! She will miss you more after the wedding."

"What wedding?" she asked, looking from her mother to Vijaya.

"Your one and only sister's wedding, silly, of course. It is going to be wonderful! You can be sure of that. Obviously, everything still needs to be fixed for sure, the boy and his family are arriving in a week to look at your sister. Though it is unheard of: Someone—anyone—refusing to forge a relationship with our family? Won't happen. You see, especially since this will be the last wedding to happen from this house."

A second later, she added, "Of course, I didn't mean last. Only last for now. For now. So silly of me. Never mind me." She took a deep breath, sighed, and smiled widely at Vijaya.

Sree pulled away and Vijaya let go of her chin.

So, this was the big secret. And they hadn't deemed it necessary to tell her beforehand. When Tara got married, she'd been involved right from the start. They'd asked her opinion on everything, even what she thought of the groom. But her mother had decided that this was something to be purposefully kept from her, and her alone. They were telling her now, alongside Katya, as if she and Katya were equals.

"Why didn't you tell me?" she said.

"We are telling you now. And Katya?" their mother said.

"Dorasani?" Katya said, pausing at the passage to the kitchens.

"Tell them to start the sugar syrup for the laddus, they mustn't find a single thing to fault. Did I tell you he is a doctor? The groom. They own five hundred acres in Nalgonda. He is such a good-looking boy too. A doctor! And you know the best part? He is an only child. So, it is all his. And then, it will belong to the children. Oh, Vijaya!"

The little hairs on her arms were standing on end. Vijaya was leaving her. Again. And what difference did it make? She'd left once already, hadn't she? But their mother's tone was different from last time. The last time was a betrayal, she had seen her own anger and disappointment reflected in their mother. But this leaving, it seemed to make their mother happy. Thrilled even. This leaving also seemed concrete, permanent. Involuntary. And now that she thought about it, so utterly inevitable in a way that it hadn't even occurred to her as a possibility. It felt as though a piece of her, Vijaya was going to excise and take with. Vijaya's hands were clasped together in her lap. She was staring at her fingertips intensely.

"Aren't you thrilled Vijaya?" their mother said.

Vijaya looked up and met her eyes.

This wasn't the martyr face. The martyr face was tinged with pleasure, a secret pleasure that Sree alone could see. This was sadness. This was pain, and there was nothing hidden behind it. Sree had the sudden, fleeting impulse to reach out and touch Vijaya, comfort her somehow. But of course, she resisted it. Vijaya always smelled so good; like warmth, like wellness and clean clothes, and whenever she was around Vijaya, it was an impulse she had to fight back constantly—to not touch Vijaya, to not kiss her cheek, to not ask to braid her hair, to not rest her head in Vijaya's lap.

"What do you say, Sree?" their mother asked her.

"What?" she said.

"You have to say congratulations."

"Congratulations, Vijaya," she said blankly.

To that Vijaya said nothing.

She told her mother she needed to go back upstairs. "Why?" her mother asked. "You ask after your sister all the time. Now she's here, why don't you sit with her?"

"I *don't* ask about her all the time!"

"Yes, you do."

"I'm going!"

"Fine. Go. And what's taking Katya so long? Tell her to hurry if you see her."

Sree left the table. On the way back upstairs, she stopped outside the study. The phone was ringing. The doors were ajar, and Katya was inside. She leaned in. Katya was sorting the mail. The plate of hot puris she was supposed to have brought for Vijaya was sitting on her father's desk, getting cold again.

"Ma wants you to hurry up," she said. Katya didn't respond. The phone was still ringing.

Katya wasn't allowed to answer the phone. Sree crossed the room and picked up the receiver. "Hello?" she said.

The line was all crackly after the rains last week, the voice on the other side was slightly garbled, but she could hear distinctly a man's voice. It was polite and serene, like her father's. He said he was a professor at Osmania University, and he was looking for Vijayalakshmi Deshmukh. He said Vijaya's name in an official, unfamiliar way, as if reading it off a piece of paper.

Of course, it was a professor, a person from a world into which she wasn't allowed entry. Osmania, even she knew, was in Hyderabad. Was Vijaya going to move universities after her wedding? Why didn't anyone tell her anything.

Still, she stayed calm, answered politely. Said yes, she would call Vijaya to the phone. "One minute," she added and put the receiver down.

"Katya, it's for Vijaya," she said.

Katya did not reply. She tucked a stack of letters underneath her father's glass paperweight. She looked so angry. Why did she look so angry?

"Katya, did you hear me? the phone is for *her*. Tell *her*," she said.

"Why don't you tell her yourself," Katya snapped.

"Do what I say, Katya!"

Katya glared at her.

"What's wrong? Why are you being mean? Are you angry with me?" Sree said.

Katya did not reply. She went back to sorting the letters, separating them out into piles so angrily that the paper was in danger of being crumpled. Then she took a deep breath, shook her head. "How can I be angry with you, Sree-papa."

"Please? Tell her someone is calling from Osmania for her."

Katya stopped sorting the letters and looked up, her face blank and expressionless.

"I don't want to go near her. I hate her! I hate her so much, Katya."

Sree went upstairs, ignoring the stabbing pains that prickled her shin whenever she had to climb stairs. As she went into her room, she thought she heard the sound of the receiver being picked up again. She thought she heard what sounded like Katya's voice, not Vijaya's, saying Hello, yes, this is Vijaya. But Katya wasn't allowed to answer the phone. Then she slammed her door shut.

# FRACTURES

---

Krishna was in the hospital. He knew this before he opened his eyes. The hard mattress underneath. The smell of antiseptic, alcohol. The noises of someone moving around. The soft palm of a nurse; her white sari brushing against his face. *His skull had a fracture, not life-threatening, no permanent damage*, she was telling someone. *Needs therapy and rehabilitation.* His head swam in and out of consciousness.


Morning. He was able to sit up. The sunlight hurt his eyes, so the nurse kept the curtains of his hospital room drawn. She left the newspaper at the foot of his bed. A spasm went through him as he read the upside-down headline. An ongoing investigation. No one in custody.

A man he did not recognize came into his hospital room.

He had the appearance of a lawyer, the man. Pressed clothes and combed hair. He said that someone had paid all his hospital bills. *You are a hardworking boy, I heard, simply brilliant, came all this way from an impoverished background. Why do you want to get involved in all this rowdyism?* the man said, with what seemed to Krishna like genuine concern, a paternal tone, as though speaking to his own son.

*Why get involved in the police investigation? So unnecessary.*

*Your professor said you are transferring to the University of Bombay anyway. Listen to him. The police will come and ask you what you saw. You know what to say, don't you?*

*Won't you be the first person in your family to have a college degree, much less a PhD? They will be so proud of you. You can see them again.*

Gagan. Gagan. It felt as though Gagan would walk in the door any minute. Any second. Walk in and make the room seem small. Walk in and thump him on his shoulder, hold up his hands and say: *Krishna, you have to listen to this.* The way he said *Krishna.* Brother. Friend. Family.

The man was at the door, his hand on the knob before he turned around, looked straight at him and asked: Did he know that Gagan was stabbed twenty times?

He heard the nurse's soft, concerned voice asking him if he was okay. His head swam. It wasn't anger, and he felt ashamed when he realized what he was feeling. It was terror. He was terrified. He leaned over the bed and retched.

When he woke again, he felt his bandages. How tender his skull felt under the gauze. Dr. Ramaswamy was sitting by his bedside.

"Where's Vijaya?" he asked. "I have to go to the station to get her."

Dr. Ramaswamy shook his head. "Krishna, that was days ago."

"Where is she?"

"She didn't come."

"Where is she?" he repeated. He didn't understand.

"Krishna, she didn't come. She went back to Irumi."

He shook his head, he didn't understand.

Dr. Ramaswamy said, "Krishna, I went to the station myself. I called her in Irumi and spoke to her on the phone. She isn't coming."

# SUMMONS

---

When Sree awoke the next morning, the house smelled of sugar syrup. It was early, everything was still. A thin-legged spider was crawling up the windowpane next to her bed. She got off the bed and went to the window. She tapped the glass and the spider froze, watching her, waiting to see what she would do next.

The light outside was still dim, a dark blue. In the window glass she could even see her reflection, though only a section of her face was visible; the tip of her chin, her left eye, the outline of her left cheek. She drew close to the window and cupped her hands around her face.

Mist sat over everything. So thick it was as if she could grasp it like a sheet and pull. In the lemon grove below, a jeetha was at work already, trimming the bare branches of the lemon trees, his lips making that round shape that meant he was whistling. The grove was dying. A mysterious disease had taken hold of the trees when the vandals had hacked it, and since then, nothing they did could arrest the spread. It seemed to spread with the moving wind, from branch to branch, leaf to leaf, tree to tree. The outer edges of the grove were attacked first and of them nothing remained green; it was simply a ring of pale, dead brambles.

Underneath the hillock on which the gadi stood, hectares and hectares of spry green paddy. Brown hedgerows marking the boundaries. Beyond them, the cotton plantations, the oil seeds, the sunflowers, the cornfields, the groundnut, the chilies, the sugarcane. It was as if before her lay a sheet of brown wrapping paper, on which all the colors were stippled, then smeared. But the colors all had textures—now powdery, now prickly, now slick—textures that she could imagine touching. Of the forestland and the mountain range beyond the fields she could see nothing, it was all too dark, as if Irumi existed alone, all by itself, in a field of utter darkness, on the outer reaches of the very universe.

This was winter. A winter morning in Irumi looked like this. But in the summer, the snowy bolls of cotton cracked, and in the arid heat, they looked like moths, crouching low against that same sheet of brown paper, twitching now and then. The green paddy disappeared, the hedgerows shrank, the brown earth under them showed, multiplied, first in the far reaches of Irumi, then slowly moved closer; russet islands surfacing overnight. When the wind blew, it tumbled through the panes of dry fields and moved upwards, towards her room on the second floor, clouds and clouds of it beat against the windowpanes, forming piles of dust in the windowsills, soft like cornstarch, gathering in the gaps between the walls and the stonework, the fretworked wooden windows, smearing patches on the exterior walls. A dusty brown light filled her room then. The jeethas came around and shut all the doors and windows, stuffing moistened rags in the gaps of doorframes and window frames. Katya told her that in the village, they covered the mouths of wells, that they even buried their rice, their grain, their earthenware under layers of wet jute. In the summer, it was a sight full of desolation. Her eyes fell once again on the dying lemon grove that the jeetha was still trimming. He paused, dropped the big shears at his feet, and went to fetch the water hose.

Downstairs, she heard Katya mumbling and her mother replying. Next door, in Vijaya's room, she heard rustling, what sounded like sheaves of paper dropping on stone floors, the opening and closing of the closet, the bureau, the creak of the bedframe, the scrape of chair legs. Something like a trunk dragging.

"Sree, are you awake?"

She hesitated.

"Sree?"

"I'm awake," she said, turning to the wall that divided their rooms.

"Come here," Vijaya said.

She opened Vijaya's door. Vijaya was sitting on her bed.

After Vijaya left, she had the long mirror moved from Vijaya's room to hers. She hardly went in there afterwards, and had quite forgotten the view from Vijaya's room.

The room had that odor, of having been empty and unused for a while—like dust, like damp wood. Vijaya's teak rolltop was set at that angle she liked, looking over the fields and the mountains on one side, the banyan and the stepwell on the other. Books were piled on the rolltop, clothes on the high-backed chair. Clothes on her bed. Papers. The room was in disarray, but a pleasant sort of disarray, like when one goes away from home for a long while and returns, dropping bags and clothes and papers and travel things everywhere.

As children, they both slept in this room. She remembered, with sudden longing, the way they used to stay up late at night whispering across their cots, watching the shadows of night owls swooping around outside, the moon in the window. The perfect stillness of that memory was so tangible she felt she could hold it up to light and examine it this way and that way.

There was something in Vijaya's lap.

"Look what I found."

She stepped forward, shutting the door behind them.

It was a thing that she'd never been allowed to touch. That was all she remembered about it.

She reached forward and picked it up. Vijaya watched her.

It was heavy, the kaleidoscope.

The red silk Vijaya had wrapped around it all those years ago had retained its brilliance; it must be the gold zari that was used in the fabric, and the fact that all these years it was kept hidden somewhere in Vijaya's room, not exposed to the sun, to moisture, to changing seasons. The silk was smooth, flat, almost like velvet. The kaleidoscope made a sound when she picked it up. Like the rustling of anklets.

It came in such broken pieces, such a rush and jumble of images, that she felt as though the dark blue sky would fall through Vijaya's windows, knock the rolltop over, fall onto her.

"What's the matter Sree, aren't you feeling well?" Vijaya said, standing up and coming forward.

Instinctively, she drew back, shielding the kaleidoscope.

"I'm not going to take it from you, Sree."

"What is it made of?" she asked.

"Brass," Vijaya said, sitting back down. She seemed excited for the first time since she'd arrived. "See, I'd found this brass pipe. I don't know where it came from, I just took it from the library and I'm not sure if anyone missed it. And I ripped up the edge of Ma's silk sari—don't remind her—and broke pieces off my silver anklets. I got the colored twine in the bazaar. And the long pieces of glass . . . well, for the patterns."

"Ma used to always complain. That your anklets never chimed."

"While yours did. Even though they were identical."

"She blamed the goldsmith," she said.

"I want you to keep it, Sree," Vijaya said. "Are you okay? Please tell me if you aren't feeling well."

"I'm feeling well, I'm so fine."

"You look pale."

"I'm fine."

"Do you like it?" Vijaya said.

She nodded.

Vijaya's eyes were full, her lips were pressed together. Even as she watched, a fat tear struck down Vijaya's cheek and she turned away, wiping her face with the end of her sari. She had never seen Vijaya cry, she realized. Never. It looked so strange. Just like a normal person, crying. Human.

"I want to go to my room."

In her room, she lifted the kaleidoscope and pressed it against her eye. They were all of them triangles inside. They smarmed together, their edges soft, their manner glib, pressing together and multiplying, swelling, opening and closing like lips. She turned the kaleidoscope, the anklets chimed, the glass moved, and the pattern shifted.

"Though his name is Ravindra, everyone calls him Ravi, like the river," Katya said. She looked more cheerful than she'd looked in days. She was laying out Sree's clothes. The sun was up. Sree was at her desk, the biology textbook open in front of her again.

The outfit was a pale green tussar skirt, with a matching long blouse, all worked in bright red Kutch embroidery. Her mother often complained that the woman in the village who used to do the embroideries for them, Suma, was gone. Disappeared. And that now, anytime she needed any small bit of embroidery or stitching done, she had to send it away all the way to Hyderabad City.

Ever since she'd turned thirteen, she wasn't allowed to walk around in the clothes she'd slept in. She always had to be dressed well, even if all she was doing was reading at her desk. Her mother had Katya lay out her clothes on her bed every morning, something that she'd made Vijaya do as well. When they had houseguests, the outfit was something bright and dramatic. Today's choice of color was dull and muted. "Why the tussar?" she asked. Even though it was silk, tussar was lightweight, thin, it wrinkled easily and made a swishing noise when she walked.

Katya shrugged and left.

Around eleven, she heard cars pulling up outside. She'd lost track of time, she wasn't dressed. The outfit still lay where Katya had left it, on her bed, a part of the Kutch embroidery reflected in Vijaya's long mirror. She'd assumed that Katya would have reminded her when it was nearly time.

She hurried, slipped out of her night clothes. She was at the point of stepping into the green skirt when she stopped, went to the window and leaned over the bureau. They were already here, and no one had reminded her. There were two cars, a blue one and a black one. The black one looked new, the glossy paint rippled in the sunlight.

People began alighting. Her parents were standing in the vaakili, waiting to receive them. Her mother, slightly ahead of her father and uncle. She was so well attuned to the manner of her family's clothing choices that she knew immediately that they'd all dressed to be impressive, but in an offhand, casual sort of way; a manner carrying the suggestion that even though they'd dressed up to be respectful, they hadn't done it so excessively as to be mistaken for the petty bourgeois. They'd all gone down without her.

When the alighting group reached them, it was immediately obvious which one of them the groom was.

Ravindra—Ravi—the man who was going to be her sister's husband, had gotten out of the black car. He was wearing a navy-blue shirt, the cuffs buttoned over his wrists; pressed beige trousers; tan oxfords. He smiled at her parents. Looked around at the gadi in frank admiration. He had a broad face, a slim if somewhat pointed nose, skin that was almost mahogany but tinged red—ruddy—glowing with health. He was just as their mother described.

Hands were being shaken all around. Namastes being said, now softly, now jovially. Laughter. Crossing the vaakili, admiring the façade of the gadi, Ravi looked up.

She was holding the green skirt still. She was perfectly aware of the fact that she was not visible. Behind the fretwork windows, all he would be able to see was a pale white shadow of something, someone moving. His eyes passed over where she was, but she could have sworn their eyes met. The smile he gave now, looking up at her, meeting her invisible eyes, it was as though he knew she was there.

She was naked. He was too, Ravi. And it seemed she and Ravi were sitting together, in some vague and far away place, but on the surface of something sturdy and concrete but brambly, like a tree, green like memory. This image, of her and Ravi, together, perfectly naked, their bodies touching, was raw, powerful and perfectly hazy. She was biting his lips, it seemed. And it was pink and delicious, like the first bite of an apple. "You smell like a tree," she said.

And it felt as if her mouth was full. As if she'd sat too close to the stove, too close to the sugar syrup boiling on that stove, inhaling the swollen perfume of it. She desired something—intensely—unbearably—but did not quite know what it was.

She knew what she looked like naked, but not well enough. She couldn't close her eyes and summon an image of herself, the way she could summon the image of the courtyard, or her room, or the view outside her room in every season. Also, she was constantly discovering things. In the afternoons, sometimes there was an opportunity for her to perform one of her examinations on herself. But only when she was sure

Katya was taking a nap. She'd strip quickly and stand in front of the long mirror.

Now, she went to the long mirror and stood in front of it. Downstairs, she could hear them, moving, mumbling, chair scraping. She put her foot on the purple tufted pouf. She stood up straight. Hands on hips. Look.

Look away. That was always her first instinct. But then, why? Why should she look away when it was hers to look at. She watched the scar, the long single scar, beginning at her ankle, slithering up her shin, gliding past that misshapen knee, drifting up the thigh. At her thigh, it took a slight turn. There, it disappeared, into the edge of her hip bone. The rough brown scar was ever so slightly beneath the surface. *How long will I have it?* she remembered asking her mother, in some distant past of her childhood. She turned, first one way, then the other way, cocked her chin and just simply looked. It was like a railway track, one track instead of the two, but with that same bisecting design wherever the sutures healed, dents, dimples, pits.

"Sree-papa," Katya was calling up the stairs.

Suddenly Katya's voice sounded closer. She wasn't allowed to lock her door. "Dorasani wants you downstairs," Katya said. Her hand was on the doorjamb, only seconds away from sensing the thing roiling in her; she was sure of it. The image of them in that green place doing the secret thing, their bellies rubbing.

She slipped into the tussar skirt with the matching long blouse. She took quick smooth strides and reached the doorway before Katya had the chance to repeat herself. Careful, Katya said, holding her elbow. Don't you trip now. Why must you walk so fast? Slow down. She pulled her elbow out of Katya's grip.

She went downstairs, but waited behind the stairway doors and looked in. They were all in the courtyard, spread across the rosewood furniture. The sky over the courtyard was clear, the light soft and white, as on a morning after it rains and the sun isn't yellow or gold. She counted six unfamiliar faces. Her mother, her father. Her uncle; he was across the room, sitting in the easy chair by the gramophone. Navy shirt, beige trousers, feet bare now. Ravi.

A woven rug was spread in front of them, set against the reflecting pool, at a slight angle so that it drew the eye. The Chettinad tile had been replaced recently. The reds and greens and yellows had been matched as closely as possible to the original, and even though her mother said that no one would be able to tell, the difference was still obvious to her; obvious and off-putting; it lent a sense of unpleasant foreignness to an accustomed place.

The rug was scarlet, with a pattern of maroon paisleys. She'd never seen that rug before, certainly not in that place.

There was a lull in the conversation when she entered the courtyard.

They'd re-done the limewash recently and everything felt blindingly white, except for the scarlet rug. In her dull green clothes, she felt conspicuous, like a bug, and she felt every single eye in the room on her, following her, her progress across the courtyard where her mother was sitting. She held herself as straight as possible. She walked as quickly as possible. As smoothly as possible, holding herself at that angle that she knew hid the laziness in her leg.

It was all colors, smears, splashing all across the rosewood, now moving, now still. She felt afraid, that the image would come back to her, and that everyone might know what it was. Who's to say her thoughts were private? Who's to say there wasn't some method; some method that perhaps only the adults knew, by which her thoughts were entirely transparent, put on display somewhere, for them all to laugh at her. She felt ashamed, she felt the color seeping up her neck. Why were they all looking at her like that, all the knowing looks, at her face, at her body, running down her legs.

Then she was safely ensconced by her mother. The conversation picked up again. A low comforting sort of murmur breaking the surface of the quiet. She looked at her fingertips, the way Vijaya did the day before. It seemed like the proper thing to do.

Her father, she noticed, as she snuck a glance, was deep in conversation with Ravi across the room from her. Over the general murmur, she could overhear their conversation. They were talking about his work.

He was a house surgeon now, on "rotation," he said, that would last a year. Then what? Then it is a difficult question. A career move isn't a difficult choice, her father said. There is one cardinal rule for all career decisions. And what was that? Never make the easy choice. That's it. The manner in which her father delivered this advice? As though to a confidant. But also, in the genial tone of an advisor, a mentor, a father. And also, colored by the camaraderie reserved for insiders. This depressed her a little. She wondered why. She observed her father, the glint in his eyes, his shiny expression while talking to Ravi, a stranger.

"All daughters," someone across the room said. It was a man sitting on her uncle's right. He was bald, and extremely thin, with watery gray eyes that made her think of standing water.

Her father smiled coolly, nodded.

"But you must feel it no? The lack of sons. It would have been nice to have sons," the man said, shaking his head earnestly, with something like sympathy in his eyes.

"Oh, no," her father said.

"You're just saying that. It isn't true. A son is a son. You know it."

She was familiar with how this kind of conversation with fathers of sons went. Sree whispered into her mother's ear, in the same tone that her father usually said it: "Sons, daughters, aren't they all the same? Because in the end, all children break your heart, no matter their gender. Then you die."

"Hush," her mother said, widening her eyes, trying not to look amused.

But before her father said this, her uncle made a gesture with the tips of his fingers, telling her father not to react; done so imperceptibly that she was sure everyone except she, her mother, and her father would have missed it. This self-control, from her uncle of all people. How strange.

But the man, seemingly intent on getting a reaction out of her father, said, "See when you do die, a daughter cannot light your pyre. That's the job for only the son. If you have one. Or a son-in-law."

Her uncle's jaw tightened, but still, he did not say anything. Neither did her father. The man looked at Ravi, and she realized that he was Ravi's father. That's why.

"Sree, go to Daddy," her mother said loudly. She shook her head. Widened her eyes. She didn't want to go near them. But her mother lifted her by the arm and nudged her forward again.

"Is it your youngest?" Ravi's father said, frankly appraising her. "Oh she's a beauty. Gold. Pure gold!"

Her face was burning. Walking across the room, she felt like an ant, a little black ant under a magnifying glass. It made her feel unbearably small, and also unbearably conspicuous, conscious of every movement in her body, and then she became aware that there was a fastidiousness in her manner now, appearing, apparition-like, under the glare of the many eyes trained on her.

"But what use is just gold eh?" the man said, when she reached them. "A diamond is needed to set it. A diamond"—here, he looked pointedly in the direction of Ravi—"is required. Isn't that the truth?" He laughed and a few of the others joined in. She felt that he seemed to want to reach out and touch her, as passing, distant relations frequently did. Drawing her into hugs she didn't want, pinching her cheeks, making her sit on their laps even.

On Ravi's face, which she snuck a glance at, her own embarrassment seemed reflected, along with a resemblance to his father on the edges of his face—the shape of the forehead, the chin, the ears too.

"Sit here, bidda," her father said, making room on the small sofa, between him and Ravi. Relieved, and not even minding that she had to sit so close to Ravi, she changed direction and went to them.

"Daddy, can I go back upstairs?" she whispered in his ear.

"In a little while," he whispered back.

"Daddy?" Ravi's father said, leaning over her father and repeating, as if to grab her. "Daddy? Daddy? The English dora has left us, but he's ruined our language forever, hasn't he?"

He peered into her face, clearly intending it as an accusation. As though she had personally been responsible for the English being there, and for them leaving behind their language. *This is all your fault*, his gaze seemed to say.

When she did not respond, he looked around at the others, and seeming to change his mind, added seriously, "Nowadays everyone says *mummy* and *daddy* instead of Amma and Nanna. It falls so oddly on the ears I must say. The language of our younger generations, our culture even, it is all being horribly ruined. Such are these times."

"Oh, they don't say *mummy*," their mother said from across the room. "No. No. I made sure they never even learned that. I dislike that word too. Completely. Don't use a foreign word, at least to refer to your own mother—that's what I always say."

She said *mummy* all the time. Her mother never objected. She also said *ma, amma, mother* and once, in a jovial mood she called her *Mother India*, in reference to the film. *Oh, Mother India, bring me the Horlicks.* It had been a film she'd heard about but hadn't watched. Her father, overhearing this, said that she mustn't use words she didn't understand. And that the film was an extraordinary achievement in filmmaking; that it deliberately borrowed the name *Mother India* from a novel; a novel written by a Westerner who'd portrayed Indians as uncivilized devil worshippers and sexual perverts. The movie re-wrote the meaning of the phrase, re-claimed it to the point that nobody even remembered the novel. The color seemed to rise in her father's face when he started talking about the novel. She'd said, "Daddy, there is child marriage in India, I read about it in the paper," by way of asking for an explanation, because she'd understood very little of what he was saying. He sighed and said, "You're just a girl, You can't understand." It had made her feel horrible.

Now, in the ensuing lull after her mother's intervention, her father and her uncle and Ravi fell into deep conversation. They were leaning over her so they could meet each other's eyes, so she pressed herself against the sofa so as to not be in the way. For a while, she herself seemed to be the subject of conversation. She heard Ravi say "chronic pain management" and tuned it out.

In a minute or two the topic shifted. They were trading opinions on the stock market, grain subsidies and fertilizer subsidies, the Marxists, the congress party. Her father and her uncle were staunch anti-Marxists, whatever that meant. Her uncle was shaking his head. It was the congress that always had their support; monetary or otherwise. Ravi said he saw both sides. They were disagreeing. She observed him. His face was flushed, energized. While talking to Ravi, her uncle seemed to be vibrating with energy. How rare a sight that was.

Sree drew close to her father. She wound her arm through his, and he acknowledged it in an absent sort of way. They continued to volley arguments over her head. In the manner of having an epiphany, she came to realize something. In this light shining in her father's and in her uncle's every feature, she realized that there would remain something elemental in both of them that she would never be able to access. That Vijaya had always been able to access.

"How pretty you are," Ravi said suddenly, his gaze falling on her, sitting in between them.

She looked at him. Ravi's lips were a dark, deep, delicious pink. They were thick and wide. And she wanted to know how it would feel to press hers against his. And she wanted to know how it would feel to bite down on them.

He was smiling at her. She said nothing. She returned to look at her fingertips. Her father nudged her. "Tell him your name," he said. Of course, everyone knew her name, but it was as if a way to torment her; this need for her to open her mouth and utter her own name in public.

She said her name and also at the same time tried to clear her throat so that her voice would sound better.

And Ravi flinched, a little taken-aback twitch appearing and disappearing on his face. She realized that she had said her name in a tone as if snapping at him; her voice was rude and sharp. She felt her father's hand on her shoulder tighten, a slight pressure as if to say *Calm down*. She looked at her fingernails again and smoothed the front of her skirt, picking at the Kutch embroidery. Ravindra reached across and lightly pinched her cheek. "Very pretty girl. Which form are you in?"

"I'm going into eleventh," she said.

"Which form?"

"Eleventh," she said again, raising her voice slightly.

"Tell me the atomic weight of gold," he commanded.

Her face she knew, was bright red. Knew because of the burning sensation it gave her. That was the problem with being so light-skinned. It allowed her emotions to surface. The tops of her cheeks turned pink, her ears flushed red, her neck too. It was so maddening. So maddening to think that she could never control what showed on her face. What she showed others.

When she arrived at the answer of, "Aurum, 196.96," she lost his attention. Vijaya had arrived.

Vijaya walked, gently, gracefully, light on her feet. She was wearing an orange sari. The silk was not shiny. The fabric was rich and glossy, but flat, muted. The zari was pale gold, almost translucent. She was wearing jewelry that Sree hadn't seen before. Filigreed basket hoops and a matching necklace—a flat, wide, rectangular pendant, also filigreed gold. The design of the pendant was of two little peacocks in profile, their tail feathers joined together. Their eyes set with rubies, tails with little emeralds. They were floating, the peacocks, on the edge of a river, rippling water, a row of seed pearls.

There was so much grace in Vijaya. A grace that she could never imagine having.

That was the purpose of the red rug on the floor, at that angle, in that light. It was the place where Vijaya would sit, be displayed, visible in every direction.

"Can we ask the girl to walk?" Ravi's father said. He repeated: "To walk. Just over here and there."

Ravi objected, but his father pretended not to hear.

Her father nodded in the direction of Vijaya, and their mother went over, crouched down, obstructing Vijaya's face from them. She had the feeling that every single person in the courtyard, spread across all that rosewood furniture, was avoiding her eye. Even Ravi's father, who was up until them making her feel somewhat uncomfortable with his staring, was avoiding looking at her specifically. It was as if they wanted proof that Vijaya wasn't like her.

See? She could never control her face like Vijaya was always able to. Even now, even after that short and furious exchange was completed between their mother and her, Vijaya stood up and her face was placid.

She caught Ravi looking at Vijaya. His expression was polite, admiring, frankly interested, and apologetic.

Vijaya straightened her sari, took a few general steps across the court-yard, towards the end where her mother returned to sit, and then again towards this end, toward where she was sitting, between her father and Ravindra. Ravindra, he was trying to catch Vijaya's eye. He seemed to want to say something. His smile had a charming quality. But Vijaya did not meet his eyes. She walked like she was asked to, gently, gracefully.

And all the while she walked for them, once this way then the other way back again—twice in all—Vijaya's face was tranquil, betraying absolutely nothing. Her braid was thick and smooth. It wound around her neck, fell all the way to her waist.

"She is studying for a BA in economics at Presidency College," her mother said proudly.


She'd been allowed to go back up only when they were ready to leave. From the vantage point of her room, Sree saw Ravi lagging behind.

This was on purpose, it was plain to her. He wanted to fall into step with Vijaya. Both sets of parents let him. They walked ahead, towards the two waiting cars, not noticing them. Goodbyes seemed to take an unreasonably long time. Ravi was saying something, she could see his lips moving. Vijaya was replying. They exchanged polite smiles.

She turned away from the window. It was almost noon. The sun was high and mighty and yellow. It fell in through her windows, throwing great splashes of bright color on her desk, the biology textbook still opened to the leaf page, the bed on which the kaleidoscope sat. She went to her bed and picked it up.

She pressed it against her eye. The shapes again. It made her head spin. She felt dizzy and nauseated.

It began behind her right ear, the same place where it always began. A little crack. Spreading, widening and deepening as it went; a straight line going from her ear to her temple, then arriving at a point between her brows it exploded. She cried out and held her face to her hands. The kaleidoscope slipped out. She heard it hit the floor. She heard the mirrors inside crack.

It rolled under her bed, chinks of glass tinkling, sputtering.

She shut her eyes. Darkness. But tinged with red. Blood. Thrusting in and out of the little capillaries running across her eyelids. A sheet of red light. The soft clatter of car doors. Opening, closing. Engines starting. She fell into bed and pulled the covers over her head. The sheets were so cool against her face, it was like falling headfirst into a pool of water.

This was all so familiar, she welcomed it. Not the pain of course, but the familiar things the pain brought with it. A fat, bitter pill going down her throat, Katya by her side, wiping her face with a cool washcloth, covering her windows with quilts to block out the light, giving her little sips of lemonade, spoonfuls of buttermilk rice, all the while silent, not talking, not even whispering because any sound was like a pincer, sharp and knife-like, entering her skull, slicing into her brain. She would throw up. And Katya would sponge it off her, pull a new shirt over her head. It was all of it familiar. It was all of it a kind of homecoming.

She would miss the first day of eleventh form after all, there was no doubt about it. Her final thought was that she felt angry. At Vijaya, for giving her the kaleidoscope and causing her headaches to begin.

Katya walked in, without knocking, announcing the news that the match was fixed, the wedding would be within a month. "What does *she* think about that?"

Then she saw it.

A little rip in that sheet of red light. Within that rip was a velvety darkness. The eye of a needle, filled with lead. But lead that was porous, like sand, like quicksand. She turned sideways and slipped through it.

Sometime in the middle of the night, and it could have been early morning, she became aware of the fabric sitting against her body. It wasn't the tussar. She was wearing a cotton nightdress. And beside her, asleep on the floor was Katya, her hand stretched out underneath her in an arc. She felt hot. She pulled off her sheet and tried to stand up.

It was raining outside. Thunder. But distant now, soft, no more than a comforting sort of rumble, tiny tapping noises against the dark windowpanes. She got out of bed, and steadying herself with one hand, she threw her sheet over Katya. It didn't cover her well, her foot stuck out from under it, but she didn't go around and adjust it. Besides, Katya might wake up, ask her how she was feeling, make a big fuss, call her mother. She didn't feel up to it.

Sree went to the window and stood there, watched the rain fall. The windowpanes were wet, smeared with color.

Then it came to her. It came simply, in snatches, in a sequence of images, like catching sight of the brightly colored illustrations while riffling through her biology textbook.

How green the knoll was, how sweet the custard apples. The smell of grass she'd pulled up by the roots, the sound of blades snapping.

*Be quiet! The tiger mustn't hear us.*

The sky growing overcast, the breeze shifting direction; her red ribbon; his wild, wild laughter, like the howling of wind through the tunnels of a solitary mountain.

Sree turned away from the window. In the darkness of her room, she said it aloud—his name—over thunder and the sound of rain, flowing through the years, through the hills.

"Ranga," she said, as if it were an invocation. Summons.

# PART THREE

---

# 1970

# LORD OF THE MANGO TREES

———◆———

Ranga tied up the little rowboat. The river was flowing fast, and the rowboat bobbed in place. He knelt down to check the knot, untied it and tied it up again. He couldn't lose the boat, it was the only way for him to leave Irumi without being seen. The gadi loomed over the riverbank. Its many windows, its fretwork shutters, the stained glass panes. In the midday sun, its shadow barely fell.

He'd borrowed the boat from a fisherman in the next village; he'd lent Ranga the boat for money, but also on trust.

"Are you a Naxalite?" the fisherman asked him blankly. He said no. And he saw that the fisherman did not believe him.

In some villages, saying yes meant food; they'd be fed, and housed, if only for the night. But in some villages, a small or big landlord would hear of it and summon the police. One never heard from those comrades again.

Surendra Deshmukh was not a beloved figure in Irumi. But there would still be loyalists. The reason was his brother; those in luck had their sharecropping rents reduced by him, debt erased even. On festival days, they would be fed, given some grain, even money for this or that expense if they caught him in the right moment. Because of this one would never tell, who was loyal to the Deshmukh family, and who wasn't; who'd come to their rescue, who wouldn't. In the charity of Mahendra Deshmukh had always been the family's safety; there was a measure of respect for him, even a peculiar type of affection, as one has towards a tyrant prone to bouts of kindness. Born out of familiarity, if nothing else.

"Why do you need it?" the fisherman had asked, even after pocketing the coins that Ranga had given him. The fisherman seemed curious. And suspicious. He looked Ranga up and down, wistfully, even sadly. Though cash was scarce, and he'd been paid well, he was unwilling to part with his boat for even a day. He wanted to know exactly what use his boat would be put to.

Ranga hadn't prepared a lie, and he said the first thing that rose to his lips.

"For my brother's ashes."

"Oh?"

"I want to go out into the river so I can pour out his ashes into the river."

"What did he die of?"

"Malaria."

Less curiosity. More sympathy. "I had a little one once," the fisherman said, "a girl. She was three when she got it. She always wanted to come out on the water with me. And I let her come once, took her all the way up to the reservoir. Just the two of us. A crocodile came up, almost got us in the water. She was so scared she never asked to come again. She died. Malaria. We buried her. She would have been this high by now."

He asked again, "Are you a Naxalite?" as though hoping to surprise him into answering.

"No."

There was such doubt in his eyes. "I don't want any trouble with the police. Our lives are too small for trouble. If they catch hold of the boat, who it belongs to, they'll put me inside as a sympathizer. Do you know what they do to you? One man from our hamlet was taken like that. They beat him in the cell until he bled out of his ears. They lashed him, strung him up by the feet. Put chili powder in his eyes and pressed it into his wounds too. All because of a suspicion. Now tell me, if he doesn't know the whereabouts of a squad, how can he tell them? How much ever he is beaten? I don't want to be beaten."

"I'm not a Naxalite."

That was the second lie he'd told in as many days. The first one had been for Suma. "Promise me you won't go to the gadi," she'd said, handing him the baby, so carefully bundled in its black wool blanket. Its clean muslin clothes, its smooth hair. Where had she gotten the muslin clothes? The squad had found a tribal midwife for Suma, a place to have it. A place, the midwife insisted, away from any water body so that the tigers that came to drink at the pools would not smell all the blood, hear the terrific screams.

"Won't you look at him?" Suma asked. "Won't you, Ranga?"

He didn't.

"I wanted dignity," she said. "I thought I'd have dignity if I joined the movement. Where is the dignity in this?"

An activist cannot feel regret, he told her. Can only feel pride that every sacrifice made on behalf of the party contributes to the revolutionary liberation of the oppressed masses of this country. Everyone in the squad had touched the baby. Viplavam: *Revolution*.

Govind asked to go instead of him. Anyone else in the squad could go, Ranga mustn't risk it; if he was seen, he was as good as dead. He said no. He'd go himself. "Don't go to the gadi," Suma told him. "I want your child to see you again one day." He said he wouldn't.

He'd reached Irumi, his mother's cottage. The baby bundled in its wool blanket, muslin clothes, smooth hair. He stayed at his mother's cottage for two days. On the third, Katya had arrived. Saroja-dorasani has sent me, she said, to ask after you. His mother went out into the palm grove to talk to Katya. Told him to stay hidden. She'd send Katya away.

Listening to Katya and his mother talk, Ranga had known what it was—why he'd chosen to come himself even though being sighted in the vicinity of the village meant certain death. He'd been guided towards this moment his whole life. And now it was here.

"Because everyone was coming home this year," Katya said. Tara—and Vijaya too, who never came for Diwali but was coming this year because; well, you know why, Pichamma—even Surendra Deshmukh wasn't remaining in the city this year. Because when Vijaya came, he came.

"It is all for her," Katya said. Then a pause. "It has been such a hard year for her, and—" His mother interrupting, saying Katya mustn't think that way.

"It would make her so happy, Pichamma," Katya said. "To have it like the old days. The entire family together. Being all dressed up. With fireworks for the children. And they are doing it all, everything she wants. Even the goondas—well, most of them—are being sent away this year. It will be just the family."

And Ranga turned to the baby, asleep on the cot. He picked it up, looked into its face, ran a finger between its brows. This is why this puny thing was born. Its life was predestined. A stroke of divine intervention. So that he could hold the decision of whether the Deshmukhs would live or die in his hands. Balanced like the blade of a sword.

He'd tell his squad: "I did the recce work myself, Comrades. We will go on the night of Diwali. We will kill them all, and we will put them on spectacular display. I want the Deshmukhs as an example of what happens if you stand in the way of the red flag—for their oppression of the proletariat, for their willful spreading of the doctrine of the imperialists and the class enemies, their heads will hang in the paddy fields. Our chance has finally come."

Maybe he believed some of it, maybe he believed none of it.

"I want to tell you my daughter's name," the fisherman had said. "Bullemma was her name," and he touched a point in his chest, as if that was where she lived.

At the riverbank, Ranga gave the rope another tug to make sure it was secure. The trees on the bank were old and tall. They sprawled thickly overhead, blocking out the sun, sunlight falling only through the gaps between branches. He looked at the boat one last time and made his way up the hillock. The ground was damp and cold, the leaves wet. There were some tuniki berries in his pocket and as he made his way towards the orchard, up the slope of the hillock, away from the tree, the boat, the river, he began to eat the berries, spitting out the seeds one after the other. He waited to catch sight of the orchard, but even after reaching the top of the hillock, the orchard did not materialize. He looked down at the bank, the boat.

Most of the orchard was dead, he realized. Long dead, by the looks of it. The closer he moved towards the gadi, the louder his footsteps became; the dry leaves, the dry earth, his feet no longer muffled. The cicadas were trilling. The dead leaves crunched. The branches bare, birdless. Was there ever a time when the orchard had no birds?

He tried to orient himself. He always used to know exactly where he was, anywhere in the Deshmukh household, anywhere in the orchard. He knew each and every single inch of it like the lines in his own hands. But amongst all this dead vegetation, he felt disoriented.

The copse of mango trees was on the northern edge, right underneath Surendra Deshmukh's study. He counted the third window from the left and made his way towards that section. Soon enough, he found the copse. A small group, a gray scab covered all the branches, the trunk, the stems. Leaves wilted and brown. All dead.

Could he climb one?

He tested the branch above him. It creaked threateningly but did not seem likely to crack. Its surface was the color of flint. He pulled himself up, swung his foot over a fork in the trunk. The bark rasped under his fingers. Sitting in the tree, a sense of elation spread through him. He realized that he'd been holding on to a pit, unconsciously grinding it under his rear teeth. He spat it out and watched it fall in an arc, disappear among the dry leaves. He surveyed. There he was again, lord of the mango trees. Lord of the orchard.

In the room above, Surendra Deshmukh used to sit smoking his cigars in the afternoons. The shutters were closed. Would it open? Would he be seen? What if he shouted, made a noise?

The temptation to draw attention to himself was almost too much to bear. He willed himself to get back down quietly. The walls of the gadi were made of stone, they were fat and wide, but the orchard had a rear door. He needed to make sure they could get in through that. He knew that door so well. Even though shut and locked, the latch could be shaken loose with a single nudge in the right place, a nudge timed precisely, so that the jangle of the metal chain would be drowned out by the screech of a night owl.

In his mind he marked off all the sections with which he was familiar. The places that used to be intentionally burned down around festival days to make room for the firewood, the outdoor kitchens that fed a hundred people a day. *Remember, remember*, the orchard seemed to say. *Remember.*

There used to be beehives in the Deshmukh orchard. So many of them that they had no need to buy honeycombs off the tribes. But now there were only wasp nests. There were also mealy bugs. The cicadas. A lemon tree, dead too, insects pierced on its long needles.

Back on the ground, he made his way towards the rear door of the orchard. But he stopped again. He couldn't help himself. He had to find the gunja—the tamarind tree—the whipping tree.

There was a charred section of the orchard, closer to the gadi's western wall, roughly where the tamarind tree used to be, as though an attempt had been made to burn down the orchard and then abandoned. The tree trunks were black, as was the brush on the ground. It was also the only place where new groundcover was emerging; a few bright green leaves, wild plants, tender stalks just beginning to shoot out of the earth. He bent down and pinched a leaf, put it in his mouth, chewed and spat it out.

He heard the distinct clatter of a window. Movement. But when he looked up, there was no one. All the windows were still shut.

He began walking away from the charred section. The dead brambles crunched underfoot, but closer to the orchard door the cicadas were so loud that the noise of his footfalls was barely audible. It was as though their trilling began to come at him from every direction, as if even the grains of soil underneath him were vibrating, ready to rise up and hide him. The closer he got to the door, the more he felt out of control, but also safe; protected by his adulthood, his pistol strapped to his waist.

In his adulthood he had killed men. He had taken lives. Seen blood gush out of necks, scrubbed it off his hands, washed his clothes of it, chewed betel leaves to get the smell out of his nostrils. But all that spilled blood had meaning behind it. There was sense in it—a sense that in the end, it would be worth it. In the end, it would bring him here.

He was approaching the door. Again and again, he looked at all the shut windows. A face with too many eyes. The clatter of the window echoed around in his mind. Who was that? Had they seen him? And who was he? He was ten yards away from the door. There was something new there; a stone platform, raised slightly aboveground, running alongside the orchard wall, as if it were a place to sit and admire the vegetation in the morning time. Closer and closer he went, watching for scorpions, watching for snakes. Who was he? He was Ranga. He was Comrade RK. Krishna's lost brother. His mother's firstborn son. A lost son. He looked at his hands, at his feet, at the earth underneath them. Who was he?

Once in a while, the cicadas fell silent. It was a hushed, sudden, unexpected silence. Not a heavy silence, not a lush silence, but an anemic one. He was only a few feet away from the door. He had the keen sensation of being watched.

This was how they would attack:

They'd come down the river on rowboats, small ones like the one he'd borrowed from the fisherman. They'd come in the dead of the night. They'd go through the orchard, tracing the path he was taking now. They'd surround the gadi. Comrades near the rear door leading to the orchard so that no one could escape. The gadi's main doorways were thick, too sturdy for them to enter. In the end, they would open. They will open, hinges pried off the frames. He knew where the safes were kept, their exact locations. They would take cash. Gold. Burn all the land deeds. Then, they would burn down the gadi.

There was someone standing at the rear door.

She still looked the same. The same slender neck. It felt like he could reach it and hold it, snap it like a wet green stem, between his thumb and his forefinger, and the milk would run.

"Ranga, are you Ranga? You are, aren't you?" Sree said.

*Don't go to the gadi*, Suma had told him. *One day I want your child to see you again.*

He hadn't set eyes on her since that day in the jungle, the after. How slight she was in his arms. Soft, little, caked in mud. Like a thing trapped. A moth. A butterfly. A thing to care for simply by the nature of its beauty; its utter, complete vulnerability. Its frailty.

He didn't know how much of that day she remembered. How much, it was in his power, to leave her there. To leave them both there. Return home with Krishna. Tell no one. Two missing girls, a loss to plague the Deshmukhs forever. Surely a just punishment? Why then did he save her?

She was standing on the edge of the orchard, in a little charred clearing by the rear door. On that stone platform. The cicadas started up again. She looked frightened. This was the hand of fate, testing his resolve. It had to be today, it had to be her.

"Ranga," she said again. "It is you, isn't it?"

He reached her. When he touched her cheek, she looked frightened, she shut her eyes.

He felt for her scar, behind her ear, running alongside her chin. *I saved you*, he thought. *And your life is mine. Do you know this?*

She scrunched up her eyes tighter, angled her chin away, as if something heavy were being swung her way and she couldn't get away in time.

If anyone saw him, that minute, the expression on his face, they'd know. His reappearance, years after the factory had burned down, years after it had become truth that he was a Naxalite with a bounty on his head, they would know. If she told anyone she saw him there, they'd know. The answer was clear, the way to prevent it from happening. The way to make sure that their mission would be successful.

Would it be murder if he killed her now?

In this dead orchard, while she stood in front of him, trusting, guileless, lamb, pale, lily.

Was it her humanity that day, that made him save her at the price of losing his brother, his everything. Or was it *his* humanity?

Would it not be murder if he killed her in two weeks, when she stood alongside her family and he stood alongside his. He, divorced from his individual conscience but part of a collective consciousness, feel only what the collective consciousness could feel? If it wasn't murder then what would it be, what was its name? Justice; vengeance; the greater good? The death of all those who stood on her side. The lives that would be bettered from those deaths. It would be one brotherhood destroying another, not him destroying her. Then what was his humanity, what was hers? When he killed her, he wouldn't think of her face in the grass, the soft, soft grass of the knoll, the blue sky reflected in the blacks of her eyes. Guileless lamb. Lily. He wouldn't think of her like that because she wasn't Sree then, and he wasn't Ranga. He was Comrade RK. And today would be the day he would glimpse his humanity, the last and final time, in this place, and she would be the witness. This was where his pain lived. This was also where his humanity lived. She was its home.

Are you well? he asked.

There were purple half-moons under her eyes.

I'm tired, she said. I'm so tired.

He drew close and pressed his lips against hers.

After all, wasn't it the one thing he'd wanted to do all his natural life. This touching of his lips against hers.

# TIGER CLAWS

---

The colt was losing the last of its milk teeth. Her uncle was holding the colt's mouth open, and sure enough, Vijaya saw a large gap between its scalars and molars, the last teeth to go. "How tall is it now?" she asked him. He let go of the colt's mouth. The colt shook its head, sniffed. Immediately, it went back to gnawing at the knot in its leash.

"Sixty inches?" she guessed.

"Almost sixty-two," her uncle said.

"Stop that," Vijaya muttered, pulling the colt away from the leash, brushing the spot between its eyes. There was a snowy patch of white there, longer and more oblong than a spot, but not quite a lace either. An in-betweenness that was enchanting. The color matched the socks on its front and hind legs. It was going to be a beautiful trail horse in a few years. Seeing it grow had been one of the few pleasures of returning to Irumi.

The colt pulled away, nickering softly, moving towards her uncle as though asking him to make her stop. "He's spoilt," her uncle said, brushing the same spot more roughly. "Never stops gnawing at the leash. What horse does that? And when I let him out, he prances around like a big shot," he added. "Do you want to see?"

She nodded.

"Lead him," he said, pulling it out of the stable and handing her the reins.

The colt looked at her appraisingly. She shook her head.

"Why not?" he said.

"We could let him loose for a while," she said.

All the while her uncle loosened the knot, it puffed its nostrils impatiently, snorting and tugging. When the leash finally came off, it sprinted out, first trotting, then cantering playfully, its body velvety black in the sunshine. It had a beautiful gait.

"Look how he does it," her uncle said. "The rascal."

She smiled.

"But the shoes aren't sitting right," he said.

They sounded all right to her, but she didn't say it.

Then he said, "Only Ranga could do it properly."

She knew what he meant, knew he didn't want her to acknowledge what he really meant. That he wished Ranga would return.

"I'll go and check on Sree," she said.

He took his eyes off the colt.

She turned to leave, but he said, "When did you get all those?" He was pointing at his temple.

"What?" she said, touching her hair.

"You aren't even thirty."

She realized he meant the gray hair.

"Tell Ravi to test your blood. Maybe it's an iron deficiency," he said.

She said she would. Then she left the sheds, crossed the courtyard.

Ravi never came with her because she asked him not to. Usually, she returned only once a year, for Sree's birthday, stayed for a month. But this year, Sree asked her if she could come a second time, for Diwali. Sree made so few requests nowadays that she couldn't say no. She was planning to stay two weeks, till the day after Diwali, and leave the morning after.

She went back into the gadi, went upstairs to her uncle's study. They had continued to call it the study, even years after it had been transformed into Sree's room. Her father and her mother were both standing at the door. "She's sleeping," her mother said.

She still wanted to go inside, sit there awhile. But her mother did not move out of her way.

"Where's the pendant?" her mother said. "You've lost it, haven't you!"

Her father nodded once in her direction and left.

Vijaya asked her mother if she meant the one she'd lost in Madras all those years ago—the round gold one with the ruby that had been made for her first birthday. "No, not that," her mother said. "The one with the tiger claws."

She said, honestly, that she did not know where it was. She'd never even laid eyes on it.

"Liar," her mother hissed. "You always were such a liar."

Vijaya moved away from the door, not wanting to disturb Sree. She wasn't sleeping well.

"Don't you walk away from me. Who do you think you are?" her mother shouted, and followed her, all the way down the corridor, to her old room.

"Ma, I'm only going to look in my room," she said.

"What *used* to be your room."

She stopped, turned around and said, "Why did you have to say that? This is still my home."

"You don't know where anything is anymore. Katya! Katya, come with us. Only you know where everything is," her mother said.

In what used to be her room, she and Katya went through the drawers in her bureau, one after the other, while her mother stood at the door, her words continuing to assail Vijaya. There was so much jewelry. She opened box after box: there was the emerald and diamond set, the ruby choker that belonged to her grandmother, there were the golden anklets, the bunch pearls with the matching bangles, the old gold-wire earrings strung with Basra pearls that her uncle had given her. She kept looking.

"Why don't you have children?" her mother said suddenly.

"What?"

"The tiger claws were for your firstborn child. You've been married for three years now. Why don't you have a child?"

She didn't know what to say, so she said, "I don't know."

"You don't know? Liar! *Liar.* You have always been one. Even at this age you've kept your old habits. I *know* it is your doing. I *know* you won't have children because you are so 'unhappy.' *Ravi's mother told me!*"

Vijaya stopped. She was sure Ravi wouldn't have told his mother, or hers. He wasn't like that.

Then she remembered. Ravi's mother had visited them in Hyderabad. It had taken all her strength to just look presentable, clean clothes, cheerfulness. To make sure the cook had prepared the meals, the tea. The driver had the tank full in case she wanted to go shopping. Then she was overcome by such exhaustion, she lay down for a nap. And by the time she awoke it was the middle of the night, and Ravi was crouching next to the bed, still in his hospital clothes. He'd just come home. He smelled like clean metal, antiseptic. He stroked her forehead, his hands were cold. Was it a bad day today? he'd asked. Sorry I couldn't be there. Then a muted conversation with his mother out of her earshot. How long has this been going on, Ravi? his mother said. Don't interfere, he said. It isn't your job to look after her, his mother said. It runs in their family.

"And what reason do you have to be unhappy?" her mother said now. "Even on your wedding day, I had to wipe the tears off from under your veil without anyone noticing, without Ravi noticing. I had to explain away how morose you were, how dreary, how sad, as if you were condemned—a death sentence! Is that what the wedding was for you? Do you know how much you have? Look at Ravi, how good he is to you. If it were anyone else they'd have left you on the street—and oh, remember, Katya? She invited that disgusting, honorless girl from her hostel to the wedding?"

"Don't speak that way about Asha."

"Scheming! I had to scheme, at every juncture, to explain away and hide you away, to make sure no one thought you had a mental problem. Oh! Now she is crying, see Katya. So convenient, crying. Crying all the time. Why do you cry all the time? Katya, look at her."

"Ma, stop."

It was all so painful. All the memories were so painful. Her fingers were shaking. She didn't want to remember. She turned around to face her mother. "Please, Ma. Don't remind me. I don't want to remember."

Her mother took a deep breath, and said: "Where is the tiger claw pendant? Katya!"

"I'm looking, dorasani."

Vijaya sank down on her bed. She looked out of the windows. She wiped her face. There was an electric pump now, for the stepwell. And she could heard the soft, mechanical thudding, the sounds of water gushing out.

"Look how she is sitting, Katya. Queen-like. Tell me, where are the tiger claws?"

"Ma, I promise, I really don't know."

"I know it is your doing! You must have lost it. Or it is an omen. The pendant was supposed to be for your firstborn child! *Even* Katya has one. Oh, I know what it is—something is wrong with you. Isn't that so?"

Katya continued opening and closing the drawers, but Vijaya knew she was listening.

"You aren't telling me, isn't it? Maybe you aren't *supposed* to have children. Katya!"

"Dorasani?"

"Katya, stop. Stop. No need. Turn and look at her. Look at her: how boldly she is sitting there, this barren woman."

Vijaya bit her lip and turned away from the window. She looked at her mother, how much older she looked now. There were thick locks of white running through her hair, which her mother wore in a low bun now, instead of a braid. She looked gaunt, especially her eyes, which were shapeless and sunken. She looked physically smaller, but remained just as frightening. It occurred to Vijaya that her mother might have been as old as she herself was now, when Vijaya was born, but she could not imagine it, how her mother must have looked like as a younger, happier woman. Age, life, time, had all passed her mother by, and it had brought no change.

"Ma," Vijaya said, "why do you hate me?"

"Don't talk nonsense."

"Ma, can I never be deserving of your love? Will you never love me, the way you love Sree?"

"Katya, tell her not to talk nonsense."

Katya was looking at her with a peculiar expression. It was that look she used to give her when they were children, as though trying to puzzle something out.

"Don't talk nonsense," her mother said again, and left the room. But Katya stayed. They looked at each other in silence for a moment longer, then Vijaya got up and went to stand at the window.

Behind her, she heard Katya rummaging still, then the noise ceased. She heard Katya's footsteps. When she heard the sound of the door closing, Vijaya's knees gave out. She sank to the floor, drew her knees close to her, the world a blur, shapes and smears, like waves lashing the shore. She sobbed, and didn't know for how long. She felt only aware of the cold plaster of the window ledge against her forehead, her head throbbing, her eyes growing sore, her chest heaving. She didn't care if she was heard, because no one *would* care. How familiar this too was.

Eventually, she took a deep breath and calmed herself.

Sree was refusing to eat. She wanted to check if Sree was awake, ask if she wanted something. She thought of the Eclairs candy she'd brought with her from Hyderabad. Though Sree wasn't allowed sweets, she snuck them to her, a secret between them. She wiped her face with the end of her sari, wiped her nose, her cheeks, the hollow of her neck where her tears had gathered, dampening her blouse. She wiped her forehead; she knew the limewash from the wall left a shadow there. Her lips were stinging, and she realized that the edges of her lips were cracked. The salt in her tears was making them sting. She pursed her lips, waited for the pain to fade.

When she turned around to leave the room, she saw that Katya was still there. All this time, she had been there.

Katya was standing with the door closed behind her.

Then Katya said, "I took the tiger claws."

Vijaya stared.

"What did you say?"

Katya did not repeat herself. She said, "But I don't want them anymore. When you look in the case tomorrow, they will be there."

She could barely register her shock.

Katya said, "Do you want to know why I took them?"

She couldn't understand. Katya took them? And she didn't want them?

"Look at my face. *Really* look at it. Do you see why?"

She looked. How pale Katya was. Such dark eyes, such sharpness. Beauty. And a lifetime of hard labor hadn't dulled those traits. She'd never really wondered about that, or even noticed it; nobody ever did—but really, how unusual that coloring was, that sharpness. Beauty. How come? she thought now. Why not? And it was so much like Sree, wasn't it? Why didn't anyone ever say so? The tiger claws were for your firstborn child, her mother had said. *Even* Katya has one. *No.*

The motor on the stepwell stopped. A sudden silence filled the space between her and Katya.

Katya said, "Your mother can never love you, Vijaya. And it isn't because of what happened to Sree-papa. It is because you weren't born before me. She punishes you in the way she wishes to punish herself. In you, she sees the hate she has for her own self."

Vijaya clutched the edge of her bed and sank into it. She stared at Katya. It couldn't be. *It couldn't.* Katya was the girl who had always lived with them, swept the courtyard, ate from the beaten aluminum bowl she kept in the kitchens next to the gunny sacks and the floor brushes, slept on the floor next to Sree, smelling like hay, served them their meals, laid out their clothes, their jewelry. Always there.

"Birth means so much to you people," Katya said. "It is *everything.* You think it is your right—your absolute right—to violate anyone whose birth is inferior to your own. And all my life, I wanted *your* birth, Vijaya—to replace you, claim my rightful place as your father's firstborn child."

Vijaya's head was throbbing, she felt numb.

"I took the tiger claws because I knew you weren't coming back. *But you came back.* And I thought, *Well, I can only ever be the servant, nothing else. But now I can fulfill the vow I made.* Remember? I told you that one day I would find a way to punish you, cause you as much pain as you caused Sree. And I did. It felt right. *Just.* To punish you for everything, even for the sins of your family."

Katya turned the doorknob and drew the door open. They could hear her mother's voice drifting down the corridor, talking to Sree.

Vijaya realized that she was holding her hands against her mouth, pressing forcefully. Her fingernails were digging into her cheeks. How could she have been so blind? She lowered her hands and opened her mouth. But what could she say? What could she say that could atone for the sins of her mother, her father, her own? All her life, her own sister had been made to live as her servant. She felt ill.

For a moment Katya stood at the door, without turning her way, without leaving. "I thought it would make me happy," she said. "Watching you suffer."

Then Katya shut the door, came back into the room. She sat down. On the floor in front of Vijaya, the way she always sat; balancing herself on the soles of her feet.

Vijaya recoiled.

"I used to go into the sheds," Katya said.

"What?"

"All the time. I used to sleep there, it was the only place I could sleep soundly. It took me years to realize why. The animals, Vijaya, and only the animals in his house have any humanity. Not the people. I was always able to recognize that. *Why?* Because I'm not a piece of this family. I'm a piece of my own mother. As is my daughter. And the only way for my mother to live again is through us. I *won't* belong to this family. I refuse it."

Katya stood up. She went to the door again. At the door, she seemed to hesitate, but when she spoke, her tone was soft, the way it was when she spoke to Sree, never her. "No one ever tells you this, but you look like your mother."

"I look like my mother?" she said.

Then Katya said, "Krishna didn't come because he couldn't, not because he didn't want to. You are worthy of being loved, just not by your mother."

# WEIGHTLESSNESS, VERTIGO

I n the three years since arriving in Bombay, there were two constants in Krishna's life.

The first was his journal, and the second was Gagan's steel trunk. The journal he'd seen in the shop window, walking past the stationers on MG Road. It was leather bound, the kind to which one could add pages, and bind the covers together with a ribbon of leather looped around twice or thrice. At his desk at the university staff office, he kept a stack of white letter paper in a cardboard box, alongside some binding glue, a three-hole punch. He wrote in the journal every day, a page or half a page. In time, his handwriting acquired a small, cramped quality. He hadn't known that handwriting could change. Whenever he encountered some old papers—loose sheets of class notes he'd made as an undergraduate, or old letters he'd never posted—he barely recognized the writing on them.

This was his daily routine: he'd wake up and ask himself: *Is this going to be a good day?*

Some days were better than others. The pain appeared. Sometimes suddenly, without warning, apparition-like. Without Gagan, without Ranga, without Irumi, without Vijaya. All the things he was now without.

On his first day in Bombay, he'd gotten a letter from his mother. He was being shown around the campus by Dr. Godrej's assistant, a young woman by the name of Uma.

Uma had a head of very thick, very curly hair held in place by barrettes and ties and variously colored hair clips. He had opened the letter while she was still hovering, rearranging things on his desk, fussing, placing the file with his class roster this way, the paperweight another way, a covered water glass on the coaster. At the very end of the letter, his mother mentioned Vijaya's wedding.

Reading her words, it felt as though something sharp had pierced his heart. His chest hurt. He felt physical pain, an ache as tangible as the sheet of paper between his fingers. The pain made him realize that he'd been holding out hope still, hope for a world in which he and Vijaya could be together. And everything would be better. She could heal him. How grand it was, his mother wrote. The groom, she wrote, is a doctor. And so handsome too. Think of the children.

The color must have drained from his face because Uma said, "Are you sure you're okay, Krishna-ji? Shall I have the peon fetch you some tea and biscuits?" and again, "Are you sure? Are you sure?"

Eventually Uma left him, casting doubtful looks over her shoulder. Within a few minutes, the peon came bearing a tray, a white cup filled with tea sitting on a saucer, a small plate with Parle-G biscuits arranged in a semicircle. He noticed the peon; his khaki uniform, the little round hat. That there was a peon who came to him. Bearing a tray, serving him tea and biscuits. What it said about his changed position in life. This was his mother's dream. Ranga's dream. Why wasn't he happy?

"I'm not naive enough to suggest that you forget the past or put it behind. The past isn't like that," Dr. Ramaswamy had told him, before he left Osmania. "But, Krishna, it is possible to live alongside it, to manage it. Every day, try to remember one good thing, one good memory, write it down in a book somewhere. And when enough days have passed, read it all and see how far you've come."

So, he'd bought the leather journal. And he wrote. But the trunk—Gagan's trunk, now his, emblazoned on the side with the name G. GUPTA—remained in the corner of his room at the chawl. He'd come close to opening the trunk a handful of times. But he hadn't.

Dr. Ramaswamy had been right, though. He had been able to manage the pain, had indeed been able to live alongside it. He'd smile at Uma in the morning, he'd go to class, teach, he'd go back to his desk, tip the peon on Sundays, to the library, to his desk again, meet with Dr. Godrej, then he'd take the train back to the chawl. And no one could tell what was going on within him. The battle he had to wage every single day simply to get up and walk around. What an extraordinary accomplishment it was that he was able to do all these things. The regret over lost things was paralyzing. Everything had been within grasp, a life in Bombay with Vijaya, Gagan, and all at once everything had vanished.

Gagan appeared before him sometimes. That laughter, the way he hunched his shoulders while lighting his cigarette, like a schoolboy afraid of being found out. It happened without warning: *Why don't you open my trunk?* Gagan asked. It was physical pain, what he felt then too, shooting out his spine and up his neck. He'd sweat. That hot night would come back to him and lay over his consciousness like a shroud. *Let's go out, you and I. You want to remember this, believe you me.* Gagan. Gagan, in his room, a lit cigarette between his fingers, his feet propped on his desk, grinning at him, blowing smoke out of the corner of his mouth. Gagan, in his crisp white linen, balling up his fists as he spoke at a rally, the crowds chanting his name. A summer morning on the lawn outside the arts building. Gagan, poring over cricket scores. Gagan, asleep in his room after a night out, groaning into his pillow that his head was ready to burst. Gagan, face down in a pool of blood.

The tremor would pass, the images would withdraw. Gagan, his laughter, his anger, all of it.

These were the motions of his life in Bombay: after finishing his doctorate, he was now a reader at the University of Bombay. He taught. Commuted to campus in the packed local trains, then after work he'd sit at the marina and watch seawater spraying; the Arabian Sea slamming against the pilings. Then he'd walk the same route back to the chawl. His room on the third floor. A single gas oil stove in the corner. A cot. A closet. The trunk. On the first floor of the chawl was a general shop run out of two rooms, selling everything from rice to kerosene to children's craft paper. He had found neither the desire nor the need to explore that vast city thrumming with life. Only once he'd gone to the Gateway of India, stood under that basalt arch and read the inscription.

ERECTED TO COMMEMORATE THE LANDING IN INDIA OF THEIR
IMPERIAL MAJESTIES KING GEORGE V AND QUEEN MARY ON THE
SECOND OF DECEMBER MCMXI.

A guide was bellowing at a group of tourists that there used to be a statue of George V opposite the monument. Krishna looked to where the guide was pointing and saw that instead of George V, there was a cast-iron statue of the Maratha warrior-king, Shivaji. Astride his horse, sword drawn, head held high. Someone had put a fresh garland of marigolds around the statue's neck.

Also standing over the grounds of the gateway and the marina was the Taj Palace hotel. How he would have loved to bring Vijaya here. On an impulse, he walked all the way up to its golden doors. But he did not enter. Instead, he walked back to Victoria Terminus and caught the train back to the chawl.

Sometimes he'd sit on the beach, wondering what Irumi looked like now. The hills, the jungle, the village fair, the vegetable market, the dirt road leading to the bazaar, the mud houses; all the walls stippled with dung cakes. Cowbells. Palm trees. The big sky. He supposed that Vijaya didn't live there anymore, supposed that she might live in Hyderabad now, and if he'd still been there, they might have crossed paths again. Three years, maybe she had children, maybe a girl who looked the way she did as a child. It made his heart break to think like this, and he told himself to stop.

How easy it would have been for them here. Bombay was not a quiet place, it was made for people whose desire was to move, rapidly. To achieve. Although of the same country, its people seemed to be cut out of a fabric entirely different from that of the deccan; the plains of Telangana where he was from, where one could stay still enough, quiet enough, to hear leaves falling. They could have lived here, in this place where humanity swarmed, rushed past in great big waves. Then, he'd see Vijaya. Standing amidst the crowds on the train platform. Her beautiful face, her round child-like eyes. Her fine clothes, oddly out of place there. If he looked again she wouldn't be there. Occasionally there would be a moment when he could not recall the particulars of her face, the shape of it, the smell of her skin. And that would bother him too. Gagan and Vijaya. He felt plagued by both of them. He'd never be free of them. To him, they were both equally dead. And although he felt alive, it was only so much, just enough.

"Do you have a pen?" Dr. Godrej asked him.

It was late in the afternoon. Krishna was in the staff office. Everyone had left already.

Dr. Godrej was in his late sixties. A whole foot shorter than Krishna, he possessed the cultivated demeanor, the polished diction of a boarding school education so reminiscent of Gagan. He had a trimmed, snowy beard and neatly combed hair that was never once out of place.

"Here is the address, Krishna. It should be easy enough to find."

In the years since Krishna joined him as a doctoral student, then later in the readership, Dr. Godrej had invited Krishna home for tea more times than he could count, but he'd never once accepted, kept his excuses ready. Now Dr. Godrej handed Krishna the slip of paper. "At the entrance to the building, on the ground floor, there is a doorman," he said. "Give him my name and he will let you up. See you then."

"Yes, sir," he said.

Krishna went back to his room to change.

The smell of the tea he'd made in the morning on the gas oil stove was still lingering, as did the smell of kerosene. On the floor was the morning paper; pushed underneath his door after he left. He picked it up, skipped the headlines, went to the sports pages. Australia beat India by 146 runs in the first Test Match in Adelaide. "Horrid performance," Gagan would have said.

He changed his clothes, his shoes, but took his time with the laces. He wondered if he should polish his shoes. He hadn't worn the good ones in years. But he decided not to, he was running late. The train was in half an hour. The walk to the station was ten minutes.

In the corridor of the chawl, he realized that it was a bank holiday. Nearly everyone seemed to be home. The chawl was full; men, women and screaming children running up and down the corridors, chasing one another out between threats of "If you fall and hit your head, I won't take you to the hospital." He recognized most of the children. Nearly every child from the chawl showed up at his room during the half-yearly exams, on Sunday mornings, bearing bowls of cooked potatoes or flat rice, or rice pudding, or vermicelli upma with peanuts, asking for help with revision. "Dada, let us in," they'd call, knocking on his door with their elbows because their hands were full, and their shoulders heavy with book bags. He'd run out of place to store all the food the mothers sent. He told them to not bring anything, that he'd tutor them either way. Then they showed up with stuff that would last; like grapes, half a dozen bananas, but only one or two apples because apples were expensive.

Now, because of the holiday, they barely glanced at him, the children, even going so far as to ignore him and look the other way when he rumpled their hair. He was a mathematics teacher, and a mathematics teacher, even one in a seasonal capacity, can never be a favorite teacher. That post was reserved for English teachers.

He could hear the hard clacking noise that the cricket bat made against the ball in the courtyard below. Now and then, someone shouted, "Catch it" or "Howzat" or "Sixer."

"Krishna, kuthe jatoes?" Mrs. Desai from next door said, looking up from the clothes she was wringing out of a metal bucket at her feet.

"Professor," Krishna replied, and held up his hands to make the shape of a roofline. He did not know how to say *house* in Marathi. "Chai," he added.

"Aaj sutti aahe na?" she said, turning up her palm at him.

"University not closed," Mr. Desai said, before he attempted an answer, looking up from the newspaper he was reading, leaning against the parapet wall.

"Aha. Chor! Mulgi baghayla jatoy toh!" Mrs. Desai said.

He had learned bits and pieces of Marathi over the years; words that meant *curd* or *milk* or *vegetable*, and more important phrases like "When will the water come?"

He tried to understand what she was saying, but he must have looked puzzled because Mrs. Desai added, "Beautiful girl? When coming to marry?" and made a sign of a necklace around her neck. She laughed.

Walking past her, he managed a polite smile.


The trains were empty. Which meant that there was enough room to stand comfortably, without bumping into anyone or leaning onto anyone. Across from him in the compartment, two young men were sitting. They were speaking in Telugu.

The subject of the conversation seemed to be the flat owner of one of the men, who was fleecing him for this or that bill. Water. Electricity. He said, "Each and every day there is a new thing that's broken." He touched the tips of his fingers to his temple and made that typical motion, a little tapping, and said, "Karma, karma." The vowels of even that grumbling complaint fell so softly on his ears. Their friendly quality. How long had it been since he'd last heard anyone speak Telugu. His heart felt warm and full.

The friend replied: "Do you know that guy? Why is he smiling at you?"

Krishna stopped smiling and looked away.

"Maybe he is a Telugu fellow. He looks like one. Or a south fellow, at least."

Krishna stared out the window, angling his face away from them. They'd probably ask him to come over and join them. Ask whether he'd watched the Chiranjeevi movie that was showing at the talkies. Whether his living situation was difficult too. He checked his watch, then took a few steps in the opposite direction, out of their sight.

He found an empty seat by the window and sank down in it.

A small girl across the aisle from him said, "Dada, kiti wajle?"

He checked his watch again and replied, "Quarter past six," but in Marathi, like she had.

Outside the station, he glanced at the card on which Dr. Godrej's address was written in spiny cursive.

Marine Drive. It was in a part of the city that Krishna hadn't been to, on the eastern edge of the city, against the shoreline.

Krishna rounded the corner and entered the street on which the Godrej residence was. It was a promenade. Walking along the marine bollards, he heard seagulls wailing and cawing above him. The wheels of cars against the cobbles, the tar road smooth like pressed starch. On Marine Drive, storefronts had gold lettering. Clothing merchants, watchmakers, jewelers. ESTD. 1901. ESTD. 1923. The glass doors were thick. Doormen stood outside the art deco bungalows, white-gloved, red-hatted, facing the sea.

A gentle sea breeze was blowing in, and with it came a cool drizzle, drops of seawater that clung to the slick pavement, to his eyelashes and his hair. A tall, slender woman was walking towards Krishna, her skirt billowing around her knees, her heels clicking against the street. She seemed not to notice him and he moved out of her way.

At the building, he gave the professor's name to the doorman, who in turn gave Krishna a look, from his face to his shoes. At his damp hair, at his unpolished shoes. His shirt collar was beginning to fall and he smoothed it, attempted to force it to lie flat.

"I'll take you up," the doorman said. He led Krishna inside, past a square, open-air courtyard full of trimmed border hedges, potted rose-bushes and at the far end, a lift.

He had never been inside a lift before. The doorman held the door open for him. He stepped in and the doorman shut the lift door behind him.

"What floor, sir?" he asked.

Krishna checked the card that was still in his hand. The floor was written next to the door number.

"Seventh."

He experienced a peculiar sensation. Weightlessness, vertigo. He pressed his hand against the wall of the lift. A whirring and clicking noise. The lift stopped. He stepped into the corridor.

The Godrej apartment was the last one in the corridor. He pressed the doorbell. The doorman stood behind him, at his shoulder. After a pause, he heard footsteps approaching, and the door opened.

A young woman appeared at the door. She was a foot shorter than he was and dressed just like the woman who had passed him in the street; a gray silk skirt that fell to her calves, a cream blouse with buttons, tucked loosely into her skirt. She had pale skin, a slender neck. Her hair and her eyes were both a shade that was not quite black; a shade too light to be black, brown, copper, maybe even red.

"You must be Krishna," she said. Her voice was sweet, her manner of speaking cultivated; soft and low like that of a newsreader on the radio. "I'm Ada."

She stood aside. He heard the doorman walk away.

Inside, he flattened his collar again, his neck felt warm. He looked around the apartment for something to do. Ada called for Dr. Godrej. "He's here," she said.

The apartment had large windows that faced the sea on both sides. The place felt airy, cheerful, blue. There was a look of disarray about the place. A squashy green sofa almost in the middle of the room, wicker easy chairs alongside the windows, poufs grouped together without order, cushions on the floor, records on the floor, stacks of books on the floor.

"Come and sit out in the balcony."

Walking past it all, it occurred to him that there was a method to this disarray. The easy chairs and the poufs and the cushions on the floor were placed so as to catch the views of the sea at various points in time during the day.

It did not look like a place where Dr. Godrej lived, with his mild manners, his gentle, orderly way of speaking, walking. He wondered if Ada was Dr. Godrej's daughter, or if she was his wife. Or his girlfriend. Either way, everything in the apartment looked like it belonged to her.

Out on the balcony, where Ada led him, there was more furniture, white wicker with pale blue cushions.

"Please, sit down," she said.

Auburn. That was the name of the color. Her hair was auburn.

The view from the balcony was breathtaking. The sun was setting, sinking into the Arabian. Sailboats cruised directly into the horizon. It was intense, but also serene. He felt very calm; calmer, it struck him, than he'd felt in a long while. Looking into the sunset from this balcony belonging to Dr. Godrej, he came to the realization that he would never set eyes on Irumi again. As long as he was alive. Irumi, his home, his homeland, there it would remain, on the shores of his memory, with the palm trees and the birds in shadow. He'd come too far.

He sat down on one of the chairs. He could sense Ada moving around in the apartment, he could hear another voice murmuring, calling to Ada in a matronly tone. He turned around. Her back was to him, her thin calves. She was talking to someone who was out of sight; a cook based on the conversation. Ada brushed her auburn hair out of her face, swept it across her shoulder. He caught sight of the nape of her neck, thin and pale, disappearing into her shirt. He blinked, looked away. The pilings along the shoreline were covered in dark moss that, even from that height, he felt he could smell.

"Krishna!"

Dr. Godrej appeared. Before Krishna could stand up fully, Dr. Godrej made a flapping motion with his hand and sat down across from him.

"How are you, sir?" Krishna said.

Dr. Godrej said, "Sit. Sit. How are *you*?"

He had never been to a professor's, or any teacher's home before. He had always had his encounters with them in school and university settings, surrounded by old books, old buildings, the requests and the exchanges, professional manners. Dr. Godrej was wearing a kurta that was open at the collar, loose pants, both white, and slippers. He rested the heel of his right leg on his left knee and sank back into the wicker chair. Krishna felt like he was sitting across from a different person, someone whose name he did not know, but who resembled someone he did know. It was like looking at the underside of a desk one used every day, and finding scribbled on the pale wood the pencil marks of the carpenter.

He did not know Dr. Godrej's first name, he realized. The apartment door just said GODREJ. Then a vague memory surfaced, of a plaque, the university endowers list.

It was Phiroze. Phiroze Godrej. It was a Parsi name.

Ada re-appeared. Behind her was a woman in a brown sari—presumably the cook whose voice he had heard. Each bore a tray—Ada, a tea set: cups, saucers, a covered sugar bowl and a small silver jug of milk; the woman: three small plates of potatoes over flat rice, yellow from turmeric, roasted groundnuts and coriander leaves, a small bowl of sliced lemons. He caught the cook noticing him, she was attempting to place him; his position, whether it was closer to the Godrej family's or to hers, but adjusted by his educational credentials. The moment passed, and she smiled at him warmly. In her smile was something familial.

Ada poured their tea. A lock of hair fell to her chin. The sunset made her skin look bronze. "Sugar?" she asked him.

"Yes. Please."

"He says that you are the most dedicated student he's ever worked with," Ada said.

Dr. Godrej said, "It's true, I did say that," pointing a finger at himself and smiling. "He *was* a student, Ada, but not now. Now he is the reader. And that too will be over soon."

"Yes, sir," Krishna said.

Ada handed him the cup. He took a sip and placed the cup back on the saucer, where it clinked.

"So. What do you think of the place, Krishna?"

"It is very beautiful, sir. The views especially."

"Aren't they?"

"I don't remember ever feeling this peaceful."

He hadn't meant to say that. It had slipped out.

Ada and Dr. Godrej looked at each other.

"This is her place," he said, nodded toward Ada. "She's done it all up."

He noted a touch of pride, a touch of ownership in Dr. Godrej's tone.

"I actually live downstairs."

He noted the kurta and the loose pants. An outfit one could wear for tea, and also for bed.

"It was a very old, pre-independence building. Art deco, I believe it is called. Very poorly maintained, very damaged when we got it. Ada had to re-do practically everything. The floors. The plasterwork, the balconies, everything. She did a splendid job, didn't she? She really has an eye for these things."

Ada smiled, looking mildly embarrassed, pursing her lips and narrowing her eyes and dipping her neck.

He wanted to make sure he did not avoid speaking to her. "You did a wonderful job," he said.

She sat back in her chair and crossed her legs. The silken material of her skirt shifted and gathered around her knees, fell around her legs. She held his gaze.

"We should take Krishna downstairs and show him my apartment. Some other time?" Dr. Godrej said, looking at Ada, looking at him.

"If you are interested, Krishna."

She said his name softly.

He nodded.

Afterwards, he stayed more or less silent, did not volunteer much information about himself. Dr. Godrej and Ada were jovial with each other. Ada was an English teacher. She worked at Bombay Scottish, and they talked about her day, joking and chatting like very old friends. After a while they fell silent.

The sun was almost gone. In a matter of minutes, it sank completely, and the sky became a moody blue.

He rose.

"Going already?"

"Yes, sir. Thank you. I had a wonderful time."

"Stay awhile longer, Krishna. We are enjoying your company. Aren't we, Ada?"

"Yes. Stay," she said, her eyes on him again.

"I have to get back, sir. The train, I have to catch it."

"Nonsense. Ada can take you in the car. Where do you live?"

Quickly, he made up a lie. That the building he lived in had rules about last entrants and that they locked the gates after. And not because he was in any way ashamed of where he lived. Ada and Dr. Godrej looked genuinely sorry to see him leave.

"You must come again." Dr. Godrej shook his hand. "Walk him out, Ada?" he added before going back into the apartment.

He and Ada stayed on the balcony for a moment longer, then the spell was broken and she walked him to the door.

"Goodbye," she said. Although he waited, she did not extend her hand to shake his. He left.

About a week later, he was at his desk.

In the staff office, the little cramped space in the corner of the general floor was his. He had several papers to grade and mark up, and go over the set exam for the upcoming mid-years. He tipped back his chair, and looked at the roof.

He'd stopped smoking, and in idle moments, like now, he felt an almost unbearable pull. To walk down the street outside, to the paan shop, and buy a pack. Wills Navy Cuts. Slit the gold foil wrap and pull a cigarette out. It would be firm between his fingers, also soft. If he pressed it slightly, he'd feel the packed tobacco, like sand underneath. The paper taste between his lips, the matches striking.

"Hello there."

Her face was upside down.

"Ada."

She took a step back and let him straighten up.

"How are you?"

"Good."

Her auburn hair was pulled back into a ponytail, its edges curled and draping the side of her neck. "I was visiting my father. And I was hoping to run into you, Krishna," she said, touching his shoulder with the tip of her finger. "Do you want to walk me to the car?"

The campus was lined with old gulmohurs, trimmed hedges, and low-growing ferns. The trees were always full of birds; mynas and koels chirruping, singing. He walked beside Ada, her car was parked only a few yards away from the building. When they reached it, she turned to face him.

"I'm having some friends over today. At six. Come."

"Okay," he said. He didn't have to say yes. He realized that he'd agreed simply out of relief. He felt relieved that Ada Godrej was Dr. Godrej's daughter.

Before she got into the car, Ada said in the tone of quoting something, "Ships that pass in the night."

He looked at her, feeling perplexed. He didn't know what she meant by that.

"We've met before, Krishna," she said.

"We have?" He couldn't remember.

"Nineteen sixty-six or sixty-seven. In Dr. Ramaswamy's office. And I remember a very strange detail." She reached out and touched his collar. "Your collar was damp."

Then he remembered. It was the day he'd written Vijaya and asked to see her. The day Dr. Ramaswamy had asked him to separate himself from Gagan.

"But we did meet again," he said. "We aren't ships that passed in the night."

That evening, he opened Gagan's trunk.

It was a steel trunk, painted green, filled with his last remaining possessions. In a different universe, a simultaneous universe, it would be behind glass, fifty or seventy years from now. The memorabilia of Gagan Gupta. A plaque. A piece in the making of a nation.

He sank to his knees. He unbolted the latch and opened it.

The first thing he saw was the framed photograph of a woman. She looked to be in her late twenties. A little girl was sitting in her lap, an arm draped around the woman's waist, head resting against her shoulder. He picked up the frame and looked closely at her face. The picture was black and white, but he could tell that it was taken outdoors, near water, based on the stretch of stony rocks behind them. The little girl was wearing a summer frock. She looked like she was cold and was drawing close to the woman for warmth.

Gagan's mother was smiling playfully at the camera, presumably at the person standing behind the camera; one who could only be Gagan's father.

Grief came differently.

He smiled. The boy Gagan who must have been around when the picture was taken, picking river rocks, too busy to sit still and be photographed.

He put the picture frame down, on the floor next to him. The trunk was packed, but neatly, everything in its place. Folded shirts and slacks.

Rolled-up socks, ties, handkerchiefs. The kind of clothes Gagan wore, clothes that would have not looked out of place in a formal dining room, a military boarding school, a cocktail party thrown on the seventh floor of an art deco building on Marine Drive.

He extracted a shirt. It was white. Fine linen. The label said MADE IN IRELAND. It still smelled new, even after the years it had spent in the locked trunk. He put the picture frame back into the trunk, on top of the clothes in roughly the same place, closed the lid and bolted it again.

He buttoned the linen shirt up to the collar, did the cuffs, tucked the edges into his slacks, looped his belt, buckled it and looked at himself in the mirror. The shirt did not fit him very well. His chin was covered in week-old stubble, but it was too late to shave.

# VIJAYA AND KRISHNA

———◆———

Vijaya was standing on the cement pavement, in the shade of the gulmohurs, on the street outside Krishna's office building. At the end of the corridor, she was to pass through the double doors and ask the peon for the reader. She'd been told this by a woman she presumed was his assistant. She said her name was Uma, and made Vijaya tell hers. Are you a family friend? the woman asked. Vijaya said yes.

Now, she'd been standing on the pavement for the last thirty minutes, trying to muster the courage to go up.

She'd purchased a leather journal at the stationery shop at the end of the street. She'd bought it, for no reason other than to have something to hold when she saw him. The shopkeeper had gone on and on about how the leather was sourced directly from the leatherworkers and the artisans in the rural countryside. She'd paid and left without waiting for change.

Her mother had called her at Asha's. "What big work do you have in Bombay that you had to leave home two days before Diwali? Couldn't you have gone after? Even your uncle came home for you, Vijaya. What shall I tell him? And Sree—you promised to be here for her, Vijaya. When are you coming back?"

"I tried to stay, Ma. I really tried. I couldn't. I need to know."

"What does that mean?" Then her mother added in a whisper, "Vijaya, Sree's not doing well at all. I'm so scared."

She guessed Sree was within earshot because it was Sree's voice that she heard next.

"But did you go to the beach there, Vijaya? Did you see the ocean?"

She said she hadn't.

"Vijaya, when are you coming?"

"Soon," she replied.

"How soon? Will you come tomorrow? Will you burn sparklers with me? Will you promise?"

She promised.

And why had she come all this way? What did she need to know?

Now she saw him.

Krishna was holding the door open for someone behind him. A woman in a green dress. Vijaya drew back, into the shade of the gulmohur trees, pressing herself against the compound wall.

They were lingering outside, Krishna and the woman in the green dress. The woman put out her hand and Krishna took it without looking. The woman said something in a bright voice.

Vijaya couldn't overhear their conversation. The woman was leaving. But, after a few paces she paused and came back, calling his name. Krishna waited, and when she reached him again, she placed her hands on his shoulders, raised herself up on her toes and kissed him. He looked pleased, he looked shy. He brushed his hands through her red hair, resting his thumb on her lips for a second longer.

# LEMON GROVE

———◆———

Krishna watched Ada go. She was treading lightly, trying not to trample fallen gulmohurs that littered the sidewalk every few feet.

Afterwards, as he was going up the stairs to his office, he passed Uma.

"Krishna-ji," Uma said, "kasa aahes?"

"How are you, Uma? How come I didn't see you yesterday?" he said.

"Oh, I was going to come," Uma said. "I packed my lunch box and everything, but suddenly my son had a fever. You know how kids get, they are happy, playing, running, and suddenly you touch their forehead and it is burning hot. And they still won't stop playing!"

He shrugged.

"Well, maybe you will, soon, god willing." Uma laughed, looking meaningfully at him.

He nodded politely at her, and was about to go through the double doors of the staff offices when Uma called back, "Krishna-ji, did you meet your friend?"

He must have looked puzzled, because Uma waited a moment, adjusted the large barrette in her curly hair, and said, "You know, she was waiting for you outside. She came yesterday too, the peon said. I asked her to come in and wait, but she said no."

"An older woman?" he asked, wondering for an irrational second if his mother was somehow here.

"No, not old. Young," Uma said. "As tall as I am. She has brown eyes. She said her name was Vijaya."

He was aware that Uma was still speaking, telling him that she could go downstairs, or send the peon, to see if she was still waiting. Maybe they'd only just missed each other.

The staff room was empty.

From where Krishna sat, behind the desk on which there was a small plaque with his name and his post at the university, he could see a sliver of the street outside, the branches of the gulmohurs, laden and yellow, waving gently in the breeze.

Vijaya walked into the room behind Uma, and he couldn't find his voice. He grew keenly aware of the pace at which his heart was beating, how it seemed to continue beating, as though nothing was the matter. It would betray him. He felt out of breath.

"Your sari color is very nice, Vijaya-ji," Uma said. "Such a beautiful pink. It is like the color of a bougainvillea in bloom."

He felt as though his skin was on fire. He got up, went to the window, and tried to push it open. It was painted shut. He heaved and shoved. It was taking everything he had, to keep away the image of the little white house on the northern edge of the campus where he was supposed to have made love to her, to not allow it to flood his mind. He managed to crack the window open a few inches. The ledge left dull red stripes on his palms.

Then, Uma left. And they were alone.

He went back to his desk, sank into the chair. He couldn't look at her, he couldn't find his voice. But he must have spoken, asked Vijaya if she wanted to sit down, because she took the seat across from him.

"Your assistant is very nice," Vijaya said.

Now he looked at her, met her gaze, and felt unable to look away. It was the same face that had plagued him all these years, all of it exactly the same except for the strands of hair that had grayed near her temples, the way his had. It was unbearable to look at her.

"She's Dr. Godrej's assistant," he said.

"She's very nice."

He said, "Do you want some tea?"

"Yes," she said. Then it occurred to him that the building was nearly empty, the peon must have gone home too, like Uma.

She was wearing a gold chain. On a pendant hanging from it were what looked like tiger claws. He caught himself in time, looked away. "How is Sree?" he said.

Vijaya's face fell. She shook her head. How could she look exactly the same? He saw her now, and it was as if they were standing across from each other in the lemon grove again. She was holding out her palm, asking him to promise. How did she do this? How did she make time stop, fall backwards.

He said, "Do you go home often?"

"Once a year," she said.

"For Diwali?"

"No. Not usually. Just this year."

"Isn't it tomorrow?"

He wanted to ask her why she didn't go every year; if she had children for whom she needed to stay home, light firecrackers, sparklers. Her husband. But he didn't ask. Instead, he said, "When are you leaving then?"

"My train is in the morning. Sree made me promise to come."

Then she opened her mouth as if to say something, as if to say the thing she came all this way to say, and he knew what it was before she said it.

"Krishna, must I remain? Tell me, and I will," she said.

She said his name again, but he couldn't take it anymore. "Why are you here?" he said harshly, cutting her off. He felt so angry with her. He stopped himself from saying her name. He didn't think he could say it without betraying himself.

"I met Dr. Ramaswamy, he told me where you were."

"I asked *why* you are here. Now. Why you are here, now, Vijaya?"

Vijaya stood up abruptly. She looked unhappy, as if there was an emptiness in her, as though the life force had been taken out of her.

He stood up, too. He was aware that his fists were balled up, his nails were clawing into his palm. She was looking at him intensely, as if trying to commit his face to memory. Then the moment passed. She was at the door.

"Where are you staying," he said, trying and failing to keep the anguish out of his voice. She turned, said the name of the place. It was on the other side of the city.

"Shall I take you?"

She shook her head, then she was gone.

An entire minute passed. He remained standing. The very air he breathed felt impressed with her presence. All his life, he had been running towards her. All his life, he had been calling her name, loudly, recklessly, not caring if anyone heard. And she was calling him now, waiting for him, waiting in the lemon grove with her arms crossed. What was fate? Fate was to never have been parted from her. To have been born another away.

He wished he had never set eyes on Vijaya. Where would he be if she hadn't existed for him? Ranga—his mother's longing for Ranga; where would Ranga be, if they'd been allowed to grow up together, look after each other. He'd never have left Irumi, his family would have been whole. Her family would have been whole. He'd fated himself to yearn for her, and this was the reckoning. This was the price being demanded of him. The price of being able to live without looking back.

He went downstairs.

Vijaya wasn't on the street. He ran across the pavement, passing tree after tree, trampling the fallen gulmohurs, not caring. He rounded the corner. Then he saw her, she'd dropped her book, and she was bending down to pick it up, her face wet with tears. He called her name. He called again. And Vijaya heard him. She straightened up, clutched the book to her chest, looking at him as though she knew he'd come.

# IN BOMBAY

Krishna was at Asha's apartment, to get Vijaya's things. Vijaya was in his room at the chawl.

She had been almost at the door when she asked him if she could stay behind. She could have gone too, there was no reason for her not to have. But Krishna didn't insist, he took Asha's address from her and left, saying that it would take him about an hour to return. She needn't worry about locking the door, and there was a phone booth downstairs if she needed to call him at Asha's. And Mrs. Desai was next door if she needed anything, he'd let her know that Vijaya was there.

Vijaya felt an inexplicable reluctance to leave his room and all the small things that belonged there. The single gas oil stove, the washed teacup drying next to the sink, the green trunk printed not with Krishna's name but with G. GUPTA, a small chest of drawers next to the neatly made-up cot. The footsteps of children racing in the corridor outside. Pressure cookers whistling now and then, sewing tins clattering open, the smell of lentils, laundry soap and all the warm, beautiful things that went into keeping a home.

She went to sit on the cot. On top of the drawer was a shaving kit. The box was slim, wooden, chipped at the corners like it had been knocked around inside a trunk for years, taken out, put back again. She opened it, the lid was loose at the hinges. A frayed shaving brush, a metal razor with the blade still inside. Vijaya could smell the castile soap on it, the hot water he'd run through it before he left for his office this very morning. Krishna must have bought it as a teenager. How alone he had been in the world.

An hour later, Krishna returned.

She went to the door and attempted to help him bring her suitcase inside. He placed it over the threshold, and cast around as if to find the best place to put it, but stopped. He straightened up, brushed the hair out of Vijaya's eyes, asked her if she was hungry, if she wanted to get something to eat. He could bring food here, if she didn't want to leave.

"Vijaya," he said, taking her hand. What was he going to say? What was there to say that needed to be said right now, today?

Nothing. He knew how she felt, understood exactly why she didn't want to leave this square room full of the things that showed only that he'd been waiting for her, that he'd never stopped waiting for her.

There was a knock on the door and Vijaya turned to see it being nudged open. She let go of Krishna's hand. But he took it again, placed it over his chest. The children at the door giggled.

There were three of them, all boys, roughly the same age, their shoulders coming up to the door handle. The boy in the front was wearing a red cap. He was holding a tiffin box. One of them had a cricket bat tucked underneath his arm, he was craning his neck to get a good look at Vijaya, but when she smiled at him he looked away shyly.

"Dada, Aai ne Diwali mithai pathavli," the boy in the front said, holding out the box to Krishna. "Abhinandan bolli ti tula!" they chanted in unison, falling into a fit of giggles.

Krishna said, "Nothing misses your mother's eyes, does it? Tell her thank you. From both of us." The boys scrambled away before Krishna could ruffle their hair.

They left the door ajar and sat on the floor next to each other.

Krishna opened the tiffin box. It surprised neither of them that the milk cakes were still warm. Krishna picked a slivered almond from the sweet, they never did eat the almonds. Vijaya held out her palm and he placed the almond on it. She closed her palm around it, letting it sit against her skin like so much happiness.

# RIFLES IN THE GADI

———◆———

S he's not coming?" Sree said. "Ma, she promised. Why isn't she coming?"

Her mother ignored her. She was talking to Vijaya on the telephone. "Have you no shame?" her mother hissed.

"Ma," she said.

"You've left your husband and you are living with *a washerwoman's son*. How dare you, Vijaya! How dare you. It would have been better if you'd died. Or if we'd died, so we wouldn't have to see such a thing happen. How dare you, Vijaya. Have you no shame!"

Then a moment later: "You shut your mouth. *Katya is not your sister*. How dare you say such an outrageous thing. Enough! This is what you did to yourself—throwing away a good husband—throwing away your family—don't you dare blame me. Enough! Listen to me, Vijaya, and listen carefully. When I die, Vijaya, I don't want even your shadow to fall across my corpse. That's my last wish, you hear? And if you die before I do, Vijaya, I will come, but only to spit on your dead body. And you will never step foot back here. You will never see Sree."

Then her mother hung up the phone, held her face in her hands and sobbed.

"Ma," she said.

A moment later, her mother called Vijaya back. "Please, Vijaya, don't do this. Please, I'm so scared about Sree. Please don't do this. Please don't do this. No one knows yet, right? You didn't tell Ravi yet, right? Go back and we never have to tell anyone. It can be our secret. Please, Vijaya, please don't do this. It isn't too late yet. Don't tell anyone, go back to Ravi. Tell him you were here all this time. I'll lie for you."

"Ma," Sree said, but it was as if she wasn't even there. A moment later, her mother hung up the phone once more.

"Ma," she said again, but her mother did not respond, did not even look at her. She sank back into the easy chair.

"Come, Sree-papa," Katya said, appearing at her elbow, helping her to her feet. "Let's get you back upstairs. It's evening now."

She turned back to look at her mother. In the reddish light spilling into the courtyard, her mother looked like a statue. "Lean on me now," Katya said, "careful."

This was the ceremony with which her day ended, the climbing of the staircase.

It was a pretend ceremony, because the truth was that Katya had to bear most of her weight, hold her firmly around her waist while still allowing her to put one foot after the other, stair after stair, evening after evening. After reaching upstairs, they made their way down the corridor. Today had been a good day; a day she was well enough to sit downstairs and not have to stay in bed all day in her room; what used to be her uncle's study.

It was sometime after Vijaya's wedding that she'd moved rooms.

Though she didn't remember exactly how long after the wedding; more than a week definitely; she remembered the smell of wilting marigolds, wilting mango leaves, things used in the wedding like silver and betel nuts and the sweetness of rosewater perfume. All of them still detectable in every room. Her mother refused to have them taken down, the flowers and the leaves, from all the doorways, until they were well beyond the first blush of wilt. And by the time she'd settled into her new surroundings properly, the flowers and the leaves were crisp and golden. She had never even been inside her uncle's study before then because absolutely everyone was forbidden from entering it. And it was simply given to her, with no hesitation.

She did question it, though not at length. After stopping school, losing her room didn't seem like a big thing; a small battle as battles went. Katya said that the doctor wanted to keep her away from too much sun, because the sun was making everything worse, and her room, facing the front of the gadi; the vaakili and the village underneath the hillock, got so much sunlight. So they'd found for her the darkest room. And even then they kept the drapes drawn on the windows. These drapes she secretly drew open when she was left alone in the afternoons when everyone napped for an hour or two. The only time of day she was ever alone.

Katya settled her into her cot. "What's the matter?" Katya said.

She hated the smell of her sheets, even though Katya made it a point to change them every day. "Nothing," she said, sinking into her pillow, trying to ignore the hospital smell, the doctor smell, the stench of alcohol and syringes that pervaded her sheets.

There was the tiger head mounted on the wall opposite her. Her uncle's large teakwood desk with the many drawers stuffed with old papers and receipts and promissory notes and other things like that. One drawer, she knew, was full of pencils and pens, and an antique inkpot. Another slim drawer was empty except for a single item: the kaleidoscope Vijaya had given her.

Even though she knew that it would make Katya feel bad, she said, "Katya, I want Vijaya."

But Katya did not look like she felt bad. She smoothed her covers and said, "Soon, Sree-papa. Soon."

"She promised she'd come."

"Not today, but she'll come, just wait. She'll come back. She promised, didn't she?"

At the end of each of Vijaya's annual visits to Irumi, for her birthday, Sree could never say if Vijaya was happy to leave, or unhappy to leave. But on the day of leaving, she came into her room—formerly the study—unasked, and just stubbornly sat around, saying almost nothing—on the window ledge or on the large desk, not looking at the tiger's head. Vijaya would sit around until Sree stretched out her arms, and then she'd come close, draw Sree into a hug, hold on to her so tightly that she felt momentarily breathless, she'd kiss her forehead, and then they'd part.

All the while Vijaya hugged and kissed her, promised her that she would come back soon, to take good care of herself, to remember to eat, she'd avoid looking at the tiger's head looming behind Vijaya. It scared her, especially during sunset when its eyes went all angry, like a real tiger's, the red color swirling inside its glass eyes eerily, hypnotically. Its spirit and its life. Looking at it, she felt a little pit open up in her stomach, a whooshing sensation, her heart beat a little too fast, there were even little tremors at her fingertips. And the smell of the room was brought into sharp focus. What did the room smell like? Like oil.

"Gun oil," Katya had said once, when she asked. And where are their guns? Oh, Katya shrugged. Who hunts nowadays?

They'd put so much effort into making this unfamiliar room familiar, all the touches, a kind of softening around the edges that was disorienting. Closing her eyes, she could sniff out the gun oil, the varnish from the teakwood desk. Old animal pelt. Red ants nesting inside what remained of its flesh. But opening her eyes, there it all was: the stack of her old schoolbooks, the covered water glass, the rose saucer for her tablets, floating around her as though defying gravity. On her bedside was a pen and some writing paper. She'd written Vijaya a long letter.

"Katya, will you post this letter to Vijaya?" she said. "Ma said I can't write her anymore. Will you post it without telling?"

"Tomorrow," Katya replied, gathering the pages. "Will you eat something now?"

"No," she said, hoping Katya wouldn't force her to eat today. She'd lost the taste for food, not that she had particularly enjoyed eating to begin with. But at least the food she used to be allowed to eat had a certain magical glint, like the pools of melted ghee in her upma, leaking into the silver plate in transparent puddles. The doctor said that it might be a good idea to avoid silver, and so her food now came to her in earthenware plates. Dull and cold, brown like the orchard outside. The threat of eating now hung over her day: bland white rice, with some turmeric. A small, imperceptible dollop of lemon pickle if Katya was in an indulgent mood. The meals, three long shadows.

"Katya, will you stay with me tonight?"

Katya did not stay nights anymore. She'd moved out of the gadi, and was living in the village, with her husband and her daughter. Sree never asked about him, never asked to see her daughter even. For inexplicable reasons, she felt angry with these people she'd never met. They'd taken away Katya. During the daytime hours, while Katya was there, she did her best to ignore her altered appearance, the toe rings, the yellow necklace, the vermillion in the part of her hair, distorting and altering the version of Katya that she'd always known. Like everyone else, Katya too was leaving her.

Katya shook her head. "Go to sleep," she said, handing her the rose saucer with her tablets. "You will see me in the morning. I'll be here before you wake up."

She swallowed her tablets, and a drowsiness came over her. As she drifted, she was aware of Katya moving about the room, shutting everything up, all the windows, tight, like she did every night before she left the gadi.

At night, the sounds in this room were different too. Since the orchard was dead, it seemed to attract different birds. There was the magical cackle of some bird she did not recognize. There was the night owl that went *whoop whoop whoop*.


When she awoke again, it was not morning, it was sometime in the middle of the night. She felt strangely alert, wide awake. Her stomach was rumbling, she realized that she was hungry. How long it had been since she'd felt truly hungry? She couldn't remember.

The tablets were still working. Though she felt light-headed, she felt no pain. She got out of bed and stood up gingerly. The room was dark, she opened the window latch and unbolted it. The moon was high in the sky. Round and full, its pale white light flooded the room. Not quite knowing why, she went to her uncle's desk, drew out the slim drawer and fished the kaleidoscope out.

She got into bed again, sank back into her pillow, pulled up the covers and turned the kaleidoscope over in her hands. Could she send it to Vijaya, along with the letter? Would she want it back, something for her to keep until they met again. She looked out of the window.

They were far away, near the riverbank.

First she thought it was fireflies, the little pinpricks of light, going in and out of focus, moving in an almost straight line towards the gadi, towards her. How strange it was. Then she realized that it was light from flashlights; people with flashlights. She sat up. Surely, she was imagining it. But she knew straightaway that they were all carrying rifles. She gripped the kaleidoscope. *Oh, who hunts nowadays?* Once, there was a king. *Are you listening, little children? Listen, listen. Pay close attention.* Once, there was a king, and on a hunt one particular morning, the king came across a doe. All he wanted to do was to capture it.

There was a crash, downstairs, the sound of wood splitting, glass splintering, shards scattering across the stone floors, heavy furniture being upturned. Shouting—her uncle's voice—her mother's voice—Tara's voice—her father's voice. *Barricade the doors!*

There were tremors at her fingertips, a whooshing sensation in her stomach, as if she were falling from a great height, as if she were looking into the tiger's eyes. She must get out of bed, she knew. She must run— down the corridor—down the stairs, leap across the pool of water in the courtyard. Help. See what the matter was, see what the matter was. She tried to move, but the sheets remained pulled up, the kaleidoscope remained in her lap, and the noises continued to rise up the floors of the gadi—glass breaking, shouting, wood splintering. *Barricade the doors!* The king gently tugged on his horse's reins. Luckily, the doe didn't hear them. It was looking at its reflection in a pool of water, a glen, now and then dipping its neck low and drinking from the pool.

Then a smell—distinct, malodorous, like the gun oil, like the old animal pelt, like the remnants of the wilted marigolds that she'd continued to smell long after Vijaya's wedding. Petrol. Thick splashes of petrol falling across wood furniture, spilling across the stone floors. Silence. Must *she* remain silent? Must she shout? She gripped the kaleidoscope in her hand. Then she shouted. "Ma!"

"What's the matter!"

Then she shouted, "Is there a fire?" What was she supposed to do if there was a fire? Fetch water. Fetch water. "Water, water!"

Her call was answered. The door crashed open and people burst into her room. She caught sight of silver wire-rimmed glasses on the face of the man who entered the room first, he was almost as thin as she was. Behind him were two others, a woman and a man, all wearing green clothes and caps: a uniform almost like the military's. When she caught sight of the man who entered the room last, her voice caught in her throat.

Like the others, Ranga was wearing green clothes. Like the others, a rifle was slung across his shoulders.

Ranga moved towards her cot, stopped at the foot of her bed. "Ranga," she said. "You are here," she said. "Is there a fire?" she said. "Water," she said. "Fetch water." The doe was still staring at its reflection. Bhairav waited, his eyes fixed on the doe. It was utterly quiet. "You are here," she said again. "Ranga," she said again. "Who are they?" she said. "Is there a fire?" But Ranga continued to stand at the foot of her bed, looking at her, his face impassive. Behind him, she saw the others rummaging through her uncle's desk, upending drawers, the papers fluttering across the floor. It was a small or large wild animal. It made a frightening sound the very second the king's arrow left the bow. "Why are you touching my uncle's things?" she cried, and then Ranga looked away.

"Comrade Suma," he said. The woman moved away from her uncle's desk and came towards her. Her face was round, her cheeks pink and swollen.

"Stand up," the woman ordered.

"Who are you?" Sree said. "Why are you in my room? Is there a fire?"

Again, the woman said, "Stand up."

"Where's Katya?" she said.

The woman's hands were not soft, like her mother's, nor were they rough yet gentle, like Katya's. They were calloused, they scraped her skin. The woman pulled her out of bed, then dragged her down the corridor by her hair. Once they reached the stairway, the woman ordered her to walk, she couldn't, and she felt the woman's hands grip the back of her head, push forcefully, felt her feet leave the landing. The sodden, cracking noises her head made, hitting stair after stair after stair, now muffled, now hollowed out, now feeble. She cried out for her mother, she cried out for Katya, she cried out for Vijaya. Gleaming tendrils of pain rushed towards her, a terrific brightness erupting in her skull, pouring down her spine before the world went dark.


Once, she'd made Katya open up all the windows of the study, and it felt like she was both inside and outside at once, and the study smelled like old leaves. Not newly dead, the wilt with the green, citrusy edge, with the tang of rot, but the dead of absence. How does the color brown smell? she'd asked Katya, and before she answered, "Like this," she said, "Like old, crisp leaves."

That is what she smelled now. Leaves; the dry, crumbly leaves of the orchard against her face. There was a taste in her mouth; acidic, like bile, and underneath it, something sweet and metallic. Was it raining? Her face was wet, but it wasn't rain. She swallowed and realized it was blood, dripping down her face, into her mouth. She retched. And there her mother was. There her father was. Tara. And her uncle. "Ma," she whispered. Why were they all kneeling, here in the orchard? And why was the orchard so bright? Why did the air smell like ash. She tried to stand. A tremor passed through her body. She retched again. She shuddered. "Ma," she said, trying to stand up. "Ma, I can't walk."

There was a dull ringing in her ears. Surely, this was a nightmare. One that seemed to continue, because they were all still there—the people in the military clothes—the thin man with the wire-rimmed glasses, the woman who'd thrown her down the stairs, and three others she hadn't seen before, all surrounding them; one of them was crouching on the balls of his feet holding a scythe. Ranga was standing in front of her uncle. He'd been speaking all this time, she realized. She hadn't heard him, because all the while, over the dull ringing in her ears, over the sounds of the river, over the sounds of the timber rafters burning and falling, his pistol loading, there was her mother's voice rising and rising, octave on octave. First her mother begged, then she bargained. "She's too ill. My Sree's too ill, she's like a child. What did she ever do to you? Please don't kill her. Let me touch your feet. Please don't kill her. My Sree's like a little child. She's innocent."

"The letter," she whispered. Katya said she'd post the letter tomorrow.

Her home was burning. But the letter was safe with Katya; it was four pages long; with all the little details that Vijaya so loved; how the golden ear of the gramophone vibrated when she played a record, the music dropping a note when she laid her hand over it; the little pocket watch she'd found in one of the drawers of her uncle's desk, how she'd fallen asleep with it clutched tightly in her fist, the watch ticking like a hummingbird's tiny, metal heart. She'd asked Vijaya, if she could visit her and Krishna in Bombay. If they would take her to the beach, if she could touch the sea. Water, she said. Letter, she said. Ma, she said.

But the king broke his silence. "You're blinded," he said, trying to stand up. How much he loved that dog. "You don't see it. Ranga—"

Ranga braced his pistol against her uncle's head and fired. A crack, like a whip snapping through the air. A flash of light. And there was a river of blood, and all around the king fell his regalia: his ruby-encrusted sword, his filigree dagger, his bow and his quiver of arrows. The king became unconscious. *Are you listening, little children? Listen, listen. Pay close attention.*

"Ranga!" her mother screamed. "Ranga! It's you, isn't it? It's you. Don't you remember me? Remember? We always took care of you. Mahendra, you always took care of them!"

"Ma," she said. "Fire, water."

Ranga's pistol went off again. Her father.

Again. Tara.

"Don't you remember Sree?" her mother screamed. "You saved her life, Ranga. Remember? Remember? Please don't kill her." Ranga's pistol went off a fourth time. And over the dull ringing in her ears, over the sounds of the river, over the sounds of the timber rafters burning and falling, Ranga patiently re-loading his pistol, the bullet shell falling softly on the floor of the orchard, there was an echo of her mother's voice. Falling, receding, vanishing, octave on octave.

A memory. This was not a story narrated to her, patched up here and there. But a clear one. A perfectly preserved one. Of sitting by the stepwell with Vijaya, her ear pressed up against the cool stone, the walls roaring inside. The earth underneath her is baked, the leaves of the banyan are yellowed, but the branches are still chirring with crickets. It was the sweetness of late summer, strumming through her like music, like the water in the stepwell, glinting merrily in the afternoon sun. She remembered the brightness of that day, but more than anything, she remembered being well. Being happy. A life she did not get to live.

It occurred to her that she was screaming. But when Ranga came towards her, the pistol with which he'd killed her family in his hands, she fell quiet. In the moment before he pulled the trigger, she shut her eyes and whispered the same thing as when he kissed her for the first time, for the last time. *Be still, be still.*

# 1990

---

# IRUMI, TELANGANA

# KANAKAM'S TALE

—◆—

lthough their place kept the name as "the way over there where
the tanners live," nearly all the old tanners had left, moved to
the city, or changed trades. Irumi had expanded outwards,
reached them. Though it was narrow and muddy, it was a street now, with
streetlights, where Kanakam lived. For Sankranti, the harvest season,
Kanakam's wife, along with the wives of those on their little street, drew
these elaborate patterns outside their home with rice flour, as large as she
could manage—intricate curves and loops, grids, geometric shapes, pots
full of frothing milk, wheat bundles, peacocks. They were allowed into
the temples now, so she went every evening without fail, as though to
make sure no one ever forgot.

Nearly all the houses on his street, including his own, had tiled
roofs—two rooms, with a cowshed in the back. Mostly they were farmers,
including Kanakam. He possessed a bit of dry land. He sowed groundnuts. During planting season, he paid a man in the village who owned a
tractor to come and plow it. Each year, his daughter threw a tantrum on
the plowing day, weeping, asking to miss school and come to the field.
Even though his wife said no, he let her come. So she could watch the
furrows being made, the sump pump gush water.

"Katyamma is coming!" Kanakam's daughter said. It was late afternoon. She was pacing back and forth outside their house, her hands on
her hips, her brows drawn together, her slippers slapping against her feet.

"I told her about *it*," she said, speaking with the conviction that only children had, that everyone understood exactly what they were talking about without having to name it. "She wants to see *it*."

Even though she was called Katyamma now, it didn't leave anyone's memory that her old name was Katya, only now it was propped up by a set of softer vowels, to better fit into the mouths of everyone in Irumi. Nor did it leave anyone's memory that she used to live in the gadi, with the Deshmukhs, and that she was a child of Mahendra Deshmukh. She ran the only village shop with her husband, sold oil and soap and medicine.

"Your mother's at the temple," Kanakam said. "I don't know where she kept it."

"Katyamma is coming!" his daughter said again. "You have to look!" She bounded up and down on the balls of her feet, followed him inside.

He'd known Katya for years. The first time he met her was at her shop when his daughter was only a few weeks old. He'd stood a few feet away from the shop entrance, put a two-rupee note on the ground and asked for baby soap. Katya held out the bar of soap and beckoned him towards her. Take it, she said. She didn't put it on the ground for him to pick up. The way the saukar did when he went to borrow farming implements, or the potter, or the tailor, or anyone else in the village who didn't want to risk touching him accidentally. Katya didn't care, she'd never wanted to belong to the village. And that evening, she and Pichamma came to his house, bringing along food and old baby clothes and the boy Pichamma was raising, her grandson, now a grown youth. Ranga—that was his name too.

But this was new, this intense fascination his daughter began to have with Katya, and with the old ruins over the hillock. It had started when there was a proposal in the panchayat, to convert the gadi into a public school. Plans since abandoned because of what the restoration would cost. Instead, the panchayat had summoned a fellow from the archeology department, and supervised the removal of the large carving of the chariot from over the doors of the gadi, the teak carving had miraculously survived the fire, and was sitting in a warehouse somewhere, with red paper tags, waiting to go on display.

Kanakam lit the kerosene lamp and glanced around their two-room house: the stove in the corner, the jute basket that dangled from the ceiling and held the milk out of reach of wild cats, the neatly rolled-up beds, the smell of camphor and incense from his wife's altar. He pulled a tin box from an alcove behind the stove: a rusted blue box that once held baby powder, with a fading illustration of a brown-haired baby absently sucking its thumb. The blue box held all his wife's orphan objects: her spare bangles, her small tub of katuka for lining her eyes, a spool of thread. The box also held a collection of entirely useless things that she could not bear to throw away. Bits of split ribbon, shards of multihued glass bangles. The kaleidoscope.

He had given it to his wife. And never looked at it again. Now it had been years. Now he was thirty-one. He'd fulfilled all his mother's dreams.

The silk had faded. What was once bright red, like freshly drawn blood, was muted, grown dusty with age. The gold zari did not catch light. Even in the yellow light of the kerosene lamp, he could barely make out the pattern of paisleys.

"It isn't here," Kanakam said, putting the lid back on and pushing the box back into its hiding place. "Go tell her we don't have it."

He didn't want to be parted from it, and surely she'd want to take it. In the years they'd known each other, he never told Katya he had it.

"But I told Katyamma we have it. She's coming."

"Why today?" he said.

"Because!" she said, sprinting out of doors again.

Sure enough, he heard Katya greeting his daughter. "She's here!" his daughter called.

Katya came in. She was dressed in her best clothes. She was even wearing her special necklace, the one she only wore once a year. She smiled warmly at him. If Katya thought badly of him because he hadn't told her about holding on to the kaleidoscope all this time, she didn't show it. She seemed to understand.

"Sit here, Katyamma. He'll show it to you!" His daughter tugged Katya towards the spot near the window where she usually sat.

"All right," Katya replied, following her lead. "As you say," she said, sitting down, holding his daughter's chin and squeezing it playfully.

His daughter sat down next to Katya and said again, "Show it to her!"

"Are they here yet?" Kanakam asked Katya.

"No. Not yet," Katya replied.

He was glad he hadn't missed them. He'd been putting off going up to the ruins all day.

"Is Ranga packed?" he said.

"We'll see. *Uncle will take care of it*, is what he says whenever I ask him if he has this or that thing. Everyone came to see him last night. To wish him well, even the old farmers who'd spent half their lives chasing him out of their orchards." She laughed, before adding softly, "He always was such a rascal. Like his father."

"Wish the old woman could have been alive," Kanakam said. Pichamma always said that she named the boy Ranga because the name was unsullied. That even in death, nobody had called her son that.

Katya said, "She raised him the way she wished she could've raised his father. 'Katya, I'm hungry. Give me something to eat!' he says, walking in my door. And for a second, I look at him and forget how much time has passed."

After what happened with the Deshmukhs, they were told that every last landlord in the region had fled to the city. It was in the national newspapers. First the police came. Then the army. Suma came to see her son in the middle of the night during the army sweep, when the baby was only a few months old. It was through Suma that they learned that Ranga had only made it till the morning after.

All throughout the night, Ranga had refused to wash the blood off his hands. "I keep seeing her," he'd said. "I keep seeing her lying there in the grass." Again and again, he turned up his palms and looked at them and said, "This is all her blood."

At sunrise, Ranga had walked into the center of the clearing and shot himself with the same pistol.

It was raining when they buried him, Suma said. In the jungle they couldn't perform his last rites, not without the fire giving away their position. So they found for him a place in the hills, a cliff side overlooking a ravine, a place where the grass was green, and the earth raw and fertile. They closed Ranga's eyes against the earth and the rain, took off his boots, but placed his pistol on his chest.

Suma tried to hide in her mother's old village. Even managed it for a few days, but the army found her; found every last one of them. Killed, jailed, executed without trial. How long ago that was; Kanakam had been young enough to escape the interrogations.

His daughter widened his eyes at him. Stop delaying, she seemed to say.

He took the kaleidoscope from the box and gave it to Katya.

Katya ran her fingers over the silk, touched the little silver anklets. But she didn't press it against her eye the way he'd done. She already knew it was broken. Absently, she wiped her cheeks with the end of her sari. "She would have been thirty-nine years old today," she said.

"Don't you want to keep it?" his daughter said, when Katya made to hand it back. She shook her head. Kanakam took it, put it back in the box.

"Even now, I cannot bear to look in the direction of the ruins," she said. "I don't know how Vijaya does it every year."

Katya had gone to Bombay, to help care for Vijaya afterwards. Vijaya couldn't move or talk for months, Katya had told him. But, for better or worse, she had something of her uncle in her, the good parts, Katya said. Spirit. The will to survive. Nobody but Vijaya could have endured such a thing. "And she is so good with them, her children. Always worrying over them, dressing them in matching clothes."

Katya stood up.

"Are you leaving already?" his daughter cried.

"Oh, why don't you come with me?" Katya replied. "Your mother won't mind. You can sleep there if it gets too late. You can wear my daughter's old clothes if you need."

Kanakam watched them till they turned at the end of his street. Then he set out himself.

Every year when Vijaya and Krishna came, he went up to the old ruins.

He walked through the village. It had been drizzling all day. Even though the rain had stopped falling, the air was misty and cool. He cut through the cornfields in order to reach the hillock. The rainwater was dripping steadily, sliding off the cornstalks, the smell of wet corn silk. He went up the steep incline of the hillock. The river was full, and even from the stepwell he could hear the rushing sounds of water over stones.

He sat down, his back to the old stepwell, the ruins rising over him.

There was now a large gaping hole between the double arches of the main entryway, where the chariot carving had been. The doors were gone, and he could see straight through the gadi, at the fat trunks of trees, the vines and shrubbery and undergrowth that sprouted from its very floors. He could even see all the way through to the orchard, the mango trees, their oblong, leathery bunches of leaves. All of it green and wet.

The blackened half walls still standing throughout the complex looked unsteady, porous even, the stone blocks having slid over one another but still holding together, like a pack of cards. Though the rock walls were graffitied with arrows, hearts, initials of vandals, he could still make out the sunken carvings, green like aged copper: the dancers holding poses, the horses, the birds, the flame palmettes. The flagstones of the courtyard were covered in bright green moss, with large sections missing. The gadi looked unsteady, as though it was balanced precariously on the surface of water, at sea, sinking.

Kanakam knew why Vijaya and Krishna came back each year, why they brought their children. They came to remember, to see the gadi with the lights turned on in every room, the stained glass windows glowing like jewels, the way Sree would have seen it.

He heard their car pull up. Trundling up the hillock slowly, it stopped a little ways from him. It was a gray Fiat Padmini with windows so clear he could see straight through: the family of four; Krishna in the driver's seat, Vijaya beside him, the children in the back.

Vijaya got out, followed by the two children, girls in matching yellow frocks. Vijaya told the children to be careful, gesturing at them to come around and show her their shoes, so she could check the laces. Krishna leaned out of the window and touched Vijaya's arm. She said something in response, holding her hand over his. Kanakam couldn't quite overhear.

Then Krishna reversed the Fiat, turning it around and parking at the edge of the courtyard. In all that time, Vijaya didn't take her eyes off the

# ACKNOWLEDGMENTS

I've had the good fortune of learning from extraordinary teachers and mentors, each of whom had a hand in helping me bring this book into existence. I'm indebted to Lan Samantha Chang, for guiding the manuscript through its most formative period, for her kindness and generosity and seeing what I wanted to create better than I did; Natalie Bakopoulos, at the writing program at Wayne State and later, for her faith from the very beginning, for her mentorship and friendship and caring so much; Margot Livesey, for teaching me how to read for essentials, and the vitally important skill of separating the cutting from the revising; Charles D'Ambrosio, for seeing the faults beneath the sentences, an incalculably valuable gift that helped me swim the last mile; Angela Flournoy, for showing me how to think about minor characters, for all the sound advice about new motherhood; Donovan Hohn, for the keys to using rhythm in sentences; Ethan Canin, for teaching Alice Munro; and Tom Drury, for teaching Chekhov and fairy tales.

I'm grateful to Jin Auh, for sharing in the bones and the ambition of the manuscript, for her supernatural ability to give voice to my instincts. Also, for not accepting anything less than my absolute best. My wonderful editors, Kukuwa Ashun and Megan Lynch, for falling in love with Krishna and Vijaya and Ranga and Sree at exactly the right time, for the razor-sharp editorial advice and for being such champions for this book throughout.

My dear friends: E Jeremijenko-Conley, trusted reader, for all the time spent interrogating my characters; Kirsten Johnson, for talking me down from despair, for such faith; Anisha Desai, for twenty years of friendship, for all the Telugu-Marathi translations, any errors my own; and Sudhamayi, for always being there.

I'm grateful to the Iowa Writers' Workshop and the Truman Capote Literary Trust, for their support in writing this novel. The Stanley Award for international research, and the Iowa University libraries, for making archival materials available to me; particularly newspapers from this period; reportage related to the Sain family killings of 1970; the oral history project of the Stree Shakti Sanghatana: *The Life Stories of Women of the Telangana People's Struggle,* which inspired portions of Suma's childhood; and crucially, a volume of folk poetry: *Telangana Porata Patalu;* and the unnamed poets and singers of the rural countryside who cataloged the everyday lives of Telangana peasants.

I'm grateful to my parents, Rajagopal Rao and Shylaja, for fostering my love of reading and writing, for buying me any book I've ever wanted no matter how hard the times. Thank you for the lifelike details, and for the truly invaluable gift of remembered history. My sister, Tapasya, for her constant friendship. My mother-in-law, Sabitha, for taking excellent care of my son while I worked. My grandparents Sanjeeva Rao and Tirumala, and my extended family in Warangal, for the steadfast affection, for the summers; always a source of creativity and respite. Most of all, my spouse and my son, to whom everything is owed: నా కథకి, నా కళకి, నా జీవితానికి, ప్రాణం పోసేది మీరే.

# ABOUT THE AUTHOR

**Ruthvika Rao** is a graduate of the Iowa Writers' Workshop, where she was a Truman Capote fellow and recipient of the Henfield Prize in fiction. She was born in Warangal district, Telangana, and grew up in Hyderabad. Her short fiction has appeared in *The Georgia Review*, *The Southern Review*, *New Letters*, *StoryQuarterly*, and elsewhere.

ruins. But now she glanced around at the stepwell. Kanakam observed her, the gold watch on her wrist, the starched cotton sari. He saw her face, he saw the family resemblance. After all, she too was Katyamma's sister. Her eyes slid over where he was, she looked at the banyan over him. Then she looked away.

The girls moved across the courtyard, first uncertainly, then enthusiastically, towards what was once the rock fountain but was now a pit filled with stones. Don't go too far, he heard Krishna say, shutting the car door. But when the children entered the ruins, armed with fallen tree branches, neither of them called the children back. Krishna came to stand by Vijaya. She knelt and cleared a spot on the ground, brushing away wet leaves with her hands.